ROAR VOLUME 11

ROAR VOLUME 11

INNOVATION

Edited by

IAN MADISON KELLER

ROAR Volume 11

First publication 2022

Edited by Ian Madison Keller

Cover by Fresaboba
Copyright © 2022

Published by Bad Dog Books

www . baddogbooks . com

BAD DOG BOOKS

CONTENTS

FOREWORD

I spent a lot of time agonizing over the theme to choose for my first ever time editing ROAR. I settled on INNOVATION, because at its core innovation is merely the introduction of something new. A fitting theme for a passing-of-the-torch volume.

Going through the slush pile meant making some hard decisions. I had to reject quite a few stories that I loved, which was harder than expected. It was great seeing all the various forms of innovation taken in each story. Some were expected, and some were a delightful surprise. And I hope to take you on the same journey as you read this volume.

The fifteen stories in this collection will take you from invention to discovery, the thrill of exploration to the bitter sting of failure. So join a god in introductory computer classes. Journey with a horse as he struggles to invent a new type of boat lift. Blast off to space with a foxhound cosmonaut. Compose music with a teenage opossum. Experiment on a mysterious hole with a village of crows. Or just sit back and fight digital dragons in virtual reality.

But at the end, innovation is what you make of it.
—Ian Madison Keller

DRAUGHT HORSE

HUSKYTEER

Innovation can come in many ways and forms, but sometimes a good, old-fashioned invention is what you really need. Magnus the shire horse is an artist at heart, not an inventor, but he has a grand idea and maybe the will to make it happen.

Magnus placed the steel-handled pen back in the inkwell and licked his cold lips where they had held it. He stretched his neck, shaking out his mane and snorting gently, and walked to the window. The rain had stopped, and the sunset turned the wet grey roof tiles to a carpet of autumn leaves. You could see clear to the docks.

Kip, the weasel engineer who employed him, sprang on to his shoulder.

"Claws," Magnus protested half-heartedly. Kip coiled up to his neck, burrowing into the black tangle of his mane, and peeped out at the world beyond the window.

"Won't it be grand when this loading crane of ours hops off the drawing-board and we can see it from here? Hey?" He gave the mane a little yank.

"Mm? Oh, yes. Grand."

As a foal, he had sketched small. Leaves. Flowers. Now he drew machines that towered above buildings. His nose wrinkled in a smile.

"All right, horse. I see you snuffing that country air already. Go and catch your train." Kip bounced off and across the room, leaped up to pluck Magnus's bowler from its peg, and tossed it so it landed between the horse's ears.

Magnus adjusted the hat brim, then snapped off the sleeve garters that kept the long hair at his fetlocks from trailing in the wet ink and dropped them in a drawer. Carefully, with hooves and mouth, he rolled up the technical drawing he'd been working on, putting it aside for the next week.

For the working week he had lodgings in the suburbs, in a respectable boarding-house presided over by a hedgehog landlady, but today was Saturday, when he caught a tram, then a train, then walked to his parents' cottage to stop the night. If he hurried, he could catch the 5.02. He flared his nostrils and broke into a trot.

"Giddyup there, Dobbin!"

He looked around, ears flat, but it was only Mattie, her chestnut sides shining with sweat as she pulled her hansom cab. Ignoring the obvious displeasure of her passenger, who would probably have preferred a dignified silence, she stuck her tongue out at the black shire horse, and wiggled her ears.

"Still pulling that thing? Learn to drive an omnibus!" he called back. He raised his hat to her and heaved himself onto the tram just as it began to move.

The jostle of commuters on the tram and the train gradually thinned out. Nobody else alighted at the little country station, and he stood a moment to let his eyes adjust to the darkness of the lane, snuffing the smells of wet earth and water, before taking the path that led to the canal.

As he clopped along, he pulled leaves and late blackberries with his lips from the top of the hedge, where the fumes from motor cars could not reach. He was always hungry in the city.

Bed and board, I offer, and you, my lad, account for as much board as the rest of my boys put together, Mrs Pearce, his landlady, would say, as she ladled out his porridge.

I'm sorry.

Oh, eat up. It's cold out. I won't hear anyone say that I starve my boys.

She was a decent old biddy, really. He'd bring her back a present.

Magnus ducked his head to enter the lock-keeper's cottage, built in the previous century for some family of smaller animals, and stood with his back to the fire.

"Here, put a blanket round your shoulders. You're steaming the place up." His mother stretched her grey neck to kiss him on the cheek. "Look, Reggie! Here's Magnus home again."

The old horse swung his head towards Magnus. His pale-blue eyes weren't quite looking into his son's, but past him, towards some other time or place. Magnus felt his skin twitch, as if flies were landing on him.

"Have you had a good week, son?" his mother asked into the silence.

Gratefully, Magnus told her about Kip and the design they were working on, the crane that would transfer cargo from dock to ship's hold. About his landlady, and Mattie. About the busy city streets, the trams and the increasingly common motorcars.

"You and this Mattie." Her ears perked forward. "I like the sound of her. Are you stepping out?"

"No! She's…" Was she even a friend? Or simply a friendly face he could stop and chat with? He didn't even know where the cab horse lived. They just nodded to each other over the heads of smaller folk, trading smiles and insults.

He steered his mother off the topic and on to his work.

"You always were drawing," she said. "Birds and flowers and things. Do you still do that?"

"I don't have much time to myself. You should see my technical drawings, though."

"I'd come and visit," she said, "only…"

"Pulling's all I know," his father interjected, as if this followed with perfect logic from the conversation.

"And you're very good at it. But our son knows a lot more than that. He's a clever one."

"They work you to death and then make your hoof into an inkwell," grumbled the stallion.

"Nobody's going to do that, Dad."

"Dead right they're not. I'm not ready for the glue factory yet." He pulled himself up and out of the armchair. Magnus whickered and turned sideways to keep his father in full view, as he would an enemy.

"Don't excite yourself, Reggie." Magnus's mother kept her voice steady, but her ears were flicking. "It's about time you were in bed." He followed meekly when she led him into the cottage's second room.

"How is he?" Magnus asked when she returned.

"It'll kill him, one of these days." His mother spoke more freely about her husband when he was in the next room, even though he could have heard every word through the wall. "But stopping would kill him too. And Heaven forbid he should let me help him."

When I married your mother, I promised her she'd never work again. It had been one of Reginald's favourite phrases when Magnus was growing up. The foal had supposed that cooking and cleaning and housekeeping weren't proper work, because you didn't get paid.

"Not that we get many boats, anymore," she added. "Walk me to church in the morning?

"Of course I will. Then I thought maybe I'd pick some fruit and nuts to take back."

She looked sad at the reminder of how short his visit would be, but said "I'll help you."

They nuzzled each other's necks. Magnus settled for the night by the fire, while his mother retired to join his father in the cottage's other room — the room where Magnus had been born.

The rain streamed into Magnus's eyes from his mane — nobody wore a bowler hat in the country — and bounced off the surface of the canal. His father stood in a cloud of his own breath, watching the water. Sometimes his tail flicked, sending droplets in an arc up and down, and sometimes he stamped his great feet, but otherwise the old horse did not move.

Magnus had watched him stand like that since the first time he was able to toddle after his father up the towpath. Together, they had seen the barges travelling from the docks, laden with coal or cotton. Back then, horses like themselves would tow the barges; more and more often, these days, a noisy motor propelled them through the water.

"One day, son, you'll be doing this." Magnus remembered the way the black stallion's muscles had moved under the glossy coat as he turned the wheel that operated the first in the series of locks. The colt Magnus had cantered after him on long, unsteady legs as he moved on to the next lock, then the next and the next and the last. Each had to be filled with water to float the boat up to the next level of the canal. The process took nearly two hours. By the end, there was sweat on his father's shoulders and foam at the corners of his mouth.

Over the years, Reginald's flanks had hollowed and the proud tilt of his head had lowered. Magnus had grown, but not enough to equal his sire. In the city, he stooped constantly to make himself look smaller. Next to his father, with his hooves like upturned buckets, he still felt like a colt.

A family of otters in a brightly-painted houseboat had entered the lock. They chirruped happily to each other as Reginald opened the sluice gate and the boat began to rise. Magnus waved and wrinkled his nose. The two older children waved back, while their mother held the baby up to see him.

His father snorted. "Huh. Day trippers."

After that, he saved his breath. Magnus could see his ribs heaving as he turned the wheel. The otter children grew restless at the delay.

"Let me help, Dad," Magnus said at last.

Reginald stared directly into his son's eyes, back in the present for perhaps the first time in weeks. He laid his ears against his skull and blew down his nose. Magnus took a step backwards, so his hoof rang on the cobbled towpath.

"You?" his father snorted. "Save your delicate hooves for the city streets. You've made it very clear you don't want to take this job on when I'm gone."

Then he turned his back as if he had forgotten Magnus was there, and who he was.

Magnus thought back to the first time he was allowed to touch the wheel. Determined to make it turn, he had put all his teenage strength behind it, locking his arms and back.

At last, the water began to trickle through the sluice. The trickle became a stream, became a torrent that foamed and swirled in the lock as the water level rose. It terrified the colt to hold so much power over nature. Eager for approval, he turned to his father.

"Keep at it, son," his father had said flatly.

Magnus knew that he would never be good enough.

After that first time, turning the wheel was just a chore like any other. Reginald set him to chopping wood and carrying the shopping home from market, to build his muscles. In private, Magnus worked on his own system, improving his eye and tuning the muscles that let him move a pencil in small, delicate strokes. His mother might reassure his father that their son would settle down, that this was just childish rebellion, but Magnus knew he didn't want to spend his life opening and closing, with nothing ever changing.

At last, all five locks had opened, closed, and opened again. The otter mother started the motor, and her pups' squeals of excitement faded as they steered away.

"Needs oiling," his father grunted, leaning against the rail that guarded walkers from falling into the depths. He could still talk sense about locks and canals, at least.

Magnus touched the lever and felt how easily it would move with a little pressure. It was his father's muscles, not the mechanism, that had stiffened and warped.

His mother had written to him about the change in Reggie, after he left. For a long time Magnus didn't come home, pleading that he was busy with his studies, then hunting for a job, then working.

When he visited at last, confident that he had a home of his own to go back to, his father still loomed over him. Sometimes he knew who Magnus was and sometimes he didn't appear to see him at all. The white around his lips and nose had begun to turn silver, and spread back along his muzzle. In the cottage he stood like a piece of furniture. On the canal he worked the locks, with limbs that held less power every time

Magnus came. Magnus couldn't hate him, but he didn't have to love him, either.

There was no more traffic. When the light faded, his father fastened his locks with chains and keys, so mischievous paws couldn't meddle in the dark. Up and down the canal, the barges would be mooring for the night, their pilots lighting little stoves to cook their dinner. The otter pups would be snuggled up in their bunks.

"You'll break your mother's heart!" his father had roared, the day Magnus announced that he had won a scholarship to art college. "Your own mother! You'd like that? Would you?"

He was moving to the city with the money he had earned from chopping wood and carrying shopping all over the village. His father's ears were flat and his nostrils flared. His mother thundered into the room, and placed herself between father and son.

"Go on. Tell her what you've just told me." Reginald spoke in a breathy whicker that was more frightening than a shout.

Magnus told her, stumbling over his words.

His mother's eyes filled with tears.

Then she hugged him.

"I'm so proud!" she squealed. "You clever, clever boy! I always loved your pictures, ever since you were a tiny little foal… You'll visit, won't you?"

———

"Treats!" Magnus dropped a bag of hazelnuts on Kip's desk. The weasel gave a happy squeak, tore the bag apart and began to nibble, dropping crumbs and fragments of shell all over his work.

Magnus leaned over to inspect the chaos of doodles and sums. His snort blew hazelnut debris in all directions.

"This is a mess, Kip."

"Luckily for me, I've got you to turn it into something sensible."

"Listen. I've got something to ask you."

He had rushed to the office, only sparing a minute to call on Mattie at the cabbies' shelter and present her with a bag of windfall apples.

He'd had plenty of time to think, on the slow Sunday stopping service city-bound. He was an artist, and thought in shapes, but he had spent enough time with Kip for a little of the engineer to rub off on him. He saw the landscape not so much as a thing of beauty to be captured, but as an architectural problem to solve with his pencil. So, walking back to the station with his mother, he had turned his engineer eyes on the five locks.

"A lift," he said. "To take the boats all the way up in one go. Works faster, see? More traffic in a day." He didn't mention how little traffic he had seen on his visit.

Kip sat and listened, munching away on his hazelnuts. "It could work," he said, his mouth full. "They have one in France, I believe. I can look up the plans. And I happen to know that the County Waterways Authority is worried about the railways taking away from their revenue. I think they'll like this."

His weasel brain moved faster than Magnus could talk, and the little brown paw was already flying over the paper, covering it with the squiggles and swirls Magnus had learned to interpret.

"If the balance point is here, and the counterweight here...then...yes. The water displaced by the boat starts the mechanism moving. Bigger boat, more water. So you use the same amount of force, whatever the cargo. You could do it with a small engine."

"Or a horse," Magnus said.

"But — oh. Yes, of course."

"If my father stops working, my parents lose the cottage, and there's nowhere for them but the poorhouse." Magnus had been pacing the room as he talked. Now he stopped to look out of the window, rather than at Kip. "But the work, it's killing him. If he could carry on just a few more years, till I make senior draughtsman, I could afford to set them up somewhere. Near the water."

Kip nodded absently, his paws already reaching for a fresh sheet of paper. "I'll do the arithmetic and sketch it out. You'll draw it up."

"It'll mean a lot of extra work. We still have to deliver the crane contract on time."

"Don't worry about that," Kip told him, tapping his claws affectionately on the big hoof. "You just keep the hazelnuts coming."

It was a dark month. They burned the gas lamps all day, and blow the expense, to help the strain on Magnus's eyes from peering at figures and angles in Kip's tiny scrawl. Magnus brought chestnuts from the country, and they roasted them on the paraffin stove.

Sometimes, to stretch his neck and limbs, he stepped away from his desk and stared out of the window at the blank white paper of the sky. It was overcoat weather, and the people below were wrapped up in black or grey or brown. Mattie's chestnut was a bold flash of colour whenever she went by, taking a passenger to or from the station. She looked small and fragile from above, clopping determinedly along between the steam or petrol powered cars and refusing to budge when the drivers tooted at her.

His parents' cottage seemed smaller and darker when he visited, and the journey longer. He didn't see his own home in daylight from one week to the next. On the Sundays, walking the canal with his father, he took care to keep his strides long and his eyes on the hills. His body and mind needed the room.

One Monday morning, he arrived to find Kip bouncing about the office on the balls of his feet, waving a cream envelope in the air.

"You're late!" he said. "Look! It's our appointment to speak to the transport authority about the boat lift! Today!"

Magnus snorted gently, and his hooves fidgeted on the floor. They had spent so long planning, and talking, and drawing, he had almost forgotten there would be a time when their creation of pen and set square was scaled up to life size, to tower over them in wood and cement. When his mother asked him what he was working on, he talked about the crane down at the docks. The boat lift was like the Christmas presents he'd made and stored in secret when he was a foal, knowing that his mother, at least, would be grateful and proud.

Now Christmas was here.

"I was thinking," Kip said. "You might need to go and supervise. You could stay with your parents and help out with the locks. I'd keep your position open!" he rushed on when the horse frowned. "For as long as you need."

"No!" Magnus stamped hard enough to make Kip jump. They both examined the dent his hoof had made in the floorboards. "I'll pay to have that fixed."

"It's fine. We'll get a rug."

"I can go back for a night," Magnus said, slowly and patiently as if explaining a tricky technical aspect in one of his drawings, "but I can't stay longer. I just can't."

"All right, Magnus. That's all right." The weasel waited for his employee's black flanks to stop heaving, and for the white surrounds of his eyes to disappear.

"I thought you left for the city because you had big ideas and ambitions," he said at last. "Dreams of machines to make life easier."

"No. I left because of him."

Kip waited.

"Because I wouldn't be the horse he wanted me to be, he always had to let me know I was no horse at all. Whenever my mother wasn't there, he pushed me around. I think I was supposed to fight back, but I wouldn't. Sometimes he'd nip my shoulder or smack my flanks. It didn't even hurt; he just wanted to show he was in charge. I thought it would stop when I got bigger, but it didn't. Then, when I told him I was going to art college…"

"You poor little lad," Kip said to Magnus, who could have sent him flying across the office with one tap from his hoof. He wrapped his arms around the horse's fetlock, stroking the white feathers. Magnus blew warm breath across his head.

"He was so angry, it burst something in his brain, we think," Magnus continued. "The next time I saw him, he was like he is now. I can't go back there to live, Kip, even though he can't hurt me anymore. I have to help them some other way."

"You can start by speaking to the Waterways Authority," Kip said.

Magnus lifted a hoof from the floor and stood poised, as if he might have to gallop out of the office to safety. He looked down and sideways at Kip. "Me? Why can't you do it?"

"It was your idea. You're the one who's passionate about it. You can talk through those diagrams better than I can. And besides…"

Kip stood still, which he rarely did, and seemed at once to

fade into the background, against the dark wood-panelled walls. Magnus pictured the weasel standing up at the meeting, his whiskers barely clearing the table, squeaking at the top of his voice to make himself heard, while the politer members hid their smiles behind their paws and the rude ones laughed out loud. He rushed about so, and talked so much, that Magnus forgot how small he was.

"I can do it," he promised.

Kip patted his nose. "Remember when you started here?" he asked. "You were so shy you barely spoke!"

Magnus didn't explain that the city had cured his shyness, not caused it. He'd grown up in a village where everyone knew you by name from the day you were born, knew more about you and your family than you did yourself. In the city, there were people everywhere and no obligation to talk to any of them if you didn't want to. On the tram and the omnibus, sitting quietly in the warmth and scent of the other passengers, he felt secure. He might be head and shoulders above the rest of them, but if he kept his head bowed and his knees together, nobody gave the shire horse a second glance.

———

They were glancing now.

The table in the wood-panelled room was shaped like a horseshoe, with paintings of former board members looking down from the walls.

Magnus looked at the faces turned attentively to him: an otter, two dogs, a cat, a donkey, and a Clydesdale horse. The County Waterways Authority in full. Kip sat to his left, fuzzy tail curled around his haunches, watching the faces with his beady little eyes. Magnus could almost hear the weasel's heart racing.

"We'd like to talk to you about our idea for Three Elms Locks." Straight away, he reconsidered the sentence. It sounded too humble, not confident enough. 'Idea'? He should have said 'plan'. Nothing for it now. He ploughed on.

As he outlined their proposition, his words gathered strength and power, rolling forward from his slow start until they were an unstoppable force. Just as their lift would gather momentum to hoist the boats uphill. He saw the faces light up with interest, and Kip visibly puff up with pride. The donkey was smiling at him.

He finished by unrolling their plans across the top of the horseshoe.

His meticulous lines and shading covered a sheet of paper that took the full span of his arms to hold open. Ears flicked forwards and necks craned to see. The Clydesdale held down a curling corner with his hoof. The size of it reminded Magnus of his father.

"That's lovely work, lad," the donkey said softly. "I'm sorry we can't help you build it."

"What?" Kip jerked upright, bristling. Magnus slid a hoof onto his tail, pinning him to his seat.

"Barge traffic's dying," the donkey said. She adjusted the purple bonnet that sat on her stiff mane. "We can only afford to spend on the locks we have, and paying the keepers' wages."

There was a murmur of agreement.

"We'd be throwing good money after bad," the Clydesdale concluded.

And it was over, after all those months of planning. Christmas gone, and no present for his parents.

His landlady didn't ask why he was back early, just gave him a cup of tea and an oat biscuit.

"Your blankets are aired. I'll put fresh sheets on for you."

"Thanks, Mrs. Pearce."

"And thank you for the sloes." The hedgehog's bright little eyes gleamed above the moist, black nose. "Wicked boy. You know I like my sloe gin."

She did like her sloe gin. And Mattie liked her apples, and Kip his hazelnuts. Nobody ever left the countryside behind. Magnus himself hadn't managed it.

Huh. Day trippers.

Magnus grabbed his hat and kissed his landlady on the cheek on his way to the door, managing to avoid her prickles with his soft nose.

"This boat lift," he said to Kip as he burst through the door. "There won't be another one like it in the country."

"You're talking as if we were going to build it after all." Kip, for once, was sitting still at his desk, while Magnus was the one who paced the room, tossing his mane and snorting with excitement.

"We are. We'll build it for tourists. Who wouldn't want to take a boat up in a lift? They'll use the waterways and bring trade to the inns."

Kip's tail flicked. "I like it. We'll talk to the council first thing on—"

Outside, a mechanical screech of brakes mingled with the animal scream of a horse in distress. Kip, his fur on end, bounced to the windowsill to see, but Magnus was already thundering down the stairs.

Mattie lay among the wreckage of her cab. Her left flank was scraped and filthy where she had been dragged along the street. A motorcar, dented and steaming, had mounted the pavement on two wheels. To Magnus, it seemed to loom over Mattie's body, the bonnet open in a crooked smile.

"Can you move your legs?" he asked. He laid his nose on her neck.

The other horse flexed each limb in turn.

"The cab was all I owned." Mattie's eyes, with their blonde lashes, closed.

"Mattie. Come on. There's nothing broken. Get up."

"Pulling's all I know."

Her lips were drawn back from her teeth, and Magnus realised the chestnut was older than he'd thought. Her gums were very pale.

Pulling's all I know.

"Hey. Mattie. Hey." He nipped her shoulder. "How would you like to retire to the country?"

The mare's high, fast breathing caught and stopped, then resumed more slowly. One eye opened and swivelled to look at Magnus.

"Where the apples come from?" she asked.

Hulllo young Magnus,

I never thought I'd want to be a country horse, but it's lovely here. Trees with room to grow, and trunks not blackened by soot! Space to stretch your legs and have a bit of a gallop if you like, nobody to see you and poke fun. Grass everywhere, just to nibble when you fancy it.

Your Mam is an absolute pet and we get on like a house on fire. She's been lonely and it's good for her to have another girl around. It's good for me, too.

Your Dad is doing fine. He might not have the first idea who I am but he lets me order him about like a foal. When you're a cabbie for as long as I was, you learn to do a bit of shouting and not take any nonsense. You can stop worrying that the locks will be too much for me, or dangerous! He's shown me exactly how it's done. We work as a team, me and your Dad, and I'm stronger than you think. A lifetime of pulling built these muscles, my lad, and don't you forget it.

He speaks of you sometimes. 'My son, who does fancy art in the city'. He's proud, you know. I'm sorry he won't show it when you're around. My Dad was the same, rest his soul. Maybe that's why I rub along all right with yours.

We all wanted to wish you and Kip good luck when you apply to the Waterways Authority again. Your Mam framed your sketch of the boat lift and hung it over the mantle. Your Dad goes over to it every now and then and studies it, peering down that long whiskery nose of his.

"Won't it be nice, Reg, when you're lifting all the boats up and down?" says your Mam, and he nods. He's happy, we think. He'll be happier when he can do a one-horse job again.

"Our son thought of that. For us," she adds.

There's been an otter and a donkey up here already, looking around and asking questions. Talk of building an inn, if things really got going. I think your Mam would like to run an inn, and so would I. A warm bar for your Dad to sit in when he retires. A place for you to stay, too, so you could visit for as long as you wanted.

You'll be here before then, though. Supervising. Bring Kip when you come. Your Mam will love him to bits and want to feed him up. He'll love her, too.

The leaves are out on the apple trees, and now the buds are starting to come. I'm looking forward to a real Spring. Visit soon!

Yours,
Mattie

Magnus folded the letter and sat back in his chair, breathing the scents of tea, toast, and porridge as the rain pattered on the windows. It was Sunday, and he could stay where he was, cosy in his lodgings, without any need to feel guilty.

Mrs. Pearce shuffled in from the kitchen and spooned an extra helping of porridge into his bowl.

"Eat up," she told him. "You need something that sticks to your ribs, this weather."

Magnus ate up obediently. After breakfast, with a mug of tea at his side, he opened his sketchbook and began to draw. The page began to fill with blackberries, acorns and mushrooms heaped on autumn leaves. He'd frame it, he decided, and give it to Mrs. Pearce.

BOILER ROOM BEASTIES

GUSTAVO BONDONI

The world goes on, and the elders must bow down to the will of the younger generation. But they might not like what they discover beyond the confines of the boiler room.

It had been years since they'd last seen a human. Sher-Nal suspected that many of the youngsters didn't actually believe in their absent masters, although they'd never admit it out loud. So it made the mother-protector proud to see how well Unit did his part. The young analysis cat had been still as a statue, perched for hours above the single opening that remained.

All the signs were present, and Unit would soon get to test his reflexes. The air around the hole seemed to vibrate and turn a pale shade of blue as the air molecules emitted in the visible spectrum. A quick reaction from the analysis cat would make for a quick battle — anything less than that would be long and drawn out, as it was any time the lead bug lived long enough to identify the defensive formation and give orders to its soldiers.

Seven tiny figures, each about the size of a feline head, appeared outside the hole. The cats hidden around the room stayed perfectly still, ready to act on Unit's signal.

The analysis cat waited, and Sher-nal felt apprehension. As leader, she should have been detached and prepared for anything, but the tension was double for her because — for the first time — the cat responsible for marking the leader was one of hers, from her next to last litter. She was proud that he'd been the one to master the link equipment, but paid for it in nervous watching now.

Nanoseconds passed, and her genetically optimized neural pathways kept track of each. Every tick increased her nervousness, but she knew that they were still well within the safety margin for insectoid attack. Unit was doing the right thing: taking his time to identify the leader. A mistake there would be costly.

The analysis cat moved suddenly, just a slight shift of his head, but it meant action. A beam of laser-light illuminated one of the beasties, just off to the side of the group and near the back, and the cats moved as one.

The three members of the lead team pounced from their concealment to both sides of the opening, while the backup squad took positions in a semicircle six feet beyond it.

All three threw themselves at the marked insect, and all three proved necessary. Moving with a quickness that even the modified cats were hard-pressed to match, the beasties opened fire on the defenders with some kind of particle beam that emerged from their mouths, trying to protect their leader from the strike. Two of the cats died before they came down.

But the third landed squarely on the black insect, his open mouth tearing its head off before the beastie could react.

Success! The enemy leader was down! The only questions now were whether it had been done quickly enough and, she shuddered to think, whether that was even the leader. The next few minutes — or hours, depending on whether Unit had been right or wrong — would tell the tale.

Bugs scattered, opening fire on the unarmed cats. The shots were undirected, seemingly aimed at whichever cat was nearest. That was a good sign, indicating that they might have succeeded in nailing the leader, but the beams were still deadly. Sher-Nal sighed as she saw one of the cats on the perimeter fall to the blasts.

Why didn't the humans give us technology? she wondered. *They set us to fight against an intelligent species, gave us minds so that we could match wits with them, and then left us with nothing but teeth and claws.* It seemed wasteful.

But there would be time — endless time — to ponder those questions later. Right now she had to make certain that none of the enemy made it past her position. She was on the second perimeter, not out in the open, but hidden behind specially placed pieces of equipment or boxes of stuff. She'd never known the first perimeter to fail — the cats there were chosen for both reflexes and strength — but it could happen, and it was her job to get any beasties that made it out of the trap.

None did. Unit had identified the correct leader from among the pack, and the cats had moved with their habitual efficiency. She'd never understood the analysis cat's explanations for how he picked the one bug that could think independently of the queen. Something about chemical analysis of the air and pheromone concentrations. But it worked. All that mattered was that Unit had gotten the right leader, that they'd gotten him before he (or she or it) could do a tactical analysis and transmit specific orders to the mindless drones that had come out with him, making them fall into their fallback mode of scatter, destroy, and shoot at anything that moves. It was never overly effective.

But there was always a cost and, as leader, it fell to Sher-Nal to assess it. She padded slowly out into the open. The only cats she could see were either finishing off beasties who were in no condition to resist, or else they were strutting around, marking their territory, exulting in victory.

It was time to put a stop to that.

"To me," she hissed. She'd heard the humans speak, heard the well-defined tones that cats — even genetically modified ones — could never hope to imitate, even though the language they spoke was the same.

The young warriors immediately heeded her command. They might be the true line of defense, but a mother was always a figure of awe to most of them, even if some of the young females might one day challenge for a place among the ranks of the breeders.

Unit was the last to arrive, after climbing carefully down from his perch. He was the last cat one would have expected to be a protector: not quite the runt of his litter, but close, very close to being too weak to survive kittenhood. She felt a surge of pride in what he'd achieved. There would be no more doubt, no more challenges, no more sneers. All would see his value to the defenders.

"How many lost?" she asked.

Unit, his face concealed by the link helm, took his time. Actual seconds passed while he verified the information. "Four casualties. Three dead, and Errit has lost a leg. He's in shock."

Alive? The team shot into action. There was little consideration for the weak among the cats of the *SS Oppenheimer*, but an exception was made for those wounded in battle. They would be revered until the day old age took them onto the next of the nine roads they had to travel.

They dragged Errit, whimpering, by the scruff of the neck to the warm spot beside the tap that dispensed painkillers and antibiotics. One of the few good things about the rays of intense heat that the beasties used to fight back was that they immediately cauterized any wound they created, making infection unusual. Errit would survive once they got him warm and stabilized. As she watched, Sher-nal wondered, for the millionth time, why the humans hadn't modified their bodies when they spliced the genes that mapped their brains; paws that could actually grip things would have been extremely welcome.

But humans moved in mysterious ways. She'd always accepted that, but now it was beginning to create a problem. She ordered the members of the second perimeter to pick up the rest of the casualties, and move back towards the den, wondering what she would do to solve it.

———

The humans called it the boiler room. Every sign with instructions on equipment maintenance said 'boiler room this' and 'boiler room that.' But, as far as Unit, or any of the analysts before him could tell her, there were no boilers in this room. There was, however, something they referred to as 'nuclear reactors,' which they'd never been able to explain adequately to any of the fighting cats, and which had consequently simply been referred to as 'boxes' ever since.

Of course, none of the fighters was really all that interested in what happened inside the metallic elements that defined the contours of their world, which probably explained why they never stayed around to listen to the complete explanations. When the subject turned to the beasties, however…

But that wasn't the problem. Her first order of business on

arrival would be to check on Errit. If the bearers had followed procedure, he would be under sedation, and a cursory check would be enough. She just hoped the other mother-protectors would allow her that small service, and those few minutes to marshal her arguments.

No such luck. As soon as crossed the towering, human-sized doorway, they were upon her.

"We won't be shrugged off this time, Sher-Nal," Dae-Ñik told her firmly.

Sher-Nal was about to ask for leave to go see Errit, but that would have been a mistake. The mothers facing her seemed ready for anything, erect, alert and nervous. Tails twitched as they waited to see what she would do. She wanted to sigh, to slap them around with her paws for acting like children, but every one of these cats had shown the strength of character to be allowed to become a breeder. They were all strong, intelligent, and loved the tribe more than they loved themselves. Sher-Nal would never have dismissed their concerns were it not for the fact that she knew from firsthand experience that they were wrong.

"I know. Let's go into the den so we can discuss this." The response immediately calmed them. They might hold different views, might even believe that Sher-Nal was making a mistake that would endanger the future of the tribe, but they respected her; there was a measure of fear in that respect, of course, but it was mostly a feeling she'd earned during hours and years spent helping to transform each of them from a playful kitten to a formidable pillar of their society.

The den was warm, clean, and quiet. Ted-Lio's newest litter had been shooed out into the nursery so that the mothers could meet in peace and quiet. Someone had even laid out a bowl of synth-milk and food for Sher-Nal: a sign of respect and acknowledgement that she'd been out risking her life for the good of the tribe. But they were impatient, and she'd barely managed a sip of the milk when the other mothers began speaking.

"Can't it be possible that you might be wrong?" one of them asked, sounding surprised that she'd had the courage to speak.

"Maybe you misremember. You were just a kitten at the time. If I were to start talking about the things I remember as a kitten, you'd box me around the ears," Dae-Ñik said, the very voice of reason. She said it evenly, but the plaintive note obvious even in the limited vocal range available to the cats made it evident that the young mother wanted it to be true. *For more reasons than one.*

"No, it isn't possible," Sher-Nal sighed. "This wasn't an isolated occurrence. Humans used to come in here every day. Some would work on the machines. Others would just stand around discussing things they saw up on the readout board. There was one man who would come in every day to clean dust off the tables. We used to love him because he would let the kittens play with the thing he used, it had hanging pieces that he would hold just out of reach. And there was one lady who would speak to the mothers. She would tell us what to do, and warn us when she thought there would be an attack of beasties." She didn't tell them of the way the woman smelled, of the sharp acid scent of her perfume, of the pheromones and musk beneath it, and of the simple smell of human under *that*. It would have served no purpose.

"Why would we need her? We have the analysis cats. We've always had analysis cats. Your own Unit is one."

"We haven't always had analysis cats. The last time the lady was here, she left her control device, and showed some of the mothers how to use it. She said she might not be around for some days, that there was trouble on the ship." Sher-Nal paused, remembering those times of turmoil. "I wasn't there, of course. I wasn't even old enough then to be a defender, much less a part of the mother's council. But those mothers have passed the story of the meeting on to me, and I've done my duty to them by passing it on to you."

The rest of them shifted uncomfortably. They all knew what Sher-Nal was implying. Subtlety was no part of tribal politics.

"And they also passed on the injunction against trying to get through the door?"

"Of course. It came from the humans themselves. They know the beasties are dangerous if they can get beyond the walls of the boiler room."

"Of that, there is no doubt. What we doubt is whether there are any humans out there for them to be a danger *to*," Dae-Ñik said. "We think the time has come to go back out there and have a look."

"I won't oppose you," Sher-Nal said. It wasn't diplomacy, it was a bow to the inevitable. She would be defeated if it came to a vote, something that would serve no purpose other than to undermine her position. And judging by the turn things were taking, her wisdom would be necessary in the days ahead. "But have you thought of how we'll manage it? That door has been closed since that very day. Even all the kittens born since then have been unable to open it, despite their best efforts, and their mightiest leaps."

"That won't be a problem. Unit has come up with a solution. I couldn't really understand how it worked, but he seemed convinced."

Unit? One of her own? He knew full well that Sher-Nal was against the idea of outside excursions, and he was one of the few that believed humans had been there relatively recently. He said his evidence showed him it was true. And still, he'd gone behind her back and cooperated with the other mothers. Sher-Nal was tempted to accuse him of the deepest betrayal, but she knew it wasn't the case; like nearly every cat of every generation, he wanted to explore, thought there had to be more to life than the endless vigilance against an enemy that wasn't theirs to begin with.

She felt old, tired and anachronistic, but she showed none of this to the mothers. To them, all she said was: "Then let's get on with it."

————

The mothers had been telling the truth. Unit had devised — using some abandoned straps that could be manipulated with paws and claws — a system with which he believed he could get the door open. Pride mixed with anxiety once again as Sher-Nal watched the young analysis cat as he studied the round iron ring which made up the only mechanism that might conceivably be used to budge the door. He stood under it, moved to one side, moved to the other, and then began hissing orders.

Young cats, some too young to fight, even, began running about, dragging lengths of strap in their teeth and jumping from nearby flat surfaces to string the straps through the ring at precise places on Unit's command. Soon, the metallic cross in the center of the ring was strung with multiple lines.

How Unit decided when the straps were all in place was a mystery to Sher-Nal. It looked like a hopeless tangle to her eye, but Unit was soon satisfied. The next step seemed to be to get every single able-bodied cat in the warren to take one particular strap in their teeth and pull.

Nothing happened, and Unit ordered them to stop. He climbed up the tense line and observed the ring from up close for long moments, hissing softly to himself as he did. Finally, he walked back down and calmly told the cats to pull harder.

They did, to no avail.

"Harder!"

Sher-Nal could see the strain in the cats' eyes, in every twitch of their tails, in the hardness of their muscles. They slipped against the metal deck and often lost their purchase entirely. The seconds took eons to pass as she watched, not permitted even to pull.

"Harder!"

Suddenly, a crack like something breaking shook the room and the line surged forward. Cats stumbled and fell with the sudden movement. The wheel on the door seemed to have moved about a quarter of a turn.

Unit ordered his workers to repeat the movement with a different line, and then again with another. The motion came quickly, easily, as if, with the initial resistance conquered, the door's spirit had been broken. They turned the wheel until it turned no more, and then Unit ordered the cats to pull on all four straps at once.

The huge, ponderous door screamed as it parted from its moorings for the first time since Sher-Nal was a kitten, revealing a dimly lit passageway.

She spoke. "All right, we've got it open. Now get over here so we can talk about what to do next."

She was glad to see that impetuosity among her kind was still tempered with caution, and they all crowded around her, each wanting to say their part.

———

Sher-Nal darted across the hallway. While it was obvious to all the cats in the group both from the way the passage looked and the way it smelled, that it had been deserted for a long, long time, they had decided to take no chances, and she was determined to lead by example.

Only the enormous respect the other members of the tribe still accorded her had allowed Sher-Nal to come at all. The group consisted of Unit, Dae-Ñik, two senior fighting cats, and herself. Everyone knew that the only indispensable member of the team was Unit, the only one who could solve any unexpected problems that might crop up. The rest of them were there to protect him.

So far, the great adventure that the younger generations had imagined had proved anticlimactic. There was evidence of human habitation everywhere: discarded articles of what Sher-Nal gleefully informed her companions was clothing, scattered sheets of paper similar in texture to the ones that the cats carefully guarded and preserved inside the boiler room except these were soiled and ragged, and other items that none of the cats could identify.

Even so, their progress was tortuous. Sher-Nal had insisted on one small exploration party and that it was to move slowly and cautiously. For once, no one had argued.

Perhaps long experience with the insectoid beasties was finally paying off in the cats' hunting methods. No feline knew what the beasties were, exactly, but lore handed down from humans to Sher-Nal's elders and from Sher-Nal to the next generations said that they were a plague: hive-minded insects capable of short quantum teleports that the *Oppenheimer* had picked up on one of its many ports of call. They lived deep within the radioactive cooling cores, out of reach behind the reactor shielding, and only came out occasionally by way of that single gap in the lead — which they had presumably created themselves — that allowed them to jump into the ship proper. Unit's equipment was able to pick up the quantum disturbances minutes before the beasties attacked.

The lore said that the humans, knowing that the bugs were intelligent, had once tried to reason with them, and many men and women had been killed in the attempt. So, after hunting down the pests, they had created the modified cats to do the fighting for them. The legends also said that it would take the ship nearly eighty years to reach another planet where equipment was available that could decontaminate even the most radioactive parts of the ship.

But no one was thinking of the legends and their duty. Sher-Nal could almost read the thoughts of the other cats in her group as they surveyed the debris: the humans were all gone, and they could be masters of a much larger domain.

"Careful, children," she warned, feeling old even as she spoke the words.

They ignored her, and she could see the discipline break down as her troops became more and more convinced that some unnamed cataclysm had left the cats as sole masters of the ship. When the forward scout hissed that the way was clear, the rest would follow out in the open, as if they were walking back into their own dens.

The endless hallways and the single echoing chamber they encountered reinforced this behavior. Everything was empty, and even the room itself, though it held all manner of equipment Sher-Nal couldn't identify, showed no signs or scents of human habitation.

Finally, after a sharp right turn, the passage came to an end in a colossal empty space. It was filled with furniture, not equipment. Tables like the one in the boiler room repeated a few dozen times stood in rows and yellow chairs were standing or lying on their backs beside them. Dim red light, quite unlike the usual white glow that illuminated everything else on the *Oppenheimer*, cast no shadows into the vast space. It simply seemed like the more distant reaches faded into darkness.

The cat whose turn it was to be the point scout bounded onto the nearest table in a mighty leap. He hissed inarticulately and his head appeared from the edge of the table to look down on them from above. "You guys need to see this," he said quietly.

Sensing the tension, they jumped up silently, one by one.

"Is this what a human looks like?" the scout asked when Sher-Nal arrived.

She stared. "Maybe on the inside." They'd all seen enough bones to know what bone was like — cats died all the time. This was bone. Polished, clean, and with no flesh on it whatsoever; the bones of a creature long dead. The skull, sunken and formless, gave her the only clue, but it was difficult to reconcile the warm flesh she'd seen on their masters to this gaping emptiness. "Yes, that was once a human," she replied, finally.

"There are lots more of them," the scout observed. The young cat wasn't being disrespectful; he was just pointing out the obvious. Every table in sight was crowned with a similar mound of bones, carefully arranged to form the semblance of a living master, but all devoid of flesh, picked clean by time or a respectful hand.

A whistling sound came out of nowhere and suddenly the scout disappeared off the edge of the table.

When they dropped to investigate, they found the young cat dead, transfixed on the end of a long metal shaft. The heavy pounding of something approaching could be heard in the distance.

Or some*one*, Sher-Nal amended. The smell of human, not soft and covered by artificial scents, but raw, unclean and stronger than she'd ever imagined, could be sensed. There were no pheromones here, no musk, just the stink of immature flesh. She could see shadows moving, much smaller than the humans of her memory. They were coming her way.

"Hello!" she said loudly. "I'm glad we finally found you!"

The nearest shadow hissed and threw a shaft at her. Her genetically modified reflexes saved her and it flew harmlessly past, gouging the floor where she'd stood an eye-blink before.

Unit materialized behind her. "They don't seem to be coherent, mother," he said. "I think it would be best to study them from afar for a time before attempting to reason with them."

"What? Those are humans out there. They created us, modified us. They built this ship, they're responsible for feeding us."

"I have a feeling that most of that is completely auto-mated. Besides, according to my database, those humans are juveniles. They shouldn't be able to design or create much of anything."

"So where are their parents?"

"I don't know. Dead, perhaps? They certainly don't seem to have been around long enough to teach the children to speak." He paused. "We need to run. I have to think about this for a while."

Sher-Nal ran. There was little else that she could do.

Another ineffectual shaft landed behind the fleeing group.

————

Unit knew he was getting old, but until Gener was old enough to fight, there was nothing he could do. They needed a cat well adapted to the data link to keep the tribe alive, and Gener was the only one with the necessary skills to be born in the last five generations. *It was a pity that Freeweight had gotten himself killed in a beastie raid,* Unit thought. *That one had enough potential to let me retire.*

But it was impossible. Only by interpreting the information, knowing when the humans were massing to attack, and predicting where the beasties would emerge from one of their quantum micro-jumps could the cats stay alive, caught between two relentless, almost mindless foes. He'd forbidden attacking any humans, but the younger generations didn't seem to follow his reasoning. They were too fast for any single human to subdue, so why not strike back? After all, didn't the humans hunt them for food?

He'd heard the suggestions. Let the beasties take care of the humans for them. Move to another sector of the ship and barricade the door behind them. Strike back, and strike hard.

So far, with the help of old Dae-Ñik, the venerable crone of the mother's council, he'd been able to reason with them, keep them focused on doing their duty to defend the ship against the beasties.

His greatest hope was that they would arrive at port soon. They needed to be somewhere where civilized humans could reason with the savages that the children had become, where they could clean out the beasties and give the cats somewhere safe to live. Unit suspected that the human adults had died in some catastrophe, and that only some isolated nursery crèche had survived, but he didn't know what had happened, or how the young ones had lived.

He knew that he would probably never learn the truth.

But his greatest preoccupation was that it was time for him to leave his post. He could no longer communicate effectively with the rest of the tribe. The younger generations would soon choose their own path, and he thought he knew what it would be.

Only that morning, he'd overheard two of the warrior cats speculating as to what human flesh would taste like.

He had a feeling that it was a taste that cats would come to know very well long before he moved onto his next life. A shudder ran through him which he had no time for. The future would take care of itself, and there was an attack of beasties due in a few minutes.

He had work to do.

HANGING BY A THREAD

NENEKIRI BOOKWYRM

Sophie the spider has always loved movies, and now she has a chance to work on a real, live set! Now if only she wasn't the janitor...

There it was! The shot Sophia had been waiting patiently for. The light of sunrise bounced off of the nearby pool of water and created a wonderful ripple effect that she knew would be perfect for her new film. She carefully made her way over to the web where she had her camera set up and delicately adjusted the tilt of the lens. Then with a trembling leg, she clicked the record button and scuttled out of the way of the shot.

The sun rose painfully slow for Sophia's taste. Sophia shook her head as she tried her best to refocus. She wasn't used to staying up this late, but she had envisioned this shot obsessively in her head. She couldn't stop thinking of trying it out since her last shift at work. She was experienced enough with setting her camera up on her web now that she could try these more adventurous shots.

She didn't breathe as the sun made it to the middle of the

sky, signaling the pivotal moment. The sun would reflect off of the water and create the effect of one circular sun that existed in both the water and the sky. But before she could celebrate, she felt a slight twinge on her web. She whirled her head around to see where the disturbance was coming from only to find a small fly had managed to get caught right next to her camera. She tried to raise her front two legs and make a calming gesture to the fly. The fly, however, had decided that it was a great idea to try and struggle as much as its tiny little wings would allow and began to tug at the web. This of course bounced the camera quite a bit and in the next moment, the camera had become dislodged from the web and was rapidly falling. Sophia ran as fast as she could across the wooden beam of the barn and dropped down by a quickly spun thread to catch it. She missed with her front legs but managed to just barely catch it by the strap with her mandibles. As she slowly worked her way back up the thread she muttered curses to herself.

"Damn! I was sure I would be able to get that shot this time. Now I'm gonna have to stay up again tomorrow."

She sighed as she caught her breath back on top of the wooden beam. She was familiar with setbacks in her passion's work, but she couldn't dwell on it long. It was already getting to be early morning and she had work tonight. If she didn't get any sleep it would make her sloppy at work and she couldn't afford that. At least she had something to take for lunch tomorrow. She quietly wrapped the fly up for later and ate down her old web so it wouldn't get in the actors way.

Her alarm woke her up a few minutes before 9PM, just in time to get ready before her coworkers showed up. Sophia had the shortest commute out of all of them. Being a barn spider had its share of difficulties, especially living in a world where all of the jobs were offered by species much bigger than yourself. But filming a movie on location at a barn? That was much too good an opportunity to pass up. Sophia had loved cinema ever since she was a spiderling. She desperately wanted to direct but she didn't have the experience to get hired. She had hoped that her current job would give her more experience, but they were only interested in having her keep the bug population down so as not to disturb the actors during shooting.

As Marge walked into the barn, Sophia could see that she seemed more tired than usual. It was harder for the other actors to be up all night than it was for Sophia. Most of the main characters in the movie were diurnal and had to fight their nature every night. She couldn't blame them, though. Anything to make their shot.

"Evening Marge, are you doing alright?"

The hippo turned quickly in the direction of Sophia, but couldn't find her. She squinted her eyes and called out, "Sophia? Is that you hon?"

Sophia let herself down by a thin thread and dangled in front of Marge's face.

"Good morning!" she exclaimed while waving one of her many legs.

"AHHHHH!" Marge cried out in surprise.

"You know one of these days you're going to remember I'm a spider before 10PM," Sophia said sarcastically.

"I certainly hope so hon, for your feelings and my heart both" she said as she held her chest. When she had calmed herself down enough, she turned towards Sophia and held out her hand.

Sophia landed in it and Marge brought it closer to her face so that she could hear Sophia better. She spoke softer so Sophia wouldn't be uncomfortable.

"It's hell on me getting my body to wake up for these

shoots. I'm just in need of a good night's sleep, at night prefer-ably. How's your camera work been? Did you get that shot you were talking about?"

"No, of all the times I'm not looking for a meal one comes waltzing into my web and ruins the whole thing!" Sophia crossed her front legs in a huff.

"Aww, I'm sure you're gonna get it hon. I've seen your stuff and it's good. Maybe you can talk to the Director about getting some pointers?"

Sophia had tried to broach the subject of working with Greg before but he brushed her off every time. He was of the opinion that she had been hired as pest control for the set and that was what she was there to do. Nothing more or less. And, as if on cue, he walked into the barn. He was a gruff looking boar with an average build but carried himself like he was as tall as a giraffe. His right tusk was coated in a cheap but shiny gold plating that glowed soft yellow whenever he stood under-neath the moonlight. He didn't say anything to Marge or Sophia as he walked past them and began to set up for the night's shoot.

"If he's here, then the others aren't long behind. We'll catch up later?"

"Sure! I don't want you to get in trouble."

Marge gently set Sophia back on the top rafter of the barn and walked over to the prep station to finish getting ready. Sophia still couldn't believe how well she and Marge had gotten along since the start of this movie. When Sophia first met Marge, she was intimidated by her size and was afraid of getting crushed. But now, she knew that Marge was more careful than anybody else on the set.

The other actors and employees came through the barn door entrance shortly afterward and before long everyone was ready to begin filming. Sophia had finished setting up her web traps for any errant bugs that might wander on set, so she could take a quick break. The movie they were filming for was a horror movie and the entirety of it was set within the barn itself. It was heavily implied at the beginning of the movie that some evil force had trapped the three main characters in the barn and was waiting for them to turn on each other. It was also not an accident that the three main characters were animals known for being terrifying in their own regard. Dale, the laid-back lion, was frightening to most larger animals. And Chris, the long-eared owl, was scary to most smaller animals who didn't want to get caught in his razor sharp talons. Marge was scary when it suited her, which meant you never really knew when she would snap.

All three of them were giving a great performance but Sophia couldn't help but notice the camera work out of the corner of her eye. It seemed so stiff and steady, especially in the moments where it would make more sense to have some movement. It didn't hurt that she had eight eyes to give her a few different angles on each shot as it was happening. Before long, she started to plan out better versions of the shots for the scenes as they were filming. By the end of the night, she was furious that Greg hadn't once tried to do something creative with the shoot. The characters were dealing with some supernatural evil and the camerawork made it look like a low-budget Halloween special!

Once the camera crew had packed up the equipment, Greg came out into the middle of the barn and bellowed out to all the remaining employees.

"Don't go home just yet! I am expecting a very important visitor and I expect you all to be on your best behavior for him."

"Who's coming through Greg?" Dale piped up as he put on his jacket.

"Only the guy who greenlit this movie in the first place," Greg said with a smirk.

Chris's eyes went wide as he cocked his head in disbelief. "You don't mean Tyler's coming?"

"Of course he's coming! I invited him personally to see a rough screening of my newest masterpiece. He's paying for it after all, I only figure it's fair to show him how much money it'll make him."

That was just like Greg, bragging before thinking. But Sophia couldn't help but be intrigued at how the movie was coming along. Maybe she had been wrong about Greg's decisions as director. She hurried up and wrapped the remaining bugs from her web traps and started to clean up early for their visitor.

Tyler managed to be a whopping three hours late to his own private screening. When he did arrive, the barn doors burst open and a small red carpet was rolled out into the center of the barn. Walking down it was a weasel dressed in a suit so expertly tailored it could keep up with his slinking movements effortlessly.

"Tyler baby! So good to see you!" Greg beamed.

"Yeah, yeah Greggy. I wanna know two things. One, do you have my movie? And two, do you have any refreshments?"

"Not to worry sir, I have both for you in spades."

Greg clacked his hooves together and a pair of interns began to set up a projector in the back corner of the barn to project onto the wall. Another intern brought out a carton of eggs and opened them in front of Tyler. He looked over them for a time and after some careful consideration picked one from the middle. Without missing a beat, he reached into his pocket, pulled out a straw, and stuck it into the side of the egg taking a long sip.

"Ahhh, that is some good egg."

"Only Grade A for you sir!"

Satisfied with his snack, Tyler and Greg moved over to the back wall of the barn and the movie began to play. It was tough for Sophia to get a good read of Tyler as he was watching the movie. The rest of the crew had stuck around to watch the movie as well. If her suspicions were correct then Chris, Dale, and Marge were not enjoying it, but from her vantage point in the top of the barn, she could only see the backs of everyone. Sophia tried to turn her brain off and just enjoy the movie for what it was, but it wasn't working. How could someone who had this much experience be making this many rookie mistakes in composition and shot framing? Thankfully this cut of the movie was much shorter than its actual run-time.

With the movie done, the projector was switched off with a click and Greg looked expectantly over to Tyler.

"Well, what did you think?"

Tyler looked over to Greg and shrugged his shoulders. "It was OK."

Greg's brow furrowed as he asked, "OK? Just OK?"

"Yep, just OK."

"Now wait just a damn minute…"

"Greg, your movie is horrible. I was trying to be nice for once."

"HORRIBLE!" he shouted, lowering his head down to get in Tyler's face.

"Yes, horrible. It's a horror movie, right? Then why am I not scared? Give me something that'll really make me squirm. Then we can talk."

"Well what do you suggest I do then? The movie's almost finished!"

"I don't rightly care what you have to do. But I do know

that if I don't see something scary by tomorrow morning, then it'll be your job."

And with that, Tyler crushed the eggshell in his hand, wiped the resulting mess on Greg's shirt, and walked out of the barn.

Greg stood there speechless for a few minutes before stamping the ground and storming out himself. The rest of the crew were left to clean up the set and get ready for the next night of intense and frantic filming.

Except when night rolled back around again, Greg was nowhere to be found. Dale tried calling him on his cell phone but he wouldn't pick up. By 10 PM it was all but decided that he had ditched them. Sophia tried to get everyone's attention, but in the confusion, it was much too loud for them to hear her. Save for one person in particular.

Marge stepped out into the barn and slowly opened her mouth wider and wider until she let out a roar so loud that every occupant of the whole barn stopped cold.

"If everyone would stop panicking for half a second, I could hear what Sophia has been trying to tell me!"

"We can still make the deadline! I have some ideas of how we can fix the shots that Greg did, but I'll need everyone's help to get it done."

"And just who do you think you are to be giving us direction?" Chris hooted from across the room.

"I'm the spider that's gonna make the best horror flick you've ever seen Chris! And it's going to be so good it just might save all of our jobs too."

Dale stepped forward and stuck out a paw towards Sophia. "Where do you want us, Director?"

Sophia's eyes lit up as she said, "Well first, we're gonna need a few more cameras."

For the rest of the night, the barn was a blur of activity.

Sophia jumped from rafter to rafter, giving direction to each of the camera operators as they re-shot integral scenes in the movie. She scuttled around her webs and positioned each camera to catch the perfect shot. She used her small size to her advantage too. Taking large and imposing ground level shots of the characters for moments where it looked like they were losing their minds. She managed to suspend herself by a single strand of silk to film Dale charging straight into the camera without the fear of him accidentally breaking the more expensive stand cameras. Even Chris pitched in at the end, helping Sophia edit the new material into the existing film so that it would be ready in time.

By the time the telltale red carpet was rolled into the barn, they had their movie done. Tyler strode in without saying anything and held out his hand. This time the intern handed him the whole carton of eggs and slumped down into the audience in an exhausted heap. Sophia was nervous throughout the whole screening, but felt better when she looked around the audience and saw how everyone was reacting to the new edits. She caught Tyler breaking an egg in surprise more than once during the show and hoped that was a good sign. When the projector light faded this time, Tyler stood up and clapped.

"Now *that's* what I call a scary movie!"

From the back row, a familiar boar stood up and rushed over to Tyler.

"I told you I wouldn't disappoint you Tyler baby. You should have more faith in me!"

The rest of the crew was dumbstruck as they saw their Director taking credit for all of their hard work. When did he even get into the barn? Had he snuck in during the screening? Sophia tried to get Tyler's attention but both him and Greg were turned away from her. It wasn't long before Marge got out of her seat and walked over to Greg. Since Marge was a hippo, she was used to places being too small for her. As a result, she tended to crouch down whenever she was inside buildings to keep from intimidating her coworkers. But as she stepped in front of Greg, she unfolded to her full height and looked down at him.

"If you think I'm going to let you have the credit for what Sophia and the rest of us did, then you've got another thing coming hon."

Tyler slinked around the base of Marge's leg and said, "Oh not to worry, I know that Greg didn't film this. It's far too good for that! What I do want to know is who did?"

Sophia lowered herself from the top rafter slowly as she said, "That would be me sir."

"Well kid, you've got a real good eye for pictures. Real innovative shots you showed off here today. How would you like this smuck's job?"

"Now wait just a second!" Greg bellowed.

Tyler looked up to Marge and said "Ma'am if you wouldn't mind…"

The barn doors were flung wide open as Greg crashed through them and tumbled to a stop outside. A satisfied Marge dusted off her hands and headed back inside.

"Well I've got business to attend to out of state, so I trust you all will be able to finish the film for me." And with a flourish Tyler packed up his carpet and left the barn.

Sophia couldn't believe that she'd finally get her chance to show what she was truly capable of. She looked to her crewmembers and felt good about the future. Over the horizon, the sun was just beginning to rise.

"C'mon folks, I have the perfect shot for ending this movie."

THE MANELESS

DAVID M. SULA

Can innovation give this lion something that nature never could?

"For my good friend Joey, who inspires me to keep innovating every day."

They called themselves the Maneless, a small but intimate pride of lions all of whom lacked the hallmark of their species, all born with different names than the ones they called themselves now. Among the strongest and eldest of the pride was Marrow. Though tall and heavy with muscle, he still bore the residual curves of childbirth from the three cubs he'd mothered before breaking free of his old life. Because of this, he grew his fur out thick, and when he smoothed it just the right way, his breasts were less noticeable, and the hips he disdained looked thinner by comparison. With a mixture of rich dark loam and acacia sap, Marrow teased and spiked the fur circling his broad muzzle. A wreath of gelled umber jags could resemble a trimmed-down mane from a distance on the golden Savannah; however, up close, the stickiness and graini-ness was quite apparent. Still, Marrow committed to the prac-tice. He had learned to accept such limitations, and the effort put in far outweighed the cons of not trying at all.

Appearances were important. Especially on the Savannah. The Maneless only consisted of nine members, which was fewer than average. For this reason, Marrow always ensured his pride projected the appearance of strength, knowing it was just as important as possessing actual strength. He would always prefer to deter conflicts than endure them. When imparting such wisdom to his pride, Marrow often explained that strength was like a wall. If it looked imposing enough, no one would challenge it, but attacks wore it down, and the more attacks a wall endured, the likelier it would crumble to a weaker attack later on. That was a gamble he never wanted to open himself or his pride to.

Snugly squeezed on a narrow stub of peninsula within the crescent of a winding river, the Maneless' camp prospered well enough to make do. They had access to clean water, and the river wrapping around them on three sides made the camp easy to defend from scavengers or other hostile prides. Brush was plentiful, and two slanted trees on the banks provided shade on particularly hot days — tents could be stuffy at times. Despite the many useful affordances provided by this location, it didn't come without its disadvantages. While there was safety in distance from more populated sects of the Savannah, the other prides out there, especially the large ones, could benefit from a close proximity to the Water Hole. The Maneless were fortunate enough to have access to regular clean water, but the Water Hole offered more than a place to drink. As a location of eternal armistice, it was the only place where predators and prey, warring tribes, and animus loner barbarians sheathed their claws and weapons to engage in bartered trade under a banner of truce. Medicine, weapons, tools, shelter supplies, art, goods of comfort, and more could all be acquired and sold there.

Marrow sat in his tent carving a fresh spear from a flat spade of rock. Their food reserves were dwindling, so two of the younger lions had ventured earlier this morning to hunt. It wasn't uncommon to lose a tool or two to general wear and tear on hunts, especially considering Dusty's carelessness. Shaded from the sun, seated on a striped pelt of zebra skin, Marrow clacked rocks together over a sheet of dried leather to catch the shaled chips.

There was something about working with stone that the lion found pleasurable. It was rigid and sturdy and tough, and yet with the right strikes he could alter its shape into whatever he wanted. He could chip away the undesirable parts.

With another spear point completed, he set it aside before reaching for another flat hunk of stone to begin shaping when the tarp that hung over the doorway of his tent thwapped open. A young male, barely more than a child, stood hunched over gasping for breath.

"Dusty?" Marrow dropped his materials as he scrambled to his feet. The young lion's eyes were wide. His fur was smeared with mud and dirt. "You're supposed to be out hunting. Where's Karma?"

"She's been hurt!" Then his eyes widened larger. "I mean *he's* been hurt. Sorry. I'm sorry. He's been hurt."

Marrow embraced the younger lion's shoulders, helping him stand upright and also ground him out of his panic. "What happened?"

In between gasps of breath, Dusty explained, "We were hunting, and his foot lodged in a meerkat hole, and he fell. He can't get back up."

Marrow stepped around him and pushed his way into the

47

mid-afternoon sun. Shielding his eyes, he scanned his distant surroundings, naively hoping that the accident had happened close by. He knew better than to hope for something like that. Karma had a tendency for wandering off farther than he should. "Where is he, Dusty?"

Dusty pointed off to the northwest, along the river.

"Take me."

A few other members of the pride had crept towards Marrow's tent to investigate. "What's happening?" "Where's Karma?" "Did you say Karma's been hurt? Was it the Kutoka Pride?"

"Calm down, everyone," Marrow reassured them. He raised his paws to ask for quiet. "There's been an accident. Nothing more." The last thing he wanted was panic. Panic was easy to exploit.

Spotting Ridge in the back of the growing cluster, Marrow singled him out with a point. "Come with me." Dusty wouldn't be strong enough to carry Karma home if need be. Ridge was the only lion in the pride who rivaled Marrow's strength.

Ridge bore a hard soul. Not only was he one of the first to join the Maneless, he was the oldest among them. He spent a long time wandering the Savannah alone after leaving the Kiume Pride. His old pride was legendary. Nearly thirty lions large, enviable masculinity pumped through all of their veins. In fact, Ridge named himself on account of the thick ruffs of speckled blond and umber fur that haloed his face and shoulders. Out of all of them, he was the closest to having a natural mane. It rose up into a spike between his ears that descended all the way down his lower back. It was actually a common genetic trait among the biological family he left so long ago. While he was a bit shorter than Marrow, he made up for that with thick and powerful muscle. When living with the Kiume Pride, he led the hunters, second in status only to their King.

With a delegation of aid chosen, Marrow urged Dusty to lead the way. The trio of lions ran off down the river bank, Marrow promising a swift return over his shoulder. Soon the encampment of the Maneless was behind them, a cluster of sand-colored domes of animal skins that sank beneath the yellow grasses of the Savannah.

Dusty quickly put a bit of distance between himself and the older lions, spritely fellow that he was. They thundered a mile through the ocher fields before anyone finally said anything.

"Karma is a fool," Ridge grumbled, just quietly enough that Dusty wouldn't hear him disparaging another member of their ranks. "No one should ever hunt alone."

"He wasn't alone," Marrow chastised. "Dusty was with him."

"That's basically being alone. Dusty is still very young."

"He has to learn to hunt at some point." Marrow struggled to keep his voice even, which was admittedly difficult while running so steadily. His lungs stung, and his thick fur only added to his exhaustion in this heat. Ridge seemed to keep pace just fine. Perhaps his irritability kept him going.

"At his age, Dusty is a liability. Karma routinely takes unnecessary risks and should have brought someone else along."

"It will be fine," Marrow insisted. He was not fond of such platitudes, but he needed Ridge to have a level head now; although, Ridge didn't seem convinced and snorted contemptuously.

It was two more miles before they finally broke away from the river and arced further west. They were uncomfortably close to the Kutoka Pride's territory. Ridge noticed this as well and passed a sideways glower towards Marrow as they ran. The look made it clear that his opinions about Karma had only strengthened.

They were all exhausted. They hadn't brought any water with them in their hurry. Marrow's fur spikes were softening in the heat. The sap was running thin, and sticky mud started oozing down his forehead. His makeshift mane was good for appearances, but offered little practical stability. As his outward portrayal of his own masculinity melted down his back like honeyed candies in the sun, Marrow did his best to focus on the task at paw. There were obviously more pressing concerns at the moment, but he couldn't help but worry what would happen if a patrolling Kutoka lion saw them encroaching on their borders. Would they wonder who these filthy ragged-looking lionesses were? Or would they recognize them as Maneless? Knowing all too well what that pride was like, Marrow wondered which would bring about a more violent response.

"How much further, Dusty?"

"We're close." The young lion was gasping for breath again. He had uncanny amounts of energy most of the time, but burned through it rather quickly. He needed to learn how to moderate his endurance better. That was one of the reasons Marrow assigned him to hunt with Karma. For all of Karma's faults, the reckless lion understood the concept of balance, risk, and reward. Marrow had been around enough cubs to recognize that Dusty needed someone like Karma to help him hone those energies and teach him how to self-moderate. Karma made snap decisions, and that sort of quick thinking was something Dusty would benefit from. Ridge didn't see that though. While Marrow looked for potential, Ridge obsessed over outcomes. Everything had a cause of blame.

Upon passing an acacia tree that Dusty recognized, the

three spurred themselves to sprint the last of the way there until they saw a bronze paw wave in the air above the grasses. "Hello, boys," a high voice drawled.

The three exhausted lions came upon the scene gasping for breath. Karma lay on the ground propped on a boulder. His shoulders were hunched in hapless guilt. He forced a smile, though he was still wincing from pain and embarrassment.

"Are you alright?" Marrow asked in a forced calm before Ridge could interject a rebuke. Health was the most important, and Marrow wanted to emphasize that to the whole group.

Karma lifted his left foot, which hung at an awkward angle, and roved his paw up and down the joint above it. "I'm alright, but I can't really bend my ankle."

Marrow knelt at his side.

"We should get out of here as soon as possible," Ridge said anxiously.

"Not until we know what we're dealing with." Marrow gingerly lifted the foot in question and craned his head around to get a look at it from all angles. When he twisted it towards him, Karma hissed sharply through his teeth.

"Fuu—" He chomped the curse into his lips and squeezed his eyes shut.

Marrow didn't like the sound of that cry. Leaning down, he blew gently on the joint, moving the lion's short fur around to see the skin beneath without exacerbating the injury with more physical manipulation. Dark blue splotches discolored the flesh beneath his follicles like he'd been smeared with berries. Appraising it against his other ankle, there was noticeable swelling. "First things first, we have to get this elevated as soon as possible. It could be a sprain, but it looks like a break. There's some minor hemorrhaging around the joint." Marrow actually didn't know for sure if it was "minor." The coloration was deep, which meant it could be even worse than it looked. Marrow only knew the basics of healing, but he still wanted to provide some reassurance about what they all could see quite clearly.

"Damn meerkats," Karma muttered. "Ridge, will you do me a favor and piss in that hole over there?" He nodded towards a small burrow entrance nestled between two towering fans of yellow grass.

"You can get your revenge later," Marrow placated. "Let's get you up."

Karma was a slight for a lion. Nimble and quick, he was good at sneaking up on and chasing down prey. Marrow knew that with Ridge's help they would have no trouble carrying him. The two of them crouched on either side of their injured comrade and lifted him up by the armpits. This would be a difficult trek. Ridge grunted as he shouldered a good portion of the younger lion's weight.

"What should I do?" Dusty asked.

"Stay out of the way," Ridge snarled.

"Run along ahead and tell Harvest the situation. Have him set up everything he needs to mend a broken bone so that we can get to work as soon as we get back."

"You got it, Marrow." Though clearly fatigued, Dusty started off at a brisk run back the way they had come.

Meanwhile Marrow and Ridge helped Karma hobble along. He kept his injured leg aloft and hopped along on his good one with one arm draped over the powerful shoulders of his elders. He kept his eyes down, abashed by the situation.

"I'm so sorry," he admitted. "I should have paid closer attention to where we were going."

"Yes you should have," Ridge snapped.

Marrow swallowed his own feelings. "I'm just happy you're alright."

"Not being able to walk is far from alright," Ridge grumbled.

Marrow heaved a sigh.

It took almost two hours for the three of them to return home. Marrow could tell the pain was growing in severity. Now and then, Karma's claws dug into the two other lions' shoulders before he retracted them and offered a strained apology. Marrow understood. That said, when they finally entered their camp, he was relieved to finally remove the weight from his shoulders. Several other lions came to greet them and take the burden from them. As a pride, they helped carry Karma to Harvest's tent, leaving Ridge and Marrow at the edge of the peninsula under the shade of the trees. The older lion fell to his knees at the bank and splashed water in his face. Marrow on the other paw, abstained. Sap was smeared through the fur all over his face. As refreshing as a splash of cold water would be, it would just cause loam to bleed into his eyes. Instead, he leaned against the tree and arched his aching back. Then he surveyed the camp. Everything still looked the same as when they'd left a few hours ago. Every minute he spent away from his pride though, Marrow worried over their safety.

"This pride is too small," he said to the river's breeze.

Ridge snorted and rose from his crouch. "And what would you do? Proselytize and recruit?"

"Our pride is infamous. Surely there are other lions of manelessness out there. We should be seeking them out. We need numbers, for our own protection."

"Our hunters hurt themselves on the landscape, and yet you would send us out on missionary work? How many would need to travel together to be safe? How vulnerable would that leave us while they were away?" Ridge demanded.

"It's not like I haven't thought of that." Marrow wished he could strike the perfect balance between accessibility to others like them and the isolation that kept them out of harm's way. "But what about those who don't know how to find us? What about those who can't get away?"

Ridge rounded on Marrow. "Today we narrowly avoided a disaster. What if a Kutoka lion or other enemy found Karma before we could? And you want to split our numbers further?"

"No!" Marrow raked his claws through his head fur and looked down at his paw, smeared with amber slime and gritty soil. He grimaced at the stickiness of his palm before smearing it on the smooth bark of the tree. "I'm just being wistful is all. It's exactly because our pride is so small that I worry. All prides would say something like, 'If something bad happens to one of us, it happens to all of us,' and that sort of brotherhood is just as strong among our ranks if not stronger, but practically thinking, *if* something bad happens to one of us, something terrible actually could happen to all of us. I know there is no simple fix to this problem that doesn't divide us and put us at risk, but it would be such a relief to comfortably know that if something *were* to happen to one of us, the rest of us could still be safe."

After a contemplative pause, Ridge said, "We need to move the camp. We need to go farther away."

"That's not the solution, and you know it," Marrow argued. He pushed past his peer and stepped closer to the camp while still standing on its edges. Almost everyone was gathered outside of Harvest's tent, curious and concerned for their fallen family member.

"Then we need to stop letting our pride venture so far from the camp."

"We hunt how we have to."

"Marrow——"

"Ridge," he interrupted. Then he took a deep breath. He was too tired to have this argument again. Ridge's heart was in the right place, but further separating the pride from others wouldn't help anyone. As it was, their distance from the Water Hole was already dangerously far.

"We live on a precipice of animosity, and you would rather we teeter into harm's way if given the ultimatum." Stealing the last word, Ridge turned away and headed towards his tent. His tail lashed. His fists were clenched. Marrow had several retorts he would have loved to fling at the other lion's back, but what use was it? Instead, he took a deep breath to steady himself and went to Harvest's tent to check on Karma.

———

"It's not good," Harvest admitted. They stood outside the healing lion's tent. Karma's faint grunts of pain could be heard through the taut walls of skins. "I've got the leg elevated, so I hope the swelling will go down, but it's definitely broken. Possibly in multiple places." Harvest had never mothered any cubs himself in his old life — he always felt averse to carrying a life inside of him even at a young age — but he had a strong bedside manner and still spent a lot of his time caring for the cubs of his old pride, which was where he picked up his adept healing skills. "He's going to be in a lot of pain, so we'll need some of the proper herbs. I've compiled a list, but our own stores won't suffice. I have enough bandages to wrap it up for the time being, but in order to set it properly, we'll need more."

"How long will it take to heal?" Marrow asked. He internally prepared himself for the worst.

Harvest bit his lip and swiveled his eyes to his tent as if he could see Karma's injured form through the wall. Or maybe he just wanted to avoid eye contact with Marrow. "Best estimate? Two months."

Marrow raked his fur again, once more smearing earthy sap onto his palms. Two months without their sneakiest and most adaptable hunter would not bode well for food supplies. The pride was low as it was. Karma was also the most optimistic, and Marrow couldn't help but wonder what impact it would have on morale for the pride if Karma had to spend a majority of his time resting in a tent rather than socializing with the rest of the group. And of course there was the logistics of feeding a mouth that couldn't contribute. Of course Marrow wouldn't deign to think of one of their own as a burden, it was still going to be worth considering.

"Marrow?" Harvest asked. The young healer yanked him out of his piling concerns.

"Yes, yes. Sorry. What do you need most of all?"

"I'm going to have to go to the Water Hole."

"Out of the question," Marrow said.

"But I know exact—"

"You said you had a list. I'll go."

"But—"

He cut off the healer with a paw, and he stopped short. *Dammit, Ridge,* Marrow thought. The older lion had wormed into his head. Harvest was right. If anything, with Karma's injury, Marrow should stay put in the camp. It was his job to protect the pride should something happen, but he'd been to the Water Hole enough to know that for all its graces of cooperation, there were also dangers for them all there. If there was one lion in the pride Marrow would have trusted to go to the Water Hole alone, it was Karma. This was a place where even the gazelle and the cheetah could let bygones be bygones and greet each other amicably, but it was different for the Maneless. Their pride did not receive such friendliness.

No, Marrow decided. He would go. "I want you to stay with the camp. Tend to Karma whatever way you can. Prepare the list. I'll head out at first light."

It was too late in the day to go now. From their camp, the journey to the Water Hole took a little over half a day each way. Between the hyena packs, the warthog barbarians, and other aggressive prides like the Kutoka, the Savannah wasn't safe after dark, especially for them. Leaving Harvest to complete those orders, Marrow went on his way through the camp making preparations while also assuring the others that Karma would be fine.

He found Dusty in his tent and barged in. "Dusty."

Surprised, the young lion looked up at the leader of their pride. His wide eyes wordlessly bore the question of what this was about.

"I'm going to the Water Hole tomorrow. You'll accompany me." It was the most tactical option. Dusty had not been to the Water Hole since joining the Maneless. It would do him good to get used to the changes he would have to start expecting, and Marrow could keep him safe. Also if something *did* happen while Marrow was away, their youngest and weakest lion wouldn't be a liability.

Dusty nodded.

"Rest up. We leave at dawn." Dusty was also the most energetic, and a trek like this would get him that much-needed practice of endurance moderation that got cut short this afternoon.

Now Marrow just had to convince Ridge.

———

"I want you to protect the camp while I'm away."

"This is foolish!" Ridge sat on his bedroll, cross-legged and hunched forwards.

Marrow crossed his arms and sat down across from him. "I didn't ask for your opinion on the matter, only a reassurance you can take care of everything around here."

"Just let Harvest go."

"Harvest isn't ready to go alone."

"Then *I'll* accompany him," Ridge argued.

"There are tactical reasons for this," he reminded the older lion. "Others are less likely to harass a pride King, even one like me."

"If you trust my skill enough to leave me in charge of defense here, then I should be trusted to take care of myself at the Water Hole."

Defense though was exactly the role Marrow *wanted* Ridge to serve. It would be harder for him to pick a fight with someone miles and miles away from other people. "You said you wanted distance, so that's what I'm giving you."

"*You're* the one who I want distanced from that place; not me," Ridge growled.

A silence hung in the air. Marrow stared at his comrade incredulously. "What is that supposed to mean?"

Ridge heaved a sigh and rubbed the broad bridge of his muzzle. "It's nothing personal—"

"Of course it isn't."

"Would you let me talk?"

Marrow offered an upturned paw for the other lion to continue.

After mulling his words a moment with a bite of his ebony lip, Ridge said with a carefulness almost uncharacteristic, "I think… you're trying to hold on too hard to what we've lost."

"Ridge—"

"Ah ah ah." He waggled a finger. "None of us had a more difficult break from our prides than you. I think you want to stay in these lands because deep down, you're as stubborn as I am. The Kiume Pride didn't understand my choices. They don't understand *me*, but they let me go."

"And they also said you could never go back," Marrow reminded him. His throat grew tight. He didn't like thinking about his old life. None of the Maneless did.

"That said… the lions who inherit their gender by birth go far to start prides of their own. You want to think yourself King of this pride? Then you need to start acting like a King."

"Or what?"

Ridge looked down at his feet scratching the thick ruffs of fur that covered his chest. "Or maybe let someone else do so."

The tightness in Marrow's throat clenched tighter. Deep down, he always knew Ridge wanted to be King. He long suspected that was one of the reasons he left the Kiume Pride. The highest he could have amounted to there was second best, and after discovering his new self as a lion, it surely had to grate on him that he still couldn't rise higher than that, but Marrow steeled himself, balling his fists at his sides. He stood up and smoothed his fur down to cover the parts of himself he loathed. This was *his* pride. "You're right, Ridge. No one here lost as much as I did. That's why I know what I'm doing. Good night."

Marrow left the tent before either of them could say anything else to each other. But as he started off towards his own tent in the center of the camp, he heard the faintest of mutterings from within Ridge's tent about cubs. Marrow clenched his teeth and forged on. He needed rest.

———

The next morning, Marrow stood at the edge of the camp, rocking on the balls of his feet. Grey light crested across the Savannah. It was still chilly outside, but the heat would bear down on them soon enough. The whole pride had gathered to see them off, with the exception of Karma who was resting in Harvest's tent. Harvest ran down the list with Marrow one last time.

"I've got it, Harvest. Tell Karma to hang in there."

Dusty yawned and stretched. He stood close to Marrow. He looked weary, but once they got moving, he would be his usual alert and energetic self. He shouldered his pack. Marrow had charged him with food for the journey. Marrow's shoulder satchel held what little they could spare to trade: the spear points he'd made yesterday and some salted meat. Marrow bid farewell and good fortune to his pride, reminding everyone to mind Ridge, who stood at the back of the cluster with his arms crossed.

"He's in charge until I get back." Then Marrow locked eyes with him and pointedly added, "He knows what's best." Ridge looked away, knowing what that meant. Don't do anything Marrow wouldn't approve of. With that, the two set off towards the Water Hole.

It was quiet at first. The Savannah could be sleepy in the morning, but soon the caws of birds flapping high overhead pierced the dullness of dawn. Color returned to the world as the red globe of the sun lit up the sea of grasses.

"Can I have something to eat?" Dusty asked.

"You have the food pack."

The young lion reached over his shoulder and pulled out a flank of cooked meat and chomped into it vigorously. He tore off a chunk, chewed, and swallowed.

"Just remember. No eating once we get there."

Dusty nodded. "I know. I know."

"I know you know. I just want to emphasize. We have to be on our best behavior. We are representing the Maneless today."

Again, the young lion nodded. "I'll be a man you can be proud of."

"You already are," Marrow said with a smile. That smile was a facade though, something forced on his lips to cover up the ache of what was to come. He knew that the folks at the Water Hole would not see him that way.

———

The Water Hole featured some of the most innovative infrastructure for miles and miles around. The moon-shaped reservoir of shining grey water sunk into the ground next to two single-story buildings hewn from multi-colored striated wood. Small rooms were available for use while traveling. The establishments were collectively run by a council of several species to maintain a sense of equality. One was managed by a rhinoceros and a wild dog. Another sold bowls of ogogoro, distilled from the juice of the local palm trees that sprouted up at one corner of the Water Hole. On the other side, a bloated dead baobab had been husked out and was used as a store room on the rare occasions of fierce rains. Along the outer curve of the crescent, surrounding the tavern and hostel, were numerous stalls where various animals hocked their wares. The stalls weren't individually owned; whoever showed up earliest in the morning with their supplies to trade could secure an unclaimed spot. When Marrow and the other Maneless came to the Water Hole, they often had to scout around for the best deals as nothing was ever static.

Marrow and Dusty approached the baobab from the south. It was busy today with all sorts of animals hustling about the arced arrangement of stands, tarps, tables, and carpets. Marrow's heart thumped fresh anxiety into his veins. Busy days were often a mixed bag. On the plus side, they would blend in easier, but on the other, there were more people to cause trouble.

"Want me to refill the water skins?" Dusty's eyes were already on the reservoir that he was able to sneak peaks at between the marketplace gaps.

Marrow knew that look. The young lion wanted to galli-vant off and explore. "Stay close to me," he instructed as they passed the baobab. The huge gaping hole in its trunk showed that it was currently full of shelves covered with clay pots. As they passed, Marrow spotted a cheetah inside weaving in and out of the stacks of pottery. Perhaps the council turned it into a permanent fixture of some sort. It smelled of herbs. *Might be worth checking out first,* Marrow figured, but as soon as he started to traject his path towards the tree, the cheetah inside looked up through the doorway and growled. Marrow paused and put his arm around Dusty. "Come," he said steering them back towards the first row of stalls. "We need some fresh canvas to help set Karma's ankle."

There were so many people. They shouted over each other. They pushed each other. Marrow took Dusty's paw like he was a cub who might get lost in the crowd. A body brushed against him, broad, grey, and leathery, a mountain of person, and though they didn't seem to notice them as anyone other than a regular face in the crowd, Marrow still mumbled an apology before worming deeper into the throng.

"Marrow, slow down," Dusty begged.

The older lion ignored him. He tugged his comrade along, eager to get in and get out as soon as possible. The density of bodies made him disoriented. He scanned the various tables for what they needed. There were some artisan goods, fruits and nuts in bowls, and folded stacks of tanned leather. The number of refined goods had increased since the last time Marrow had been here. A new anxiety crippled him as he searched desperately for what he needed, that what they brought to trade would be insufficient in comparison.

"Marrow!"

Dusty's shout snapped Marrow back to the present. He stopped and looked at the young lion who looked back with concern.

"You okay? You're acting... weird."

Marrow swallowed and nodded. "Yeah. Just..." He let go of Dusty's paw and sidestepped between two tables out of the main path of foot traffic. Dusty squeezed next to him.

After a pause and a cursory glance in all directions, the young lion admitted, "It *does* seem different."

This hadn't been what Marrow meant. It wasn't just the bigger crowd. When he looked around he saw wooden masks meticulously painted, clay beaded jewelry, and tapestries of orange and yellow threaded with geometric designs. It had only been a couple of months since the last time Marrow made the trip here, and everything was so much more advanced. This was what he'd worried about. Ridge was so obsessed with moving farther and farther away. They were already outsiders to this community. Now Marrow felt like they'd been left behind as the world evolved around them.

Aside from the cheetah in the baobab, no one had even paid any negative attention to them. Most people were preoccupied with their own affairs: hocking goods or haggling. Nearby, a zebra argued with an antelope behind a stall of shawls that they would be better off trading one for the zebra's stack of rare parchment than the adjacent water buffalo's fresh spool of wool twine. Eventually the antelope shooed both of them away claiming his art was too valuable for either offer. Once they did, Marrow sidled in and occupied the antelope's attention.

"I'm looking for… well… cloth scraps," Marrow admitted.

The antelope raised an eyebrow. He then gestured his detailed crafts with both arms, a look of indignation souring his already irritated demeanor.

"Yes, I see they're very lovely, I'm not trying to besmirch your work. I'm just looking for fabric that could be used to wrap an injury. Do you have anything like—"

"Why are you talking like that?"

"Sorry?" Marrow paused with confusion.

"You sound sick."

"That's just my voice," Marrow assured him. He started to suspect where this was going, and he took a deep breath. Clearing his throat, he continued, "I'm just looking for some sturdy rags."

The antelope folded his arms. His eyes roved up and down Marrow's form with a critical eye, like he wasn't sure what he was looking at. Those critical yellow eyes paused around his upper chest and then glanced at the gelled spikes of his mane. "Oh. You're one of *them*. The man-actors."

"We're called the Maneless," Dusty piped up.

Teeth clenched, Marrow hushed the younger lion with a flippant wave of his paw.

"Oh. I see," the antelope drawled. He rubbed his lithe tan fingers down his cheeks, up his face over his forehead and down his back. "Hey look I'm maneless too. Great accomplishment."

"Liste—" Marrow started, but Dusty leaned up against the table and spoke up again.

"It's not about what we don't have. It's about being proud

of what we can be without." *Stupid boy.* Marrow sighed. Those were talking points he'd instilled in Dusty to help him become more comfortable with himself, but it wasn't sufficient to convince someone like this.

The antelope's snort made Marrow's tail lash. What he wouldn't give for five minutes beyond the Water Hole's border with this arrogant—

No, Marrow. Keep it together.

"I've heard of your little girls' club," the antelope went on. "Honestly, I feel bad for you. It's sad. I can't imagine being so confused about yourself that you'd choose to live like this." He said this to no one in particular as he inspected a loose string on one of his tapestries. Then he turned his focus solely on Marrow. "Or is this old lady just that good at brainwashing cubs."

The lion's lips parted in a snarl, and his claws escaped from the sheaths in his fingers. Without showing even the slightest sign of concern, the antelope said, "Careful, lady. You know the rules. Of course I understand why you'd be so aggressive towards me. Hunting is the prime instinct of a lio*ness*."

Marrow hated him. He wanted to drag him from the Water Hole with his neck between his teeth. When Marrow hunted, when all the righteous lions and lionesses hunted, it was never personal. That was the difference between hunt and homicide, but Marrow wanted to rip him apart for disrespecting him, disrespecting Dusty, disrespecting their pride, and disrespecting their way of life. He would love to see him run his mouth against someone from the Kutoka Pride. They'd rip his tongue out, and people would say, "Serves him right for pissing off the most fearsome pride in the Savannah."

But Marrow had to take control. Other people nearby were starting to pay attention to them, and things were different for him. If he lashed out, the sentiments of the crowd would be different. "Typical of *those* people," onlookers would say. They needed to keep a low profile, get the stuff on their list, and leave. Taking a deep breath, Marrow retracted his claws and smoothed the fur of his chest. He put his paw around Dusty's shoulders. "We'll find someone else to trade with."

"Someone with lower standards, I'll bet," the antelope called after them as they turned. "You freaks aren't even worth my scraps."

Marrow pushed his way through the crowd, dragging Dusty along with him. Once they had escaped the eyesight of everyone who'd been in that vicinity, Dusty asked, "What was that all about?"

"*That*," Marrow stated, "is what I tried to tell you about. It's the new norm with this place for you. That's life for us now. It will feel like everything's changed, but in reality, it hasn't. That's how people have always been."

Dusty's muzzle drew into a grimace as he looked down at his own body. He didn't exactly glare at his own form. He just looked miserable. It was like his own body was something he loathed, but was too depressed to do anything about. "I was here once when I was a cub. My mom took me. When she and Dad kicked me out of the pride, and I met you guys... I guess I hoped that my parents were the weird ones. Like that wasn't normal, and everyone else would be nice like you guys to make up for the fact that they weren't." He ran his paw up his arm, and when he dragged his fur upwards, it revealed the double crescent of scars that usually was covered. Dusty's own father bit him when he tried to express himself how he wanted to, and that wasn't abnormal. Most of the Maneless bore scars like that.

"*You're a lioness. You were born a lioness. You'll always be a lioness, and you need to learn your place in this pride as a lioness by any means necessary.*" That had been the last thing Dusty's father ever said to him. After the blood was drawn, Dusty fled. It was only by sheer luck that Karma and Ridge found him while hunting. They gave him food and brought him back to the pride, and Marrow did his best to give him a home. He was barely more than a cub. But he was strong and optimistic in his own way, and Marrow hated seeing that jovial optimism dashed.

"Why are they like that?" he asked as they continued through the crowded market.

"I don't know," Marrow sighed. In truth, Marrow knew. Hatred. Fear. Judgment. But each of those felt as random and irrational as no answer at all.

"I hate them."

Marrow wasn't sure what "them" he meant. The people like that antelope? His parents? It didn't matter, though. So instead, Marrow just said, "I know." After a pause, he added, "You will always be a lion where it counts. People will tell you that you aren't, but they don't know what you're really like, what you really feel on the inside." He gestured broadly at the diverse crowd. "Everyone here? Their gender was handed to them. We had to *work* for ours. And they don't have the power to erase that effort. You understand?"

"I guess," he said dejectedly. "Then why do you spike your head fur?"

Now it was Marrow's turn to grimace.

"Because if it's all about how you feel inside—"

"It is," Marrow interrupted.

"But then you—"

"It's complicated. You don't have to prove anything to anyone about how you want to live your life."

"Is it because you're pride King?"

DAVID M. SULA

"A little. I don't know if anyone else in the Pride ever told you, but I didn't leave my old pride on very good terms."

"I get the feeling not many of us did," he mused, rubbing his arm.

"I had three kids before I became Marrow. I loved them with all my heart. But I hated how I looked when I was pregnant with them. It felt wrong. Nursing them felt wrong. When it was just me on the Savannah, with no one watching, I could let go. It was easy." He sighed wistfully, remembering back to the days of his youth, the feel of earth beneath his feet. The thrill of the hunt. The freedom of it all. "I don't regret being a mother, but it forced me to view myself in a way that I hated. And after the third, I didn't want any more. But I wasn't a huntress anymore. I was one of the pride mothers. Raising young... and making more. When I talked about it with our King, he didn't understand. He thought I was committing some sort of aspersion on him and my children, when all I wanted was to resume control of my own life and body. I didn't want to be what he wanted me to be. He turned my kids on me. The things he threatened... it was like he was a different person, but he wasn't. This was who he always was. I started the Maneless so that no one would have to feel what I did. We do what we have to, to feel like ourselves. I spike my fur so that in just a little way I can look on the outside how I feel on the inside. You do what you have to, to feel comfortable in your own fur."

"I see." Though the way, the smaller lion looked down at his feet, the way he shuffled them through the trodden dirt, Marrow wondered if he really did.

"The point is, you do it for you. No one else. If you look at your reflection in the river and feel at peace, then that's all you need. No matter what, you'll be Dusty to me. Because I hate to say it, but it doesn't matter how much effort you put into it.

68

Those who hate us will hate us no matter how much effort we put in."

Dusty nodded. "Does it get easier?"

"No. You just get stronger."

———

They finally found the herbs they needed, but they weren't going to be able to sell meat to the rhinoceros who had them. Against his better judgment, Marrow sent Dusty out on his own. Hopefully, they could cover more ground among the carnivorous sellers and find the best deal on something that would catch the herb seller's eyes. Marrow restricted himself to predators' stalls, the ones who didn't chase him off with leers, taunts, or insults.

Eventually he came upon a hyena, another artist who greeted him with a smile. "Hey! I recognize that mane," he greeted with a jubilant point of his finger. "You're one of those Maneless fellows. I've heard a lot about you lot. What can I do for you today?"

Marrow bit his lip. "I'm just looking for someone who'd trade more refined goods for cooked and salted meat."

"Well then, you have my attention."

Marrow shook his head with a rueful chuckle. Typical hyenas. This was perfect though. Hyenas were the worst hunters on the Savannah.

"What can I get for fifteen pounds of zebra? We also have paw-made spear points. Might be useful to catch your own food." He hoped the rib wasn't too much, but the hyena in typical fashion cackled along with the joke.

"Why spend time hunting when you can devote yourself to the arts?" He gestured at his table: masks carved from various types of wood. Every species on the Savannah was represented in elongated and intricately adorned shapes. Marrow picked up one of a cheetah. Its moon-shaped eye holes stared blankly. Yellow dye was smeared across the cheeks in a soft blend before fading to the wood's natural colors. Black spots covered it all over, and a nose was pointed in an upturned triangle. Marrow set it down and picked up another of an elephant. Its trunk was only a few inches long, but the trapezoid shape still looked authentic in its own exaggerated way. Soft leather flaps were nailed in place for the ears. The masks were light, but sturdy.

"They're very lovely," Marrow complimented. He wasn't sure this was what he'd want though, or more specifically what the rhinoceros would want.

"They're great for story-telling. My nephews love them. They also look nice as decoration over the front of a tent."

"I'm seeking more practical needs. Can you tell me anything about that rhinoceros who sells the herbs? Truth be told, that's what I want. I have an injured lion back home who needs supplies, and all we have is meat and rocks."

The hyena waved his paws. "A lion at home. A rhino across the Water Hole. You're so busy looking at what other people want—"

"It's a need actually," Marrow emphasized.

"Want? Need? That's not the question. The question is: what do *you* want?"

Marrow made a strained face. He knew the answer to that question: to get his supplies and head home to his pride. But that wasn't the answer this hyena was looking for.

The rambunctious predator dipped below his table and withdrew another of his wares, oblivious to Marrow's dwindling interest.

"Ta-dah!" His paws brandished another mask, and for a moment, Marrow was about to write him off completely. This hyena was clearly more interested in making a sale than actually helping.

Then Marrow really looked at the mask and something in his chest halted. It was a lion mask. The cheeks were painted in beautiful detail of reds and oranges. The muzzle was broad and strong. The oblong eyes were ringed in black like the kohl he'd seen jackals wear on their faces. It added a sense of dimension to the face. An open maw revealed intricate teeth carved from blond-colored wood. Its expression was fierce and majestic. But the most striking detail was the mane. Dried grasses had been woven through a series of finely drilled holes all around the circumference of the face. Marrow ran his fingers over it. Extending out in all directions, it fwished like the grasses of the Savannah. Each piece was cut for perfect symmetry. Marrow turned it over to inspect it more. It was domed over the top to fit neatly over someone's crown.

"Go head," the hyena urged.

Marrow licked his lips and then eased it over his skull. It was a perfect fit, settling into place across the bridge of his own nose.

"Absolutely stunning," the hyena appraised.

Marrow looked around through the mask's eyes. His vision was barely hindered; it was so expertly shaped. Then he delicately raised his paws to the sides of his head and felt the mane of grass ensconce his head. All at once, he found he was short on breath, and he steadied himself against the table. He wasn't maneless anymore, but it couldn't last.

"No no." Bending forward, he let the mask slide off his face and into his paws. He laid it upon the table among the other wooden animals. He wiped his eyes. Why was he tearing up? This was stupid. It was just a mask. Just wood and grass. "I... I *need* medical supplies."

The hyena frowned. This man's craftwork was beautiful,

but Marrow couldn't spare an ounce of their own supplies for something frivolous. This wouldn't interest the rhinoceros. For all the hyena's encouragement, kindness, refreshing good nature, Marrow had to distance himself from this table before the temptation lingered a moment longer. In a rush he turned around, bumping into another blond body and started off when a familiar voice stopped him dead.

"Banou?"

The word nearly rended him in pieces like a lightning bolt striking a tree. His throat clenched. Marrow looked straight ahead, but his eyes saw nothing as the distant past flooded him. *Just keep walking*, he told himself. *Just find Dusty and go.* The waft of the familiar smell harpooned into his memories: rich earth and lush greens. It had been so long since he'd been exposed to that scent.

"Banou? Is that you?"

That loathsome word cracked him again. *Just walk away. They'll think you're just someone else. But who else would it be? Who else in this whole damn Savannah smears dirt and sap in their fur?*

Marrow turned to face the lioness he'd bumped into. After a deep controlled breath, he strained out, "Hello, daughter."

The hyena still within earshot leaned forward over his table. "Oh this is your daughter?" he asked unnecessarily with an enthusiastic point. He looked her up and down like she was a piece of wood he was ready to start carving. "Ah yes, I see the resemblance. I was just showing your uh… your parent this lovely mask." He hefted up the lion mask again and addressing the young lioness suggestively encouraged, "Wouldn't he look lovely in it?"

"I was just leaving, Binti." And with that, Marrow turned and submerged himself back into the crowd. He made it to the end of the row before the young lioness shoved her way through as well and grabbed his wrist.

"Gah!" Marrow yanked himself away. "What?"

With eyes of disbelief, Binti stared at the lion. She upturned both palms, stunned. "What do you mean 'what?' After all this time... I..." She trailed off

"I see you have as many words as I do." Snarling, Marrow turned to leave, but then Binti gave out a childish cry that betrayed her age. "Mom!"

Binti was old enough to be a mother herself now, but when Marrow faced her, a soft whimper replaced the strong woman he'd raised.

"I'm not your mother anymore," Marrow spat. "You made that very clear when I left."

The lion stormed away, but Binti followed like a lost gazelle. More people were starting to stare. This was not a situation Marrow wanted to be in. More eyes on him always made things worse.

"I'm very busy, Binti," he tossed into the crowd over his shoulder.

"Too busy for your own daughter?"

Marrow stopped. Then he looked around. The tavern was just up ahead. Knowing that he wouldn't be well received inside, he could at least get some seclusion for a private conversation if they went around back away from the trading tables. With a sigh, he beckoned the lioness and headed over there. In the gap between two of the buildings where barrels of water were stacked and refuse amassed in sloppy piles, Marrow leaned against one of the walls. The rancor of the crowd was dimmed just a bit by the isolation between the two structures, but it was still quite loud. Binti stood up straight, just over an arm's length away. She looked good, healthy. Her fur was sleek and groomed. A leather satchel hung over her shoulder, adorned with strips of clattering beads of teal and orange. It looked stuffed to the brim with goods.

Marrow adjusted the worn strap of his own bag and slid it behind his back. "I can't stay long. It's a long trek back home, and it's urgent that we get there. My pride needs me."

"*We* needed you," Binti said with a heartfelt emphasis.

"And yet you could afford to cast me out."

"I was just a child when that happened. That's not fair."

"Nothing about what happened was fair, Binti."

"I don't... I don't want to fight, Mom."

"Please don't."

"Don't what?"

Anger building, he shouted "Don't..." before trailing off. He took a deep breath and said in a more restrained voice, "don't call me that. I am *not* your mother anymore."

"Because we meant that little to you?"

"That's not—"

"Because being your daughter doesn't mean any—"

"Dammit, Binti!" Marrow exploded. The lioness stopped, and finally he felt like he could breathe since seeing her. "I just don't like that word."

"Okay, fine. If that's how... you are now?"

Marrow shook his head. "It's not a *now* thing." He wondered if it was even worth it to try to explain it to her after all this time. She was older now, but that didn't mean she was more understanding.

Then she nodded. "Okay."

"And you can't call me Banou either."

Paws went up in the air. "You're *impossible*."

"*Impossible*? That's where your limit is? Three words to not use about me? For all of your pride's prosperity and might that leaves most of the Savannah in awe, it's quite sad how slim your definition of 'impossible' is. Do you know what *I've* done? I've been a hunter, a mother, and now a *King*!"

Binti turned away and then spat, "You're also a deserter. That's something *I* find impossible to be."

"Is that what you think? So that's why you stopped me? To tell me how disappointed you are with me?"

"You hated us!" she cried. Tears built up in the corners of her eyes, and Marrow's eyes were on the brink of matching. "You left us. How could you just leave us? Was being a King that important to you?"

Marrow rubbed his temples. "Being a King was a necessity for me. It's never been about that. I'd shirk it in a heartbeat, but I have people who depend on me."

"More freaks like you."

When Marrow was still with his old pride, a prisoner in his own body, he never thought he could find an unkind word to say to his children, and yet today he did. "Fuck you."

"Fuck *you*!" She moved forward and jabbed Marrow in the shoulder with an accusing finger. "Where was this dedication to us? Do you know what it was like to be raised without a mother? Not just that, but to be constantly told that you're the reason your mother went crazy and ran off to play make-believe?"

"Shut up!" Marrow shouted swatting the girl's paw away. "You have no idea what was going on when you were a cub. You have no idea what it was like to live with your father."

"Yes I do. I was *there. He* was there. The rest of your kids were there."

"Your father lied to you. I know that's not convenient to hear, but I would have stayed if I could." His voice broke with a tearful shudder. "I loved you kids."

"Except having us made you miserable."

"No, Binti. Trying to be what your father wanted me to be made me miserable. I couldn't be that. I didn't want to be that. But that didn't mean I didn't want you or Kesi or Jabori!

Your father gave me an ultimatum: his happiness or mine. I know to you and your siblings I was just a parent, but I'm more than that to myself. I couldn't *just* be a parent, especially at the cost of living my life how I needed to. Your father could never understand though. He couldn't have a maneless lion in his pride. Appearances are everything on the Savannah, especially for the Kutoka Pride."

Binti turned away. Marrow threw up his paws, turning his back on his daughter as well. For a moment, the rage and the tension were all that connected them.

After a deep breath though, Marrow was able to add, "Your father would have seen me dead before he saw me as a man. That's how unimportant *I* was to *him*. So I had to leave. And he said that if I ever came back, if I ever came near *his* children, he would hunt me down. But I'm sure that's not what he told you."

Binti sniffled, cupping her muzzle in her paw. When the two faced each other again, Marrow saw tears streaking down Binti's cheeks in full force. Silent drops smeared the ruffs of her cheeks. She folded her arms across her chest, and her tail curled around her leg, and in that moment, she looked as small as the day Marrow left. "I just wanted my mom."

"But not on my terms." He took another deep breath. For all the times he thought about what a conversation like this would go, he never anticipated it would be this hard. "There's a young boy in our pride. He's about how old you were when your father and his other lionesses chased me off. And he's like me."

"Maneless."

Marrow nodded. "I suppose it's easy for him to understand it all, because he also lived it. I know what your pride says about us. I hear the rumors and the insults."

"It's not just Kutoka," Binti argued.

"True. The last time I came here, I overheard two zebras talking about me. They said, 'A zebra runs from a lion so that he'll live. A zebra runs from the Maneless just to make sure those freaks starve.'"

"A zebra? I would have dragged them away by the neck."

"That's because you're my daughter. But I ignored them, because I didn't want to cause a scene, or give these people a reason to ban us from the Water Hole. So I went about my business, and then I saw a lioness from the old pride who used to be one of my closest friends. And she threw a rock at my head."

Marrow locked eyes with Binti, but she had no words to respond with. Uncomfortable, she looked away, rubbing her arm.

"I was afraid I'd turn out like you," she said finally.

"That what your father told you?"

"And others."

"And if you did, that would have been bad?"

"Yeah! No... I don't know. There was *so* much that people said, and I hated it. And I hated *you*. I didn't want to deal with all of this. I didn't choose you to be my mo—parent."

"But I chose to have you. And then I chose to have Kesi. And then I thought, maybe it's just me. Maybe I'm the problem. Maybe I'm not happy because... I just don't know how, and so I had Jabori. And eventually... I realized it *was* me, but there was nothing *wrong* with me, just with how I was trying to *be* me. I'm sorry you felt like you lost something or were denied something. I'm sorry for what you had to go through. But I'm not sorry for who I am. And I wouldn't trade my new pride for anything, just like I wouldn't have traded you kids for anything."

A quick glance at the sky and the position of the sun told Marrow that he had to be on his way. Dusty would be looking for him. They had to figure out their trades and head home. "It's not safe for a Maneless after dark, so we have to get going if we'll beat the dusk."

He headed towards the gap in the buildings to rejoin the crowd. "Wait!" Binti shouted.

Marrow paused, though he didn't turn around.

"Are you... are you happy now?"

"Sometimes," he said without turning back to face her. "Usually. Yes. And I have my pride, and that helps too."

"And you're happy with what you are?" A crack of doubt and tearfulness choked the words.

"Who," Marrow corrected. "Yes. Sometimes... usually... but yes."

There was a pause, and Marrow wondered if that was the end, but before he could take another step forwards, Binti admitted, "I don't... I don't think I could call you 'Dad.'"

"I wouldn't want you to, to be honest."

"Then what *can* I call you?"

"The rest of my family calls me Marrow." And with that he walked off.

———

While Marrow had been distracted, Dusty found a good enough deal for the meat and completed the trade with the rhinoceros.

"It's a bit slim; I tried my best to haggle, but this was all I could get." He opened the canvas sack he'd gotten for Marrow to appraise, and he nodded.

"It's more than I expected we'd get. Good work."

"Where'd you scuttle off to? I didn't see you."

Raking his fur with his claws, Marrow just shook his head. "Just got distracted. Nothing you need to worry about."

Marrow eventually managed to trade off the spear points for some bandages and other materials. They'd have a hard time for a few weeks, but they'd get by. They always did. If Marrow went on some extra hunts, they'd have no difficulty picking up the slack from Karma's injury. Hopefully they could find some time to procure other goods to trade next time.

"The world is changing," Marrow said as they left the Water Hole behind them. The same cheetah glowered from the same hole in the great baobab. Some things would also stay the same.

"I saw some nice-looking beads. They looked a little girly, but I would love to get some, someday. Maybe even make my own. It's just clay after all."

"I wouldn't worry about what's girly," Marrow said fondly. "It's like we talked about: whatever makes you feel most comfortable in your own fur."

Dusty nodded thoughtfully. "Yeah. I'm happy being a boy, and I love the Maneless, but sometimes... I guess I want a little more. I don't know how to explain it."

"You're young. You have plenty of time to figure it—"

Marrow froze and grabbed Dusty's shoulder. The young lion tensed under his elder's grip. "Wha—"

"Sh!" Marrow crouched low in the grass, dragging the young boy down with him. They were far enough from the Water Hole that the banner of truce no longer applied, and this was still open lands to which no one could claim. Yet somewhere on the wind, he could smell the scent of a lion. It was earthy, salty, and a bit lush with fresh foliage. "Kutoka," he whispered.

He twisted around slowly, looking for the subtlest shifting of grasses, searching for whoever was lying in wait. When he couldn't spy anyone, he announced, "We want no trouble! We're just on our way home!"

The silence made Marrow's hackles raise. Dusty gulped. Then there was a dash of movement behind a nearby tree. Marrow unsheathed his claws and charged. He wouldn't wait to be ambushed. When he reached the tree, the smell was stronger, but when he rounded it, there was no one there. Off in the distance, a lioness ran east towards Kutoka territory. Then she was gone. Dusty joined Marrow at his side, a snarl on his lips. "Let me at them!"

"Calm," Marrow assured with a touch to his shoulder. "She's gone."

"Good. What'd she want though?"

Probably just to gawk at the freaks, Marrow mused. Then he looked down and gasped.

"What's that?" Dusty asked.

Marrow stooped to pick up the maned wooden lion mask. He turned it over in his paws, tenderly, afraid he might break it. A note on a scrap of parchment was tied to one of the large wooden fangs. It simply read, "For Marrow."

Marrow ran his fingers over it with longing before looking up at the final glimpse of a lion's tale vanishing into the grasses.

"That's really pretty," Dusty said. "It has a mane and everything. Where'd it come from?"

Marrow tucked the note into his shoulder bag. "I guess you could say it's from the past, but also the future."

Dusty scrunched up his face. "What's that supposed to mean?"

"You'll understand when you're older."

He shrugged, and then he changed the subject. "Are you going to wear it?"

And Marrow grinned. "Mhmm."

The trek home was uneventful, but Marrow preferred it that way. He could take his time to reflect on what all had happened. Dusty strode ahead of him, and as Marrow watched the young lion through the eyes of the mask, he finally felt like the King his pride saw him as. He finally possessed the mane he'd always wanted. He didn't know everything that would come his way, but maybe it could be more hopeful than he originally thought. Ridge was wrong, and when Marrow returned home, they would have to discuss what was best for the future of the pride. He knew the Maneless would always face challenges no other lion or lioness could imagine, but the world was changing in strange ways, and it would not be fair for anyone in their pride to miss it.

As they walked towards their home, the two lions left feet prints in the sandy earth as they swept through the grasses. The world was big and hard and often cold, but that was the nature of stone, and even if the world wasn't fully ready for the Maneless, they still had a personal responsibility to carve out a space for themselves where they would fit and thrive.

COMPUTER LITERACY FOR DEITIES

LINNEA CAPPS

Learning new things is a great way to expand your worldview, even for a god.

"Gaahhh!"

With a frustrated whinny Edain smacked the side of their computer with a hoof. It had been quite generous of the company doing the installation work to provide them with one of the electric boxes that used the 'wee fee', but how did the Filgaians find fun in a nebulous black screen that showed nothing? They had been told the internet thing was working in their private room. Something must not be right but they couldn't figure out how to make the blasted thing work!

Edain let out an annoyed snort, wondering if their decision to let this newfangled technology be installed in the temple had been the correct one. It seemed each year that more visitors brought their electrified rectangles with them and seemed puzzled when they couldn't connect to whatever "the Internet" was. Even if the acolytes had begged and pleaded to have it, Edain was unsure it was necessary.

Edain certainly wouldn't allow visitors to use the silly things inside their temple chamber proper under any circumstances. They would only distract from what Edain believed should be a sacred moment. When families came to the Temple of Edain to see the deity themselves in horselike form they were asking for a blessing. Edain would perform miracles, giving any family that asked the opportunity to have a child to cherish and raise together.

Each upturned ear, wagging tail, deep purr, or whatever a species did to express their joy at these miracles uplifted Edain in ways they never knew possible. Some even brought their infant children to visit, and the sight of adorable tiny faces affirmed Edain's love of what they did. Edain did not want to imagine what would have happened had they not done what no celestial had done before: stay on a world once it had been formed.

Edain imagined something like that was happening now. A couple made of different species unable to conceive. A troubled otter trapped in a body that did not fit their gendered needs keeping them from parenthood. A family tree unable to sprout into life as more than two creatures came together to share their love, wishing to have their child reflect all of them. All of these families coming to the temple only to be turned away, told by the acolytes that they must wait longer. Crying as they left, waiting for the joy only Edain could offer them.

The "internet" installation had already taken three days. Edain's sunrise meditation had been interrupted earlier that day to tell them it would take four more days. Instead of raising their spirits by basking in the wondrous moments nature provided on Filgaia they had been put into a worse mood by the news.

Anger brewed within Edain for those imaginary families forced to wait over something so pointless. This stupid internet thing on these inoperable electronic boxes that no one really needed. Just like this infernal box right in front of them.

Edain's body began to glow with a harsh red light. The coat of their fur rose into spikes. Small knickknacks in the room floated into the air. Energy crackled loudly as if a thunderstorm was suddenly forming in the room, sparks from it rocketing off their form singeing the marble walls. Edain was about to force the stupid box to life or eliminate it from existence, unsure of which option they would ultimately choose.

A timid knocking on the side of their door distracted them from the task.

"S-S-Ser? Is everything all r-right?"

Edain looked towards their door, mortified to see they had left it open and a poor shivering canid had witnessed them in this altered form. Their red glow turning bright pink in embarrassment, Edain reformed their usual appearance in a flustered state.

"Oh goodness everything is fine! I…"

Edain looked the canid over, recognizing him as a dog, a papillon to be exact, by the patches of gingerbread-colored fur that extended from his ears to over his brown eyes. His tail was tucked between his legs, creasing his khaki pants. Along with that he wore a blue polo shirt with the name tag reading, "Guy". Edain lit up with excitement.

"Oh goodness you're exactly who I needed! You're the 'it' guy I keep hearing about from the acolytes! From the way they talked I thought you were multiple people."

Guy's ears turned down a bit more in confusion, though his tail began to make its way back to proper position. The deity was less terrifying in their usual form.

"Th-The 'it' guy? D-Do you mean IT?"

Edain pondered a moment, placing a hoof on their muzzle. "That may be it yes, the eye tea guy!"

"M-My name is just a coincidence ser, it's Guy. We have several information technology experts here at the temple today."

Edain nodded as if in understanding, though they still weren't entirely sure they did. "Okay Guy, Do you know if the small cost is working?"

"E-Excuse me?"

"The small cost! The... Oh blast what is it called, the wee fee? The small cost?"

The canid was trying his hardest to suppress an incredulous woof, ears upturned in curiosity as if expecting a joke. "The Wi-Fi ser?"

"Ah yes, the 'why fie' or whatever it is. I can't understand why this infernal box won't do anything!"

Edain's hoof collided against the box once more causing Guy to wince. Still, he tried to stand tall, using some manner of professionalism to guide him through such a unique situation.

"Ser that equipment is somewhat fragile. You may break it if you continue to um... strike it so. Have you tried turning it on yet?"

Edain blinked at him. The last major renovation to the temple had been to wire the temple for electricity a hundred years ago, and they had only just started to get the knack of it. Even then Edain had refused to have an electric heating system put in, still preferring the temple to be heated by the ancient hypocaust. Though Edain personally had no need, being able to see in the dark, lights could be plugged in if desired during the rare times they had diurnal visitors to their room in the evening.

"I plugged the box in but nothing happened. Is there some other ritual I must perform?"

Guy wiggled nervously. Could he even ask to enter Edain's

room? They were a deity after all and he was just a random Filgaian. He figured there must be some protocol where only acolytes could enter.

"May I? Well, that is to say, I don't mean to offer any offence, but might I join you in the room? I could show you how the computer works."

Edain considered the offer. They weren't sure they liked this newfangled box nor the rectangles that every Filgaian seemed to carry these days. Still it was likely important to get at least a rudimentary understanding of these new inventions. Edain did not like the level of confusion and frustration they currently felt around it all and education might be the only way to eliminate those feelings.

"Alright, you may be my official eye tea Guy, by my divinity. Please perform the rituals to make the electric box 'turn on' or whatever it was you called it."

"It's u-um, a computer ser, it will likely help if you learn the name. There's no rituals either, you just press a button."

Guy tried to hide the incredulity in his voice at just how insulated from technology the deity had become. He entered the room, pressing a paw pad to the power button. He wondered how stubborn Edain must be to not have been able to learn these things from their acolytes over the years. It was possible, he thought, that the acolytes were simply afraid of facing the same wrath the computer might have, had he not been in the hall to intervene.

The fans inside the computer tower whirred to life, and with a small beep the monitor flicked on with a little static. He could see Edain marveling at the screen as various company symbols for the operating system appeared, changing to bits of text and code as the software began to boot.

"Have the Filgaians mastered magic? How did you bring this to life?"

Guy could see a sparkle of energy dance its way over Edain's eyes, something like what he had seen earlier but far more playful and curious. Still he wasn't sure how to respond. When he had gone to school as a pup he had learned that the deity Edain could use magical powers. He had no idea how that magic worked, only that it was not at play inside of the computer.

He would have to keep things as simple as possible for them.

"So when a computer is built we take many pieces of electronics and put them together. When some are turned on, they do certain things like make a part of the... Um... Window into the computer, which is called a screen, a certain color. When other parts are turned on they might make a sound. We choose all the parts to put in for things we want the computer to do, then turn them on and off to make the computer do what things we want."

More of the happy sparks began to fly from Edain, one jumping onto Guy's fur. It made his skin tickle so strongly he almost laughed. He had never heard stories about Edain acting this way, not in school or on the forums he had visited online, being naturally curious about the deity living in Filgaia.

"That sounds just like making a world though. Are you sure this isn't magic? We gathered resources knowing if we put certain things next to each other they could combine for certain reactions. Everything from making the earth form to bringing life to you Filgaians. All there to control with a bit of our magic."

Guy's jaw dropped, his tail going still. To his knowledge Edain had never spoken about the creation of Filgaia to anyone before. Had no one in all their years on the planet ever thought to simply ask? Were they afraid Edain may punish them for seeking forbidden knowledge? Or was it complacency, just accepting Edain had created the planet, never caring to ask how or why?

A realization crashed over him more powerful than an ocean wave. They had said we. Were there more deities the Filgaians had never met? Guy had felt a combination of honor and excitement when he had been assigned to a job as high-profile as working for the deity. He had thought maybe he would see them if he was lucky, not have the entire foundation of his knowledge of the world rocked to its core.

He was about to open his muzzle to ask more questions, but his curiosity was hampered by a moment of existential panic. Did he truly want to know all the secrets of the universe?

"The electric b—er the computer," Edain said. "On the screen you called it? The pictures on it stopped moving. What is a… Password? Why would I need it?"

Guy decided that the only way he could keep asking questions was to keep answering theirs. Even without his curiosity to learn more he now wanted to help them understand how the computer worked since they now seem enamored with the 'magical' device.

"You see Ser—"

"Please eye tea Guy, call me Edain"

Guy held in a sigh. He would find a better way to explain his name later.

"Okay. You see, Edain, most people want to keep what they do on their computers private. A password is a word that only they know and don't tell anyone else. The computer won't show anything else on the screen until you type that word in."

Guy was met by a look of puzzlement from the deity.

"I thought people liked to share things, unless they are

embarrassing or bad... Wait, are there bad things on the internet? I wouldn't have let you 'eye tea' people install it if I knew that!"

Guy allowed himself a soft low woof. This was going to be harder than he thought. "You may be getting ahead of yourself Edain. How about we start at the beginning and I teach you how to type?'"

———

Guy hadn't been able to find an open moment to ask more questions. Between Edain blurting out password ideas, defeating the purpose of them being private, and them breaking the keyboard in half when they pressed too hard on the keys, he had too many other things to focus on.

Edain had profusely apologized and asked that Guy return the next day to continue teaching. His boss, once they learned of the request, instantly approved. At least he would get another chance for questions, though he only had three days left on the job and wanted to make them count.

So he strode towards the temple, footpaws chilled by the stone walkways. He was carrying the oldest keyboard he'd been able to find at a thrift store in town, hoping some old-school construction might be strong enough to hold up to a deity's excitement. He also carried a mouse better suited for creatures with hooves. He smiled as he approached their room, remembering just how adorable Edain had thought the name for the device that controlled the cursor had been, even if they didn't exactly understand why it was called that. He noticed their door was open once more, so he used his claws to gently tap on the marble wall.

"Edain? Ser? It's Guy. I brought you a new keyboard!"

He couldn't help his curiosity and peeked into the room,

but was startled by what he saw. What had to be Edain was simply a large ball of glowing light. As if a star had fallen from the heavens and now burned brightly inside this small room without turning the possessions inside to ashes. Somehow he could still tell it was turning towards him, sparks flying off the bright mass as a single hooved chestnut brown leg slid out from inside it.

"Just one moment eye tea Guy, I need to form!"

Guy averted his eyes, worried and embarrassed that he may have essentially seen Edain in the deity's equivalent of undress. No wonder they usually chose to take a Filgaian form. If Guy hadn't seen them yesterday prepared to smite the computer, the glowing orb would have been too much for him to comprehend.

"Okay eye tea Guy I'm ready for you to enter!"

He turned and entered the room, looking over Edain's form. They weren't wearing clothes but to his knowledge that was usual for the deity. They always had taken a horse's form but without genitals of any kind, a flat and smooth chestnut coat from chest to groin. Guy also read on the forums that they didn't understand why the Filgaians wore clothes as apparently they hadn't in the past. He suspected that thoughts on modesty had changed a great deal since the earliest years of life on the planet.

"It's just Guy, there's no need for the IT before it. It's not a title of some kind, just the job I do."

Edain nodded in what he hoped was understanding. "Got it, just Guy! What will I be learning about the computer today?"

Guy set the new keyboard and mouse on the marble slab they were using as a desk and reached into a khaki pocket for a flash drive. He wanted to try and show the deity games on the internet but was concerned what they might find if they tried to explore once he was gone. He had brought the flash drive to install parental controls so that they wouldn't run into the more scandalous websites. He also figured setting it up with antivirus software and an ad blocker might also be wise, with the deity likely not even comprehending scams on websites.

"Let's start by getting this new keyboard plugged in and typing in that password you thought of. A bit more gently this time okay?"

Pink sparks danced along their form as they nodded. "Of course jus—er, Guy."

Guy's tail wagged at the deity's progress. He plugged the new keyboard and mouse into the tower.

"Alright, do you remember how we turned off the computer yesterday with the power button? Can you press that button, gently, to turn it on again?"

Edain was practically bouncing with excitement as they reached for the power button and pressed it with their hoof. Guy was thankful they didn't manage to break the computer itself and it began to whir to life. He was impressed when Edain actually managed to type in the password and get to the home screen.

"Ooh I did it Guy! I did it! What now?"

More tickling sparks bounced onto Guy's body, forcing him to laugh in delight. It really was marvelous seeing a divine being so excited over the things he had grown to find mundane. He plugged in the flash drive, letting it automatically start its work.

Guy saw his opportunity and knew he had to take it. "I know it's less fun but I'm going to install some things on the computer to make it even easier for you. It's going to take a few minutes so I thought we could just chat a bit? Maybe if I get to know you better I can show you things on the internet you would enjoy more."

Edain was quick to hide the pouty look that crossed their face but not so quick that Guy didn't notice. He honestly found it adorable and couldn't help but put his questions on the creation of his world aside for a moment to ask another.

"Please forgive me if this is rude to ask but I've never heard of you being so animated when you are performing miracles."

Edain whinnied in amusement. "I thought when Filgaians were not working they behaved more casually and I am not currently doing my job! The acolytes always treat me strangely even when I'm enjoying my time at the temple. I thought if I acted this way you might treat me a bit more like any other person you knew. I didn't want you to feel frightened of me simply because I am a deity. Is my knowledge of Filgaians incorrect?"

Guy's tail went still in surprise. He hadn't thought the deity lacked intelligence in any way, just that they were perhaps out of touch with parts of the world. He realized he needed to readjust his expectations once again. "No you're absolutely correct and I appreciate how considerate you are. I have to admit I was a bit nervous to work in the temple." He paused. "Were the other deities as fun loving as you?"

Edain looked wistful and it could be heard in their voice. "Yes, we celestials always were so happy coming up with ideas for other worlds. By the time we finally created one we would make the sun and stars so all could enjoy the most phenomenal lightshow in creation. It was a wild celebration before leaving to work on the next world."

Guy had so much to unpack from their statement. So there were multiple deities, celestials, Edain called them. Still for some reason they didn't leave with them once Filgaia was complete. Edain was such a part of life for all people on the planet he couldn't imagine what it would be like had they not stayed.

Guy was burning with curiosity and wanted to ask more questions but the sound of a bell chime from the computer signaled his installations were complete. Still he thought he could be creative and learn a bit more. "So you made the stars to be a lightshow, like we do fireworks?"

"What are fireworks?" Edain's head tilted to the side in curiosity. Guy had got them hook, line, and sinker. Still he was surprised they didn't even know what fireworks were. When was the last time they had left the temple?

"I can show you using the internet! See that little blue symbol that looks like a fox? And see how here is an arrow on the screen? Keep gentle like with the keyboard and use your mouse to guide the arrow to that symbol and click."

Edain was whinnying in delight over the name of the mouse once more but nodded, slowly doing as he suggested, clicking on the icon.

"Great job! This is what we call a web browser."

"Web brow sir?"

"Close, but don't worry. We'll work on pronunciation! We use this to see things on the internet. Here let me borrow the mouse for just a moment."

Edain moved their hooves and Guy tried to fit his paw awkwardly around the mouse better designed for their appendages. He moved to the search box on the screen and clicked on it.

"See this box here? You can type things into it and the internet will bring up all it knows about a subject. So if you type in fireworks…"

Edain got the hint immediately and began to type in the

characters. Guy was pleased to see that they were getting the hang of the keyboard.

"Now click the key that says enter and we can see them!"

Edain did as they were told. After a moment of loading the search results came up. Some pictures of fireworks displays were shown on the top, Edain's eyes went wide as they stared, enamored by the images.

"You told me Filgaians can't use magic! These look so close to how we made the stars. Are you absolutely sure this is not magic?"

"Yes I'm very sure. This is just a different kind of technology. Besides you're only seeing them still. What if I could show you them in action? Moving even?"

Guy swore he smelled an overpowering scent of flowers as Edain bounced in their seat. "There are moving paintings somehow? Guy, I must know all the amazing things Filgaians have made!"

The excitement was infectious, Guy's tail wagged harder than he could remember since he was a puppy. "Type in 'MooTube Fireworks' into the search bar. You've got a lot to see and learn."

———

The rest of Guy's day had been filled with the imagination and wonder of the deity. He had found himself answering questions instead of asking them but this time he hadn't been remotely disappointed. It was starting to become apparent Edain was quite lonely without the other celestials around and with the acolytes treating them so differently. These lessons and all of the things he could show them were making them so happy. Deity or not, Guy knew everyone deserved this kind of joy in their lives.

He had planned to show them games for sure this time today, certain they could find something enjoyable. As he walked towards their room his ears lifted, hearing what sounded like…

"Oh no…"

He ran as fast as he could towards the room. Those sounds were unmistakably the sounds of love making. Had he forgotten a website with his parental controls?

He burst into the room panting deeply to see Edain watching a scene where two canids were enthusiastically enjoying each other's bodies.

"I must say Guy, the child making you Filgaians participate in seems to be quite rigorous!"

Guy's jaw dropped. Edain was making it quite apparent that they had no idea of the social norms surrounding what they were watching. This was just another video, like the fireworks they had watched yesterday.

"Edain p-p-please t-t-turn that off. Th-that's n-not uh, um."

Edain just seemed to get even more confused at his embarrassment. "Guy are you alright? I haven't frightened you again have I?"

His ears turned down, trying to drown out the sounds from the speakers, not wanting to accidentally excite himself.

"S-S-S-Ser w-we um, d-don't watch these videos w-with others a-a-around. This is a private thing."

Edain seemed to light up with understanding, clicking the little x on the browser to close out the window as he had taught them the previous day.

"Oh so this is the kind of thing the password is for! Now it makes sense. When I typed in 'making babies' as I was curious if anyone discussed my miracles, the web browser asked me for my password before I could see the… websites? They're called websites, right?"

One part of Guy wanted to be impressed with just how quickly they were learning how the computer worked. The other part of him felt like an idiot for using the computer's password for the parental controls. He hadn't thought Edain would be able to figure out exactly what was going on and would just go to different sites.

"Y-Yes, Edain, they are websites. Those k-kind of websites are only for adults to, u-um, enjoy in private. W-We don't share those with others."

Guy was doing his best to improvise a simple explanation, his head turning down to not look Edain in the eye. There had been canids on screen, his own species. Why did Edain have to find a video like that of all things?

"It seems like they were having so much fun though! Don't Filgaians like to share fun? Have you ever participated in such a ritual?"

Guy felt more heat creeping beneath his fur than his embarrassment had ever summoned in his entire life. His tail curled down between his legs and he couldn't summon words to speak. Edain had their usual curious expression, completely clueless as to the situation they had caused. Guy did his best to manage the shortest response he could.

"N-No I haven't."

"But children are so precious and adorable! They bring such joy to the lives of the parents I meet. Why haven't you tried to have a child of your own?"

Guy knew he was going to become too much of an awkward mess if this line of questioning continued so he desperately tried to change course.

"W-Well I mean h-have you ever made a child of y-your own?

Edain paused, as if pondering a thought so deep Guy could not comprehend. They kept silent long enough that Guy began to feel awkward over the silence itself instead of the previous situation.

"No celestial has ever had a child to my knowledge. We have always just existed."

Guy found himself confused at the answer. A large portion of their previous day on MooTube had been spent trying to find videos of children doing things. Edain so adored children, befitting the deity of fertility. He had just assumed they had helped make so many Filgaian children that they maybe had some of their own eons ago.

"Well, have any ever tried? If you love Filgaian children so much it would seem to me a child of your own would bring you so much joy."

"None have even tried before. I do not know how it could even be done." Edain pondered. "This would be creation the likes of which has never been attempted in the history of the cosmos."

Edain looked thoughtful, once more considering something incomprehensible. They then broke the silence. "Guy? Would you help make a child with me?"

Guy had been wrong. It was possible to feel even more heat beneath his fur than he had earlier. Did Edain not understand just how huge a question that was normally, let alone coming from the most powerful being in the known universe? He woofed and spluttered, trying to form words for a proper response.

"N-No I—"

Edain interrupted his pathetic attempt at speaking. "Don't people want to have children with people they really like and care about? You have been so kind and helpful to me, I enjoy your company far more than that of the acolytes."

Guy tried his best to get his thoughts in order, knowing he needed to manage to turn the conversation in a different direction. This was beyond unprofessional and far out of his depth.

"W-Well yes Edain th-that's usually how it w-works."

"Do you not like me Guy? Is my company not enjoyable to you?"

The room itself felt as though it grew unnaturally cold, the sorrow that painted Edain's features sobering Guy out of his self-conscious induced befuddlement. They truly did not understand the line of their questioning. Guy didn't want to hurt their feelings, not just because they were all powerful, but because he had seen just how much joy Edain could feel.

"Edain I do enjoy your company and like you very much. However, children are a large commitment and we've only known each other for a few days. I would need more time to get to know you. Usually Filgaians go on dates with each other for quite some time and slowly progress towards having children. There may be a Filgaian you like more out there that you just haven't met yet to consider, too."

"No, everyone else ends up afraid of me. You're the only one that has treated me like any other on this planet. You remind me of my days with the other celestials. I feel like myself when I'm with you."

It was Guy's turn to be stunned into silence. Was this really happening? Had he accidentally wooed the deity of his world just by showing them basic kindness? He felt honored and saddened at the same time. Edain had been giving selflessly to everyone on the planet all while missing their own kind for more years than Guy's brain could comprehend. They deserved better.

The silence was broken by a light rapping of claws on marble, and a black cat tilting his head around the doorway.

"There you are Guy, the boss said you would be here. O-Oh and thine deity! Such an honor to be in your presence!"

The newcomer bowed deeply towards the floor, tail flicking behind him. He kept the position, awkwardly waiting for Edain or maybe at least Guy to respond. When neither did he rose back up to his usual height.

"I, um, I guess I was sent here to tell thine deity that we have completed our work a day early! So we'll be able to be out of your way so temple activities can resume. I'm supposed to take Guy here and get him to help load up equipment. If that is okay with your blessing."

Guy looked toward Edain who gave an almost unnoticeable nod. "I will send him once we are finished speaking."

"Thank you thine deity for being so gracious!" The cat bowed once more, slipping away from the doorway before the soft pattering of his foot paws rang through the halls as he sprinted away.

Guy returned full focus to Edain and was terrified to see their features were melting; a blue mournful glow radiated from their body.

"Edain? Are you alright?"

Edain's melting form quivered, ice crept across the floor of the room, then the mournful sobs began.

"Guy... I don't want you to leave forever!"

Guy hadn't even considered daring to touch Edain before when they seemed to be holding their form well. He hadn't known if his body would be burned, they might be offended, or whatever other kind of magical craziness might happen. He was terrified still of what might happen but his instincts told him that when someone was this upset you comforted them with a hug.

He tentatively reached out his arms to wrap about Edain. As his paws rested on their deformed shoulders it was as if the world around him melted away. This was not the ticklish happiness from an errant spark from their form. He could feel the full depth of the sorrow Edain was feeling. Tears burst from his eyes outside of his control as his body was wracked with misery.

Still in this sadness he couldn't help but laugh. Edain's glow turned from blue to red, their form returning to a more sightly appearance. The sorrow that flooded Guy's every sense was turning into anger.

"Does my sorrow mean nothing to you Guy?"

The dog continued woofing in laughter. "Edain I live in the town next to the temple! I won't be leaving you forever."

"Because you don't want to upset the deity…"

Guy released them from the hug, needing to make sure Edain's emotions weren't so overwhelming he couldn't properly examine his own.

"No, because you are the most selfless being I have ever met. You have such enthusiasm for things in life I thought were boring and commonplace. You find wonder in everything, something I wish I could do."

Edain's form returned to its usual self, the red glow returning to the usual gold. "Guy… That is what you truly think? Please do not lie to me, I won't smite you. I promise."

The promise forced him to burst into laughter once more. Just a couple days prior he wouldn't have believed them. Now he just felt silly that they had thought they needed to make that promise at all. They were such a pure and kind being.

"That is what I truly think. I can try to visit some days after work. I could even teach you how to talk to me on the computer for the days I can't come."

This time Edain reached to embrace Guy. Purest joy quickly began to engulf his every sense and he burst into wheezing woofs.

"Edain p-p-please it tickles! Oh my gosh, it tickles so much!"

Edain made a shocked whinny and released him, and Guy fell to the ground in a fit of giggles.

"I'm so sorry Guy! I didn't mean to, I'm just, um—"

"So excited! It's okay I understand." He was still chuckling as he got himself up from the ground.

"You know the acolytes won't be ready to prepare the temple for visitors tomorrow since you were done early. Would... Would you come to watch the sunrise with me?"

Edain was glowing a bright pink once more, their head turned away as if they were shy. Guy's eyes widened in realization. "Wait, are you asking me on a date?"

Pink sparks flew from their cheeks, with Guy carefully dodging them.

"You said Filgaians went on many dates before things like children!"

"You know just because we date doesn't mean we'll have children right? I don't even know how we could, let alone if I want to in the future. You understand this right?"

Edain nodded. "I think I do. You gave me the idea of a child of my own, something no celestial even thought of. No matter what comes of it, I wish to know someone with such magic inside them better."

Guy was flabbergasted. He was actually being asked on a date by the deity of fertility, the being all others on the planet learned about in schools from the youngest age, that all revered. He paused just to be sure, would he want to date them even if they weren't an all-powerful being?

He easily found the answer. "Yes Edain, I'll take off work tomorrow and come watch the sunrise with you."

———

LINNEA CAPPS

Several years had passed and some things hadn't changed. The sun still rose to the heavens each morning, the light making dew sparkle as it clung to the curves of leaves. Ribbons of warm oranges, soft pinks, and dazzling golds overtook the soothing lavender of a nighttime seeking slumber as sunlight spilled over the mountain peaks.

What had changed was that Edain, the deity of fertility, had a new way to share their favorite moment of the day with everyone in Filgaia.

"Thank you for joining our sunrise stream today! If you enjoyed the view and having your questions about the universe answered be sure to give my channel a follow!

"Also don't forget I'll be taking a weekend break to enjoy a little vacation time so I won't be streaming tomorrow. Any questions you leave for me I'll answer on Monday. Until then, have miraculous days!"

Edain waived a hoof goodbye to those that had tuned in as Guy moved a paw pad on his laptop's touchpad to end the stream. When Guy had begun teaching Edain how computers worked he couldn't have imagined just how far they would come. He also couldn't have pictured what beginning fatherhood would be for him.

He woofed happily as an acolyte helped Edain put away the camera. When Edain had promised him a miracle that would start their family it hadn't been what he expected. Edain had kissed him then purest ecstasy seemed to take form in every fiber of his nerves. If he had been surprised by that then he was downright startled months later to notice the belly bump indicating a baby was forming inside him.

It was new, it was different, but as he had slowly taught Edain, new and different weren't bad.

Edain approached him, placing a hoof gently on his belly.

He could feel the curiosity and wonder radiating from their touch.

"Do you think we'll have a boy or a girl?"

Guy couldn't help but laugh. "I still haven't figured out if they'll be a horse, a dog, or a glowing celestial who chooses their form like you."

"I suppose in that case we wouldn't have a boy or a girl, but something entirely outside the binary celestials created."

Guy closed the laptop, holding it in one paw while allowing Edain to help him stand with the other. The two were heading back towards their shared room in the temple before Edain would go to perform miracles for the day. It had taken time to get used to sharing a space together. It had taken considerably less time for Edain to warm to the idea of cuddling, practically insisting on it happening every evening.

Guy still was helping Edain feel less guilty about taking vacations so they could explore, seeing what 'magic' that had come from their creation all around the world. He had told them it was good practice for the time Edain would need off to help raise their newborn. Even if he still wasn't exactly sure how the birthing process was going to work.

"All I know for sure is that they will be something the entire universe has never seen before. That and no matter what I'll love them with all my heart," Guy said.

Guy could feel through the kiss Edain gave him that they felt the same way.

BLIND

FRANCES PAULI

Marley knows that her bad luck with dating is because of her bald head.
And she has just the solution.

Luther opened the door and caught her crying. Marley ducked her head, trying to hide her bald face beneath one black wing. The alley air carried a chill. Her bare neck prickled and, no doubt, made her look even worse than usual.

"What's the matter, cutie?" Luther always called her that, as ironic a nickname as was ever uttered. He followed her out the bar's rear door and into the shadowed back alley. "Everything okay?"

The osprey tended bar at the Aerie Grill. He always had a kind word for anyone, even a vulture like Marley, but his broad shoulders and the perfect white feathers on his head made her feel self-conscious. No matter how many times Luther called her cutie, his soft eyes, surrounded by silky black, always managed to force her gaze to her feet.

To remind her how ugly she was.

Just being within wing's reach of him made her think of

every awkward pinfeather she'd ever sprouted, and tonight, she didn't need any more hits to her ego.

"I'm fine, Lu."

"Anything I can do to help?"

"No." Marley's laugh came sharp and as ragged as the rest of her. "I'll get through it."

Luther pulled out his cigarettes and lit one, offering the pack to her and winking when she shook her head no. "I take it the date didn't go well?"

"Let's just say blind dates don't really work for me... unless he actually turns out to be blind."

"Don't do that." His voice turned serious, dropped to a huskier note.

"Do what, Lu? Tell the truth?" Marley hopped into the air and fluffed her wings to the side. Her red dress clung to her breast like a scab, like her moronic bald neck and head. "I've lived in this plumage long enough to have no illusions."

Luther shook his head, took a drag off his Eagle Gold, and opened his beak to argue. Before he could get out a retort, a trio of teenagers fluttered, cackling, into the alley mouth. They linked wings and staggered from one building to the other. When they caught sight of Marley, they stopped cold.

"What the hell is that?" The stout owl in the middle clicked his beak and let out a low whistle. "Holy crap."

"'S' a buzzard, stupid." His falcon buddy wore a leather jacket. He puffed out his chest and bobbed his head. "Super creepy."

"Is not a buzzard." The owl screeched and pushed the other bird into the far wall.

Marley's wings tightened around her body, hiding the dress she'd been sure looked fine before she'd left the house. The third kid was some kind of parrot, full of color but slimmer than his friends. He said nothing, but his head tilted to the side, and his neck extended, one big yellow-rimmed eye fixing on Marley as if it could see through her.

"I'll think of it," the owl said.

"Get out." Luther appeared in front of her. He faced the kids, effectively blotting them out. His voice held no softness now, but the fury in it only wormed beneath Marley's feathers. Luther witnessing her embarrassment drove the sting of it all the deeper. "Go!"

"What's your problem, man."

One of the boys was either brave or stupid. Marley couldn't see much, but when Luther stepped forward, she heard the scrabbling of their clawed feet as they retreated. The osprey's wings mantled, making slick waterfalls at his sides. He clicked his beak and shouted a final, "Move!"

"Vulture!" The owl's hoot echoed back through the alley. It surrounded Marley, pinning her in place. She hugged her wings tighter and glared at her long toes. She'd painted her talons to match the dress, and now her feet looked bloody. "It's a vulture."

"Are you okay?" Luther's wingtip drifted near to her beak, not touching, not quite that. "They're just stupid kids. Marley, I…"

"Don't do that."

"Do what?"

"You know." She scuffed her toes against the gravel and shrugged away from him. "I'm a big girl, Lu."

"I know that." He shifted his weight from one foot to the other. "Can I walk you home?"

"No."

"It's not out of my way."

"I'm fine, Lu. I'm used to it." She eased backwards, keeping her customary hopping as subdued as possible, tamping down the vulture as much as she could. When Luther opened his beak to argue further, she held up a wing and shook her 'super creepy' head. "I kind of need to be alone."

"Oh." He nodded, and his eyes grew shadows. "Right. Sure."

Marley hop-stepped down the alley, backwards until Luther looked away again. Then she muttered, "thanks," and retreated as fast as her ridiculous toes could carry her.

———

She bought the wig online in a fit of self-loathing. It was supposed to be cutting edge fashion, a top-of-the-line full hood with invisible seams. The feathers had been donated by some molting raptor, and they almost matched the ones covering the rest of her body. The mesh itched though. It had cost her two week's salary, and yet the plastic irritated the soft skin on her neck and head and left her with tons of prickly bumps if she kept the thing on for more than fifteen minutes.

Marley stretched it around her hooked beak and pulled the edge over her head and down, all the way to the bottom of her red neck. She glared into the full-length mirror, tilted her head to one side, and adjusted the eyeholes.

Not too bad, really.

She used a scaled foot to reach for her wine glass, balancing on the other and squinting past the unfamiliar feathers at her own reflection. Just a tuck around the beak there and smooth the feathers down to blend in with her own. Nearly the right color. Not bad at all.

Marley could see almost as well as normal in the thing. The eye holes had sticky plastic around them that made it hard to look too far in either direction, and the smaller feathers in her peripheral would take some getting used to. But if she could tolerate wearing it, limited vision was a small sacrifice to pay for how much she liked the fluffy face staring back at her from the mirror.

She lifted the wine to her beak and sipped it while admiring her new appearance.

Now to take a picture before she lost her nerve. She set down the glass and hopped across her studio apartment. Her phone sat beside the computer. Marley settled into the office perch and posed for a selfie... or six. She flipped through them slowly, cringing at the less flattering angles but still impressed with the overall effect.

The wig worked. She finally looked normal.

She'd had it for over a month and just never summoned enough nerve to try it on. Tonight's disaster pushed her that much closer to desperate. It wasn't even the rotten date so much. The hawk left with a thinly veiled excuse before the entrée was even finished, but Marley was used to that. Far worse was having Luther try to console her. As if he didn't notice what anyone with eyes could easily see. And he'd had to defend her against a bunch of idiot kids. Her cheeks puffed in embarrassment just thinking about it.

The phone rang while she was uploading her pics. Marley frowned at her mother's number and considered not answering. She didn't need this, but long habits of obedience won out and she flicked a feather over the green circle.

"Hi, mom."

"You sound sad. What happened?"

"What?" Marley reached with one wing and smoothed the new feathers down her long neck. "I don't know what you're talking about."

"We just want you to be happy honey, right? Your dad and I."

"I am happy, mom." Marley dragged the wig up, over her

head and got it caught on her beak. The sticky eye holes pulled at her skin. "Ouch."

"We don't like to see you so lonely."

"I'm not lonely." She lied.

"Maybe if you weren't so picky."

"I'm not picky." Marley ground the halves of her beak together.

"I'm just saying. I don't see why you can't date a nice vulture boy. "

"You mean like Aunt Agnes's dry cleaner?" Marley rolled her eyes and straightened out the rumpled wig.

"Whatever happened with Joe?"

"He's a jerk, Mom." Marley could hear the sigh on the other end of the line. She imagined her mother's bald red face, scrunching up in disapproval. "He told me vulture males prefer to date up."

"What's that supposed to mean?"

"It means he's not into me." The jerk's exact words had been worse than that. He'd spent their dinner explaining in detail how an enterprising young vulture like him earned enough money that he could date girls with feathers all over. "It's not like when you and Daddy were dating. What did you call for?"

"Oh!"

Marley turned to the computer and checked on the upload status. With a profile picture in her new wig, she was ready to try that dating site again.

"Your father bought one of those newfangled perches. He needs help installing the horrid thing, and it goes way up on the roof of his shop. You know I can't get that kind of altitude since I dislocated my wing."

"I thought the therapy was helping?"

"Oh, it is, dear. But flying to the top of the shop so your

father can spy on the neighbors seems like a ridiculous risk at this stage in my healing."

"Right." More like mom's accident had given her a case of the nerves. "Is Saturday okay? I can be out there in time for breakfast."

"Of course, honey. Saturday's fine."

"I'll see you then."

"Unless something comes up. If you're busy…"

"I'll see you Saturday morning." Marley swiped the call to an end and ran a wingtip over the skin on her neck. Itchy prickles after only a few minutes. If she wanted to post a fully feathered profile pic, she'd need to build up her tolerance to the wig. If she meant to wear the thing on a date, she might just have to live with a rash.

She settled lower on the perch and glared at her computer. It wasn't worth it. Dating vultures or hawks, what did it matter? For the hundredth time in her short adult life, Marley thought about giving up. A single bird did just fine these days.

She might get used to the loneliness eventually.

Of course, getting used to the wig would be easier. She found the uploaded photos and scanned them for the best profile. The wig would help. Maybe.

One more try couldn't hurt.

———

Luther didn't recognize her when she walked in. He worked his bar rag deeper into a tall glass and gave Marley the generic, quick-nod customer greeting that he used on strangers. She'd dressed more conservatively in an ivory skirt and blouse, and even when she stepped up on the perch in front of him, it took a few seconds before his eyes widened.

"Hey, Lu. Can I get a Throwback on the rocks?"

"That's a new look for you." He poured the drink without adding anything, and his flat tone gave her no hint how to respond.

When he passed her the tumbler, Marley muttered a thank you and focused on downing some courage. The whiskey warmed her insides, but her outsides had already begun to itch beneath the plastic mesh. She closed her eyes, resisting the urge to reach up and scratch at the back of her neck.

It'll be worth it. Just ignore it. Focus on something else.

Marley worked on the drink while Luther tended to the rest of the bar. She watched the front doors, the trickle of birds entering the popular Aerie, already crowded for a work night and full of the chatter of its customers.

The restaurant was usually more subdued than the bar and offered varied cuisine at reasonable prices. It was a great place for a first date, or for a series of horrendous blind dates. Marley usually suggested meeting there, as if the Aerie had become her safe place somehow.

It had certainly witnessed enough of her low moments.

When a sleek-feathered merlin wandered in, Marley sucked in a breath and prayed tonight would not be another in a long string of failures. Soft gray feathers showed around the collar of his pressed suit, and his speckled head bore dark stripes behind the eyes that reminded her a lot of Luther. His profile picture hadn't done him justice.

Marley shot her last swallow of Throwback and caught Luther's eye as she stood. "Wish me luck?"

Luther rolled his eyes. She couldn't blame him but carried the sting of it across the bar to the entrance. Even Luther thought she should give up. Maybe the osprey and her mother were right, but Marley didn't want to quit, to resign herself to an empty nest forever.

She caught the merlin's eye on the way to the door, and he

smiled and smoothed his crown feathers with one wing while sizing her up with sharp eyes and a soft tilt to his head.

Very nice.

Marley smiled and approached with as little hop as she could muster. Her neck itched, flaring beneath the plastic into a creeping tickle. She forced her wings tightly to her sides and joined Stewart at the front kiosk.

"You must be Marley." He clicked his beak softly. "Lovely to meet you."

"And you." She held out a wingtip, and their feathers brushed lightly together. "I'm glad you could find time before your trip."

According to his profile, Stewart worked in finance. He'd messaged Marley only a few hours after she uploaded her picture but was leaving for the weekend on a business trip. Also according to his profile, he liked old movies, wine, and adventure and described himself as a "risk taker."

Life was too short, in Marley's opinion, not to take risks. She preferred new movies, but definitely enjoyed a good glass of wine.

The new girl was hostessing tonight, a pretty flamingo with legs that definitely didn't hop when she walked. She led them to a table deep in the restaurant half of the Grill, far enough back that Marley couldn't see the bar. Stewart held out her perch and didn't check out the flamingo even once.

"Want to start with some wine?" His eyes reflected the light from the electric candle in the center of the table.

"I'd love a glass."

Stewart ordered them a bottle of Pinot and they discussed varietals while going over their menus. He knew his wine, likely better than she did, and talked with such an animated fervor about oak and bottling, good years, and late harvests that Marley could almost forget the burning sensation at the back of her neck.

Her limited vision proved more problematic. When she reached for her wine, Marley nearly knocked the glass off the table. She grabbed it in time but banged her wing hard enough to make her wince. The Pinot sloshed and dribbled a bit, but Stewart only widened his pretty eyes and made no comment. The wig's feathers ruffled with the overhead fans, and Marley tried to blink them away without being obvious.

Her eyes watered. The skin underneath her wig cried out to be scratched.

"Hoping to pick up a few bottles while I'm in LA." Stewart sipped his Pinot, and Marley tried to catch up with the conversation and forget her neck was on fire.

"Is it a conference?"

"My boss is meeting with the managers of a bank we're considering a merger with."

"Oh, that's exciting." She squinted away a fine layer of tears and blinked until his face clarified. "Are you in negotiations?"

"Well." Stewart leaned back and, for the first time since they'd met, looked uncomfortable. "I know my profile said I work in finance... and I do, really. But..."

He looked up toward the fan and then down at his lap. His beak ground together, making a soft grating sound.

"It's okay," Marley said. She reached one wing up and rubbed as gently as possible at the back of her neck. "You. Can. Tell. Me."

The burning eased for a second while her wingtip worked at it, but the second she stopped, the fire increased. The prickles raged, and her eyes teared and leaked around the edges where the sticky plastic met her skin.

"I'm more like a personal assistant," Stewart confessed. "But I'm in line for a promotion soon."

"I think that's wonderful." Marley blinked frantically, but the tears pooled in the short feathers and made her blind. She gave her head the smallest of shakes, and quickly, scratched at her neck again.

"I suppose no one is totally honest on those profile things," he said.

"I think people want to put their best foot forward," Marley agreed.

Their waiter arrived, and Marley ordered something fresh that was not her favorite. Her usual would be a dead giveaway, but considering Stewart's confessions, she almost picked it just to see what he'd say. After they ordered, she watched the pigeon waddle away with their menus and wondered if he had as much trouble dating, if pigeon women liked ducks, if the whole world was as messed up as her life.

At least tonight was going well. Except when she turned back to Stewart, she found him staring at her. He held his wine glass in mid-air, as if he'd lifted it and forgotten to take a drink.

"What is it?" Marley's chest tightened. Her pulse hurried and the fire under her wig throbbed.

"I think you may be allergic to the wine," he said. "Your eye's all red and puffy."

Marley reached on instinct. Her wingtips daubed at her eye, felt the lumpy soft skin around the wig's eyehole. Her heart seized. The tears had loosened the sticky stuff, and the skin around her eye was poking through.

She slapped her wing over her eye and groaned.

"Are you okay?"

He only sounded concerned, but Marley's skin flamed in

embarrassment, a subtle heat compared to the burning of her growing rash.

"I need to… excuse me."

She hopped from her perch, bumping the table hard enough to spill the rest of her wine. She couldn't see the damage and didn't stop to look. Instead, she hustled to the ladies' room dodging tables and waiters alike, with her wing covering one eye and the other straining to see around a veil of feathers and filmy tears.

———

Marley peeled off the wig and lay it beside the sink. She perched on the low counter and squinted into the bathroom mirror, cringing at the inflamed bumps, the streaks of red on red, and the puffy swollen skin around her left eye. She looked like a nightmare.

At least the air felt good on her skin. The fire dimmed once the plastic was off, and Marley turned on the tap with her foot and lowered her head, splashing cool water over her face. It dribbled down the back of her neck. She patted water up and down her irritated skin.

The prickles looked like angry volcanoes, but their fire faded enough that she stopped crying. Her face was raw, but less puffy, and she couldn't see the streaking on her cheeks or neck anymore. Only a faint pattern of mesh lines marked the top of her head. Much better. Except, of course, she'd have to put the thing back on.

She used her claws to pick it up and cursed. The counter had been wet and now the feathers on one side of the wig hung in a soggy mat. It looked like a dead thing, like the feather wads she'd pull from her drain during a molt month.

Marley shook it, and water rained to the sides. She hopped

to the auto dryer and pressed the button, using a foot to hold the bedraggled wig underneath the heat. It worked beautifully. The wet feathers fluffed before her eyes, but the plastic softened under the assault. The melting mesh burned her foot, and Marley cursed and dropped the wig on the floor.

She stared at it. She tilted her head far to one side and poked the hot wig with a claw. She'd ruined it. The mesh barely held together in places and the feathers refused to lie flat. She picked it up and waved it back and forth to cool the plastic down. A few of the feathers fluttered free and wafted to the bathroom tiles.

Somehow, she had to get the thing back on. No way could she go back out there without it, and even if she tried to just sneak out of the Aerie and make a run for it, she'd have to get past their table. Stewart would see her.

She tested the stretch with her feet and then tried to smooth the remaining feathers back down. Carefully, she eased the wig up and over her beak. The sticky around the eyes had totally vanished. It felt looser and looked a lot puffier than it had before she'd subjected it to the dryer's heat. Still, she managed to get it back on. Marley patted, and smoothed, and managed to convince herself it wasn't completely obvious.

At least it didn't scratch her neck now. She fluffed the feathers around the eyes to hide the gapping and looked askance at her reflection. It would have to do. She closed her eyes, inhaled slowly, and hopped out of the restroom and back to the table.

Their meal had arrived already. Stewart's back faced her, and she slid around the table and took her perch, keeping her eyes down and her beak tucked against her chest.

"It smells great." She avoided looking directly at him.

"I was getting worried." Stewart's fork clanked against the side of his plate. "Was it the... wine?"

"I think so." Marley took a bite and swallowed as gingerly as she could manage. She prayed the wig would stay in place, that she could just get through the entrée and say a quick goodbye. "Have to stick to water, I suppose."

"Sure. Sure."

She ate a few bites before she realized he hadn't picked up his fork again. With a sigh, Marley swallowed, inhaled slowly, and looked up.

Stewart watched her, his eyes failing to reveal anything. His beak was still, but the focus of his attention told her enough. He'd seen right through her, but then, with a drain clog on her head, who wouldn't have?

"I'm sorry." She set down her fork and prepared to bolt.

"You're a buzzard?" His voice gave nothing away either, and she was too tired to correct him.

"Yeah. Sure."

"I guess we both lied on our profiles." He didn't sound angry, and he didn't move to leave, only kept staring at her as if he was trying to see underneath the wig.

"You're not mad?"

"I'd be a bit of a hypocrite if I was, wouldn't I?"

Marley considered this while the dread brewing in her stomach settled. However Stewart reacted next, he obviously didn't intend to make a scene. She risked a smile and peeked at him from behind her veil of feathers. "You don't mind?"

She watched his face with all the focus of her scavenging ancestors. Even so, Marley found no mockery there, no disgust at all.

"I don't if you don't."

"Wow. Thanks." The flood of tension leaving her body felt like a balloon popping, like she might explode with relief. "I mean, that's cool. You know."

"The food is really good here." Stewart must have relaxed as well. He picked up his fork and turned back to his dinner.

"It's my favorite restaurant," Marley said. She took a few bites while her spine unraveled. Her shoulders loosened and she flicked her tail feathers wider than she had in ages. Even her neck felt better. It still burned, but without the customary stress-induced kinks. "The soup on Fridays is even better."

"Right." He stretched that word out, and now, his tone stopped her heart, caught her up in a wad of fear again.

"I didn't mean…" Marley's stomach sank. Through the feathers around her eyes, she saw Stewart cringing, darting guilty looks from side to side.

"It's not that I have a problem with it," he said. "I mean, I'm really open-minded. But, you know, the work thing. I'm up for a promotion, and I'll need to go to a lot of work events, be *seen*, by the right birds."

"And *with* the right sort of bird," Marley finished for him and wasn't surprised when he didn't deny it.

He stared at his plate while she let a new, nasty feeling settle into her bones. It was one thing to be overtly rejected, but this was insulting in a whole different way. It made her feel dirty, and it made her pity her date for once. She might not have enough feathers, but Stewart had no spine.

They ate the rest of their dinner in hurried silence. When Stewart offered to pay, Marley let him. There was no scene, no cringing, and yet, a dull ache had spawned in her chest, and even when the Merlin gave her a goodbye peck on the cheek, she couldn't shake it.

She stood beside her perch and watched him walk away. Her last blind date. Because, as much as there had been no drama, Marley would never do *this* to herself again.

———

After Stewart left, Marley returned to the ladies' room and removed the wig. She washed her face and splashed cool water over her neck until the skin started to itch. Better than on fire, but why didn't she *feel* better? Her feathers drooped, wet or not, and a heavy feeling dragged at her.

Wings and tail both sagging, she stuffed the wig into her purse and shuffled out, across the restaurant to the front doors. Luther tried to catch her eye as she passed, but Marley kept her head down, pretending not to see him. Praying he'd leave it alone tonight.

He didn't, and she'd only made six hops down the sidewalk when the osprey caught up with her.

"Can I walk you home, cutie?"

"Not tonight, Lu."

"Not ever." He sighed and matched pace with her. "Why do you do this to yourself?"

"Do what?"

He'd been behind the bar all night, and Marley hadn't ended up crying in the alley. As far as Luther knew, the date had ended better than any previous one. At least she'd left by the front door. Still, his voice carried that same, concerned tone. "Why do you keep dating guys like that?"

Marley stopped hopping. The weight across her shoulders deepened. He couldn't know how the date had gone, and she didn't owe him any explanation. "Guys like that?"

"Yeah."

"Guys with nice feathers and good jobs, guys that are out of my league?" Marley mantled her wings and turned to face him.

"That is *not* what I meant."

"No?" She felt her throat tightening, the sting of Luther's judgment. Luther, the last person she'd thought would echo her mother's sentiments. "I suppose you'd rather see me date a nice vulture?"

"I'd rather not see you date anyone." His dark eyes narrowed, flashing in the streetlamp.

Marley reeled backwards. She stumbled a few steps and blinked away a fresh sting. Anger flooded her tired body. She held her wings to the side and let out a low hiss, bobbing her naked head up and down.

"Marley." He reached out a wing, and she feigned a lunge. Luther snapped his limb back to his side, shaking his head.

"Don't worry, Lu." She hopped sideways down the street, and the osprey made no further move to stop her. "You won't have to *see* me at all."

"Marley!"

She ignored him and took off down the street as fast as she could hop. Her purse slapped a rhythm against her hip, and Marley's heart played a sad, stuttering counterpoint. Her chest felt like a hand had wrapped around it. Her throat was tight and dry.

A shadow crossed overhead, turning the night dark for a breath. Luther landed directly in her path.

"Are you insane?" She skidded to a halt and glared up at him.

"I like you." He said it fast, like an accusation.

"Well you've got a hell of a way of showing it."

"You're nice, funny, kind, and usually really smart." He took a step in her direction with each declaration, and Marley backpedalled to match. "But you can be really stupid about some things."

"Thank you so much." She snaked her neck lower and puffed out her feathers, making herself as large as possible and hissing again. "That's what I really needed to hear tonight."

"It is," he said. "But you're still not hearing it."

"What?"

"Me, Marley. You're not hearing me." Luther shook himself from beak to talon and stamped one foot against the pavement. "I'm crazy about you!"

"You're..." She clacked her beak shut and squinted. "Wait. You're what?"

"I have been for a long time." He shifted his weight from one foot to the other.

"But..." The sidewalk felt less solid of a sudden. Her knees wobbled and she shook her head and put her wings out for balance. "But it's me. I'm..."

"You're a vulture, Marley. And you're bald." He stated it without judgment, like he said anything, with a note of sincerity and, tonight, a tremble of something else. In the open, the words passed between them and felt... less potent somehow. "People like different things, you know. Everyone likes what they like."

"I know, but—"

"It works for me." Luther looked at his toes. He clicked his beak softly. "Not in a freaky way or anything. The bald thing. It just... works for me."

"Lu." This time she stepped forward, and Luther shuffled back a step.

"So anyway." His voice came out too high, and he cleared his throat and tried again. "I can't tell if you're really so blind about yourself or if, you know, I just don't do it for you."

Marley's throat tightened. She gaped at him.

"I hate the way other birds treat you, but I hate it even more that you believe what they say."

"Oh, come on, Lu."

"Because you're beautiful, Marley."

She tried to say something, opened her beak and found no sound left in her. Her breath barely whisked in and out.

"It's okay," he said. "You like what you like, you know? I just had to say it. A long time now."

Marley stood in the streetlight and stared.

"It's all good." Luther side-stepped back toward the bar, keeping his eyes on her, and his feet moving. "Maybe we just pretend I never said anything, and maybe, sometime when you're free, I can buy you a drink. Up to you."

She watched him shuffle another step, turn, and head back to his bar. Her chest pounded, and her wings had wrapped tightly around her body. She had no words, had never imagined for a second. Luther.

Luther. Walking back to the bar.

"Wait!" It came out as a squawk, and she choked on it. One wing reached into her purse, pulling out the fancy half drowned and half melted wig. She hop-skipped after Luther with the thing dangling in one hand. "Luther, wait. Lu!"

He stopped under the next lamp, allowing her to catch up but not turning around to face her. Vulnerable. She knew exactly how that felt. Her heart raced. She scrambled for the right thing to say. *Up to you... Maybe... It's okay.*

There was a defensive edge to the set of his shoulders, a prickly aura that she knew too well. Every time, Luther had been there for her. *Can I walk you home?* How had she never seen it? *Sometime when you're free...*

"Luther?" Marley held her breath until he turned around. His eyes flashed in the streetlamps, and she threw the useless wig into the street. "I'm free *now*, Lu."

He clicked his beak softly, nodded once, and held out a wing for her. The streetlamp flickered. From the Aerie, the sound of clacking laughter reached them. Marley brushed her wingtip against his and stretched her neck as tall as it would go. She walked beside him, back to the Aerie, with her eyes wide open.

SHARKS AND DOLPHINS

PRIYA SRIDHAR

The sharks just want a place free of dolphins, on their own terms.

There are stories that cartilaginous fish share with each other. I am sharing it with you, human, out of rage. Probably I will memorize this, wait for the tides to change, and then decide to forget it because you will probably not listen. There's no point sharing a story if you don't listen.

We are sharks, the fish that roam the sea with sharp teeth. You may know us as those that never sleep. There are other fish that never sleep, and those that have a sharper bite. Talk with a lamprey any time; they will eat you alive without any concern. Yet we get all the bad publicity.

Sharks are no strangers to this feeling of being unwanted and seen as a threat. After all, we like the occasional fish or seal. That is why some of us hide.

We all visit the megalodon sometimes, where they have hidden. Those fish are still around; you just can't see them. They have grown old, and under the water, they do what they can to keep up with the times. Sharks scratch messages onto coral reefs with our teeth and leave telltale bite marks on the skin. It's not perfect, and we need to change. So we did what sharks didn't do before: held counsel.

———

We got the message from a few floating, basking fish: dolphins, finding new ways to hunt us. So we met in the cove to discuss this new development. The basking sharks let their mouths hang open, which let them catch every gossipy krill and sea bug. They heard the news and passed it on by scratching words in the reefs. The waves carried on the message, and I added for us to meet.

The cliffs are jagged above us, casting shadows blending with the sunlight. We gathered, in a huddle of fins, just below what you humans call the surface. Normally sharks don't meet like this unless there is a giant carcass. But we are desperate and scared. No matter what we do, we always will be.

"It is the dolphins," I said. "They have changed their behavior. We try to avoid them, and they would do the same. But now they are hunting us. There was a group of whitetips that tried to escape a pod. Only one survived."

As if to confirm this, the whitetip in question came to the center of our huddle. We swam a distance away, to give him space. Under the rays of light and shadows, a pattern of scars and bite-marks danced on top of his skin. There were bloody red gashes.

"We didn't see them coming." He twirled to show off an impressive bite-mark. "They are swift, with oil and teeth as sharp as ours. The blue ones are clever, for they spread out and blocked the escape routes."

"This is terrible," I said. "I am of the Bluefin and I say that they would wipe us all out if they have a chance. The humans with their traps are bad enough. If dolphins decide to wipe us out, then no place in the ocean is safe for us."

We all considered this. Our lateral lines quivered with the concern, rippling the water in the cove.

"Pray, what shall we do?" One Mako asked. The Mako sharks are the fastest in the sea, but also the most scared. They have the least in numbers.

"Create a better warning system," I replied. My fins shimmied through the water. "We need to know when they are going to attack before they arrive, and to warn others of pods that are in the vicinity."

"Who made you the leader?" one dogfish asked, all black and scaly. "I say we lead them into a lake of oil or human traps and leave them to drown."

"But we would also get caught in those," a wayward great white pointed out. "They are faster and more likely to escape."

"I am only a leader for now because I have ideas," I said. "Truthfully, I would rather cede control to another shark. But I want to talk about how we can change our systems. Scratching on corals is not enough, and we cannot make sounds apart from these conversations in close proximity and thrashing our tales. How can we better communicate with each other?"

"There are the basking sharks," the great white brought up. "They are not attacked, because they are not seen as prey. We can ask them to convey the messages to sharks that are set up as messengers."

"That won't work," the dogfish objected. "We cannot be placed as messenger fish. What if a dolphin were to attack one of us? The message would be lost!"

"We could scratch a message onto sea turtle shells on the

currents," another lantern shark brought up. "They are swift and not eaten by dolphins."

"Have you tried to catch a sea turtle without eating it?" the great white interrupted. "It is hard. You just want to chomp and swallow; there's your dinner!"

We all started to argue. On our bellies, the remoras listened with interest as they chewed at the sea bugs that nibbled at us.

"Excuse me!" the one on my underbelly said. "We have an idea!"

The sharks stopped. When a remora spoke, they often delivered pearls of wisdom. That and them cleaning our parasites were why we kept them.

"We remoras could deliver the messages in the case that a dolphin is in the area," my little fish said. "On a relay line, we could go from shark to shark and deliver the message. That way if a shark gets attacked, the remora will be able to escape and pass on a warning."

We considered this. Dolphins would not seek out to destroy the remoras if they were attacking a bigger fish. They were tiny, swift, and practically invisible. If a shark were attacked.

"But if you do this, you risk yourselves," I said. "We are indebted to you already."

"We can try it," My remora said. "After all, if you die then we have no food."

———

Dolphins are often seen as the good guys. It's not hard to blame humans; you can train a dolphin to jump in the air on command. Sharks at best will swim toward a thing and bite. We have that failing. Dolphins also have a history of rescuing sailors or gently trying to nudge them toward the shore. Sharks will take a bite out of what's in the water. We do not mean to hurt. You are in our way and sometimes you look like a fish or a clam.

As you surmise, dolphins get the press on saving their species. Sharks only receive it belatedly. Our fins are cut to make soup, and people are scared of our bite. When we all decide to retreat into the waters where you cannot follow us, it's because we want to live. It's not our fault that you have decided to dive deeper with your equipment.

With dolphins, we try to create spaces where they are not welcome. This is not always possible. An orca may come into the area, and we have no choice but to flee. An orca does not have the word "Go away" in their dictionary. And why should they? One bite and a shark will lie dead, floating in the water. We may be able to grab a calf in the pod, but only if we are desperate and hungry. I for one cannot claim to eat the flesh of such a dolphin. My taste is for schools of fish.

There is no compromising with a dolphin. They quite clearly want to kill us if they are given the chance.

———

My remora's plan seemed to work. The little fish conveyed messages in between cleaning us. We learned how to avoid the dreaded fish. I stopped thinking how I would scratch my will on the coral reefs.

As you can imagine, it disconcerted us when this particular cove used to be sharks only, and one day there was a dolphin in the rippling waves. We did not realize at first because the fins are similar.

"So far there are tiny complications in the message relay,"

I said. "Some remoras have trouble with the distance. We can refine that."

"It's also not fast enough," the dogfish said. "A dolphin is swifter than a shark."

"Maybe you should seek another solution," an unfamiliar voice burbled.

We stopped. The newcomer had a telltale snout and fin.

"Hello," it said, leaving for a quick breath of air toward the surface.

Fear shot through our lateral line. The waters in the cove were narrowed by the cliffs, giving us little chance to flee. One Bluefin shark had a glint in her eye, perhaps of opportunity. Little pup; she had no idea what damage she caused.

"Please listen," it asked. "We merely have words. As you know, dolphins are growing in number. And maybe we can live together."

"Why are you here?" I asked, taking charge. As I said, I didn't want to be a leader, but my fins were sharp and intact, and I wanted to keep them that way. The other sharks' blue and yellowing eyes rolled.

"You are in our way," the dolphin said. "And yet you obviously don't want to be. We can work with you in mapping out locations. There will be fish, and sufficient prey for you, water full of nutrients."

"And what if we say no?"

"You may like agreeing better," it replied.

We all felt the vibrations in the water. A pod swimming, with no calf in tow. That only meant one thing.

"FLEE!" I shouted. We all scattered. The waves frothed as our fins dashed back and forth. Despite our scattering, the dolphin kept close on my tail.

"You need to listen!" it shouted. "I am not like the others; I don't want to eat you all! This is a chance to save you."

I couldn't outswim it, but I could outsmart him. Ahead, there were familiar tendrils in the water. My tail angled, and I dove below. A choking, spluttering sound, as a human net with tentacles, caught the dolphin. Its tail was tangled, leaving him tethered to a wreck of glinting rocks.

"That was a bad deal," my remora said.

"Aye; a shark does not exist at a dolphin's mercy," I said, with pity and fear. Then I moved on, to rejoin the others.

———

"Did we lose them?" I asked, miles away at a distant mangrove island. We hung just off the coast, for it was a group of trees and dirt in the water. None of us would be beached.

"We did," a whitetip reef shark answered. Normally the whitetips were not afraid of the dolphins, but they had joined in the splashing panic. Some of them were turning their snouts, to go in the other direction.

"Who invited them?" I asked bluntly. "You would only know about the cove if you were told."

Everyone spun in circles. No one wanted to lay the first bite. But we knew a shark had revealed our place because the dolphin had arrived with purpose. The Bluefin would not be part of message relaying anymore.

"But what is the problem?" one shark asked. "They do not want to eat us now."

"Aye," I said. "But at some point, a few of them are okay with eating us. We try not to eat dolphins because we do not want to die. And we want a space to talk about them freely. They are uncomfortable that this space doesn't belong to them."

This hung over us with the seafoam. We thought and pondered.

"Let us designate this space as dolphin-free," I said. "They do not hang around these tiny balls of dirt. But no one from here on is to reveal our location. No dolphins are allowed in this area. Do I make myself clear?"

There was angry grumbling muffled by the water from the Bluefin. But we all were in agreement. I would bite the fins of any who disagreed. This is how we sharks survive, by not letting those who want us dead in our territory. The language was all-pretty but they made it clear we would survive on their terms.

I pass on this story, to tell you humans that we will never accept this from dolphins, or any animal that can live outside the water. Sharks survived by not making compromises. And we would keep learning to live as sharks should. Pass on the message to your remora. They always speak wisdom.

POYEKHALI!

CEDRIC G! BACON

Innovation never comes without a cost. For Zariyah the foxhound and Valentina the golden retriever that cost is a small price to pay for the thrill and freedom of the sky and beyond.

To Valentina Tereshkova, Svetlana Savitskaya, Judith Resnick, Chiaki Mukai, Sally Ride, Mae Jemison and all other spacefarers, those who have reached the stars and those who did not, who have boldly gone where no one has gone before, this chronicle is respectfully dedicated.

There was a great whoosh of air as she opened the hatch wide. Peering out over the edge, Zariyah said a silent prayer for luck and then she was out.

Somewhere down below was her friend, Valentina York-ina, watching her and cursing her with every breath that she could summon. The jump was already unwieldy and Zariyah realized she would once again completely miss her target. Oh well, there was no use crying over it; as long as she could land somewhere without breaking her back or drowning, that was the important part.

But still, there was a certain freedom to this life, up here. Down below, milling with everyone else, she was only Zariyah Pasternak, weaver and daughter of a poor, widowed milk-maid. But up here, she was so much more, as though she were a goddess of old fantasy looking down upon the world and holding its fate and future within the palm of her paws.

She was four thousand feet from the ground when she reached for the rip-cord on her harness and that familiar jerking motion from so many previous jumps took her, for one fleeting second, back towards the radiance of the sun before settling in and gravity held her in its grip. Controlling the steering lines of her web-gear, she was able to maneuver the riser towards the direction she needed to be.

Her feet struck the ground first and she threw herself side-ways to distribute the shock from the landing sequentially along the balls of her feet, sides of the calf and thigh, hip, and back, bending slightly at the knee with her chin and muzzle tucked into her chest to protect her face and throat. Soon the canopy fell over her head and she felt renewed even as she heard Valentina call out from her bullhorn, riding hard on her gas-powered motorcycle and cursing how far off course the foxhound had landed.

Zariyah grinned. "Nice landing though, right?"

An annoyed vein seemed to pop out from Valentina's fore-head, parting her golden fur as she buried her face and snub-snout in a paw. "That's not the point…"

"Oh, so it was a nice landing?"

"Damn it, Zara!"

"I'm just kidding around," said Zariyah, climbing on the back of Valentina's moped.

"You kid around too much," answered the retriever. "You

mess around and you'll end up hurting yourself. Or worse. You need to pay better attention or they'll kick you out one of these days."

Zariyah did take this into consideration. The truth was the Parachute Club was just the thing to enliven the dull hokum of her daily life. This was her third year in the Yaroslavl chapter, and at the time she had joined she had had to live down her mother's protestations that such activities were unfeminine. The foxhound didn't let this stigma stop her after her inaugural year and she became obsessed with jumping through the air, learning how to parachute and skydive thanks to Valentina's patient instructions. When she had jumped that first time, falling end over end through the air and landing back on the ground, she had felt a certain renewal and rebirth. Without the club, she didn't know what she would be doing with herself, besides going to work at the weaving factory and coming home to help her mother.

"Sorry," said Zariyah. "I'll get it right next time."

Valentina sighed. "Maybe I'm coming across too strong. You're not bad at this at all. You're just way too eager and want to jump into…"

"Or out of." Zariyah grinned. If she could be honest, she was a little envious of the retriever. Valentina could not only sail through the purple air as though she were not afraid of the chute opening, but she was a better pilot, understanding aircraft principal axis and commands better than anyone in the club. It was a chance both relished, to be part of the skies.

"Okay, that was funny," said Valentina with a wide smirk. "But I'm serious. You've got to do better, especially…"

She paused when they came up to the hangar, where the Parachute Club's president, a short beagle named Lagunov, was in deep conversation with two mastiffs dressed in a nondescript formal style, no different from any other businessman displaying interest in the club. And yet, to Zariyah's eyes, there appeared to be something else in their demeanor, something which hinted at them being from the military, with their standing up straight although one of the mastiffs had a slightly bent appearance and leaned on a cane for balance. The other wore a suit that was casual and bereft of the usual ribbons and honors that would be on his person. However, Zariyah saw a certain pride and honor in the way he carried himself, fore-limbs folded behind his back and the proud puff of his chest with each syllable he spoke which seemed to announced a patient purpose.

Just what that purpose was Zariyah wanted to know. "What do you think they're talking about?" she whispered over to Valentina, to which the retriever shrugged.

"I'd heard a rumor that a bunch of the skydiving club presidents have had meetings like this between here and Moscow," replied Valentina. "Must be something big if they're involving the military."

"A war?"

Valentina shook her head. "It'd have been all over TASS and the *Pravda* if there was a war. No, I think this is something else entirely."

"We need young, strong girls in good shape so we can train them for the flight within five to six months, comrade Lagunov," said the more militarily dressed mastiff. "I hope you understand what I am explaining to you."

"But of course, colonel-general Kamanin, of course," answered the club president. "But what shall I say to my members? They will demand the when and the how of it all, particularly with the speed in which you wish to train them and use them for the program."

"*If* they are chosen," quipped the mastiff with the cane.

"It is far from a guarantee that those who wish to enroll in the program will go the distance deemed necessary."

"Do not misunderstand," said Kamanin. "Colonel Karpov and I are not merely interested in advancing both our party and our country. "

"No?"

Kamanin shook his head. "No. The main reason for such rapid training and development is to leave the Americans behind. Already there is much talk of their own programs to send an American farther than previously possible. We cannot allow that, won't you agree?"

"Yes."

"Good," answered Kamanin. "Now, if you will, provide us with the records of each member who has two hundred hours flying time, or at least fifty parachute jumps, so we may proceed in screening each potential candidate for the program."

"The list won't be long," explained Lagunov. "Comrade Yorkina is your best choice followed by Kuznetsova and Solovyova, but I've several more you may be interested in interviewing. Now… what in hell…?"

The two mastiffs followed Lagunov's eye towards the corner, keeping their gaze trained on his quick, hopping steps towards Zariyah and Valentina. It was perhaps not an entirely happy moment for the disclosure, as Zariyah was half-in and half-out of her flightsuit, exposing the T-shirt she had worn beneath which revealed the perspiration clinging to the tips of her fur.

"What are you two doing eavesdropping like that?" he demanded.

"We were, ah…" began Valentina, nervous as the two mastiffs sidled up next to Lagunov. Zariyah was in awe; now that he was closer, the more military dressed canine she recognized as Colonel-General Nikolai Kamanin, whose rescue of the crew of the *SS Chelysukin* from the frozen surface of the Chukchi Sea near Kolyuchin Island had made him a Hero of the Soviet Union.

"You know these women?" asked Kamanin.

"Pasternak the Annoyance and her friend, Yorkina," answered Lagunov dryly. "One of my club's best members and one of the worst nuisances around."

"I see," said the colonel-general. "And how many jumps have the two of you made?"

"One-hundred and sixty-three," answered Valentina.

"Comrade Yorkina is your best choice," expostulated Lagunov. "She knows how to pilot small aircraft and was second in her class at the Steklov Mathematical Institute." This brought an interested murmur to both Karpov and Kamanin.

"Ah, an intellectual," Karpov said, then turned to Zariyah. "And you?"

"Ninety jumps," announced the foxhound.

"With some sixty unsuccessful!" revealed Lagunov.

"But I've never died or broke a bone!" added Zariyah. "Not like Chugunkin or Sorokin!"

"Important facts we need to know about," said Kamanin. "When one steps from danger and into danger, their probability of success hinges somewhere between twenty and thirty-five percent." He stepped closer to the foxhound and looked hard and deep into her amber-colored eyes. He had a strong scent, steady and powerful. The fire of his mahogany eyes belied some sense of inner wisdom and patience. Kamanin stood nearly nose to nose and eyeball to eyeball to Zariyah, but she did not blink or waver or crack a whimper that such a figure would have elicited from others.

"You both fascinate me, comrade Pasternak and comrade

Yorkina," said the colonel-general. "So tell us, what is it that the two of want?"

"If you are putting together an Air Force, colonel-general," said Valentina, "both Zara and I are ready and willing to volunteer our services."

"It is perhaps a little more involved than that," answered Kamanin with a wry chuckle. "What we ask of you may be dangerous."

"This whole club is built on danger."

"Have either of you seen much of it outside the club's doors?" asked Kamanin.

"We both grew up in the thick of the last war," returned Zariyah, "when the German war machines marched through Yaroslavl." A certain frost hung on these words, as all present remembered; a slight and invisible anxiety passed through all of them, unacknowledged and unspoken but still there. "You do what you can to survive."

"Well then, what say you, Colonel Karpov?" said Kamanin, looking to his companion. "You have heard as well as I that the women are interested parties to our program."

The mastiff with the cane nodded. "I am positive that their eagerness is why these two have so many jumps under their belts. Tell me, why do you both like flying?"

"I just do," answered Valentina. "Why does anyone who joins these clubs or the Air Force like flying? We just do."

"And you, comrade Pasternak?"

Zariyah shrugged. "All I can tell you is that I just want to go up there and be like the birds."

"A bird?" asked Karpov

"Yes, a bird. I like birds."

"What's your favorite?" queried Kamanin.

"A seagull," replied Zariyah. "They're expert fliers, didn't you know? And survivalists. They always survive, no matter the odds the elements throw at them. If I were a seagull, colonel-general, then the sky would become my ocean and I would be skimming its rim."

A silent scream left the muzzle of Lagunov but another chuckle came from that of Kamanin.

"Oh-ho! Such proud arrogance from this one. Her kinfolk's history flow deep from within her. Tell me, who was your father?"

"Sergey Pasternak," answered the foxhound. "You never knew him, unless you were on the front during the Winter War."

"I apologize, colonel-general," parried Lagunov, cutting Zariyah off. "Pasternak is somewhat possessed of a bold tongue and bolder temperament, unlike Yorkina here. It can be an annoyance."

"But Zara... I mean, comrade Pasternak," retorted Valentina, "is just as good. You should still consider her, and you will see that she works hard, if not harder, than anyone here."

"Well, apologies and explanations are not needed," replied Kamanin. "It's candidates that we desire more." He reached into his double-breasted suit and produced a single piece of paper. He laid it on Lagunov's desk and looked back at Zariyah and Valentina. "That is," added Kamanin, "if you are interested."

Zariyah and Valentina leaned in and examined the document. Zariyah skimmed the proposal and what was asked of them, much of it being vague in its wording. But it was the seal stamped in the upper right hand corner which caught her attention and held it. The seal was ensnared in the emblem of the Soviet Union, but instead of the familiar hammer and sickle, an image of a terrier mix with a curled tail was captured in the center. The figure looked proudly off the side, head tilted high, a grin on her face. The terrier was dressed in a spacesuit, a bubble helmet tucked under one forelimb and above her flopped ears was an approximation of the moon — Zariyah recognized the craters — and stars along with the sun.

"That's Laika Kudryavka," said Valentina.

"Correct," responded Karpov.

Zariyah breathed in. Laika Kudryavka — the first furred kin in space. The first living, sentient creature launched four years earlier, soon after the Sputnik satellite orbited the earth. That had been her only adventure; Kudryavka was now living quietly in the countryside far away from the fame which had seen her depart the earth. No one had seen the terrier in nearly four years and she was protected by the Soviet military so that she would not be disturbed, but Kudryavka's importance had not been forgotten.

Once outside, the gray skies arched over the canines heads. The clouds were lumpy and ominous, portending a hard rain on the bare horizon massed like a sortie within.

"Did you really mean all that?" asked Zariyah when they walked out of Lagunov's office.

"Mean what?"

"That I'm just as good as everyone here."

The retriever clicked her teeth together and shrugged her shoulders and said, "It wasn't a lie. You just don't pay attention to the little things that could make you better."

"Gee, thanks," laughed Zariyah.

———

In the end, a group of five from the Yaroslavl Parachute Club was accepted into Kamanin's program. They were to meet in Star City of Moscow at a location known primarily to the public as Military Unit 26266, the Cosmonaut Training Center. It was not, at first appearance, situated in the middle of nowhere, despite the dense population of trees which surrounded the buildings. It was near both the Chkalovsky Airport and the Yaroslavl railroad, the latter of which Valentina and Zariyah stepped from onto the aged platform. From there, a plain gray car whisked the canines up the well-trodden dirt path and inside the gate, where a guard checked the driver's credentials and welcomed the two newest recruits with a smirk.

They mingled with the other candidates, a noticeable bounce in Zariyah's step. Her ears were up and her tail wagged, thwapping against the leg of Valentina, who whispered harshly, "Control yourself, Zara! This is not a game!"

Zariyah giggled her apologies but the truth was Valentina was correct: when her application was accepted and she had been screened by both the Air Force and a doctor from the OKB-1 bureau, Kamanin had written each of the potential cosmonauts a list of simple instructions, the most important of which stressed the high confidentiality of what they were embarking upon. Not even Zariyah's mother and sisters could know why the foxhound was suddenly departing for Moscow, with the story she relayed being that she was chosen as a reserve member of the Soviet Parachuting Team.

Kamanin and Karpov were there to meet them and the other recruits in Room 1A. It was a vast room with a large whalebone shaped machine in the center which tapered into an odd oval at its tail. Among their group was a spaniel named Balakin, a collie named Levin, and another retriever named Nikonov. There were others behind them, many with differing accents from different cities. Zariyah had heard that this was had been screened down from fifty-eight, further down from five thousand just weeks ago, based on both age and health requirements placed on the application.

"I am sure you're all wondering what flight we are preparing you all for," said Kamanin. He gestured to the machine behind him. "This here is a centrifuge. It will simulate the g-forces one would feel upon launch of the Vostock, but also various other flight maneuvers that would be more than your typical turbulence felt within a plane."

"A Vostock?" said Balakin.

"Correct."

"What is that?"

"Why, the name of our space program."

Murmurs floated among the group. Zariyah's ears perked up — so it was true! Space; that unending, unfolding void above their heads. All theirs for the taking.

"Just like Kudryavka?" asked Zariyah.

"Just like Kudryavka," replied Karpov. "You'll step inside the gondola and will be spun on the arm. That is why we chose only accomplished pilots and parachutists, as the force of reentry, the force during takeoff, long-term exposures... the average citizen would not be able to take such punishment on their frames."

"But we are still testing to see if even *you* can still take it," instructed Kamanin. "We will begin the first round of tests this morning, beginning with the centrifuge. From there, you will be subjected to tests regarding your health, your weight, and your mental states in low pressure altitude. Now, who is to go first?"

Zariyah's heart pounded hard in her chest. She hesitated to raise her paw and when she lifted it shakily and unsure, she was overlooked, only for Valentina to shoot hers high and get noticed by Kamanin.

"Right then, step forward, Comrade Yorkina," said Karpov.

The first test lasted just five minutes. The group watched as the retriever was loaded into the gondola and strapped inside. She vanished from view once the hatch was shut. It was slow to accelerate, spinning around and around just like the carousels Zariyah remembered from her school playground. Karpov explained that the increase in speed would be equitable to the turbulence encountered, and gestured back at the control station. The centrifuge increased, spinning faster and tumbling end over end.

"How do you think she's doin' in there?" asked Balakin, leaning to Zariyah's ear. The foxhound did not answer, wondering how herself.

In five minutes it was all over, with the gondola spinning down until it came to a complete rest. Karpov, clacking with each step of his cane, strolled to the hatch and opened it wide. The rest of the candidates broke formation and dashed to see Valentina helped out from the seat, her fur mussed and the expression on her eyes betraying a grim and sickly mask, yet she offered a thumbs up towards the other women.

Each of the candidates went through the centrifuge, each one coming out with the same expression of disorientation as Valentina. When it came to Zariyah's turn, she hopped inside the padded seat and became aware of how warm and hot it was. The cushion was moist and she tried not to think which of her fellow cosmonauts could have done that.

The first movements were slow but subtle shifts from 1g to 2g, then 3g to 4g. She tensed her muscles, squeezing the blood vessels to force function back into her brain, so that her world would not suddenly go dark. Beyond 5g, it was as if her bones were splintering within her body, her fur and the skin beneath melting into the chair as the intense discomfort seemed like it would split her in half. Breathing became strained and too much of an effort — it had not been this hard when she had flown in the Anotov or tumbled through the air. Oscillating at those 180 degree turns, it was though she was becoming one with the harness as the wheel thrashed and moved.

A sudden burst of air escaped from her muzzle and then, darkness welcomed her. Zariyah was not aware of much else once she entered the ether, except the sensation of strong paws lifting her from the gondola's cockpit and then cold water being dashed into her face.

Then, laughter.

"As you can see," noted Kamanin, "sometimes even seagulls have weaknesses. Are you alright there, Pasternak?"

Zariyah made a motion to open her mouth, but as she did clutched her paw around her muzzle just as quickly.

"I think I'm gonna be sick," she managed to mumble.

———

The tests were intense, perhaps just as intense as the men's happening at the same time. Each day for the next several weeks, Zariyah, Valentina, and the other women lived in the cosmonaut dormitories and trained. They underwent psychological training, examinations of their intellectual capacity, and physiological examinations that happened concurrent with athletics testing of each candidate's endurance and stamina.

The centrifuge was hell; after the tests each of the women took note of red spots just beneath their fur, bleeding when the blood vessels of the skin burst. They were expected to spend between four and five hours in the gym, five days a week. It became clear after the first two weeks that Valentina was growing into the clear favorite among the scientists and

CEDRIC G! BACON

the program leaders. Studying her swimming and ability to navigate through the water's weightlessness, Kamanin and Karpov were impressed by her concentration and dedication.

Repeated sessions in the simulators which heated the body to extremes and mimicked the significant gravitational forces of flight put a stress on those who could not respond well to such tests. Nikonov, a Rex, was the first to drop out, receiving the lowest marks due massive dehydration during the early rounds. Kuznetsova, a calico, was deemed too sensitive while the horned gerunk Levin was next, injuring her leg during a skydiving session, although some wondered even if she had made it just how the bubble helmet would've fit over those horns.

Of the original team that met that day in the centrifuge chamber, only Valentina, Zariyah, Balakin, and a scant few others remained. The next steps were crucial in their development, as the women were enrolled in basic cockpit training under Kamanin's subordinate Seryogin, a dachshund, which would qualify them as flight-trained passengers in the Ilyushin 14 turboprop transports and the two-seater MiG-15 trainers. At most, this was to gain a feel for flying: the Vostocks in which the lucky pick would venture in to space were to be fully automated, making the necessity for a solo flight a moot point aside from piloting for reentry.

Zariyah, too, impressed their superiors, finding Seryogin a kind and patient teacher as she clocked in sixteen hours of flight time with the dachshund. She even learned Morse code, which she tried by tapping out a rhythm and laughing at its similarity to the staccato clarinet in "Rhapsody in Blue," played often over the loudspeakers by Kamanin to motivate the cosmonauts.

And yet at the end of it all, she was beneath Valentina, who quickly rose to the rank of lieutenant while the rest remained junior lieutenants or as pilot-cosmonauts junior class. The foxhound lagged behind Valentina, her breathing not quite as optimum when it came to the stresses of orbit. There was little she could do to move beyond the simple, polite nods of approval they offered her after each training session, not like what they offered toward Valentina.

All this ran through Zariyah's mind as she completed another lap across the pool. Balakin helped her back over the edge. "They've been watching and shaking their heads at you," noted the spaniel.

"I know," said Zariyah between gasps.

"They're pretty strict about the exercises. Do you think Kudryavka experienced all of this?"

Zariyah did not reply right away. Her attention went towards the two felines in military dress who had walked into the training center, saluting the scientist and Karpov. They were Popovic and Gragarin, men who had gone up and come down successfully and were training for the next orbital mission just as they were. Listening keenly, despite their hushed tones, Zariyah heard them all but say they were strongly looking at Valentina to go up around the world on the Vostock.

———

At Zhukovsky Air Force Base, thirty-five kilometers from Moscow, a windy day found the candidates at an air field where Kamanin marched with them in front of a Lockheed T-33. Explaining that the nature of the flight was the test of zero-G, Kamanin looked into each of their eyes once more.

"Fear is real and palpable," said Kamanin, turning away from them. "They are afraid that the stress of zero gravity will kill a non-pilot passenger. However, the physicians of

Korolev's OK bureau are too conservative, in my view. There should be nothing to prevent flight of you all, if desire is coupled with courage. Strength always finds a way, dears, remember that!"

Zariyah and the other candidates saluted. Yet that same fear rippled through them like the winds of that dusky day. They were to be loaded into the cargo bay of the Lockheed, and then launched into the edge of orbit. The pilots were to keep the wings as level as they possibly could, all while giving the cosmonauts their necessary training in zero-gravity.

Liftoff began like so many other times Zariyah and Valentina had taken off in the Anotov at Yaroslavl. They exchanged wary glances with their fellow candidates, hanging on to their harnesses as the Lockheed sailed higher and then ebbed and flowed, dipping low then raising and leveling. It was in the peaks and valleys, the parabolas that Zariyah became aware of the loss of motion and a sudden jerk of extra gravity as the plane reduced its thrust and lowered its nose, just before reaching the peak of 1.8gs.

Zariyah had to turn off her brain, her senses screaming at her that she was falling.

No, I'm not falling, she thought. *I'm not about to reach out and catch myself.*

Her muscles tensed and then she relaxed. She glanced over to Valentina as she made that first push off the surface. It was a little too hard — she and Balakin, who'd also come to recognize the weightless environment they were now in, both dinged their heads against the roof of the cargo bay to the amusement of the other candidates.

"No, like this, Zara," instructed Valentina, seeming as though she were swimming as she glided with little effort from one end to the other.

Always the showoff, thought Zariyah once she rose into the freedom of zero-gravity.

It was like they were skydiving, all within the parameters of the plane. They could feel Lockheed pull up again and they once more shifted around, bouncing into one another and doing somersaults in midair. Looking out the window, Zariyah could see the very edge of the world around them. The sky was dim and milky gray, although she felt no sense of danger or worry up there. Her long tail gave a happy wag as she floated towards Valentina and she drew a spiral in midair.

"Nazdarovya!" cheered Zariyah.

"Ura!" returned Valentina.

Each parabola ran by the Lockheed gave a zero G environment of thirty seconds. Staring out the window, Zariyah began to ponder how perfect everything looked — the milky and pillow-like softness of the creamy clouds spattered against the calm blue ocean of the sky — and thought how there was little up here to enjoy this serene calm except them, the earth-bound misfits who dared to trip this rift. Kudryavka had been the first up here, but why had there not been many more since? Gragarin and Popovic had followed, but they had only repeated the terrier's accomplishments and ventured into space on a similar vertical trail, not an orbital one. Balakin had mentioned a fear that they might float off into space and never be heard from again. Karpov had waved away these concerns as fantasy, while Kamanin said it was a slim chance, but one not likely to occur. It all left Zariyah to wonder if it were not possible for there to be margins of error in space-flight, the same as in a normal airplane? Everything could not be as perfect as it seemed on the surface above.

She shuddered at the thought of suddenly coming down hard and fast in the metal shell that had cocooned Kudryavka, more terrifying than the real fear of her parachute failing to open. At least then there was the possibility of a backup system, a secondary smaller chute that would deploy if the first failed. From space, what such system was there for her, or Valentina, or any of the others for that matter? If anything failed while beyond the beyond, what could do they do then?

Nothing, except prayer.

When the Lockheed landed and came to its rest, the candidates piled out and touched the ground, with Kamanin laughing, "So, my little Peter Pans, how did you enjoy flying?"

No one answered, though Zariyah and Valentina giggled lightly among themselves.

"The data will be compared and analyzed," added the colonel. "Of course, I should mention that these results are being sent back to the Kremlin. The premier is looking at you all, and while I have my favorites the final choice, of course, rests with him."

"Colonel-General?" asked Zariyah. Acknowledged, she said, "You've always outlined all of the dangers and the stresses with each test. They're supposed to simulate what could happen to us up there."

"Affirmative," answered Kamanin. "Why, I'm surprised that you would ask such a thing, Pasternak. I had thought the seagull would be brave and strong."

"And cautious. That's why I wanted to ask, has anyone ever died because of errors?"

The heads of the potential cosmonauts all turned towards Kamanin. But the colonel-general did not wince, only smiled. "Grievous injuries have happened in early years when we knew nothing. Parachutes and engines failing, things that you would be well aware of from your clubs. But each failure inches us that much closer to success. We learn something new, in order to send you all up there and do the Soviet Union proud. Don't forget that."

As training continued, word traveled to the cosmonauts of the rapid developments made by the Americans. Their Juno rockets launched orbital satellites with a far more powerful yield than the Sputniks, transmitting data from beyond the darker ranges of the moon and. Where Sputnik lasted only a few brief months in orbit, the Americans' Explorer satellites still remained among the stars, their signals ringing in the ears of every Soviet scientist like so much hurtful laughter.

The announcement came towards spring that Valentina would be chosen for the Vostock flight. It was in a great ceremony, with Zariyah, Balakin, and the others sitting at a long, velvet lined table as Kamanin and Karpov feted Valentina. There were uniforms from each branch of the Soviet military, top scientists from the various bureaus involved with the space programs, and the ministers representing the premier were in attendance. Khrushchev was originally slated to make an appearance but had to decline at the last minute in lieu of a phone call congratulating the women.

"From now on," enthused Karpov to the thunder of applause which welcomed the first furred kin in orbit, "there is nothing to worry about!" He then turned to look at each and enjoined a toast for them, congratulating them on a job well done. "The power of the Soviet Union could not survive without the strength of you all!"

Zariyah clapped her paws together, watching as her friend went to the podium in her matching dress uniform and necktie. Valentina said a few words thanking Kamanin for the opportunity presented and would trade it all in a heartbeat for another. After, she glanced over to Zariyah.

The foxhound did not meet this glance and instead rose from her seat, walking outside of the science building and into the dim light that swaths over the landscape just after sunset. Stars had not yet appeared, though Zariyah badly wished for one right now. Come on and zip across the sky, she mused to herself. I want to make a wish upon you... I don't want to be greedy. Just one simple wish.

Still, it likely would not be enough to change a thing.

Of course nothing lasts, she thought. Karpov was right, there wasn't anything to worry about now. They had their cosmonaut and the Vostock-1 would go up into orbit and circle the earth and step into the sagas of the history books. No one could've been more deserving of the honor than Valentina.

So why did it hurt so bad when it was all said and done?

She strolled towards the test MiG resting nearby and placed her paw on the silent engine. "Hello my sweet love," she breathed, leaning against the quiet hull. "Fancy seeing you here all alone. You are the one who is the worker among workers, preparing us all for this next destination. But, for once as comrade Karpov says, there seems to be nothing to worry about."

The foxhound sighed, breathing softly for a few moments as she lapped at her teacup of wine.

"We will pull ahead of the Americans and the data retrieved from such a mission will make us the rulers of the cosmos, whatever that means. Of course, nothing lasts. I should have known that it would not. After all, Valentina was always the best in the Parachute Club. Why should it not be the same here, where futures and destinies are intertwined with one another."

Another sip before continuing. "One must learn not to worry about that," said Zariyah to the MiG.

"Can I join you?" came a voice from the dark behind her. Zariyah spun and saw Valentina approach her.

"Not my decision," muttered Zariyah. "I'm the guest, not the head of house."

"I suppose that's true," said the retriever. "You left before my speech was over."

"What was the point of staying? They chose the better woman and the future belongs to Russia. We shall beat the Americans in the race for space, and it will all be because of you, Valya."

Valentina was quiet and paced around the ground. Her ears lay flat against her skull and paws folded behind her back, the retriever's brow knotted as she thought about what to say next. "Are you upset that they picked me?"

Zariyah hesitated.

"Come on, Zara. I know you and I know when you're going to lie to me. Are you offended at the decision?"

"Yes," answered the foxhound. "I am upset." She sighed again and continued. "You're good at everything, Valya. No one else could bring such honor and distinction to this country than you. I guess I just didn't want it bad enough."

"That's not true," said Valentina, sitting down on the MiG's tire. "You're good too! You left before Karpov could announce it, but you're my alternate."

"What's that mean?"

"In case I'm injured or something, you go up there instead of me. Don't you get it, Zara? All the effort you and me have put into this program and pushing the possibility that all furred kin may one day walk in space, it's all headed somewhere. It'll be us two, Zara, making history just like Kudryavka!"

Zariyah sighed looked up at the sky. It was a star-flecked night, with the moon lazily hidden behind a blue cloud. "They're looking for another Kudryavka, you know. Someone to be a symbol like she was. Accomplishing all the great things she did." She turned her glance back towards Valentina, her eyes taking on a glimmer of the darkness. "They wanted someone who could achieve all of that and more with the right credits they can advertise and rub in the faces of the Americans."

Valentina looked down. "Funny thing, sometimes I fool myself into thinking there are high ideals in doing any of this. I love my country and will do my duty, but that's not all there is to it all." The retriever then looked at the foxhound. "You had it right the first time," said Valentina. "There is no secret road to accomplishing great things, Zara. The only answer is simply not to worry."

"Don't worry?"

Valentina nodded. "You worry about the past things and you lose focus of the frontiers of the future. You can't go back, but you have to realize that all those you leave behind will still think fondly of you as you move forward."

Zariyah nodded in return, ears perking up at the thought.

"Whatever goes on from here," said Zariyah, "I want to claim it as the beginning of a new frontier. Like those John Waynefox movies from Hollywood. You and me, we're going to be pioneers."

"Ty chertovski tootin'," said Valentina, affecting an awkward impression of the Hollywood star Waynefox, bringing a mighty laugh from the both. "Come on, we're supposed to have a call from Khrushchev congratulating us all. Then, Kamanin is going to show off designs of the Vostock and announce when we're supposed to fly into that new frontier."

———

Karpov referred to it as the Chamber of Silence.

In actuality, it was a room with minimal furnishings: a steel bed, a wooden table, a toilet, an open-coil hot plate for cooking food and warmth, and a limited amount of water for both washing and cooking. In the center, just opposite a two-way viewing port, was a seat identical to the Vostock-1's capsule.

There were some leisure materials, such as magazines and mind games posted on the wall to keep the retriever occupied, as the main point of the Chamber of Silence was sensory deprivation. There was no audible communication with the test administrators outside; Valentina could only communicate by flashing lights and vice versa, one signaled the beginning of the medical tests to the retriever's body with another outside light telling the scientists when she was ready to begin. A different light signaled the end of the test.

Despite rubber shock absorbers which muffled the vibrations of movement from outside the sixteen-inch thick walls, there were always random interruptions to test Valentina's mental acumen, to see how the cosmonaut would react to a pleasurable shock such as music, usually Gershwin but occasionally Sibelius or Tchaikovsky.

For ten days, Valentina had been in this isolation tank. Eating, sleeping, and working in a pressurized environment to mimic the Vostock in flight with 68% oxygen. Meant to challenge the cosmonauts' mental stability and ability to adapt to strange situations. It was an important test, saved for last for the chosen candidate. Zariyah and the others would walk by this room and peer in at Valentina, watching as the retriever made notes and kept careful surveys of her vitals.

"That's something I'll never do," mused Balakin after a training session.

"Why?" Zariyah asked.

"They're talking about spending weeks in space when they've got enough tests and learned enough so no one will succumb to dementia or lunacy. Seeing if the body can withstand that isolation. Not me, I'm no loner. I'd go crazy spending all that time by myself."

"Yeah, I suppose."

"How do you think Yorkina's doing it?"

Zariyah looked back into the view port as the retriever began to undo her sensors. It was the tenth day of the experiment and she would be coming out. Word was going around that the launch pad was being prepared in Kazakhstan and that she would be taken to see the rocket in person prior to the big day.

Balakin shrugged and went towards a hallway leading into the mess hall. Zariyah opted to wait in the control room, watching as the scientists wrapped up the experiment in the Chamber of Silence. Kamanin was there, reading the data from the biomedical sensors. Within the Chamber, Valentina had to remove the adhesive from her shaved torso with a rubbing-alcohol-soaked cotton pad. Zariyah grinned. She bet the retriever would be happy to grow her fur back in that area again.

Within the Chamber, Valentina threw the alcohol-soaked pad towards the garbage. Instead of landing inside, the retriever missed. The pad bounced off the rim and was briefly airborne, landing on the hot plate's uncovered coil. The pad ignited almost instantly and the flames exploded, accelerated by the pure oxygen inside the Chamber. It was like being caught in a bomb blast, the conflagration touching every inch of the Chamber, concealing Valentina from anyone on the other side of the view port.

But everyone could hear her screams. And the pounding on the Chamber's heavy door, even as the flames reached an intense heat that radiated to the outside.

Alarm sensors blared all about the facility as scientists and soldiers alike worked to reach the Chamber and get the door open. Zariyah was screaming at them to hurry up, snatching glimpses of her friend's face in the view port as the fire grew into an inferno. Their expressions were grim and their ears were dropped in a somber resignation of the inevitable, so obvious to them all except for the foxhound as Kamanin put a paw on Zariyah's shoulder.

"Ne day mne eto!" shouted Zariyah as she shook him off and dashed down the hall and towards a fireman's ax. She broke the glass and quickly returned, screaming "MOVE!" as she attacked the heavy door of the Chamber, cracking both the jamb and the view port's thick glass, not minding the flames dancing around her and throwing her entire weight behind the strikes. In her mind there would be plenty of time to think about the pain later.

There was only now and now Valentina needed her.

Exposed to the air, the fire died down almost immediately. Fire officials swarmed in and hosed the last remnants of the conflagration down, then surveyed the damage.

There, huddled on the floor in a fetal position, was a severely burnt Valentina. Her wool clothes were burnt into every extremity of her body. There were many deep and raw patches where fur had previously been, now blistering and boiling; her ears had been burned to nubs and her swollen eyes were melted shut, the lips of her maw obliterated into a thick, slime-like stuff.

"Valya!" shouted Zariyah. She tried to reach the retriever but was held back by Kamanin and his soldiers. "Ne otvali! Otstan' ot menya! Valya!"

The retriever rolled her skull in the direction of Zariyah's voice. "It's my fault," she croaked. "I'm so sorry."

Valentina was wrapped quickly in a blanket and immediately transferred from the facility to a hospital in Moscow, sirens blaring. No questions asked, no answers given. Zariyah followed, growling at everyone who tried to part her from Valentina, ignoring the smell of burnt fur and flesh that came from the retriever's body. Kamanin was there when the retriever was wheeled into the hospital room and stopped Zariyah from going further.

"Let me go!" shouted the foxhound.

"You cannot go in there," calmly ordered Kamanin. "You have no gown, no credentials."

"She needs me!"

"You've done all you can for her, comrade Pasternak. We cannot do much more besides wait."

How long she waited Zariyah never knew. Pacing those linoleum floors like a caged suppliant, she wondered what was taking the doctors and nurses so long.

Every now and then her ears would perk when someone would come out the operating room and her heart would lift just a little bit. Then they would lay flat once again against her skull as they bypassed both her and Kamanin, offering little comfort or niceties. The foxhound did not sleep and declined food and drink. The wait ground on her nerves and she began to chew on her forepaw until one doctor, a Labrador, strolled out and removed his surgical mask. He took the mastiff Kamanin aside and said words to him, their tones hushed and below Zariyah's hearing. Kamanin raised his head and barked something, not in anger but in frustration, then sighed and his shoulders slacked.

———

The official report was that it was a fire in the cockpit during a training exercise.

Valentina's funeral was the first time in months that Zariyah had seen her own mother, but she sat away from her.

She was trembling and the fur was raised high against the nape of her neck from worry that she would soon let slip the truth. But what good would the truth do? Many would believe that it had happened, yes, but it would impact the gains made by the space program.

She sighed, thinking to herself how puerile it all appeared now. It had seemed so important but now it paled against the staggering loss she felt in her heart now. Valentina was to be the first and now she was dead; talk was that Zariyah was being eyed to take her place, although Balakin was a close second as well.

The truth was it no longer mattered. Balakin could have that honor and duty.

In her heart, Zariyah felt the race was over for her.

It was a day after the ceremony that she went looking for Kamanin. She found him in his office, a bottle of vodka across from him and a glass in the middle. She knocked gently and was greeted warmly.

"You've come to resign, haven't you, comrade Pasternak?" asked the mastiff, his voice thick.

Zariyah looked down and away. She had prepared for this moment, going over the speech she wanted to say many times in her head. Kamanin said nothing, instead reaching for the bottle and poured a shot to the rim. He knocked it back in one shot and gulped loudly.

"I know better," said Zariyah. "In my head I know better. But in my heart I know even more. And I can't say anything."

"None of us can," said Kamanin. "It's all part of the game."

Anger leaped into Zariyah's eyes, forgetful of Kamanin's rank in the stress of the moment. Her paws curled into fists, opened, then closed and opened again as she growled, "Is that what all this is to you, colonel-general? Some sort of Gorky Park amusement?"

"No," answered the mastiff. "Life is not." He sighed as he leaned back in his chair, the ice in his drink tinkling against the sides of the glass. Kamanin prepared to open his mouth but closed it again as he swiveled around, away from Zariyah. The foxhound chanced a look over Kamanin's shoulder and watched him reach for a framed photo on the wall. It showed him with Laika Kudryavka, the great heroine and the first to breach the threshold of space. Both were waving and smiling to the camera, the terrier wearing the same spacesuit as on the Vostock program's seal. There was a happiness in Kudryavka's eyes that did not reveal whatever fears or anxieties surely raged behind the terrier's mind. All there was, as Zariyah could see, was that chance at making history.

"You asked me if anyone had ever died during training," said Kamanin. "Do you remember that?" Zariyah nodded and Kamanin continued. "We Russians, we like heroic gestures. In some ways, had Yorkina died up there, we would have dealt with it better. It would've meant more to the success of the program and her legacy as a candidate than some fluke that happened due to accidental misfortune. It would've been just like we did back then."

Zariyah tilted her head, confused. "Back then? What do you mean?"

"We rushed into the whole thing, back in '57. Trying to keep the momentum going after Sputnik-1. Khrushchev asked for it and Korolev and his minions made it happen. I knew it was flawed almost immediately. There was no time to test the machinery, nor any chance to test the optics of risk vis-à-vis reward. Any good pilot or engineer worth their salt would never allow an untested piece of equipment from their sight, let alone into space. But I signed off and approved of it. What could I do, go against the premier's wishes?" He sighed. "My cowardice was at a cost that we all did not see."

"I don't think I'm following, colonel-general."

"Working with someone we all like and respect is a source of suffering to all of us," said Kamanin. "Especially when they die. The more time passes, the more I'm sorry about it. My report reflected otherwise, but I will be honest with you, comrade Pasternak, that we did not learn enough to justify the murder of Kudryavka."

It was like being dashed with cold water. Zariyah blinked several times, her breathing harsh, as though she were back inside the centrifuge.

"Murder?" she managed to say. "But... you brought Laika... I mean, comrade Kudryavka, back from orbit. She prefers the quiet and does not wish to be seen in public. She's guarded daily and disdains the press..."

A bark of laughter escaped from Kamanin's throat. "Kudryavka died four hours into her flight, just barely making it past the threshold and into the sphere separating earth from space. When the nose-cone malfunctioned and did not jettison off the experimental Sputnik, thermal control was difficult to manage. The heat did not disperse, her body temperature rose..."

Zariyah did not wish to hear anymore. She sank into the opposite chair with a thud, which brought Kamanin back around to face her.

"No one wished to mention it," said the mastiff. "The truth will come out later rather than sooner. Fate was on our side as the Sputnik spiraled out of orbit and decayed some-where off the coast of China sixteen hours later. A favorable phone call from the premier to Chairman Mao and we were able to hush up the whole matter. Nothing remains but bits of metal and dust at the bottom of the ocean. We thought up a lie and we thought it up quick, as no one would dare say out loud what they probably really thought."

"You did not murder her," said the foxhound. "It was all an accident. She volunteered for it like we did because she believed in the program."

Kamanin grinned. "I only wish I could tell myself that each night. Is that what your father felt when he fought the Finnish?"

"He served because he thought it was right," answered Zariyah. "He thought he was doing something to protect us, regardless of country or party."

"When did he die?"

"In the last weeks of the war. Where, I do not know, but his bones are somewhere on some grass-grown battlefield. Forgotten and alone." Zariyah then looked into Kamanin's gaze. "I saw Valya's mother and father weep deeply, colonel-general. I saw those same tears on my mother when she received the telegram that my father was not coming home. Have you ever had to tell anyone that, face to face?"

"All the time," answered Kamanin coldly. "I know what it is like to tell a wife, a mother, and a sister that their husband, son, and brother is dead. You know something, Pasternak? I still remember the ranks and the first, middle, and last names of every pilot that qualified for this program. I have to, because I do not know if it will be the final time I see them. Khrushchev honors them as heroes when they fail."

"The premier is at least compassionate about loss," said Zariyah. "Stalin presented our mother fifty rubles for each of us. Imagine that: my father's life was so worth little to the country he served. A loaf of bread cost two-hundred rubles after the war. But you know what?"

"What is that?"

"We never saw my mother cry again."

"Your mother is a strong woman," said Kamanin.

"She had no choice. In times like that, you have to be."

Kamanin listened keenly, saying nothing. He reached out to pour another drink but paused halfway, grabbing another glass. He poured another shot into it and passed it on to Zariyah.

"I shouldn't be giving you alcohol," he mused. "It's not a good look to have a drink before a space flight. Kudryavka, I once chastised her for having a cigarette and a drink right before Sputnik left."

"You should go with Balakin, then," said Zariyah. "She disdains alcohol."

Kamanin shook his head. "Balakin is not mentally or physically ready."

"And I am?"

"How are you feeling?"

"Good, considering I've never been so scared in my entire life. What will it be like when I go up?"

"Once you go up there, you'll be temporarily locked out of the controls. Automatic systems will take over; all you will need to do is pilot the craft carefully for reentry. There is still the real chance that the systems could fail in space, but you'll be provided with enough food until orbital decay occurs."

"And after?"

"We hope that you do not die. The craft does not have a reliable braking system inside to land safely and you will have to eject from the capsule at twenty-thousand feet with all the ballistic force of a bullet leaving a gun."

"That's why you wanted parachutists."

Kamanin nodded. "Who else would be able to gauge the distance between life and death but those who have seen it up close?"

Zariyah laughed. "You're not doing a very good job of convincing me otherwise, colonel-general."

Leaning back in his chair, Kamanin said, "I once watched a seagull on a flight in '43. It occurred to me that the bird does not take notice of the small, gradual changes which are bestowed upon the society below its beating wings. Only the sudden, unexpected ones with which it must maneuver. I watched the seagull for a long time... it was mindful and knowing and patient and serene all at once, hanging there in the air. It was like it knew the danger and all at once it did not want to give in to its fear. Do you understand what I'm saying, Pasternak?"

Zariyah was silent and stared into the bottom of her glass. She had it in her mind to ask for another drink but thought better of it, placing the glass back on Kamanin's table.

In the back of her mind she could imagine Valentina's voice, chastising her for not taking things seriously. She wanted to tell Valentina that she was taking things seriously.

"But you're wanting to back out of something that could make all the differences, Zara."

"Well, don't worry."

I kind of expected that. Any other advice you can give me, Valya?

"Just what I told you then and a hundred times over. You have to learn not to. Every day, every moment...it's all a frontier, Zara, to a country that knows much pain and sorrow. It's born inside of us to over-come yesterday and move forward, into today and tomorrow. Once you cross the threshold of the prepared moment, Zara, you can never return to it. Ever. But once you understand that nothing lasts, that those you leave behind you, it'll come to you that everything will be alright in the end."

"Colonel-general?" asked Zariyah.

"Yes, comrade Pasternak?"

"If I do this... if I go up there and come back... can I ask one thing of the Soviet government?"

"If we bring you back you may ask anything of the Soviet government," answered Kamanin.

"I want the government to search for and publish the location of where my father was killed in action. The individual deserves to be acknowledged, not just a pile of forgotten bones."

"Return home," said Kamanin, "and we shall see."

"And if I don't," said Zariyah, "please don't lie to my mother about what happened. Kudryavka had family too, colonel-general. My mother deserves an answer if I do not come home."

"I promise." Kamanin nodded.

———

It all reminded her of her first jump from the Anotov in Yaroslavl. Zariyah could remember the wait, the anticipation, the anxiety when Valentina — who was sitting next to her, calmly telling her not to worry — jumped first and looked like she was flying. Tumbling, she was going end over end until the chute opened. And then it was all okay and it was quickly Zariyah's turn.

She had jumped then, into something new and unknown and had loved it.

It was familiar and it was all different.

"Check your gauges," crackled the voice of Karpov over the intercom. The instrument board of the Vostock was similar to the MiG-15 Zariyah had trained in. There was the globe and its rotations of the earth in congress with the spacecraft's movement. Press a button, and a reset would occur to see where the craft would land once she turned on the descent engine. There was another, a digital indicator displaying the number of orbits the craft would make and below that all of the dial indicators for the capsule and life support systems.

Zariyah looked out the capsule's porthole above her head. It was nothing but the bare sky of Earth, clear and blue. To the foxhound it was welcoming, seeming to be ready to take her into its azure womb with open arms. She had been awoken early that morning having not slept a wink at all; she was tired but did not let on to her handlers how exhausted she was as she was assisted into her bright orange spacesuit, then transported to the launchpad by bus. There had already been a number of delays on the ground, as the string lanyard, used to arm the ejection seat prior to hatch closure, snapped when it was pulled. A gyroscope in the rocket's upper stage had failed, and there were rumblings about postponing the flight until the following day had the repair not been completed.

Baikanour Cosmodrome in the desert steppes of southern Kazakhstan had been buzzing for the last several days. Her Vostock spaceship was comprised of a spherical descent module and a conical equipment module atop the third stage of an R7 rocket. She was nervous having her back to what was essentially a missile; Kamanin had been honest when he described the number of failures over the years concerning the R7, many of them at this same launch site.

She had to wonder, would Kamanin lie to her mother too if she died? There would be no way of knowing if the old dog would honor that request. Or if she succeeded but died on reentry, would she become a fable now like Kudryavka? Regret filled her heart and head. She wished she could have told her mother and sisters goodbye in case that would be the final time they ever saw her.

Zariyah had to push these thoughts from her mind when the radio came alive, cackling a status check from her. It was Kamanin's voice.

"How is the seagull?" he asked, using Zariyah's call sign.

"The seagull is anxious," answered Zariyah. "And bored too. Can I have some music?"

"What would you like?"

Zariyah thought. "How about Beethoven? Piano Sonata Eight, that's always been a favorite."

"Of course. I think it's a good choice."

The soft piano selection came on as Zariyah waited. There was radio and audio equipment, along with telemetry to transmit her image over the hundred thousand miles she'd be away. That is, should she survive. She then turned her attention back to the lone sight in front of her.

"We are turning on the ignition, Zara," said Kamanin. "You'll feel the rumble and then the turbulence prior to liftoff. There will be no countdown."

She tapped her digits against the arm rest, heart racing and telling herself that it was a good kind of anxiety.

"Hey, mister sky," said Zariyah out loud. "Be a gentleman and take off your hat to greet me. I'm on my way!"

Inside her cabin, all Zariyah heard was a low hum, the deep rumble shaking the cabin. The main engines came up to full thrust and the solid rocket boosters ignited, kicking the foxhound back as she was blasted off the pad. The pounding exhaust from the booster shook and rattled her cabin and Zariyah gripped the sides of her booster seat tightly, unable to hear over the roar of the rocket the warnings from Kamanin about how fast her heart was racing and how she needed to calm herself. She could not tell if she was trembling or if it was the din from the rocket, one ever-growing and ever-present, as it tore itself away from the pad.

The turbulence was worse than the training in the centrifuge ever simulated. Zariyah felt as though her chest was collapsing and briefly thought she was on the brink of seeing her world spill into darkness. The G-forces increase made her flex her muscles to keep the blood circulated and soon the ill feelings subsided as the sustained acceleration held for about a minute and then was done. With the main engine and thrust cut off and dropping, the pressure on her body vanished.

"Seagull, this ground Cedar 1," crackled Karpov. "Come in Seagull, do you copy?"

"Seagull reporting in," replied Zariyah. "The shroud separation has happened."

"What do you see?"

It took Zariyah a few moments to collect her bearings, once everything became clear to her maladjusted sight. The weightlessness settled in around her almost instantly, while the wan image before was, in the briefest moment, similar to what she'd experienced when falling through the sky. Milky white clouds rolled lazily together across a grazing horizon, and through those swirling gray mists she came aware, as one does when being called across the great and gloomy gulfs which divide Time and one's being.

Then the view gained clarity and her breath was taken by the sight.

It was the world below her feet. There were the rivers, the mountains, the sloping green meadowlands that she had only seen overhead when looking at a map. There were the folds in the terrain and she could just imagine the little cars and tractors tumbling up and down those beaten paths. As she traversed along earth's axis, she became certain of time standing still around her with the blue planet reminding her of a standing glass marble. Zariyah imagined that she could simple push it off its side if she so determined, if it was in the powers of a god to do so.

But if she had the power, she determined, she would not.

"I see everything!" reported Zariyah joyfully. "Everything is good, the visibility is good. Everything… is good!"

She could hear the faint static of cheers from across the many miles of radio waves and demands for her to describe what else she was seeing, but the foxhound paid these little heed for now. There was concern at her lack of communication; yet how could they understand just what it was she seeing? Snows in the forests, throbbing volcanoes in the Pacific islands pulsating with their endless, voluminous rays of heat. It was all beautiful. Bright shining tears fell down the length of her muzzle, matching the same shine as the icecaps at the head of the Arctic Circle. Clouds rolled in and out like a film over the earth, with the tops of the mountains parting through the nimbus like jutting, razor-sharp canyons.

Zariyah lost track of time as her Vostock capsule ascended. She was high now, looking out from her windows at the sun crowning Earth. The star gleamed bright the sky against the velveteen onyx around it, the earth, and her. At this stage, sitting in its shadow, Zariyah shied from its brightness until it passed by her.

"Are you lonely up there, Seagull?" asked Kamanin over the little radio.

"I don't feel loneliness," reported the foxhound. "I almost feel like I'm one with everyone down there."

"We want you to know that we're very proud of you." In Kamanin's voice Zariyah detected the note of a smile and beneath her spacesuit she could feel her tail wag. "We have telegraphed all across the mainland the world that it is once again a Soviet who has blazed the trail to the stars. Many in the British and American media wish to know more about this child of the cosmos we have sent! Imagine, one of our girls up there among the heavens and the stars, like a goddess."

"No."

"No?"

"Like a seagull."

On the other end of the radio the mastiff laughed.

Some hours passed. Zariyah was not aware that she had fallen asleep until she heard Kamanin's voice alert her with a pulsating cadence that was both soundless and vibrant. When she opened her eyes, it occurred to her that she was not in the fantastical dream but in the stark naked nature of it all, that the inky black abyss of space was before her. Stars flecked the onyx, just as the sun rose in the western horizon. Its rays touched all like an everlasting web of eternity.

The spacecraft rotated, its Sun Orientation System working perfectly. She reported this back in. The foxhound heard the intense sigh of relief on Kamanin's lips just as the weaving of dawn continued on, meeting her eyes through her helmet's visor. The huge stars and blazing constellations trickled before her, penetrating the thick fog of black as she turned and rotated. Checking her satellite system, she was surprised to learn that she had been up here for almost eighteen hours and a grim reality settled in that, if Kamanin was not lying, she had surpassed Laika Kudryavka's survival in orbit.

Somewhere near was either Gragarin or Popovic — it was still confidential which one had launched at the same time she had — and she wondered what awesomeness they felt at being among this everlasting primeval. Were they too overawed at the bright wallow touching over all? There would have to be many questions when they both returned.

The spacecraft was entering its final orbit and according to her instructions she was nearing Earth's shadow and needed to activate solar orientation at the point of reentry.

As she attempted to take control of the manual piloting

the spacecraft kept tipping to the side, warning lights indicating a wrong orientation along all three axes.

"Cedar-1," she chimed in.

"Go for Cedar-1, Seagull," responded Kamanin. "Are you all clear for reentry descent?"

"There is a problem." The panic surged behind Zariyah's words. "I cannot point the Vostock in manual direction for reentry."

There was flurry on the other end of the relay. When Kamanin returned, he instructed, "What are you getting on the Photometer?"

"Negatives, Photometer has been disengaged," muttered Zariyah, followed by a curse. "Checking catapult toggle switch and harness locks." There was a hard jerking motion and a thunk that sounded like a hollow banging to Zariyah's ears.

"What was that?" called out Kamanin.

"I don't know," answered the foxhound as the spacecraft directed itself hard towards the earth. "I think the booster rockets have engaged. Loose equipment has been fastened."

The ship was turning hard and fast, tumbling through Earth's atmosphere like a swinging pendulum. Zariyah pulled back on the three-point controller, activating the hard brake and disengage with the booster rocket. The secondary module sputtered, like that of a backfiring engine, and again Zariyah felt the sharp motion of turbulence together with the intense gravitational forces. The heat inside the capsule flared and panic surged within her. Earth was careening around her: there was Africa and then there wasn't anything but sky. Then there was another horizon, everything was spinning.

"Seagull! Report! Come in, Seagull!" commanded Kamanin. But Zariyah remained silent, mind racing as she saw the module tumbling out the other end of the viewport. Several times the descent and equipment modules banged together like stone upon stone, striking and jarring the foxhound within almost to nausea. Passing through the realm of Earth's atmosphere, she became enveloped by a reddish light, the turbulent G-forces throwing her mind into overdrive as she checked all of her systems, making clear of one thing.

She was going to die on impact.

"It's burning vigorously," she finally said. "I'm swinging around on all axes, just swinging and shaking." Zariyah was fatigued; she could hear it in her voice as much as Kamanin and the others could. "Hard brake is useless, I'm going faster than planned."

There was static.

The antenna had burned off.

But at that same moment, she noticed the cable connecting the booster rocket and payload also had evaporated. There was a chance: none of the automatic or manual controls in front of her were dictating her exact trajectory or direction, but she was able to view the wallpaper of the earth passing by her with each second. Where she was presently was secondary as she reached for the manual ejection and smashed the glass protector over it. The maneuver was a chore with the G-forces reaching ten and climbing with the descent, but she did it.

The spacecraft's hatch flew open and the air swirled around her. She was sucked into the open atmosphere like a bird being plucked from its nest. The capsule fell empty below, the parachute on it failing to open. But Zariyah's gaze was locked by the sight of her return to the world around her as her parachute burst open. For the nearly twenty-four hours she had been in space, she was struck by the fact that there were no worries of famine, wars, imprisonment, or poverty. There were no cars, no cause for distraction, or pressures upon time.

Up there, Earth was like an innocent snow globe and Zariyah was peering through its precious glass to stare at its true beauty.

As the earth came into focus, she noticed a lake coming up below. The issued parachutes were unlike the ones at the Parachute Club, and she could not move with the extreme winds to avoid it. She barked a laugh; she was going to land in the water, the first woman in space was going to touch back down soaking wet.

The first sight of terra her eyes clapped upon as she swam was that of a nearby farmhouse. The farmer, a squat field mouse with auburn fur, watched from his tractor as the foxhound climbed from the water, dripping wet, removing the straps of the parachute and undoing her helmet. The farmer spoke in a Moldavian accent and Zariyah replied in the same.

"Are you from the stars?" asked the farmer.

"Yes, comrade, I am," answered Zariyah. "Where am I?"

"Pokuttya."

Zariyah ran the name down in her mind. She'd landed much further than planned and laughed again, imagining Valentina somewhere rushing up on her motorbike and yelling at her for landing so crookedly and off-course. Kamanin likely thought she was dead now too since contact had been lost. "Did you happen to see where a large, ah… metal thing landed?" The farmer looked at her with a blank stare until Zariyah added, "It's kind of a big round object, really big, comrade."

The farmer large ears twitched in uncertain wariness, then he raised a paw to point several meters away to the crash site.

Zariyah smiled. "Can you give me a lift to the nearest phone? There are some very anxious folks in Moscow that I need to talk to, and I think I might have twisted my leg on landing."

"There's a telephone at the magistrate's office in town,"

said the farmer, sliding over as he welcomed Zariyah into the passenger seat. "I'll give you a ride there."

"Thanks."

"So, what are you anyway, some sort of a bird or something?"

"Something like that," said Zariyah. "Do seagulls often land around here?"

VIRTUAL SIGHT

SOFOX (AND GABIFOX)

Sometimes, Innovation really is all about fun and games.

It was a cool autumn day and the wind rustled brown leaves along the pavement. As Thomas walked forward, he scuffled the leaves along with his running shoes. He was old enough that his parents could trust him to walk around the local area on his own, but a simple walk wasn't what he had in mind.

Before him, he could see the somewhat drab suburban area. He could see a tree or two of the park peeking from behind yet another cookie cutter house. He could see bushes and various cars, and the clouds in the sky.

He could also see his current health points, currency amount, mana points, energy, and player icon all at the top left of his vision. He could also see collectibles floating off the pavement that other pedestrians were obliviously walking through. He could see the occasional MechaDragon flying through the sky and a blimp with a sign advertising some other, lesser game. He could see various markers indicating challenges or minigames around the place.

Most of all, he could see his body. Not his regular old human body, but when he held up his arms he saw the yellow with black spots fur pattern that flowed down to his paws that he could wiggle the digits of. When he looked down he could see the furry pattern continue, partially covered by some brown leather clothes. His feet paws stood on the pavement, and if he angled his body he could see his tail swish behind him.

Thomas was wearing a Vizor. A pretty sleek piece of tech that wrapped around his eyes. There were plenty of programs you could download and run on it. Art programs where you could sculpt by moving your hands in the air in front of you. GPS programs that would overlay arrows and beacons on the road to help you get to where you wanted to go. Messaging programs that could distract you while you were driving so you should never, ever do that. Seriously, that's a terrible way to distract yourself.

Of course, Thomas was only running one program: ReKai. A game that transformed the world around you. Not to mention yourself!

He was Cutah, a name he'd gained after hitting "random name" several times until he'd found one he'd liked. He was about a month into the game as this character. He'd been leveling up, gaining new abilities and accessories, and even getting some territory claims.

But he wasn't the only one. On the other side of the road, he could see a buff armoured Lion walk in the other direction. He would be annoyed when he discovered Cutah had already picked up some of the collectibles that way. Cutah wondered about crossing the road to chat with him about the game, but he seemed fine on his own, striding along with his tail swishing behind him. Cutah looked forward again and carried on.

A few more turns, some passive picking up of collectibles, and he made it to the park.

There were some monsters he could fight, some too high level, and others that would give fast rewards, but he had his sight set on something different.

The race.

He'd quickly learned that if you wanted the better rewards in this game, you had to do something that no one else in your area could easily do, or do better than you.

As for what he was good at... well, there was a reason a cheetah avatar worked well for him.

He walked to the starting diamond and triggered it. Instantly a green arrowed line on the ground outlined the route to take. It followed the path to the other end of the park, swerved around along the side, and ended by the water feature.

He'd done it several times before. There was a reward for the first time you did it in a given day, and a smaller reward every time you did it, but the biggest reward was for having the fastest time by the end of the day. That's what he was going for.

Flipping up the daily high score, he could see times posted for over ten other players, and it wasn't even late evening. He didn't bother checking their times, he didn't need that worry right now.

Crouching at the starting line in front of the arrows, he triggered the warmup and countdown. The Vizor did some checking that there weren't any immediate obstructions or crowds. Thankfully the park was pretty clear. Must have been the chill in the air.

3... The numbers popped up, hovering over the path in front of him.

2... Energetic sound effects!

1...

GO!!!!!

Cutah leapt forward and bounded down the tarmacadam path. His shoes scraping the path somewhat threw off the illusion that he was a powerful cheetah, pounding the ground with its paws, but Thomas didn't mind. Hitting a regular rhythm, he focused only on navigating the route, and, critically, watching out for any sudden obstructions.

A jogger who'd moved from another path to in front of him? Easily swerved around. A woman with a pram almost as if on cue? Too slow to intersect. A man with his dog in the adjacent grass? Man wouldn't make sudden moves but watch for the dog if he suddenly bolts this direction.

Meanwhile the path flew by underfoot, and Thomas' heart started hammering, the energy of movement flooding his whole being. Focusing on the exciting, energetic ambient music coming out of the Vizor, Thomas hit the turn and started around the edge of the park. Pushing himself harder, he could feel his muscles move, his body heat up.

He took the last turn, and the fountain and finishing line were up ahead. Now it was time.

Thomas forced every single piece of energy and effort into moving forward. Not just a human but the cheetah who would run faster than any other animal in the entire world. He pushed every muscle, every fibre of being on going forward. Pounding heart, burning lungs, everything on just making it closer, and closer and...

Fwweeeeeeeee... Trumpets and roars of the crowds sounded! Streamers flew from the sky. Overhead bright fireworks lit up the already bright sky.

He'd made it, with a burst of energy he flew over the finishing line and now stumble/collapsed over to the fountain.

Leaning against a stone statue, breathing heavily, his pulse throbbing throughout his body, Cutah brought up the same daily high score table for the race he'd just been on. Right at the top was his name, and beside it his smiling cheetah face. Phew!

Only now did he check the times. He had a decent lead on 2nd place, around ten seconds. Not bad.

He checked the previous day's high score. He'd been the winner. And the day before that, and before that, and before that.

It was a good system, and he seemed all set to get that daily high score prize. Of course he could still be beaten before midnight, but then he'd have to watch out for...

"Good running!"

"Huh?"

Cutah looked up. The remaining streamers were gradually disappearing from the ground, the music had already faded out, and in front of him a squirrel approached.

Cool, another player! "Hey thanks!" he tried to say but instead just gasped as the acrid feeling of burned out lungs came up his throat.

"Are you okay?"

"Yeah just... *gasp*... give me a second..."

Cutah sat down on the edge of the fountain and looked back at the newcomer. She was casually dressed in a bright hoodie and loose trousers that went down to her feet paws.

"Sorry... *wheeze*... just a moment to... recover." He wiped the veneer of sweat off his forehead.

"You were fast!"

"Thank you!" Cutah smiled. He hoped the smile came across. Along with sensing body movement, the Vizor also had sensors for facial movement and expressions. How well it mapped to his virtual cheetah face was another question.

"You got first place!"

"Yeah ummmm…" Cutah flipped up the table again, "Oh, you're Sonni right? Oh I'm sorry I bumped you off 3rd place." 3rd place obviously didn't have as high rewards as 1st place, but it was the lowest place you could get that would give an end of day reward.

"It's okay, I mean you deserved it. It's just… how did you get so fast?"

"Oh I, well, no one's asked me that before… I guess I like running… too impatient getting to places I guess. Then at school I had a gym teacher who encouraged me for a bit, so I did some training and now… I'm trying to ace these races for good prizes. There's another track further into the city though, really popular, but there you're competing with people who might actually be athletes so… I think I got 4th one of the days there too."

"Oh okay." The squirrel was silent a moment. "It takes a lot of effort."

"Just keep doing that race, or others, as often as you can. I mean I could be burning myself out trying to hit an Olympic level or something… but just because I'm not going professional doesn't mean I can't improve, can't keep challenging myself, or have fun peeling down park roads as a cheetah!"

The squirrel giggled (guess the smiling *was* working). "Yeah, you do look cute!"

Thomas blushed, okay, there's *no way* that expression got through, "Umm… err… Thanks!" but the nervous stuttering probably did.

Then way too late he followed it up with, "Oh, and the squirrel looks good for you!"

"Oh, thank you." She suddenly turned her back and hopped from side to side. Her big bushy tail bounced and swayed to catch up with her movement.

"Haha, nice!" Cutah had a moment of hesitation

wondering what other park goers were thinking looking at them, but forced the thought out of his mind. Thoughts like that just interrupted the fun.

Sonni finished her gesture and turned back. "Sorry, it's like, every time I look down and see squirrel hands I'm like… Eeeeeeeeeeeeeeeee!"

"I totally, totally get that." Cutah smiled. "Look… do you wanna go monster slaying or something? I mean, you know, to make up for knocking you off 3rd…"

"Oh, don't worry about that… I mean… Sure, yeah, that would be… ummm… cool!"

Feeling more recovered now, Cutah leapt to his feet steadily enough. "Alright!"

———

The pair took on a few monsters. They were some PeekBats which were annoying, but Cutah was happy to see that Sonni had more area of effect attacks. Cutah preferred to stock up on single, powerful attacks which weren't as great against enemy swarms. They were better against the Sword Jackals which they also went up against. Truthfully, Cutah preferred the running. You were doing something more tangible, whereas here you were more just waving your arms about. Still, having someone to do it with helped.

As for Sonni, he'd worked out that she wasn't too far off his age but beyond that who knew? He could have briefly removed the Vizor at any time to check but aside from some randos online who claimed it was "wrong" or even "creepy" to do that, Cutah was just happy to take things as they came. Sonni was fun, seeing a squirrel was more fun than a human, and part of the whole reason you used these Vizors was to have more fun with reality.

It was after a random battle — Sonni had hit a QuadBear with a debuf, and Cutah finished it with a CyberDrill attack — that Sonni made a gasp, followed by a profanity that Cutah hadn't expected from the cute squirrel.

"Whoa, you okay? Did that QuadBear kill someone you loved?"

"No, look! Look what it dropped!"

"Let's see… 232 Creditz, one Llama Paw, a Bingo Bomb, and… what the heck is a 'Shriveled Welk'?"

"It's the Bomb, the Bingo Bomb!"

"Yeah, but bombs are consumable, you only get a single hit and they get used up."

"It's a *Bingo* Bomb."

"Yes, you said so."

"Have you not heard of them?"

"I've heard of bombs, I use them all the time."

Sonni went silent for a second. Cutah could tell she was looking something up.

"Okay," she finally said, "With this bomb we could take on the MechaDragon."

"The MechaDragon?! But there's only two of us! You need a whole group, or at least be a really high level to take on the MechaDragon."

"Not with a Bingo Bomb you don't."

"What?"

"Yep."

"You mean the bomb does enough damage to the Mecha-Dragon that the two of us could take it down?"

"Yes!"

"That's incredible. Those bombs are awesome!"

"Yes, they are!"

———

The pair split the items between them, Sonni taking the bomb, and then they started walking through the park down to the far end where the MechaDragon lay. Cutah had noticed the MechaDragon on the map earlier, but obviously hadn't even considered it at the time. It was pretty much instant death if you weren't prepared... but large challenges tended to give large rewards, at least in video games. Even if their own chance at beating it was because of a completely random drop.

"Have you ever battled a MechaDragon before?" Cutah asked.

"I've seen people online do it."

"And you're SURE this bomb will be enough?"

"Well, we'll still have to fight, but it should be a good chance."

Thomas pursed his lips. He opened up some info screens and looked through some stats, abilities, rundowns of the monster and so forth. He upgraded a few of his abilities and health, and arranged some of his consumable items to be in easy reach. Then he realised he was thinking too single mind-edly and offered to share inventories with Sonni.

"Well okay, but let's see what we... WOW, you've got a Light Slicer?"

"Yeah, I'm thinking of using it, though wait, I think one of these items has a squirrel affinity. You should take it."

"Is it the one with an acorn on it?"

"Yes, I'm afraid the developers of this game fell victim to species stereotyping..."

"Hahaha"

A few more talks, and Cutah was feeling more confident. Two adventurers on their way to slay a MechaDragon, this could be...

"It's closed!"

"What?"

Cutah looked up. Big wooden walls were built right across their path. According to the map the MechaDragon was just behind it but instead…

"It's a construction site."

"Uggggh," Cutah groaned. Walking up closer, he peeked through gaps in the slats. "Right, it's that new playground they're making. This was just grass before."

"So ReKai's maps are outdated?"

"Yeah, it's using old maps for enemy placement. Construction only started a few months ago so it thinks we can walk into this area like it's any other part of the park."

"Maybe there's a way around?"

"No, walls on this side, and it's just houses against the other sides.

"Ohhhhhhhh." The squirrel looked crestfallen; even her tail seemed to droop.

"Look, maybe we can find another way, let's take a look."

Walking around the walls, Cutah was about to give up when he noticed that one of the wooden boards had a lot of give when he pressed against it.

"Here!"

They looked through. An abandoned, mostly completed playground, surrounded by walls of stone and wood, greeted their eyes. Also, smack in the middle was the glowing red crystal that when touched would trigger an intense battle. They looked at each other.

"So… are you thinking of going in?" Sonni asked.

"Are you?"

Silence held the moment. Then they dived in.

Sonni seemed focused "Okay, we'll start with debuffs, then when I throw the bomb, you give it every attack you have."

"Got it!"

Sonni checked that they were still joined as a group and, after a mutual nod, she reached out to the crystal.

It shattered into a million pieces that flew throughout the playground. Then a rumbling was heard, cracks appeared in the ground, and suddenly a huge cybernetic dragon erupted from the ground in a cloud of flame.

"Whoa!" Cutah took a step back to admire it and nearly tripped over a seesaw.

The dragon circled around and shot down a ball of flame. It went wide and hit the ground beside them.

"I don't have anything that can attack at this range!" Cutah yelled.

"It's okay, just survive this part, it'll land soon."

"Survive?"

But there was no time for a reply. A Gatling gun lowered down from the dragon's belly and churned up the ground in a bright line of bullets.

Cutah dived to the side and hit a swing. Sonni stayed where she was, but then jumped to the side as the stream of bullets changed direction and went for her instead. Another huge fireball to dodge, and then suddenly a rain of missiles as the dragon roared overhead. Cutah tried to keep track of all of them as they rained down and despite dodging, still took a hit to his health.

"Okay," Sonni called out, "it'll be landing soon, and when he does, there will be a ground-pound effect, like the GoGorrilla enemy!"

Sure enough, the MechaDragon circled around, hovered, and slammed down onto the ground. As it did so, a shock of yellow expanded out from below him. Cutah timed it and jumped at just the right moment so that the wave passed beneath him. Sonni wasn't so lucky and lost a chunk of health.

"Okay, now."

Cutah performed the gestures for a poison spell, which was interrupted by the MechaDragon swinging its wings at them, forcing them to duck. Still he managed to get the spell out, and then quickly moved onto some single use scroll spells that did the same.

Sonni began a powerful restraining spell and did a quick sliding blocks minigame to activate it. Instantly the Mecha-Dragon was shackled for a limited time.

"I'm doing it now!" she yelled. Pulling the bomb from the inventory, she held it in her hand, then did an overhand pitch. The Bingo Bomb sailed into the MechaDragon and froze in place.

There was a flash of light, an orange ball exploded outwards and suddenly virtual smoke, flame, and debris swept by the team with a roaring sound. It cleared surprisingly quickly, revealing a cloud of smoke rising, and the dragon itself...

"It's lost like three quarters of its health!" Cutah exclaimed.

"I told you Bingo Bombs were good." Sonni grinned.

Now the fight began in earnest. With the MechaDragon shackled, Cutah could activate the Diamond Duster, done by running completely around the enemy in a vaguely diamond-esque pattern. In this case some dodging around a jungle gym was required to complete the diamond. It did serious damage and some more debuffs. Taking advantage of the weakened state, Sonni threw some grenades and some fireball spells of her own. Cutah returned to his initial position and did a Slashing Strike, done by jumping straight into the air and swinging both arms down. Even though the enemy was meters away, he could see the slashing attack connected and dealt damage.

Another chunk of the enemy's health down, but then it recovered and started a whole new attack sequence. Walls of flame they had to quickly fall back from, another missile barrage, and a Plazma laser that Cutah had to duck behind a slide to dodge, which thankfully the Vizor counted as actual cover.

The MechaDragon's health was getting low when Sonni took out the Nutzooka.

"Whoa, so will the squirrel affinity actually make that more powerful?"

"Ask the Dragon!" and with that Sonni pulled the trigger. A barrage of nut-themed missiles shot out of the wooden tube and tore into the side of the MechaDragon.

It looked painful, but more importantly, its life gauge dropped to zero. The death animation started, the Mecha-Dragon screaming out to the skies before collapsing onto the ground, and remaining still.

"I really hope it's not going to suddenly change into a new form."

"No, those are the DiamondMechaDragons, regular MechaDragons are fine."

Fanfare music blared, streamers fell from the sky, the pair's experience points shot skyward, and a loot screen opened up.

"Alright! Maybe not some of the stuff I was hoping for, but still pretty good," Sonni said.

Cutah was less fussed. He'd had a fun experience with a cool person, but his share of the reward was still looking good.

"Hey, you there!" a new voice shouted out.

Oh shit. Looking up Cutah could see someone standing in front of a now open section of the wooden wall. Maybe not a security guard, but some sort of park employee.

"You're not meant to be in here! Didn't you read the sign?"

"Ummm, sorry sir," Cutah mumbled.

"We'll just go now!" Sonni assured the man.

"This is *restricted. Under construction. No public access.* Do you have ANY idea what that means? You could get hurt, damage something, or get stuck and have no one know where you are!"

"Sorry."

"Sorry."

"You can't just trespass. I have half a mind to call your parents, or the POLICE."

Shocked silence hung in the air.

"Okay, just go, get out of here, and don't let me catch you anywhere near here again."

"Thanks."

"Thank you sir."

"And take off those damn goggles."

The pair took off the Vizors and hurried towards the now-open exit. As Thomas did so, he caught a glance of Sonni in the flesh.

She looked... human, and a nice human at that. He was looking forward to talking more.

After they passed through the opening, the man closed it behind them and moved a basic deadbolt into position, locking them out.

"Damn kids," the man muttered. He took a Vizor from his pocket and put it on. On some level of reality a buff armoured Lion now stood in his place, gazing out at the faded crystal which now had a countdown timer over it. "Now I have to wait for the damn MechaDragon to respawn!"

NOT ALL MYSTERIES

FRANK LERENARD

A village of crows learns that innovation might not always be enough.

The ravens discovered the hole in late spring. It appeared far north of their village in a clearing along the old merchant road, where, for a bird flying safely over the treetops, the great bog pool just becomes visible beyond its skirt of sphagnum and thinning red-tipped pines.

Kuri saw it first. She'd stopped in this clearing, as she often did, to set briefly down her basket full of goods plucked from the distant shore and sea. This day it was heavier even than usual; Jatu's birthday party neared, and he'd remarked more than once the day before her trip on his love of oysters. But it was also this day — a few weeks after the last of that year's crust of snow had gone — that the hole appeared to her, immaculately round and dark where it nestled in the center of a mound of bilberry shrubs.

The others knew Kuri was not prone to bombast, and so hung on her words. A perfect circle, she'd said. More perfect than any she'd seen prior, with no bottom heard through dropped pebble or rock or even stone, and no bottom felt through prodding grass blade or twig or even branch. Images of it stirred in their minds, changing size and depth and blackness to suit the personality. They knew it was a small thing overall. But it was also a new thing, and not from outside but from their own little corner. Some small new thing, like a three-winged fly or a two-tailed caterpillar, but maybe not so easy to explain away yet. So such thoughts festered in them, fermented, gassed and bubbled to fill them until, light from the inspiration trapped in those bubbles, one-by-one their wings carried them all themselves to see this hole.

The following night, all the village gathered in the boughs of the eldest birch for Jatu's party. There they mingled over heaping platters of flame-charred vendace, steaming bowls of oysters, and roasted pine nuts that the weaver Pakku, bless his wise heart, had painstakingly collected for the event. But they spoke little of the party's purported subject.

Some of the most vocal of them of course declared a lack of interest. It was only a hole, after all. Jatu himself, a practical sort, said he too could not understand the fuss. For, he proclaimed at the tail of several servings of the wine brewed from the berries he'd picked last season, the hole was clearly nothing more than a burrow. Maybe a strangely round and vertical one, but a burrow nonetheless. Dug by moles, no doubt, who were after all clever and learned folk who liked to keep themselves busy in such projects.

Some nodded. Some scoffed. The weaver Pakku spread his wings to gain their attention, and he too chose to disagree. Clever they may be, he said, but their claws were still large, clumsy, and imprecise. Not to mention, the hole had appeared during the winter, under the snow and hard frozen earth. No sane creature, even a traditional burrower, would think to dig a new den in such conditions.

A quiet fell as they contemplated. Pakku folded his wings, stuck out his chest, and took the moment to propose an alternative: the moles, he said, had once told him of great caverns that could appear underground, when pressure from the winter's ices would carve through the stone, resulting in deep hollows come the spring and summer melting. Surely a substance so smooth as ice could also dig out a smooth hole. Maybe, then, the hole was another entrance to the world below the roots.

As with the first proposal, some granted it and others did not. Tattako, the builder, knew of what Pakku spoke, but denied that this could provide the explanation here. No, no, she said. Ice may be smooth, yes, but it was still water, it was still fluid, and fluid did not — could not — play at such intelligent engineering. No, no. Perfectly round holes, she knew, were the work of great minds. And if it could be no mole or other clumsy burrower, and if it could be not ice, no no, then it could be only the spirits of the woods, who, she reminded them all, were known to enter the material realm through portals. A portal would have no bottom to be heard from even a dropped stone, yes, or touched with even a branch.

These were the loudest voices, and so it was these three hypotheses that most easily floated about. Soon they too were buffeted by counterarguments, proposed by even those who had first declared their disinterest. The dropped stone had made no sound: was the base merely soft, muffling, or was the bottom much farther below? Weren't the great caverns of which Pakku spoke found only farther north, in the lands where the earth never fully thawed? If it was a portal to the spirit realm, how would they tell it apart from merely a particularly well-engineered burrow? Could there be not artists among moles? And why, given the prevalence of spirits, was this the first such portal any of them had seen?

So it went until long after the food and wine were gone.

Kuri's mind raced. She listened to each discussion, weighed as best she could each explanation and counter-explanation, but found they all had some merit. All served equally well to explain what they knew. But all that they knew, she realized, was that there was a round hole, and that she had not been able to find its base. So, as the after-dinner torpor began to settle, she made a proposition: ideas, so long as they remained just words, were only ideas, to be argued over endlessly. What was needed were some tests, some ways to narrow down the possibilities. If the hole were a burrow, for example — a burrow being a home — why not watch and wait for its inhabitant? If it were made by water, why not try to ascertain its depth and full shape?

Jatu danced and flapped his wings. Yes, indeed, he told them. Tomorrow, in fact, he and some others would do just such a test. They would wait and watch for the inhabitant, and they would report back the following day with not just the solution to the mystery, but with precisely who had dug the hole, and maybe they would even invite the talented fellow to share a meal with them afterward.

And so it was that early in the morning, excitement over-coming lingering wine-induced nausea, Jatu and two friends took picnic baskets and settled into the branches surrounding the clearing.

There they waited.

And they waited more. They quietly gathered back together and had their lunch, eyes always sharp on the dark spot below, and went each back to his lookout.

They waited even more. The sun drifted under the tree line, throwing all into shadow, and they took their dinner. Bleary eyed, weary in talon and sore in back, they sat on their individual trees watching the dark ground until that tomorrow passed. Yet Jatu and his friends sighted no creature entering nor emerging, so they returned to the village draped in disappointment.

But, they insisted, just because they saw no occupant over the course of one day did not mean it was not inhabited. So they refilled their baskets and watched another day. And then another, and then another, staying up in shifts through the nights. On the fifth day, they even left food by the hole — meat and fruit and vegetable all, just in case — but each bit only lingered there until it was carried away by other hungry folk who lived elsewhere.

Finally, by the week of the spring festival, they all returned for good. Really, they had proven little, Jatu said. Not sighting the burrower didn't mean it wasn't a burrow. Maybe it was merely an uninhabited burrow. But perhaps, he admitted, it was time to test one of the other ideas.

The sun those days no longer really set. Instead, it would dip just a scattering of degrees below the horizon to ride out the brief crepuscular night before rising again a short way to the east. Festivities in this season thus ignored the clock. At all hours, songs were sung, nests were cleaned, doors were decorated, goodies were baked and consumed, and wine was swallowed. The Night Walkers, a band of traveling minstrel wolves, arrived and began to play their songs and tell their tales in exchange for food and a bit of coin, and the villagers were happy to oblige. For the time being, all were content merely to bask in the warming air.

On the morning of the great midair ball, however, Pakku emerged from his home with his uncle's old ear trumpet, a bag full of bells, and a new idea.

Though it had briefly left their immediate attention, thoughts of the hole still stayed close at hand, so the villagers — and the minstrels now, always on the lookout for new stories — were quick to gather as Pakku explained. Not sighting the burrower, he said, did not mean it was not a burrow. Correct. But a burrow was a home, and a home had to be accessible. What a home could not be was a deep vertical shaft or an enormous underground cavern with a ceiling prone to collapse. The rock Kuri had dropped had made no sound, but this told nothing if the bottom was soft or very far away.

Soft soil or depth would not silence a bell, however. Therefore, during many of those crepuscular nights, flying just outside the village, he had made a table containing heights and the times it took his bells to fall from them. To measure the hole's depth, he would drop the bells inside and listen for their jingling through the trumpet.

It seemed a sound plan to all who listened. And it was simple. They trusted that Pakku, whose beautiful baskets nearly all of them made use of for one thing or another, could estimate the heights of falling bells with great precision. So with renewed interest, they vowed to help him measure the hole's depth come the morning after the ball. That evening they spent dipping and weaving and exchanging partners far above their treetop homes while the beats and yips and howls of The Night Walkers rose from the ground below.

Then, once again, when the sun rose the villagers flew to the clearing, this time accompanied by the minstrels running the merchant road. All pushed in close around the hole, wing pressed into wing in front and the wolves standing up in back and leaning overhead, tails smacking together as they wagged.

Pakku retrieved a bell from his bag. He raised it out over the hole's rim.

He paused.

And he let it fall.

Immediately when it was out of sight he jammed the ear

horn down inside and listened at the other end with eyes pressed shut.

All was still and silent while he counted the seconds. One, two, three, four, five, six. Ten seconds passed.

Twenty seconds.

Thirty.

He continued counting after the others had lost track.

Finally, he removed the horn, and they pressed in even closer. But he shook his head. He could not understand it. The bell had made no sound, he told them. Though he'd flown high, his table only went so far as a minute-long fall, as beyond that he could no longer hear the bell when it hit the ground. If it didn't land in that amount of time, then the hole, he said, was likely deeper than the great northern mountains were tall.

Once again the villagers began to argue. Maybe the bell did hit sooner, but it fell into mud or flocculent soil that plugged its openings and muffled the jingle. Maybe it landed far below but in water, and because he'd listened for a jingle and not a splash he had missed the impact. Maybe his hearing was not as good as he thought it was.

Pakku huffed at this last suggestion, but his eyes shot to the minstrels, to whom he handed his horn and the bag of bells. If the wolves, with their keenest of ears, could not hear it land, then either the hole was of unimaginable depth, or Tattako was right and it was indeed a portal to another realm.

The wolf who played the hurdy-gurdy accepted the horn and the challenge. The ravens stepped aside to let him pass, then pressed right back in to watch as he gently took another bell from the bag, hovered it over the hole, and let it fall.

He too pressed down the horn and listened.

He too squinted shut his eyes.

He too counted the seconds.

They waited and watched.

One minute passed.

Two minutes.

Three.

When he finally removed the horn, their eyes fell heavily upon him. But he too shook his head. There was no jingle, he said, and there was no splash, and there was no thud. The bell, if it landed at all, had landed silently. With only these bells, he was sorry to say, he saw no way to truly gauge what was the depth of the hole.

It had been a good idea, but the villagers now saw its limitations. Pakku had counted on being able to hear the bell land, but there were many reasons why it might make no discernable sound. As such, they'd learned nothing other than how difficult it was to hear a bell land inside a hole. They saw in each others' eyes the continued frustration.

That was when the wolf held a paw up, asking for silence. Perhaps he could not hear the bell, he said, but there was something more he needed to verify. Once again he held the horn to his ear, pressing shut his eyes. The villagers found themselves holding their breath.

Yes, there, he said. Some other sound coming from deep within that he couldn't quite place. Difficult even to describe, he said as he listened, but if he had to pick a word he might call it a hum. Perhaps even a moan. He handed the horn to one of his companions, and this wolf too claimed to hear it. Very odd, she said. She might even call it — though one might always choose such a word to describe an unknown sound emerging from so dark a place — eerie.

Their eyes all met again, but now told a different story. So there was something new after all. It was not what they'd hoped, but it was something. Long twilight fell again over the forest soon after their return, and in the morning the minstrels left to venture around the gulf to the hillier lands out west, carrying now with them the stirrings of a new tale to sing to the creatures there.

More of the summer drifted past beyond the minstrels' departure. The sound of the hum had been new, but once the excitement abated, for the first time they felt the murmur of negative tidings regarding this hole. Over the passing days, some hesitation arose on whether to proceed with their experiments. An unsettling hum from deep in the earth. Perhaps a moan. Eerie. Not all spirits were playful or good. Not all mysteries had pleasing answers. Some mysteries, once unveiled, might even have repercussions, changing forever the lives of those who dared dig them out.

Among such thoughts, the bilberries began to sprout in earnest. Merchants too began their annual passages through town, following the minstrels up and out west to the other side of the bay while the weather was good. Lone critters, mostly, dragging small carts through the one road's orange muddy wheel ruts or wearing loaded up wooden racks slung over their shoulders. Foxes and bears and even one raccoon dog come from the far, far east bearing new spices and colorful fabrics and pottery.

Maybe it was the sight of these new faces, or maybe the simple passage of time, or maybe because fear can inspire as well as discourage, but thoughts of the hole began to sprout one more time. Though none stated it outright while they talked or traded or stained their beaks purple helping Jatu pick the yearly harvest, all began then to look to Tattako, that last loud voice, for one more test.

A wolverine arrived from the coast selling dried fish and sea salt. Tattako stopped him to ask for his longest fishing rod, or, at least, if he would be so kind, a line made to such a scale. It being his only such rod and quite necessary for his business, the wolverine hesitated, but in the face of her windy persistence he finally agreed. But only for her to borrow while he was in town.

Her test was ready, as it was. No one knew quite what to think or expect, but still they all came. Even the wolverine, who was curious to see such a peculiar use put to his trusty old wand.

Tattako had brought to the hole a very small cage she had crafted from twigs and birch bark string. Inside of this cage she had placed a captured butterfly. Supposing the stories were true, she explained while she tied the wolverine's line to a hook at the top of the cage, living beings might pass through to the fey realm, but inanimate objects, no, inanimate things would not. Thus, on lowering the cage into the portal, the butterfly would be transported, and the cage would return empty. Secondarily, if the bottom of the hole really, truly had somehow muffled the sound of the pebble and the rock and the stone and then finally the bell, then when the cage reached that bottom, yes, the line would slacken and they could measure the depth this way instead.

It was a charming thing, in the mind of the wolverine trader, to see the excitement with which this village of ravens treated this test. On the way to the clearing they had chattered to him the whole story, from Kuri's initial discovery to Jatu's long stakeout, to the bell drop, to the current day, the third in a series of tests that now spanned months of rumination and the involvement of now many species of animal. No small effort had these ravens spared simply to uncover the nature of a hole in the ground, and all because it was rounder than most. It was why he loved the far north: city dwellers would call such a thing childish and never spare it another thought.

One more time the village gathered around, Tattako and her cage now at their center. With the wolverine's help, she raised and steadied the cage over the hole. And she began to lower it.

Down it went. Though it caught on the edge more than once as it swayed, the line remained taut. As the spool lost more and more of its line, even the wolverine merchant began to trade his bemusement for intrigue, his dark face going slack and leaning out farther and farther over the pit.

Down it continued. Not much line remained on the reel, yet it remained taut. The air was tense. No one dared even rustle a feather.

The reel emptied.

The line remained taut.

When finally the silence broke, Tattako asked the wolverine how long was his longest cast, and he explained that while it was not so long as the mountains were tall, perhaps, it was certainly longer than the tallest trees. Who knew, truly, but maybe the bells had not merely landed in silence.

They began to retrieve the line, counting the seconds it took to reach the end of its impressive length and waiting to see the state of the butterfly. When they heard again the cage thump into the sides of the hole, they pressed even closer in to get a look.

It emerged.

And they recoiled.

The butterfly lay motionless at its base, one wing propped up slightly above the other while it lay on its side.

Everyone felt it. Thought it. First a low hum, unsettling to a wolf, rising from an imponderable depth near straight down. Now, a death, a caged butterfly energetic on descent and stilled on its return. For the second time they felt this danger. And the longer they watched the dead insect, the larger and fuller the feeling grew, fertilized by a dark and cold soil.

The wolverine, suddenly viewing the forest floor in a new

light, departed the following day. The villagers spoke little of the hole for a long time after, and though Kuri continued to pass by it on her returns from the sea, even she avoided resting in the clearing. Summer deepened, eaten away by its clouds of mosquitos, its endless fields of shrubs and flowers, until its frayed edges betrayed the first cloudberries shining bright at the rims of the bogpools. Birch leaves then turned gold, the forest floor beaded red, the sky turned dismal and gray, and the villagers gathered and dried all the fruit and fish and seeds and bugs they could before everything once more would fall under its half-year blanket of dark and snow.

As it was near eternal day in summer, then came the near eternal night of winter, and the ravens nestled in. Trapped, again, into close quarters, with little else to do but cook warm foods, tell warm tales, and sing warm songs.

Intuitively, they knew it would happen, and it did: sometime during this long night, they began again to whisper. So the hum had frightened that wolf, and so the butterfly had perished, but their village, regardless of their prodding, had continued to thrive. Perhaps bad things would arrive if they continued to prod, yes, but they would never know unless they did. And though none had spoken much of it since their last adventure, each admitted that the hole had remained firmly lodged in the backs of their minds. Despite all their experiments, they still knew hardly anything more about it. Indeed, it felt to some as though their prodding stole knowledge from them.

So they decided: come the spring thaw, they would do it again. They would revisit the hole and begin once again to probe its great depths. The painter Muupi even had an idea to fashion a system of mirrors that a brave, small cousin of theirs — he knew a white wagtail who could be up for it — might carry some ways down inside to see if it ever opened up to a larger cavern. And though this was much more convoluted, they thought that this too would be worth a try once the new year began and the snows again parted.

But this time, when the forest floor was once more clear, they found that the hole was gone.

They might have called it grief. Kuri again had brought the news, showing first hints of it in the tired way her basket sagged in her strangely loose talons when she returned to town. Again and again they asked her, really gone? Really and truly, the hole was gone? As though to change her mind might change the reality. But they came to grasp it, eventually, as one-by-one their wings carried them all themselves to see this now empty clearing.

So that was it, then. Three failed experiments, and more questions to ask than when they had started.

With time, the silts of memory settled. In some places, the story of the hole might grow and change, turning from that one strange occurrence first into a tale, then into a legend, likely full of magic and adventure. But for the ravens it did not go through such changes. A mist in their minds, from which, every so often, dark shapes would emerge to remind them of the combined efforts, the creative thinking and inspired designs that carried them through that strange spring and summer, and to remind them of what they did not then, and maybe never would, know. Not all mysteries had pleasing answers, or answers at all, in the end.

But even so, they all agreed that it had been good to look.

STEELSWORN

JUNIPER V. STOKES

Tarkus the lion will *be king, no matter who or what it takes.*

Tarkus shielded his eyes from the setting sun, looking over the armies gathered against him; for the first time in recent memory, he was beginning to question his odds. Below the short cliffside his forces camped on, the fires of at least a dozen other encampments burned. He counted at least three other notable Mirau houses among them, and recognized some Minotaur and Heskin groups as well. The bovine herds stretched far towards the horizon and the reptilians moved in much smaller groups between them. The grasslands were packed with loose alliances and enemies-of-enemies, all with one thing in common: they were coming for Tarkus' head, and more importantly, the throne to Vannarock.

The Mirauan man's tail swished to match his concern, a fuzzy ear flicking away a fly buzzing too closely. His own forces were powerful enough — loyal, trained soldiers, and some of the best Hunters known to the Steelsworn family. And it wasn't as if Tarkus was some green noble, leading forces for the first time — his prowess as a commander had kept the Steelsworns on the Vannarock throne for nearly twelve years now. It seemed now that his success had painted a target on his back; come one, come all, take a swing at the lion and win a fabulous prize!

With a chuff, Tarkus turned back to his tent, stepping through the fold with his natural feline grace.

"I've never seen so many groups rise to challenge us," Tarkus' brother, Keen, said. Keen was much more lithe in comparison to his brother, with his dark mane slicked back into a neat ponytail while Tarkus' own ran scruffily down his cheeks — a human noble once called his style sideburns, and Tarkus quite liked that.

"We'll have to sow some chaos among them if we want to stay on top," Brisa, their sister, said as she stared intently at the map spread across the war-table, placing pins and troop-pieces on it according to her most recent reports. Her fur was much shorter and utilitarian than her brothers', covered in dark spots that stood out on the tawny base. Tarkus nodded, joining her.

"We have the high ground, so our bowmen should be able to keep them off us for a while," Tarkus said, and turned to Keen, "Have your informants returned yet?"

Keen nodded. "Yes, well, a few. Apparently the Skykeep Minotaur herd have acquired a few mages to supplement their forces, so we've got an idea about their trump card."

"I'll go out on the western front then," Tarkus said, "Channel my psionics, thin the leylines as much as I can."

"Can't cast spells if there's no magic in the air." Brisa's sharp teeth glinted in the lantern light. "Real sneaky, brother. I like it."

"All's fair, as they say," Tarkus said, a ghost of a smile on his own face. "Any news on the Evershades?"

"None, as to be expected," Keen said, and sighed. "I suppose we won't see hide nor hair of them until they want to be seen."

"Keep your scouts on alert, then," Tarkus said, and moved some of the pieces on the map; it was time to start putting a plan into motion.

"The first and second legions will fan around to the east and west — we'll have to keep them from surrounding us. Send two Hunter teams with them."

"Aye, sir," Brisa said, ducking out of the tent. Keen hung back, a frown of concern on his face.

"I'm nervous about those mages."

Tarkus looked up at his brother and shrugged. "You know my psionics make channeling magic useless around me. I know you think we should have reached out to our allies in Forlaque, but they'd be just as dead in the water."

Keen grimaced and let out another resigned sigh. "Such is the price to pay for your gifts, I suppose."

He turned towards the exit and nodded at Tarkus.

"I'll be taking my leave as well; see if any more of our informants have returned."

"Be careful," Tarkus called out, and soon enough was alone in his tent. He continued to stare at the map, thinking of the best time to sneak off to the western front as he tugged at the wide collar of his leather greatcoat. His fur was getting damp with sweat from the armored breastplate beneath, and with dull surprise Tarkus realized the cooling enchantment had lost power.

Better now than on the battlefield, Tarkus thought, and with a click, he popped off a dull amber-striped blue gem from the top of his breastplate, replacing it with a similar gem glowing with much more vibrancy. Immediately, a subtle chill radiated from the armored coat. A mage might not be able to cast a spell in his vicinity, but there were always loop-holes and keeping one's cool in as many ways as possible was a key part of winning a fight, in his opinion. The other key, of course, was to know what your enemy was up to; Tarkus' thoughts drifted back to their biggest gap in information.

The Evershades would normally have shown their faces by now, Tarkus thought. *The longer they wait, the more time they give us to plan. They have to be up to something.*

He didn't want to admit it, but their absence worried Tarkus. Of all the great families in Vannarock, only they had managed to pose a significant threat to his family's position as leaders. The various Minotaur families were tough, true, but they relied too much on their physical might; too straightfor-ward in their tactics. And Tarkus was not above playing dirty if it meant securing victory — which nearly made the Ever-shades an even match for him.

Something suddenly caught his attention. His ear flicked at the slight sound of shifting dirt behind him. He whirled around, and found himself face to face with a black clad figure, the only uncovered features on her being a long, fluffy white tail with black stripes swishing behind her and two piercing blue eyes beneath a black mask.

Of course, Tarkus thought, adrenaline kicking in as time seemed to slow down, *Cut off the head right before the melee, and leave us floundering.*

Veil dashed forward — no one else had the skill to get this close, it had to be her — and Tarkus raised his arms. He cursed himself. Why hadn't he kept his sword on him? An absolutely foolish, rookie mistake. In the split second it took for Veil to draw closer a thin, hazy line of bright red smoke started to drift from his eyes. As the would-be assassin slashed with her blade, sparks flew as it hit the thin wall of force emanating from his crossed arms. It was a hasty block, but Tarkus had had many years to hone his psionic abilities.

"So much for the element of surprise," Tarkus growled, giving Veil a determined smirk. He didn't think about how, had she been only a little quieter, he'd be out of the game right now. It was a surprising mistake coming from her.

His hands glowed. The same hue of red, psionic energy drifted off his claws as he returned her slash in kind — the length of his swipes augmented by the psionic force he projected. He was careful not to tap too much energy from the internal spark he drew his psionics from — it wouldn't do well to blow up his tent. Besides, he didn't want Veil dead, inconvenienced, maybe, but not dead.

She parried, hopping back to create some distance, but Tarkus kept pace; his heart raced in his ears, kicking into overdrive as he tapped his spark. His claws flashed as he drove the attack, Veil quickly running out of quarter. She flipped, spinning in the air as her blade sliced through the tent's wall and she tumbled out. Tarkus thrust a hand back, finally having the chance to telekinetically pull his sword to him, and followed; he did not intend to let her get away so easily.

A starlit sky greeted him; the sun had finally set, and the two moons shone overhead. His eyes adjusted quickly to the night, and he saw Veil quickly gaining distance. He reached both hands forward, searching outward for her with his psionics and yanking her back. He shot forward in the air as Veil was lifted off her feet and sent flying towards him, enveloped in the same red glow.

She was his, dead to rights — soaring like an arrow through the night until they collided. His sword was drawn, a massive length of steel, and he didn't even need to slash; he let her momentum carry her across the length of his blade in a move that would normally gut a person, and he landed into a rolling stop.

A sharp pain quickly flared in his left arm, and it suddenly dropped limply to his side.

"Damn it." He turned around to see Veil gracefully hop to her feet, a second blade, a red gem set in the cross-guard, crackling with lightning drawn in her off hand. He hadn't even felt the blade connect with his arm in the clash; she had been counting on his bravado and stubbornness, and he played right into her hands. He might have been insulted if he hadn't been so impressed.

"You should learn to cut your losses," Veil spoke, tone even and controlled as she held her ground a few feet away from him. "A narrow victory is still a victory. But you've got to have it all, don't you?"

"Certainly makes it harder to argue the Steelsworn's right to the throne," Tarkus responded. "I refuse to just settle."

The assassin stared at him for a long moment before finally easing up and removing her mask. She had a short, black mane that framed the features of her striped face well, and Tarkus smiled.

"You're too fond of lecturing me, Veil."

"Maybe take my lessons to heart and I won't have to do it so often."

Tarkus chuffed, standing up straighter as he gave his opponent a wry look. "Well, then? Are you going to go for the kill? Even if you knock me out here, my commanders should already have my orders. We're much more organized than you give credit."

Veil sheathed her blades, her face betraying no emotions, "I suppose not. In truth, I just wanted to get your attention. We need to talk."

"And it couldn't wait until after the election?"

"I'm retiring."

Tarkus froze. "I... I see."

"My family doesn't know yet," she said. "I just... felt it was fair to tell you first."

Tarkus sat on a nearby rock, rubbing his arm; Veil's blades were blunted, much like everyone else's in this little wargame, to avoid deaths during the election battle. Feeling was already returning, though not as fast as he'd like, and Veil sat down next to him.

"I suppose our little competition had to end someday."

"You were an... adequate opponent," Veil said, nodding. Tarkus chuckled in response.

"Don't get too emotional on me, now."

Silence stretched on between them as they looked at the stars. He played it off, but Tarkus was shocked to hear that Veil would just... leave. He couldn't imagine himself pushing the responsibilities of House Steelsworn on Brisa or Keen and just leaving it all behind.

"Is it because of that slacker?" Tarkus asked, trying not to scowl.

Veil gave Tarkus a questioning look, "Now look who's not giving credit where credit is due. Wander may not be a warrior, but he's a good man."

"I just don't know what you see in him, Veil." Tarkus frowned. "He's so..."

Tarkus wiggled his hand in the air, not sure how to politely call him weird. Veil rolled her eyes, turning her back to him.

"None of my other suitors make me laugh."

"Laugh?" He shot her a quizzical glance. "Since when do you laugh?"

"I laugh every single day, Tarkus Steelsworn," Veil said flatly. Tarkus frowned, and the silence took over once again. Wind blew across the plains; the tail of Tarkus' coat flapped in the breeze. The distant forest treeline waved as the winds rushed past them, and a cloud passed in front of Lunarem, the smaller moon.

The moment stretched uncomfortably long. Despite the cooling enchantment on his armor, Tarkus was starting to sweat again.

"I respect that he makes you happy," he said, not meeting her gaze. "I just... wish things could have been different. We've done a lot of good together, Veil. You'll always be important to me."

"We're professionals, Tarkus. We're just good at what we do," Veil replied. "I'm... tired. Of the posturing, the politics. I just want to rest. I know you wouldn't settle for that."

"I—"

A distant crash echoed from the forest, and Tarkus jumped, his fur bristling. There was a distant squealing, and the other encampments started to stir to life. One of Veil's hands hovered near her blade.

"A direboar?" Veil said, worry just barely creeping into her voice. Tarkus shook his head.

"Direboars."

Tarkus was already in motion, waving towards the camp, "Mobilize as many pikemen and Hunters as you can, send them to the west — we'll bottleneck them between the Skykeep's camps and the ridge!"

"Got it!"

She took off towards the camp, and reaching inwards Tarkus flared his spark once more. He was a dark blur in the night, streaking red behind him as he barreled around the camp; his speed put even horses to shame. He flew towards the treeline, catching sight of a few fellow Mirau fleeing from the forest depths.

The scouts, Tarkus thought, growling as he skidded to a

halt. He raised his left hand, a short wall of translucent red force fizzling to life in front of him — the muscles in his arm twinged, but he bore it. With one foot planted on the wall as an anchor, he reached out with the other hand and pulled. The scouts flew towards him, Tarkus having to brace both feet to keep from flying forward himself.

As they grew closer he slowed his pull, and the scouts landed next to him on their feet. One of them looked to Tarkus, panting and frazzled with fear.

"Lord Tarkus, there's—"

"A direboar stampede, I know."

"Not just direboar, sir," another one spoke. "They've got an Elder."

Tarkus' eyes widened, and he looked back towards the treeline. The thunderous crashes were getting closer now, and the squealing much clearer at this distance; one in particular piercing above the masses.

"Go cast the flares," Tarkus growled, taking a step forward and bringing his massive sword into a stance. His arm twinged again — he'd have to be careful. He couldn't let the pain break his focus. The scouts stared at him, incredulous.

"Sir, you're not thinking of—"

"Go!" he commanded, eyes burning bright red. He could feel every muscle in his body crackle with energy, a star made flesh in raw power. The scouts turned, rushing towards the camp. They managed to get a few yards away before one raised a hand — magenta glyphs slowly forming into the air as she managed to escape the zone of dead magic around Tarkus. A green light shot into the air, followed by two red.

Tarkus ripped an inset gem from the cross-guard of his sword so its sharpness returned and turned back to the forest. The first of the direboar herd crashed through: a massive, hulking beast, frothing with anger between two serrated tusks and bristling with spines. Tarkus did not envy the Hunter's lifestyle; it was a constant war against similar beasts, who existed just to breed, eat, and rampage through anything that stood in their way. A boar was a tough, noble opponent; a direboar was a thing to be slain on sight. The thing felled at least two trees on its way out just ramming through them — and that was only what Tarkus could see.

Tarkus flew forward; he had no reason to hold back in this fight. The edge of his sword cut a brilliant line through the air, and when it met the direboar's flesh it exploded with a blinding red radiance. The scent of cooking meat wafted to Tarkus' nostrils, and the direboar sailed through the air from the force of the explosion. A patch of grass where it once stood withered in front of him. The effects of psionic fire unsettled Tarkus; he much preferred force.

But, like him, it was good at what it did.

Direboars burst from the forest ahead, a roiling wave of screaming flesh. In a moment, they would be on him. A wall of crackling red force sprung to life in front of him and streaked forward, barreling through the middle of the herd before quickly cracking and dissipating. Tarkus didn't need it to last; he just needed it to split the group. In a mindless rage, half of the herd ran northwest towards the encampment, where pikemen and Hunters had set up defenses.

Tarkus took on the southbound group, blade flashing with force and fire. He cut through the waves of flesh like water; he was a one man army. This was his specialty, his spark fueling his muscles past the limits of the average soldier as he ran faster, sliced harder, and took punishment that would easily break a dozen lesser men. He was the reason the Steelsworns held the throne for the last two elections: when he had a plan, he was unconquerable.

One at a time, the corpses of slain direboars piled around

him. Broken, battered, scorched and blasted apart. The grass
was a sickly brown for yards around him, boils and lacerations
manifesting on anything that he didn't manage to strike down
with an overwhelming initial blow. He moved in bursts,
keeping his mind clear lest he lose concentration on his spark
for even a moment.

Step. Slash. Push. Burn. Repeat. He drew his breath
through gritted teeth, a serrated tusk nearly clipping him as
his sword came up too slow, but with a sidestep and a spin, the
beast fell like the rest. It was almost starting to feel rote to him;
only himself, his sword, and the next creature in his way
existed to him.

The ground rumbled. An unearthly, almost intelligent
shriek sounded through the air, as a truly titanic beast plowed
through the forest.

The Elder had arrived, and Tarkus was dumbstruck by its
size. Easily as tall as a house, a creature that had somehow
avoided culling long enough to dwarf its brethren. Its hide
was marked with scars all along its sides, and one tusk was
slightly shorter yet sharper than the other. Its eyes were dark
and devoid of any sort of empathy. This thing didn't have
wants or desires. It was a force of nature.

Tarkus reached out a hand, anchoring to the Elder and
yanking himself forward as he braced his sword for a sideward
slash. The beast was too fast — it reared and headbutt his
flying form out of the air, sending him sailing. Tarkus braced
himself, flaring as his barriers took the force of the impact. He
was on his feet again in an instant, charging right back
towards the creature.

Keep it focused on you. You can't let it get to the camp.

He slashed through the air, sending a glowing red scar of
psionic fire flying towards the Elder. As it washed over its face,

the creature erupting into another fit of screaming. Its skin boiled, but it didn't slow down.

Tarkus dashed forward, darting towards the creature's underside. The sword pulsed red again, another bolt of psionic fire flashing forward to distract it. The Elder lowered its face into the charging warrior, and swung up. Tarkus tried to lift his sword, but pain flashed in his arm again, and then soon enough spread quickly and fiercely through his face. The world was suddenly dark and hazy. Everything hurt. Moments passed before Tarkus managed to wrench himself back to reality.

He tried to open his eyes, and only managed one. The right one felt too red and wet to try. There was shouting in the distance, and groaning he stood to his feet.

The camp was alight with fires, with Hunter teams trying to corral the Elder back out and gain the upper hand once more. Someone hung from the beast's side, two blades plunged into its hide like handles; a small patch of white on the Elder's mottled hide.

Come on, Tarkus gritted his teeth, *Come on, you weakling. Stand up! Those people will die if you do not get up! Push the pain away, focus up, and do your job! What sort of leader stands idly by and watches his people get slaughtered by some mindless beast?*

Tarkus tried to take a step, and stumbled, plunging the sword into the ground for support.

You can't let them die, Tarkus! You can't let her die, you owe her at least that much!

A red haze filtered over Tarkus' vision, and he reached in and squeezed another burst out of his spark. Behind him, the ground exploded as Tarkus rocketed towards the battle. A roar rang through the air: fierce, angry, and out for blood. Tarkus didn't even care to notice it was his own.

His sword glowed red, screaming through the air as he

shot true, the blade steaming with more power than was necessarily safe. The light mists of the evening vaporized on contact, and in an instant Tarkus hit home.

The blade plunged into the beast, and Tarkus released his hold on the nova's worth of psionic fire. The beast shuddered, its skin warped and bubbled up, nearly bursting. It didn't even have time to scream as its insides flash-fried, and it collapsed.

Huffing, Tarkus pulled his sword free from the beast, roaring once more into the night sky as steam vented from the wound. He took a few more ragged breaths, and then passed out.

———

Tarkus opened his eye. Light filtered through the canvas material of the tent, and his body ached like he had just been dragged tail-first through a meat grinder.

Which, considering what he had just been through, wasn't an inaccurate description. He groaned, propping himself up into a sitting position and lightly touching the right side of his face. It was bandaged up, and when the eye didn't so much as twitch under the bandage he let out a sigh. He was no doctor, but the prognosis seemed obvious.

It was a long couple of minutes before someone eventually stepped through the tent — a Minotaur medic, carrying a fresh set of bandages and a couple bottles of clear liquid. She saw Tarkus awake and frowned.

"Couldn't have had the decency to be born magic like the rest of us, eh? Make my job harder," she grumbled good-naturedly before stepping over to his cot.

"Rest of those folk, give 'em a sip of potion and they're right as rain. But no, gotta do it the long way with you."

"I'll make sure to bring it up with my parents. Clearly they followed the instructions wrong, birthing me," Tarkus remarked, earning a short laugh from the medic.

"Well, you may have lost an eye, but your sense of humor's all there it seems."

Gingerly, she removed the bandages, dabbing a cloth with the liquid — alcohol, from the scent — and disinfected the gash. He gritted his teeth, but Tarkus didn't make a peep.

"I stitched it up best I could while you were unconscious. Once that's scarred up nice, you should think about wearing a patch, probably."

Tarkus nodded, "Could you send someone to fetch my brother and sister?"

"Aye." The medic returned the nod, wrapping the fresh bandages around Tarkus' head and taking her leave. For a few moments, Tarkus was alone with his thoughts. A proper show of Steelsworn strength, numerous casualties from the direboar rampage avoided, and all he had to pay for it was an eye? As far as Tarkus was concerned, that was a clean victory.

The tent opened up once more as Tarkus' siblings clamoring through. They both seemed rather haggard, but otherwise unharmed. Brisa grinned, while Keen let out a breath that he seemed to have been holding all night.

"You're an absolute madman, you know that?" Keen almost shouted, giving his brother a wild look, tail flicking rapidly with annoyance and a healthy dose of fear.

"Why do you sound surprised?" Tarkus replied, raising his one good eyebrow. Brisa barked out a single laugh, walking over and ruffling his mane.

"Well, you certainly put on a show. Most of our competitors have withdrawn after your little stunt."

"Most?"

Brisa waved a hand. "Officially, at least. I'd give the rest maybe two, three days of deliberation before they follow where the wind is blowing."

"I must be losing my touch," Tarkus remarked, smiling once more as Brisa grinned right back at him. Keen groaned, taking a seat in the nearest cot.

"Well, congratulations on another six years of rulership."

Tarkus reached out a hand, clasping Keen on the shoulder. They shared a nod, and Tarkus' brother finally relaxed.

"I swear, if you go off and try to kill some other ancient megafauna on your own, I'll end you myself first."

"Well, so much for my kraken fishing trip next weekend."

Keen glared, and a fourth figure came to the entrance of the tent. Tarkus' face lit with surprise. Veil was out of her uniform, adorned in the loose clothes of her family's station; her shirt folded over and tied with a sash at the waist, and loose fitting pants cinched at the ankles.

"May I enter?"

Her tone was as impassive as ever, and Tarkus gestured her over. She strode with effortless grace, sitting primly on the cot opposite Keen. He coughed, standing suddenly and turning to the exit.

"I've some business to take care of, so—"

"I'll escort you," Brisa nodded, the two of them quickly leaving. Veil watched them go, then turned back to Tarkus.

"Your siblings are strange."

"Well, we can't all be stalwart rocks," Tarkus said, shrugging, "How do you fare?"

"Nothing too serious." Veil retrieved a letter from an inner pocket of her shirt. "Officially, I'm here to deliver the Evershades' letter of withdrawal."

Tarkus took the letter, carefully flipping it open to read the flowing script inside. Veil gave him a scrutinizing look.

"That was a solid plan — funneling the direboars against

the cliff-side wall, surrounding them with the forces of every other competing house," she leaned forward, her eyes narrowing, "and safely below your own forces."

"Really?" Tarkus continued to read. "Must not have thought about that in the heat of the moment. I don't suppose the post-battle fatigue has much to do with all the other withdrawals?"

She glared at him for a few moments longer, the tip of her tail barely flicking. After a tense moment of silence, she sighed. "You always have to have it all."

He gave Veil an amused look. Folding the paper back up, he settled back into his cot.

"Well, after all this I suppose your retirement is earned."

Veil nodded, and stood up to leave. She paused for a moment at the door. "Tarkus... it's been fun."

Tarkus smiled, and shooed at her with a hand, "Emotional, as always. Let me rest, I beg you, go enjoy your life."

"So long as you do the same."

He gave her a small smile, which she returned in kind. The morning sun shone around her as she stood in the tent's threshold, shielding his face from its blinding rays. And then, a moment later, she left.

No, Veil, he thought, still smiling, *I guess I can't have it all.*

SUGAR MAGNOLIA

K.C. SHAW

Can a possum, a raccoon, and a mink make music as wonderful as their new favorite band from Mongolia?

Maggie had only just gotten out of bed when Erin appeared at her bedroom window. The raccoon's eyes were round with excitement. She rapped on the glass impatiently even though Maggie was already reaching to unlatch it.

"You have to see this!" Erin tumbled into the room, letting in a blast of heat from the August evening.

"I haven't even gone to the bathroom yet," Maggie said. She grabbed the bedstead with her prehensile, hairless tail for extra leverage as she pushed the window closed. "I just woke up."

"This is more important!" Erin waved her phone.

There was no stopping Erin when she was excited about something. Maggie smiled and grabbed her comb from the dresser. "I'm paying attention but I'm also brushing my fur, okay?"

"Just watch." Erin held her phone out and pressed play on

the YouTube video. "Oh, darn ads." Her thumb hovered impatiently until the "skip ad" button appeared. "*Now* watch."

Within five seconds Maggie had forgotten all about her comb. She watched the music video, riveted. Her whiskers vibrated in time with the pounding bass drum beat and the guttural roar of the singer's voice, and her tail twitched back and forth like a cat's.

"*See?*" Erin's voice held an excited squeal. "Maggie, we have to start a band!"

Maggie and Erin had been best friends since kindergarten. Maggie understood the raccoon's leap of logic perfectly, but she was more interested in the band. "Who are they? What language is that? What are those instruments?"

"They're from Mongolia, called Eagle's Flight. They play traditional instruments as well as, you know, regular rock instruments." Erin started to pace, her ringed tail brushing the carpet of Maggie's small bedroom. "We should do that too, only with *our* traditional instruments. Star Fisher already plays banjo, and she's really pretty and has a good voice. I can sing backup too and learn, I don't know, bass. I think I'd be good at it." She stopped and struck a rockstar pose: legs apart, head down, paws holding a low-slung air guitar — although the effect was marred by the phone in one paw.

Maggie took the phone. She wasn't allowed to have a smartphone yet. She opened a new tab and typed "Eagle's Flight band members."

Erin said, "We might ask Jess too. We're in chorus together."

Maggie glanced up from her intent study of a band photo. "Jess would never want to join our band. She's — you know. Perfect."

"Perfect for *us*. Look, do you want to meet Eagle's Flight one day or not? We have to be a really good band to get them to notice us, and that means we need Jess. Anyway, the best bands always have a carnivore as lead singer. They're charismatic."

Maggie looked at the Eagle's Flight photo again. Their lead singer was a wolf, his fur almost black, his eyes smoldering with passion. His voice still echoed in her head. She felt a flutter deep in her belly.

"Who's your favorite?" she asked Erin.

Erin joined her to look at the picture too. She was silent for a moment — a small miracle, since Erin was as talkative as Maggie was quiet. "The lead singer is really handsome," she said thoughtfully, "but that animal with the — what is that thing, do you think? It's sort of like a skinny cello. I don't know what he is but I like him. Do you think he'd think I was pretty?"

"You're beautiful, Erin," Maggie said loyally. She enlarged the photo so she could read the caption aloud. "'Eagle's Flight from left to right: Altan, a Corsac fox, guitar and backing vocals; Tuguslar (Tugi), a yak, drums; Borjigin, a wolf, lead vocals and morin khuur; Yisu, a manul (Asian wildcat), tovshuur and backing vocals.'" She stumbled over the unfamiliar names and words. "He's a cat! He looks more like a raccoon, with those stripes on the sides of his face and all that fur."

"I love his fur." Erin ran her fingers through her ruff to make it stand out properly. "Who's your favorite?"

Maggie studied the photo again. It was no use expecting any of them to be possums like her. The only marsupial musicians she'd ever heard of were some old guys from Australia that her mom liked. She looked at each band member in turn. The wolf was handsomest, but she understood how these things worked. She wasn't pretty enough to choose the lead singer of a band as her favorite. She liked the cat too but Erin had chosen him so she couldn't. That left the fox and the yak.

The fox was the obvious choice. He was good-looking in a different way from the cat, slender instead of sturdy with a mischievous grin instead of the cat's rock-n-roll scowl. He looked like he'd be fun to hang out with.

But she kept remembering the video, the steady heartbeat rhythm of the bass drum. The video hadn't shown the drummer much, just a few quick shots of him tossing his head. He was bigger than the others, hulking behind a massive drum set. He had magnificent black horns, a shaggy mane of black hair, floppy ears, and muscles in his arms as he pounded the drums.

Maggie said, "I like the yak. I want to play drums."

———

Erin tried to talk Maggie out of the drums, but Maggie was adamant. She unlocked the toy safe where she kept her money and said, "I can afford a drum set so I get to be the drummer."

Erin's eyes widened again. "What about your motorbike?"

"Mom won't let me get one anyway," Maggie said, which made her sound sulky although she was only telling the truth. She and her mom had argued about it for the last two years. "By the time I go to college I'll have a job and can buy one then."

Erin still looked doubtful, but she only said, "If you're sure. Get dressed so we can go talk to Star."

Star was a mink who lived a few streets over in their quiet subdivision. She was two grades ahead of Maggie, one ahead of Erin, and had only lived in the neighborhood a few years anyway. Maggie barely knew her, but Erin was much more outgoing.

It was still early, the light fading but nowhere near dark yet. All the diurnal animals were returning home, and all the nocturnal animals were going out, so traffic was as busy as it ever got in Coalfield. There were no traffic lights so they had to wait to cross the street every time, with heat radiating from the sidewalk until Maggie's fur prickled with sweat.

She had worn one of her new dresses she'd bought for school when it started next week, in hopes of looking more polished than usual. It was a pretty pale green that set off her gray and white fur. Erin wore her usual shorts and a blue "Coalfield Cougars" T-shirt.

They arrived at Star's house panting and sweaty. When Star's mother opened the door, Maggie sighed with longing at the air conditioning that swirled out at them.

"Is Star up yet, Ms. Fisher?" Erin asked.

"She's eating breakfast. Come on in out of the heat. Star, you have friends to see you."

Maggie smiled at Ms. Fisher, who was tall and elegant with jet-black fur. Star looked a lot like her, but with a tiny spot of white on her chest that resembled a diamond pendant. Next to the minks, Maggie felt short and dumpy.

But Star was hunched over a cereal bowl, looking half-asleep with ruffled fur. She was still in her pajamas. "Hi," she said to Erin, and glanced at Maggie with a polite but confused smile.

"Star, you have to see this," Erin said. She pulled a chair up next to the mink and held out her phone. "Darn ads. Wait a second. Oh — this is Magnolia Tate. You know her, right?"

Maggie stood awkwardly nearby. Her ears and whiskers twitched as the video started and she felt herself relax into the song. It was different from what she was used to, but familiar enough that she could appreciate it — just the right balance of new and old. She wanted to be part of the music, part of the excitement that rose in her when she heard it. She wondered how much drums cost, how long it would take to learn how to play. She wondered where Mongolia was.

"That's amazing," Star breathed when the video ended. She had put her spoon down, cereal forgotten. "Who are they?"

"A band from Mongolia. We want to start a band to do what they're doing, combine our musical traditions and instruments with rock. Are you in? We need a banjo player."

Star said, "There's already bluegrass rock."

"Not like that." Erin waved her paws in frustration, as though whatever vision she had for their future wasn't something she could express in words. "Eagle's Flight took rock and traditional music and made something totally new with it. We could do that too. Not bluegrass rock, just — just rock flavored with the *spirit* of bluegrass."

Star glanced over Erin's head to meet Maggie's eyes with a wry smile. Maggie returned it.

"What instruments do you both play?" Star asked.

"I'm going to learn bass," Erin said. "Maggie likes the drummer of Eagle's Flight so she's going to learn drums."

Star hesitated a moment with another glance at Maggie, then said, "That's great. I can sing, although I'd rather not do all the singing."

Maggie noticed her tail had wrapped itself around the leg of the nearest chair. Just because Star and Erin both thought she was too small and weak to play drums didn't mean she couldn't. She didn't need to be the size of a yak to hit a drum, for Pete's sake.

Erin said, "We thought we might ask Jess to be our singer." Confident as Erin was, she sounded more doubtful now than she had half an hour before. "She's got an amazing voice and the star quality we need. Maybe if you called her?"

Star said kindly, "She's pretty busy with other projects, and with school about to start..." She trailed off, then added, "If you had instruments and were starting lessons, that would be better. We don't have to start the band immediately. Just hold onto the idea and when we're in a better place to approach Jess, I'll talk to her."

Erin looked relieved, or at least her ears relaxed. "That's a great idea. You can sing for us in the meantime, okay? Will you practice with us?"

"Sure. Just call me when you want to get together."

"Thanks, Star!" Erin jumped up. "Come on, Maggie. Let's see if Mom will drive us to Knoxville to look at instruments."

———

Erin's little brother demanded to come with them, which meant Ms. Linwood had to come into the music store too instead of waiting in the car. When she found out, Erin said, "*Mooooom*" through clenched teeth in a way that would have gotten Maggie grounded for life.

As soon as they were in the store, though, Erin's brother went straight to the guitars, Ms. Linwood trailing after him. "We can pretend we don't know who those embarrassing raccoons are," Erin whispered, which made Maggie giggle.

A husky who looked like he'd just come from the groomer said, "Can I help you?" His glance flitted right past Maggie and settled on Erin. Maggie was used to her friend getting all the attention, but it still stung.

"I'm looking for a bass," Erin said in the giggly-flirty voice they both despised. Sometimes it just happened, though.

"Oh yeah? Played long?" the husky asked with a tail wag.

Erin twisted the hem of her T-shirt with a nervous smile. "Just starting, actually. Do you give lessons here?"

"Oh, sure. Come on over to the basses and take a look at what we have. You need an amp too, I guess?"

"I guess," Erin said, and abandoned Maggie.

Maggie stared around the store in a sudden panic. It was full of gleaming musical instruments and shelves of equipment she didn't even recognize. An otter dressed in torn jeans and a black T-shirt flipped through a display of books as though looking for something specific; a cat with grizzled gray fur settled a guitar strap over her shoulder and played a few notes. Two more clerks, both college-aged and handsome like Erin's bass player, chatted behind a counter.

She didn't belong here. She was just a possum who started ninth grade in a week. She might as well just go back out to the car.

Another clerk approached, a goat with short brown fur and short brown horns. He was older than the other clerks and scruffier, although he wore the same red polo shirt with the "Universe Music!" logo blazoned on it in yellow. "How can I help you?"

Maggie had started edging back to the door, but she stopped and looked up at the goat. She had to lick her lips and clear her throat before she could talk, and then her voice came out in a whisper. "I want to buy a drum set."

"Great. The drums are back here."

Maggie followed him to the back of the store, where three kits sat in a row with more displayed on shelves. The kits were all huge.

"Do you play yet or are you just starting?" the goat asked. His name tag said "John."

"Just starting," Maggie whispered.

"We carry some beginner kits. What kind of budget do

you have?"

Maggie swallowed and stared at the nearest drum set, a beautiful blue sparkle. She counted *seven* drums with a stool behind them, plus three cymbals. "Not enough, probably," she said.

"We have payment plans available. Come down here and look at this one." John led the way to the third drum set. "This is one of our beginner kits, but it comes in different configurations. You probably only need a four-piece kit to start. That means bass drum, snare, twelve-inch tom, and floor tom. It comes with hi-hat and crash/ride cymbals too, and a throne." He pointed to each item as he spoke.

"How much?" Maggie clutched the little purse she carried over her shoulder, which was fat with two years of birthday, babysitting, and odd-job money.

"Three-ninety-nine."

Four hundred dollars. Maggie felt sick. "I only have three twenty," she said, her voice shaking slightly. "I— I'll have to come back after my birthday next month." She started to back away.

"We can work something out." John regarded her with sympathy. "Do you really want to spend all your money on a drum set or is this your raccoon friend's idea?"

Maggie took a deep breath. "It's her idea, but — I want to learn. I really do." She thought of the Eagle's Flight song, of the yak tossing his mane as he drummed.

John nodded. "Okay. We always have some odds and ends of returned merch in the back. We sell it used. I can put you together a good four-piece kit for two-fifty if you don't mind that the drums won't match, and I'll tune it for you and show you how to set it up. For another fifty bucks I'll sign you up for six half-hour beginner lessons to get you started. That leaves you with twenty dollars and your next month's birthday money so you're not totally broke. How's that? Please don't cry," he added quickly.

Maggie giggled, although her eyes really were watering with gratitude. "Thank you. You're really nice."

"I've got a daughter about your age." John smiled. "Give me a minute to find those drums."

———

Maggie had her first drum lesson while Erin went to lunch with her mom and brother. It was mostly how to put her new kit together, including putting heads on the drums and tuning them. The snare was black, the bass drum and rack tom were purple, and the floor tom was white. The hi-hats and crash cymbals were made by different companies. But it was hers.

Every time John finished tuning a drum he'd hit it with a stick and say, "Doesn't that sound better?" Maggie nodded and didn't let on she could barely tell the difference.

After her lesson, John showed her what parts to disassemble to transport it, then helped her load everything into Ms. Linwood's SUV next to Erin's shiny red bass and small amplifier.

"We're in a *band*," Erin said on the way home. "This is so exciting!"

Maggie smiled, but inside she was less certain about her decision. John had given her a lot of exercises to practice and although he'd been encouraging, she knew she hadn't played a single one right. What if she'd spent all her money on a drum kit and turned out to have no talent at all?

Ms. Linwood looked at her in the rear-view mirror and asked, "Do you have a spot picked out to keep your drums, Magnolia?"

Maggie hadn't thought about where she'd put her drums

or what her mom would say. She shook her head, paws clenched in her lap.

Erin said, "Why don't you keep it in my room? That way we can practice all the time."

Erin's room was upstairs with windows that looked out over a tree-filled back yard. Even with her brother helping, it took them several trips to bring all their new gear upstairs, and even longer to clear a space for the drum set. It hadn't seemed all that big in the music store, not compared to the other kits for sale, but in an already cluttered bedroom it looked enormous.

John had told Maggie not to be scared to hit the drums hard. "They're meant to be banged on," he'd said. "They won't break." But she was still terrified she'd mess them up somehow if she set them up wrong.

Erin, meanwhile, only had to plug her amp in and plug the bass into the amp. She played open chords and practiced posing in front of her full-length mirror while Maggie adjusted her drums. "What do you think? Pretty awesome, huh?"

Maggie glanced up. "You look so cool."

"I need to get some stage clothes. What do you think about a denim jacket? Old-school or lame?"

"Old-school." Maggie sat on the throne — which seemed like a weird thing to call a stool — and picked up her new sticks. "You can put badges and pins all over it."

"Good idea!" Erin tried another pose in the mirror.

Maggie adjusted the sticks in her paws the way John had showed her, straightened her back so she wouldn't slouch, and hit the snare drum. It sounded *really* loud.

"Oh, Mom made me buy earplugs," Erin said. "Here's your pair. They're supposed to fit mammals of all kinds."

"Thanks." Maggie screwed them into her ears. "What

should we play first?" Her voice sounded weirdly muffled with the earplugs in.

Erin plugged her phone into its external speaker and turned the volume all the way up. The Eagle's Flight song started.

For a moment Maggie froze. She tried to remember everything John had told her, but it all flew out of her head.

She managed to hit the snare in time and occasionally stamped on the bass drum pedal. Erin didn't do much better. She didn't know any chords yet so just strummed in rhythm.

When the song ended Maggie's heart was pounding as though she'd run a mile. She knew she'd done terrible — but playing along to the song made her feel like a part of it. She grinned at Erin.

Erin started giggling. "Oh, we're so bad! Never mind, we'll get better. Want to try a different song next?"

"Sure! Something really slow."

———

They played on and off all night, until Erin's claws were worn down from the bass strings. In between playing along to songs, they watched YouTube videos for beginner musicians. By the time Maggie went home at dawn, Erin could play two chords reliably and Maggie could play a simple groove without it falling apart after a few measures.

Maggie helped her mother with supper, and after they ate she practiced John's rudimental exercises with the drumsticks she'd brought home with her. She used a book to practice on until her mother complained about the noise, then switched to a pillow. She didn't fall asleep until almost noon.

The day before school started, Ms. Linwood took Maggie and Erin to their music lessons. John was their teacher, to

Maggie's pleasure. He didn't make her feel small and clumsy like the husky. He taught them together and was enthusiastic about their progress. "I can tell you've been practicing. Are you having fun?"

"Definitely!" they both said.

"Have a band name yet?"

Erin giggled and said, "We've argued about it all week." John laughed.

Ordinarily Maggie would be terrified about the first day of school, but she had drumming to look forward to once she got home. Even when she realized ten minutes too late that she was in the wrong English class, she didn't panic or die of embarrassment. She just thought of Tugi, the yak drummer, tossing his mane. He had confidence. She could too.

At the end of September when her six introductory drum lessons were over, she paid for six more out of her birthday money. Erin gave her an Eagle's Flight poster.

East Tennessee's long summer shaded into a glorious autumn. The maple trees outside of Erin's bedroom window turned red and yellow. By the time November wind and rain shook the trees bare, Maggie and Erin decided they were good enough to invite Star to play with them.

Star had forgotten all about the band, but brought her banjo over after school whenever she didn't have basketball practice, swim lessons, yearbook or student council meetings, work, or a date with her boyfriend. Maggie had grown used to playing along with just Erin's bass and the addition of a new instrument excited her all over again.

The banjo sounded silvery and quick. It reminded Maggie of light shining on moving water. Star could really play, too — she'd taken lessons for years — and she encouraged them to play along to more than just their favorite songs. She loaned them CDs of her favorite modern bluegrass bands, and when

Maggie grew interested she invited her over to listen to actual records on a turntable in her room.

Erin's family always went out of town over winter break. Maggie took her snare home so she could practice, and Star invited Maggie over almost every day to listen to records.

Maggie was embarrassed at how much she loved lying on the tufted pink carpet in Star's room, a bowl of chips within reach and music she'd never heard before floating from the big speakers. After they listened to a record, they discussed it — sometimes for hours. They talked about what the soul of a musical style was, how to capture its essence. Maggie sometimes imagined she and Star were college roommates.

Maggie's grandmother gave her a gift certificate to the Universe Music store on the solstice. Maggie spent it on six more lessons with John and a new pair of sticks, since hers were getting chewed up by the edges of her cymbals. Erin returned home excited about her new do-it-yourself grooming supply kit. She started talking about becoming a professional groomer after high school.

Eagle's Flight released a new album. Maggie listened to it constantly. She listened to other Mongolian music she found online too, traditional and modern, along with the bluegrass Star recommended.

But even as Maggie dug deeper into music, Erin drifted away. By the time March arrived with daffodils and greening trees, most days after school Maggie practiced drums by herself. Erin occasionally joined in on a song, but just as often the little red bass leaned against the wall while Erin trimmed friends' fur in the back yard or applied claw polish while sprawled on her bed.

On the first day of spring break, Maggie said, "Hey, Erin. Can we talk about something important?" It was early evening and the two were in Erin's room as usual. The weather had turned warm and they'd opened the windows. Tree crickets chirped merrily outside.

Erin had a new fashion magazine open to an article about earrings, but she set it aside. "Of course. What's wrong?"

Maggie retreated to the throne of her drum kit. She felt more comfortable at her kit these days, more herself. "I know you're not really interested in the band anymore, but it means a lot to me. Can we play together more often? Star said she could come over tomorrow too."

"Sure. What time?"

"After she gets off work. I mean, could the two of us play together all week? Like we used to?"

Erin hesitated. "Okay."

To ease her guilt Maggie said, "You can pierce my ears if you still want to."

Erin brightened. "Yes! I have a pair of little gold hoops that would look so cute on you. And — hey, rock stars always have piercings and things, right? So it would be on brand for you."

They smiled at each other.

Erin kept her promise, playing music with Maggie a few hours each night. In return, Maggie ended up with pierced ears, claws painted pale coral, and crimped whiskers that they both agreed was not really the right look for a possum. "They'll grow out before you know it," Erin said. "The earrings look really good on you, though."

Maggie and Erin still mostly just played along to songs, but when Star joined them they practiced without recorded music. Occasionally it clicked, and the rock song they played felt subtly infused with the spirit of bluegrass — not often, but often enough that Maggie kept yearning to try harder.

———

After spring break, suddenly Erin was bored with fashion. "We don't read enough," she announced one night. They were at Maggie's house for a change, since Erin's brother had friends over. "Let's go to the library and sign up for the book-a-week pledge."

"Okay," Maggie said, but she knew it would be the end of the band. Erin couldn't read while her friend played drums in the same room.

Erin wanted to spend lunch the next day in the library, sitting in a study carrel with a book. She'd worn a new plaid skirt and a white shirt buttoned up to her throat, an outfit that announced her as a Studious Future Librarian.

Maggie went to the school's lunch room, but she didn't feel like eating. Instead she approached the tables nearest the windows, where the school elite ate together.

Ordinarily Maggie would have died rather than disturb them. But she had to act now or Erin would lose interest in the bass forever.

"Hi, Magnolia," Star said. "Need something?"

"I'm actually here to talk to Jess," Maggie said.

Star raised her eyebrows. "Oh, of course. Jess, you really need to listen to her. Trust me on this."

Everyone else at the table stared at Maggie. Jess, a bobcat with exotic green eyes and perfect poise, glanced at Star and said politely to Maggie, "Pull up a chair. What's up?"

Maggie stumbled as she pulled the chair out and nearly fell into it. She had never felt so clumsy, so scruffy, so small and insignificant.

Tugi would never feel this way. But Tugi was a yak. He was huge and handsome. He'd probably sat at his high school's elite table and ignored whatever they had in Mongolia instead of possums.

But Maggie was a drummer, just like Tugi. She straightened her back as though she was sitting at her kit. "Sorry to bother you, Jess. I know you're busy, but I'm in a band with Star and Erin Linwood and we need a good vocalist. Erin always says you have the best voice in chorus."

Jess didn't so much as twitch an ear in surprise, but she also didn't smile at the compliment. "That's sweet of you, but my schedule is pretty tight right now."

The fox to Jess's right turned away as though dismissing Maggie. Star opened her mouth, then shut it again as though she'd thought better of commenting. Instead the mink gave Maggie a sympathetic look.

Maggie remembered Tugi in his latest video, the only one where he featured for more than a few seconds. He had Eagle's Flight's logo branded on his shoulder now and knotted red cords tied in his black mane. Maggie's favorite part was where he gave the camera a fleeting smile. Sometimes she pretended he was smiling at her, one drummer to another.

Maggie said, "We're trying to create a new genre of music, rock with a subtle flavor of bluegrass — sort of the spirit of Appalachia, but more accessible to people who aren't from around here. Have you heard of the band Eagle's Flight?"

"Star mentioned them a while back," Jess said. Maggie could swear she hadn't blinked once yet. Cats were weird.

"They're our inspiration. If they can combine Mongolian folk music with rock, why can't we do the same with our folk music?" Maggie's pulse thundered in her ears. Why was she still trying to convince Jess? It was obvious the bobcat wasn't interested.

Jess glanced up and Maggie realized someone was beside her. "There you are," Erin said in a subdued voice. "Hi, Star. Hi, everyone."

Maggie scooted over and patted the other side of the chair. Erin set her lunchbox and a stack of books on the table and sat down with her, the raccoon's leg warm against hers. Maggie said, "I thought I'd talk to Jess about joining the band. I was just telling her about Eagle's Flight."

Erin fumbled her phone out of her purse. "One of my favorite bands," she said, sounding more like herself. "Look at their lead singer. Isn't he gorgeous? They're from Mongolia. And listen to them!"

She pressed play. Maggie relaxed at the familiar song. These days when she listened to it, she mostly concentrated on Tugi's powerful but intricate drumming, but the lead singer's voice still thrilled her.

Jess flicked her whiskers — a tiny movement, but better than the polite stillness she'd demonstrated so far. The others at the table, who had mostly been pretending to ignore Maggie, turned back to listen. The bear a few seats down, who was stuffed into his Coalfield Cougars jersey as though he'd burst its seams if he flexed, said, "Hey, that's good." The leader of the cheer squad shushed him.

When the song ended, Maggie said, "See? We want to do that for *our* music."

Star said, "We're getting pretty good, honestly. We just need someone who's a better singer than I am."

Maggie found Erin's paw under the table and squeezed it hard. Erin squeezed back. Jess said, "When do you get together for practice?"

Erin said, "Oh, we can work around your schedule. You and Star are busier than we are. We have a lot of fun, though — it's not all work. But we are serious about the band."

Star nodded. "I think it'll make an interesting addition to our college applications, especially if we place in the school talent show once or twice. There's still time to enter this year."

Jess finally smiled, which made her look like she belonged

on all the covers of Erin's fashion magazines. "I'll try it. What's our band's name?"

Erin gave Maggie's paw another squeeze. "Sugar Magnolia," she said. "Named after our drummer, of course."

———

It took Maggie a week to find someone online who could help her with a translation, and another week before she dug up Eagle's Flight's address. She knew her letter would probably never make it out of their PR manager's office, but it felt important to send it.

She spent ages copying the translation properly onto a piece of lavender stationery. Even the script they wrote with in Mongolia was different.

She'd written, "Dear Tugi, I learned to play drums because of you. I love your music. Thank you." She signed her name at the bottom as neatly as possible.

She folded the letter, addressed the matching envelope, and took it to the post office the next day. Then she forgot about it. She didn't expect a reply.

As she'd hoped, Erin's interest in the band surged now that Jess was a member. It was her idea to write an original song for the talent show, and while they all came up with the music, Erin wrote most of the lyrics. It was so catchy that Maggie sometimes caught herself humming it during class.

They came in second in the talent show in May. "First place next year," Jess said, the steeliness of a competitive carnivore in her expression despite her grin. "We've got all summer to practice."

They were in the school parking lot, which still radiated heat from the sunny day although it was well past midnight. Jess had her own car and sometimes gave Maggie and Erin a ride home from school, but tonight they were going to an end-of-school party. It was invitation only, held at Tom Barton's house — the football team's quarterback.

Maggie couldn't remember the last time she'd been invited to a party. Seventh grade, maybe. But tonight was even better than an ordinary party, because Tom wanted the band to play a set and was even paying them twenty dollars each. Maggie's drums were piled in the back of Jess's car.

Maggie planned to use the money to buy a pair of Tugi's newly released signature drumsticks.

———

It was mid-morning when Maggie got home. Her mother was asleep and Maggie crept inside as quietly as possible.

A letter with her name on it sat on the kitchen counter. Maggie yawned as she picked it up, then noticed the Eagle's Flight logo.

She tore the envelope open with shaking paws even though it had been mailed from New York, not Mongolia.

Inside was the generic form letter she expected, along with a sticker of the Eagle's Flight logo and a glossy photo of the band. Maggie grinned. Then she noticed the writing at the bottom.

The large, awkward letters were the writing of someone who didn't speak English and had big hooves, more used to holding a drumstick than a pen. "THANK YOU. DRUM IS LOVE." The N was backwards. Below that was a signature that Maggie couldn't read, but which she recognized as Tugi's.

She looked at the letter for a long time, smiling. Then she went to bed.

After all, she needed her rest. Her band was practicing tomorrow.

UNITY ON THE DIVIDE

JUAN CARLOS MORENO

Crash landed in hostile territory, acting Captain Palis Ponderosa's day can't get much worse. Or can it? An alliance with her sworn enemies, the bloodshirt humans, may be this kit fox's only hope.

With the last of her strength, Air Captain Villalobos pulled her first officer close. "Bring everyone home, Ponder. They're counting on you," the wolf rasped.

Commander Palis Ponderosa heard every word despite the airship's blaring alarms. The kit fox always felt proud of her ears, slightly larger than those of her fellow vulpines, but now she wished she could blunt all her senses. Fading sunlight cut through the shattered windshields, blood started to mat her rusty tan paws, and the bitter scents of fire and leaking cloud-whale gas filled her nose. All valid excuses for the tears already on their way.

"I won't let you down," Palis whispered as she squeezed the grey wolf's paw. Captain Villalobos forced a smile across her muzzle and closed her golden eyes.

Another explosion rocked the ship. Palis dried her tears

and let the captain lay among the rest of the fallen bridge crew. And their killer.

Palis' ears twitched at the pained cry of rending metal. Shudders reverberated up through her bare hind paws as she stood and headed for the radio. *Not much time left now.* She threw a passing glance at the lifeless mechanical insectoid in the center of the room, smoke wisps still wafting from the bullet holes she had put in its neon green shell. The three black, wavy lines on the machine's back only confirmed what the vixen feared most: the falling fireball that clipped the ship's midsection wasn't a random relic from space and it wasn't a human attack. It was an Aura Network hive.

Palis picked up the radio and began transmitting. "Mayday, mayday, mayday. Calling any Radan Vanguard stations, this is Radan Airship *Unity*. We were attacked by Aura units and are going down in the middle of the Divide." *Unity's* nose dipped, forcing Palis to steady herself on the radio station. She mustered enough resolve to finish the distress call, but a sinking fear gnawed at the back of her mind.

Something clattered in the hallway to the bridge; Palis tensed. Her ears swiveled and locked on the noise before she whirled around and drew her sidearm.

"Woah! Friendly comin' in!" the gryphon at the door said, holding up his talons. His tan fatigues were flecked with blood and what smelled like vitafluid from an Aura drone.

"Crags!" Palis gasped and lowered her weapon. "Are you okay?"

The gryphon nodded his hawk-like head and touched his shirt. "It's not mine. The bot tore up the engineers and the generators before I took it down." Crags' gaze finally fell upon the devastated bridge and Palis knew what he felt. His feathery ears drooped, and he tucked his sandy wings.

"I— I was too late to save them," Palis said, pointing to

the machine. "That one was on top of the Captain when I shot it. The only thing we can do now is get everyone else off this ship. Are you with me?"

"Yeah. Yeah," Crags said as he steeled himself. "I mean, yes, ma'am! What's the plan?"

"*Unity's* about to split, I can hear it," Palis replied. "I'm giving the order to evacuate. Get back there and help the crew to the life pods."

"What about you?" Crags asked. "What about the blood-shirt prisoners?"

Palis flicked an ear and felt her ashen coat start to bristle. "Don't worry about me, I'll take my chances with the crash foam. We'll hit harder if someone's not at the helm. As for the humans, their drop-crate has foam packs, too. They get the same odds as us." *Unity's* groaning framework left no room for debate. Every second was precious now.

"I understand," Crags said. "Good luck, Captain." His tawny, feathered cougar tail disappeared through the hatch as Palis turned back to the radio.

Paws flying over the controls, she switched on the intercom and hoped the airship still had enough power. "Attention, all personnel," Palis said, "this is acting Air Captain Ponderosa. We've lost Captain Villalobos and the bridge crew. I am assuming command and ordering everyone to abandon ship. I repeat, abandon ship."

The vixen's voice echoed through the corridors, leaping out of every working speaker and thankfully carrying over the alarms. As far as small comforts went, it was the least she could ask for.

"If possible, grab your weapons and individual kits," Palis continued. "This is the Divide; expect Aura contacts to be waiting for us. Reach the surface, rally at the crash site, and watch each other's tails." A few speakers crackled; others went totally silent. "When you hit the dirt, come out with your teeth bared! I'll see you on the ground. Good luck."

Palis dropped the microphone and scampered to the helm. Outside the shattered window, the setting sun washed the pine forests and scraggly grass fields of the Divide in a fiery orange glow. Crimson clouds overhead held the dying day's light as *Unity* steadily fell toward a rocky hill.

"Come on! Come on!" the vixen growled under her breath. Palis tugged at the controls, feeling the airship's resistance, or perhaps fear, towards turning. At last, *Unity* veered away to the left and Palis aimed for a meadow ringed by trees.

Life pods and drop-rafts launched in groups. Ears twitching at the sound of each successful departure, Palis smiled faintly. *That's it, land in the clearing*, she thought. However, when she went to the port window to watch her crew, she was just in time to see why *Unity* felt afraid to turn.

The strain was too much. With one more terrible screech, the ship finally ripped in two. A second later, the prisoner drop-crate launched. Debris rained upon the meadow, and the tail's first gas cell ruptured. Whatever winds or momentum guided the rear half made it clear Palis couldn't help that part of the ship anymore. For the time being, the tail's crew was on their own.

Unity's altimeter hardly told Palis anything she didn't already know. They'd be on the ground in a minute, and at their speed, the impact would hurt. It would hurt a lot.

Palis closed her eyes. *We're gonna need every scrap of this ship we can spare.* Her eyes darted to the power gauges. *Here goes nothing!* Russet ears flattened against her head, Palis gritted her teeth and diverted all remaining energy to the engines and grav units. Outside, the nacelles angled downward, the propellers whirred, and the AG thrusters hummed to life one last time. *Unity* complained from the effort. *We're almost there, you can do it.* The altimeter calmed itself somewhat. Not much, but the vixen hoped it would be enough.

Before Palis strapped herself in for the crash, Crags swooped past the windscreens. Palis gasped and jumped back as the gryphon aimed for the broken window. He flapped hard then tucked his wings long enough to shoot through the hole and crash land on the bridge floor.

"Are you insane?" Palis barked as she helped Crags to his paws. "I told you to—"

Crags grabbed the kit fox in his talons as *Unity* made her final approach. "No time! Just hold on!" With Palis close to his chest, Crags leapt through the windshield again. He spread his wings the instant they were through and banked hard. If Palis' eyes had been open, she would've seen the ground rushing up to meet them just before Crags pulled up.

The pair got clear of the airship as it scrunched its nose into the earth. Still, the shockwaves of exploding power cells, debris clouds, and venting gas rippled their fur and feathers as much as the wind did.

Palis opened her eyes at last as Crags glided to the ground. Standing together on a hill, neither could believe their eyes. Both halves of *Unity* lay in heaps of metal and envelope fabric at either end of the meadow. Pink impact foam oozed from every opening. In another few moments, it started to dissolve, stunting some aspiring fires. However, the vixen and her crew-mate watched as flames still found a way to spring up again throughout their half of the ship.

"You were almost in that," Crags said.

Taking a moment to feel the grass and dirt under her paws, Palis caught her breath. "Thank you."

The gryphon chuckled. "I wasn't about to lose two captains in one day," he said, "or any more friends."

Distant movement caught the pair's attention through the

building twilight. Landing craft were scattered around the meadow and the crew were already on the move. Someone closer to the nose's crash site sent up a holoflare, beckoning the survivors. However, the shell's red glare also illuminated just the figures Palis hoped to avoid.

"I thought we'd have more time," Palis growled as she watched Aura drones converge on the nose. Crags saw more of them, too, and pointed.

"Over there, by the tail," the gryphon reported. Electric blue and yellow muzzle flashes flickered in the distance. Seconds later, the unmistakable reports of Radan Vanguard hybrid rifles echoed across the meadow.

"Come on!" Palis said. "Fly me to the nose, then give me a SITREP on the tail!"

Crags scooped up Palis again and took off. She was thankful she was relatively light since she knew it took a lot out of the gryphon to carry passengers. Though they flew close to the ground, Palis appreciated the brief gryphon's-eye view of their situation. A downed airship and a dazed crew were one thing, but an enemy attack and potentially loose prisoners of war were another. The vixen breathed deeply and thought on her training. *Work the problem, work the problem.* However, as they were about to land, Palis spied movement. She shoved the mantra aside and let instincts kick in.

"Drop me!" Palis shouted.

"What?" Crags hesitated.

"Now!"

At that, the gryphon let go and Palis fell. She tucked and rolled on the grass, then instantly pounced onto an Aura insectoid Crags never even noticed. One sharp tug and the machine's head plate came off in her paw. She drew her pistol and fired two shots into the vital hardware.

The robot's glowing eyes hadn't even faded before Palis

heard her next target. Four paws scrabbled through the wreckage followed by a hundred metallic feet. She focused and tried to pinpoint the sources, but someone suddenly shouted from inside the wreck. "Ponder!"

Palis recognized the voice. It was Specialist Bazil, a black-footed ferret and one of the ship's technicians. The vixen swiveled her ears and found her crewmate. He scrabbled through the ship's collapsed port corridor and twisted external walkways. By the light of a nearby fire, Palis finally saw his panicked face.

"It's right behind me!" Bazil gasped as he leapt outside. His pursuer snapped at his tail with thick mandibles before it burst from the wreckage with a harsh screech, countless legs pulling its elongated body into the open with startling speed.

Palis set her sights on the orange centipede's head and squeezed off a shot, hitting one of two luminous eye clusters. The machine recoiled and thrashed wildly, raising half its body off the ground. Its writhing head was too difficult to hit again, so Palis aimed for the machine's center mass and unloaded her sidearm. Every bullet perforated the carapace neatly, but the volley merely staggered the drone.

While the robot recovered, Palis retreated a few steps and reevaluated the situation. *Gotta hold it still and hit the head again! But how?* She scanned the wreck and nudged Bazil back with her free paw, knowing distance bought her time to think. Then her eyes fell on a solution.

Palis holstered her empty pistol and reached for something she hoped would be more potent. "Help me with this!" she shouted to the frightened ferret. "Bazil! The pipe! Move!" barked the vixen, suddenly shocking her crewmate back into action.

Palis and Bazil tore a long length of pipe from the wreck seconds before the drone stabilized itself and lurched forward.

The pair whirled around and aimed the jagged tip at the charging centipede's face. Optics damaged and moving too fast to stop, the machine ran headfirst into the makeshift spear to spectacular effect.

"Thanks for that!" Bazil panted as the drone twitched for a moment. Palis slapped a new magazine into her pistol and blasted out the machine's other eye, just to be sure.

When the centipede didn't move again, Palis finally took a breath, too. She kept listening for danger, but for the moment they were safe. "You're welcome," she said. With some effort, she freed the pipe from their downed enemy. "Are you hurt?"

Bazil shook his head.

"Good," Palis sighed. "What were you doing in there?"

"Scavenging for weapons. I managed to grab a few of these," the ferret said, removing four collapsed shock batons from his cargo pockets. He took one and sharply flicked his wrist. Fully extended, the black baton gave Bazil another half an arm's length of reach.

"Good work," Palis said. "Every bit of hardware helps."

"Yes, ma'am, but there's room for improvement," Bazil replied. He pointed to the pipe in Palis' paws and she gave it to him. As Crags swooped in and landed beside them, Bazil pulled a roll of duct tape from another pocket.

"I guess your vision is better than mine now," Crags said to Palis. "These old hawk eyes aren't the same in this gloom." He checked out the scrapped Aura drones and chuckled. "You sure took care of them and saved Bazil's tail, though!"

While Bazil knelt down over his work, Palis gave the gryphon a baton. "We still need your eyes," she said. "And your wings. We'll handle everything here, so I need you to check the tail section for now." More hybrid rifles chattered and sizzled in the distance.

"I'm on it, Ponder," Crags said with a nod before he took off.

The twilight settled in, making the scattered fires around the wreck seem brighter. By their scents and the sound of pawsteps, Palis knew more survivors would join them soon. Unfortunately, so would Aura.

"Got it!" Bazil exclaimed, holding up his new weapon. He had taped the shock baton to the end of the pipe and set it to discharge on contact. "One improv powerstaff, ready for action!"

Two sets of paws trampled through the grass and behind them Palis heard the buzzing wing beats of more drones. "Let's see if it works!" Palis said with a wave of her paw. "Come on!"

The vixen and ferret ran towards the noise and saw a cougar and a badger hauling a makeshift stretcher. A wolf lay whimpering on the board, the metallic scent of his wound trailing behind them. Green robotic beetles followed, drawn to the taste.

"Sneffels!" Palis shouted to the cougar. "Over here!"

The medic and his assistant ran towards Palis and Bazil, but their pursuers were too close. "Behind you!" the ferret shouted.

Corpsman Sneffels flicked his tail twice and the badger behind him knew what to do. They set down the stretcher together and she whirled around, grabbing the hybrid carbine slung at her side. She found the first machine in her sights and gave it two energy blasts. The last two drones bobbed and weaved in the air, dodging her follow-up shots.

Racing to help, Palis and Bazil picked their targets. The vixen caught one machine with a well-timed shot when it evaded another of the badger's bursts. As the last drone made a desperate dive to attack, Bazil zapped it with the baton's electrifying tip, frying its hardware in seconds.

"Nice one, Cap'n!" Sneffels said, picking up the stretcher again.

"No problem," Palis replied. "Find a safe place to gather and treat the wounded. We'll hold here and send others your way as they come in."

Sneffels and the badger followed the order while Palis and Bazil waited to help other survivors. Their fur bristled at the thought of more drones lurking just out of sight, but they stood their ground. After a long moment, Palis permitted herself a small grin. They'd seen more survivors than machines and about half the crew could be accounted for.

Sentries with hybrid rifles took over for Palis and formed a perimeter. As she and Bazil joined the gathered survivors, she was glad to see the sentries were all crew members with keen senses, mostly felines and canines. If Aura was going to attack again, they'd know right away.

Roughly twenty survivors were gathered close to *Unity*, handling the tasks they'd given themselves. Sneffels and the medics stabilized their three wounded crewmates by the light of emergency lanterns while technicians crawled through the wreckage. Every once in a while, a weasel or an ermine would emerge with paws and pockets full of salvage. Anyone too big to fit inside the ship sorted the supplies or rushed them where they were needed most.

"You did well," Palis said to Bazil. "Give the staff to someone and see what else you can pull from the ship. If you can, get someone to make more staffs or spears while you're in there."

Bazil nodded and scurried off as Palis took stock of what the crew had already collected. Passing each cache, the vixen mentally noted what they had to work with. Lights, some food and water rations, barely enough medical supplies, proper weapons for half the crew here, and enough ammunition and batteries for one good fight. All things considered, Palis knew they could be worse off. Between *Unity* and the forest around them, everything could be replaced with a little ingenuity and time. *Time. That's the question, isn't it?* Palis barely had a moment to sink into thought before Crags returned, nearly out of breath.

"Are you alright?" Palis asked, steadying the gryphon. She gave him a canteen and let him rest.

After squirting a few sips of water into his beak, Crags told Palis everything. "I'm fine, Ponder," he said, "but we've got a situation at the tail."

———

"If anything goes wrong, hit the deck and we'll take it from there," Crags whispered before Palis stepped out of cover. The gryphon, a coyote, and a lynx checked their rifles as Palis finished tying a white cloth to a stick.

Gazing at the tail's crash site, Palis chuckled. "Then let's hope they're willing to deal." She walked towards the lights, holding the white flag in one paw and a satchel in the other. Soon, someone saw her. A pair of flashlights blinded her, but she was more concerned with the weapons they were attached to.

"Stop!" a gruff voice shouted. "Don't come any closer, fluff!"

Palis froze and made sure to present the flag. "I come in peace," she replied. Squinting, she tried blocking the lights with her paw. "Let me speak to whoever's in charge."

"What makes you think we wanna hear what you gotta say?" the human snapped.

The vixen had expected a response like this. *Easy, Palis, easy.* She perked her ears, relaxed her tail, and suppressed the instinct to bare her teeth. "Because," Palis soothed, "Aura is a threat to everyone in this valley. Your people and mine." As the man thought on this, Palis heard someone else approaching.

"We can take care of ourselves!" the man replied after a moment. "Now why don't—"

"Corporal Hatchet!" another man hissed as he joined the sentries. "Keep your voice down. Those things could be anywhere."

"But, sir—"

"That's enough, Hatch," the man declared. "Point that light somewhere useful and watch for Aura. I'll take it from here."

The human soldiers hesitated, then obeyed. As her vision adjusted to the ambient light, Palis got a better look at them. All three had dark skin and hair, simple combat boots, and Radan hybrid carbines. They also wore fatigues similar to her own, except theirs were entirely crimson instead of tan.

Hatchet took a few steps towards the forest and grumbled under his breath. His fellow sentry stayed with the newcomer as he turned and spoke to Palis. "Now then, who do we have here?"

"Radan Vanguard Air Captain Palis Ponderosa," the vixen replied, keeping her eyes on the human but one ear to the forest.

"Ah, yes, I heard your voice before the crash," the man said. "A pleasure, Captain. I am Commander Lima of the Thirteenth Mechanized Infantry Regiment of the Gilded Tower."

To Palis' surprise, Lima slung his carbine behind his back and approached her, stopping halfway. Palis planted her flag in the dirt and stepped forward. All the while, the vixen flicked her ears and sniffed the air for any signs of danger. She felt her crewmates' eyes on her and she knew their sights were trained on the humans. If Lima suspected anything, he didn't show it as he offered to shake Palis' paw.

Palis accepted and shook the commander's hand. It was firm and rough, almost like her pads. "I appreciate the civility, Commander Lima," she said, putting on her best diplomatic affect. "Given the circumstances, I'm hoping we can reach an agreement."

"I'm listening," Lima said as his eyes darted to Palis' ears for an instant.

"Where is the tail crew? Are they hurt?" Palis asked.

Lima shook his head. "They're safe for now. We put them in your prisoner crate." Noticing the vixen's fur start to rise, he quickly added, "The machines cut their way inside after we landed. They destroyed our restraints and we thought we were free until the bigger ones started carrying us away into the woods. Your crew intervened, but in the chaos, we repelled the bots and took control."

"Keep the weapons and whatever else you find in the tail," Palis said. "Just let my crew go and we'll be on our way. Your people can have the tail and mine will stay at the nose."

Lima chuckled. "I'm afraid I can't allow that. The others think as long as we have prisoners of our own, your side won't attack."

"Tell them to put the war on hold!" Palis growled. "I don't give a damn about fighting bloodshirts while Aura picks us off one by one!"

Beyond the light, in the forest's shadows, a twig snapped. Judging by Lima's mere furrowed brow, Palis knew only she heard the sound. *Time's up.*

"Easier said than done," Lima shrugged. "We're the Lost

Children of Level One, Captain. This war is all some of us have."

"If they really believe that, soon they'll have nothing left," Palis retorted. Another faint snap from the woods and her ears flicked. "You said you were listening; I need you to listen now. The frontlines are far behind us. We're in the center of the Divide." The more Lima watched her involuntary ear twitches, the more her words sank in. "There's a reason the Radans won't retreat."

Countless sets of glowing eyes twinkled in the depths of the forest. Palis and Lima looked together and their hearts skipped the same beat. Human voices sounded the alarm throughout the tail wreckage and flashlights played across the patchy darkness. However, a moment later, the few still-glowing fires around the tail went out one by one. Each time, there was a loud hiss followed by silence and darkness.

"They're back!" Lima gasped.

Palis thrust her satchel into his hand. "A can of wound sealant and a few NOM rations," she said quickly. "We don't have to be enemies, at least not until we escape this place."

"Lima! Lotta bots comin' our way!" Hatchet reported.

Lima took the bag and nodded. "I'll consider it," he said. "Don't worry about your crew, I think the machines want us, not them."

"Commander! We gotta go!"

Glancing over her shoulder, Palis saw some of the nose's last fires also wink out. "If you survive the night, I'll meet you in the middle of the clearing at dawn," she said. "Good luck."

"You too!" Lima shouted back as the vixen returned to Crags. "You too."

———

"Twenty-five. Twenty-six. And twenty-seven. That's it," Crags said before reloading the caseless rounds. "Not even a full mag."

Palis nodded and noted it. Her own weapon was down to a single magazine, too. Daybreak approached but she didn't feel relieved. The rest of the crew reported similar ammunition counts. Most had a few rounds left or nearly depleted batteries. Some were completely dry.

Aura had retreated hours ago, leaving countless husks strewn across the battlefield. In the moment, Palis hadn't realize how greatly the machines outnumbered the crew, but the aftermath sent a chill all the way to her dark tail tip. *That was way too close, and there are more machines still out there*, she thought as she continued her battle assessment.

Bazil's technicians dragged a few metal carcasses from the clearing to an area they'd set up before the night's skirmish. Palis found him tinkering, and the ferret looked up from his work when she approached.

"With a little luck, I think we can recharge our weapons with the drones' batteries," Bazil said. "I'll rig up power converters and keep you posted. Might be a longshot, though."

"You'll figure it out," Palis assured him, "you're the best."

The ferret smiled. "Thanks, Captain. To be honest, Specialist Fennel is way better at this than me. Have you seen her?"

Palis glanced at the tail, grateful to see humans milling about in the distance. "She's most likely with the tail crew," she said. "The bloodshirts are still alive, so she's probably okay."

"I hope so," Bazil said, more to himself than Palis. "Oh, before you go, I found a few things I wanna show you."

Palis glanced over Bazil's shoulder at the green drone's

pieces spread across the crude table. Some parts were recognizable, most were beyond her knowledge, but a few were unexpected.

"It has a wound sealant reservoir," Bazil explained, "and autosyringes, bandage applicators, and a heckuva sensor suite. My bet's on thermal sights and heartbeat monitors at least."

"They're full of first aid supplies?" the vixen wondered. "It's like some kind of — some kind of—"

"Medic?" Bazil offered. "It would explain the bright colors. Red dragonflies? Orange centipedes? Easy to see in an emergency."

Medical bots? Is that what they are? Palis mused, not sure if the clue was good or bad news.

"But, that's not the only weird thing," Bazil added before prodding the insectoid's internals. "Watch this." Instantly, the green metal shell turned silvery along with the bot's wings. "Solaskin."

Wrinkling her brow, Palis stepped back and looked up at *Unity's* ruined gas envelopes. "Like the solaskin on the ship?"

The technician gave her a noncommittal nod. "Sort of. This looks way more advanced. For something this small to collect enough power for itself, it's gotta be pretty efficient."

Palis filed the findings away. "Keep up the good work, Bazil. See what we can use. For now, I'm going to see if the humans are ready to talk."

The ferret's ears folded, though he tried to hide his concern. However, when Palis saw him turn to the field of dead machines and grimace, she knew what she had to do.

By the day's first light, Palis, Crags, and two escorts strode through the short grass to the center of the clearing. Opposite them, Lima led his own party. However, the trio of humans weren't alone. A tall black bear walked beside them, carrying a pipe spear in her paws.

A gentle breeze carried the scent of blood and vitafluid downwind. Even before she noticed the bandages on their arms and the stains on their fatigues, Palis sensed the humans hadn't fared as well as her crew during the night.

"Good morning, Captain Ponderosa," Lima said. "I'll admit I'm relieved to see you."

"Likewise," Palis replied. "Everyone appears to be in one piece."

The human smirked and shook his head. "Not quite, I fear." Nodding to the bear, he added, "but without Sergeant Oakes and your crew, we would have lost many more than we did. After their performance, my troops are open to a truce."

Crags and Palis exchanged a glance. He had already told Palis what he thought of her proposal. Their whole predicament was unthinkable. Aura falling from space? A crew stranded in the Divide? Work with Gilded Tower soldiers? It was unorthodox and potentially treasonous, but it could be their only chance of survival. "And just maybe," the gryphon had said, "that heckin' AI won't see this coming." After all, in Crags' opinion, unimaginable problems needed imaginative solutions.

Once again, Palis shook Lima's hand. "I'll have our medics check your casualties while you show me your resources." One of her escorts promptly ran to fetch Corpsman Sneffels as the group started towards the tail.

"Your chief engineer, the raccoon? Specialist Fennel, I believe," Lima said, "she organized the new salvaging efforts. Your people are able to get deeper into the wreck than we can, so we might have more food, ammo, and weapons soon."

"Excellent. If we're lucky, the ship's provisions should be enough for a few days," Palis replied. "The good news is we just have to survive until help arrives. I sent out a distress call before the crash. It won't be long."

The humans stopped in their tracks. "Wait, you don't have a working radio in the nose?" Lima asked, suddenly somber.

"No, not since the crash. Why?"

"I'm sorry, I thought you knew. I wondered when you'd bring it up." Lima sighed. "There's a chance your message didn't go through."

Ears instinctively pinned to her head, Palis didn't like his tone. "What makes you say that?"

"Because," Lima answered, "I think Aura sent a different one."

———

Heads turned as Lima led the group through the tail camp. Idle conversations stopped and some humans glanced up from their work and stared. A few tried to whisper, but Palis still heard them.

"Check out the gryphon. Never seen one this close before."

"More fluffs? Really?"

"Is Lima really going through with this?"

"Half my squad got cut or taken last night. We need them."

"Lima better know what he's doing."

Unity's tail crew kept mostly to themselves with only a few humans near them to help. Mixed groups fashioned spears and powerstaffs from the scrap with recovered tools. Like at the nose, the small and nimble Radans explored the suffocating corridors and grabbed anything not bolted down. Specialist Fennel, a stocky raccoon with a bandaged arm and frazzled tail, oversaw the operation. She turned, smiled, and addressed Palis as she arrived.

"So, Bazil thinks he can use the bots to get us some juice?"

Fennel asked after Palis explained the other camp's status. "It's possible, yeah. In the meantime, we can do ya one better, Cap'n. You're just in time, too."

The engineer motioned the group over to an opening in the ship. In another few minutes, sunlight would touch the top of the last inflated gas envelope. "How we doin' in there?"

A voice called back. "Should be good. Try it now!"

With a flick of her ringed tail, Fennel then went to a scavenged control panel hastily installed next to a bank of battery chargers. She held her breath and pressed a button.

Seconds later, the gray envelope fabric above them rippled and turned silvery, twinkling as daylight reached it. Another moment passed before the battery charging lights all winked on.

A possum poked his head out of the wreck entrance and asked, "Did it work?"

"For now," Fennel said with a smile. "Well done, everyone. Now let's see what else we can get online." Turning to Lima, she told him they'd need the drained weapon batteries, so he sent one of his escorts to tell the other humans.

"Finally, some good news," Palis said.

"Yes," Lima agreed, "but we're unfortunately not out of the woods yet. Follow me."

The group left Fennel and her team for the very tip of the tail. There, they found a snow leopard huddled over a portable Vanguard radio with his long tail wrapped around it. A trio of squirrels scampered up the exposed tailfin framework above, trying to arrange wires and a bent antenna.

"Ah, morning, Captain!" the leopard said. He scrambled to stand but Palis waved him off.

"It's good to see you're alright, Tang," Palis replied. "Commander Lima said you found something for us."

"Yes," Tang nodded. He adjusted the radio controls as he

spoke. "Signal was pretty spotty when I first picked it up. Although with me, the signals are always spotty," he chuckled. "Anyway, with the rigged improvements, it should be a bit clearer." Static crackled briefly, then the radio barked to life.

"This is Radan Vanguard Air Captain Villalobos! Authentication code Foxtrot Papa Romeo Alpha Zero One One!" the voice on the radio said. The Radans turned to Lima, their eyes wide. "Our ship was downed by Aura!"

Shouts and weapon fire rang out in the background as Villalobos continued. "This message will repeat, warning others to stay away. I don't have much time. They've killed most of the crew already. Only five of us are left and we're surrounded. It's too late for

" Someone's scream cut Villalobos off. The blasts and clattering machines sounded closer. "Don't lose any more ships to this place! Aura is—" She was cut off one last time. After a moment of frantic gunfire, pained howls, and static, the message played again.

"Thank you, Tang," Palis sighed, and the leopard turned off the radio.

"How did they get her voice? Or her authentication code?" Crags asked. "Captain Villalobos is dead and buried under *Unity*. That's impossible."

"I don't know," Palis said, shaking her head. "What I do know is the Vanguard won't send anyone if they heard that. Tang, can you transmit a new message?"

"Sorry, ma'am," Tang replied, "I tested it with the short-range radios and I'm certain we're being jammed."

"What if it's that thing that hit *Unity*?" Crags offered. "It seemed to be carrying the drones that got onto the ship and the ones we've fought down here. Could it be some kind of control unit?"

"It's plausible," Palis mused. "Based on what we know of

255

the Divide's zones, the machines don't travel far from their hubs. The analysts think it's something to do with hive controllers."

"Hold on," Lima said, raising his hand. "Last night you said something about the Divide and the reason Radan forces won't retreat. Did you mean this whole land is crawling with Aura?" The Radans hesitated. "Captain, it sounds like rescue isn't coming, not while your people are still fighting the invasion. If we're going to work together, we need to know everything."

"You're right," Palis said after a moment. "A few months ago, just before the war started, our people learned about a distant Tower City, the one on the southern coast."

Lima nodded. "Yes, everyone in our tower heard that, too. Even grounders like us," he said. "A whole tower, descending into chaos and anarchy, destroyed overnight."

"Well," Palis continued, "we don't know why or how the city was destabilized, but suddenly every settlement west of the Front Range reported machines emerging from the wilderness. During the evacuations, we realized this area is dotted with bunkers from before the Blackout, and all of them woke up on the day that Tower City fell."

Slowly, the human commander's eyes filled with light as Palis shared her people's tale. "Our only comfort is the machines' curious unwillingness or inability to travel far from their bunkers. And, the different bunkers don't seem to coordinate with each other. Not yet anyway."

"Yeah," Crags scoffed, "or they would've overrun us in days."

"We made a map, and now every airship crossing the Divide has to follow a narrow path through the danger zones," Palis said. "*Unity's* made the trip several times already, hauling prisoners to the camps on the other side. Never had a problem until that fireball landed on us."

"Almost like Aura was trying to plug the gap," Lima suggested. "So, the good news is we don't have to fight every machine from here to the Front Range, just the ones that shot us down, right?"

"For the moment, that's about it," the vixen agreed.

Sighing, Lima folded his arms and surveyed the tail camp again. "In that case, what do you propose?"

Everyone turned to Palis. Just saying what they were up against out loud suddenly made her perspective frightfully clearer. *Work the problem. You know what you all need, now how do you get it?* After a breath, she had her answer.

"The basics of survival are food, water, shelter, and rest, but without security we'll all be dead long before we starve," Palis said. "My crew can help us survive, that's the easy part. After all, being alone in the woods isn't a problem for us."

"That's a relief, since hardly any of us Tower folk how to start a fire." Lima chuckled. "And the hard part?"

"The hard part?" Palis said, flicking up her ears and baring her teeth slightly for emphasis. "The hard part is taking the fight to Aura."

———

By midday, the fruits of Palis' plan began to take shape. After she and Lima briefed both camps, everyone found an assignment and went to work. The humans initially didn't know what to do, but Radan team leaders quickly folded them into their ranks and taught them how to help. Though they had scouts on patrol and none had spotted the machines yet, everyone knew they'd be back eventually. So, they did everything possible to prepare for another battle.

When Bazil and the techs took apart a red dragonfly, they found it equipped with plasma cutters in its forelegs, a fire extinguisher in its tail, and various tool attachments for its legs stored in the chassis. With a few modifications, the cutters could be removed and used separately from the robot as long as a power source went with them. The ferret, though reluctant at first, also taught a few humans how to dismantle the machines and repurpose their parts.

Once the remaining solaskin on both halves of the wreck glistened in the summer sun, Specialist Fennel and her team were finally free to join the others. She created a recycling line with the humans and Radans under her instruction. Runners brought drones for disassembly, techs stripped the machines for parts and gave the tools to other teams, then they turned the shells over to the raccoon so she could convert them into solar chargers.

Soon, hybrid rifle batteries sat under the shade of their chargers in the fields near each camp. The projectile ammunition salvaged from the tail helped, but Palis and Lima knew the batteries would last longer. Unfortunately, even with the tail's supplies, there still weren't enough weapons for everyone. At least at first.

Unity's pipes, support struts, and other pieces of internal framework were the perfect materials to start with. The survivors cut and modified the lightweight yet sturdy shafts into spears, javelins, and pikes. Most were standardized into simple skewers with sharpened tips, while others followed in Bazil's inventive pawsteps. Inspecting the tail camp's armory, Palis smiled at copies of the ferret's powerstaff but she was also pleased to see spear variants whose tips could hold plasma cutters.

Panels from the airship and the landing craft were fashioned into portable shields and barricades as the crews fortified their camps. Paws and shovels dug through the earth for hours so teams could bury spikes and traps, too. The humans sweated and many Radans panted, but piece by piece they built their defenses together.

In the field between both camps, Sergeant Oakes held what she called "Animal School," where she trained batches of humans to connect with their more primal, feral, and animalistic fighting spirit. The humans preferred to call the experience "Mauling 101," for obvious reasons.

"When faced with danger, every creature on Earth will instinctually do one of three things," the bear explained. "Fight, flight, or freeze. In the Divide, freezing will get you killed, and we don't have the luxury of running." After her intro, Oakes usually charged nervous volunteers until she conditioned them not to flee. While the endeavor was easier said than done, after a while each human class learned to wield their spears and coordinate their squads like hunting packs, countering the bear's mock attacks.

Everyone worked, trained, ate, and rested in shifts as the day wore on. Even Palis and Lima, who had to be persuaded, finally sat in the shade and shared a NOM ration.

"Nutritional Omnivore Meal," Lima said, reading the side of the packet. "Beats what the Tower sent us out here with."

"You mean those NutriMush pouches?" Palis asked. "Yeah, I only sniffed one of them once. What do they taste like?"

"Oh, they taste like food," Lima grinned. "Well, like every food at the same time." He took another bite of his protein patty and gazed at the valley for a moment. "How do you do it?"

"Hmm?" Palis asked, caught off guard.

"You, the Radans," Lima clarified. "How did a nation of farmers have the tech to blunt a full-scale invasion?"

"We're not just farmers," Palis replied plainly.

"Evidently."

"And having advanced technology is only part of the answer," Palis continued. "You could argue your tech is better, but what matters is how your people think about it and what they do with it."

"As you might have guessed, we're not encouraged to think much at all," Lima said. "Those of us from Level One, that is."

"In Radan, we're all on the ground," Palis replied. "Sure, we still have leaders, but when we built our nation out of the Blackout, we started with a foundation of respect. Respect for ourselves, respect for each other, respect for nature, and especially respect for the tech we inherited and the tech we'd create."

Lima smiled again and cleaned his hands. "That's amazing," he said. "The most we can do with what we inherited is use it like our ancestors did. It's probably why we're losing this war: we keep doing things the way they've always been done."

Finishing her own meal, Palis adjusted her tail and faced Lima. "Any idea why?"

"Too much thinking probably upsets the order the upper Tower folks are comfortable with." Lima shrugged. "Or, maybe it's because the last time humans were inventive, we created the Aura Network. Look how that turned out."

Palis didn't know how to respond, so she just sipped from her canteen. After a moment, she hopped to her paws and helped Lima up. "If it makes you feel any better, the last time you were inventive, you also made us."

Before Lima could reply, Palis heard raised voices in the tail camp. The two commanders broke into a run and found Corporal Hatchet yelling and waving a hybrid carbine. His limbs were still wrapped in old bandages except for his left arm.

"Corporal, what are you doing?" Lima demanded.

The soldier steadied himself and glared at Lima. "I could ask you the same question, Commander," he fumed, spitting the last word. "I could ask all of you!" The gathered humans didn't move. "Did you forget why we're here?"

In her peripheral vision, Palis saw Sergeant Oakes readying a powerstaff. The vixen made eye contact with the bear and shook her head. If Hatchet's carbine was charged, Oakes wouldn't make it in time.

"As you seem so eager to speak, why don't you remind us, Hatch?" Lima asked, easing himself between Hatchet and Palis.

"We're the Lost Children of Level One! Sent to reclaim the land for the human race!" Hatchet cried. "Each of us was promised our own share of Radan! Space to live, food to eat, and no city stacked over our heads!"

"That's just what they told us. You can't still believe that, do you?" Lima begged. Remembering what he said last night, Palis feared Lima already knew the answer.

Half ignoring Lima, Hatchet growled, "I take one good hit and when I come to again, there's some fluffer standin' over me and a whole lot of 'em just walkin' around like there's nothin' wrong!"

"You lost a lot of blood and were out all day. Corpsman Sneffels was probably cleaning your wounds," Lima explained calmly. "Everyone agreed to a ceasefire, Corporal, so I'm ordering you to drop your weapon."

"Why? So they can put me in a cage again, like *I'm* the wild animal?" Hatchet asked, sweeping the crowd with his weapon's muzzle. "We just wanted to go back to the old world!

Before the war, before the Blackout! Back to when they were just dumb animals and the planet was ours!"

Lima slowly approached Hatchet and tried to steady his voice, almost like a predator stalking nervous prey. "Look around you. Count the dead robots, Hatch. That's only the first wave," he said. "If anything, Aura's running this planet more than anyone. We're on the same side now." Hatchet focused on his commander, aiming the carbine at his chest.

"We don't need them!"

"But they need us. They need us to remember. We created them before the Blackout. There had to be a reason."

"A mistake. Like Aura! If we don't do this, they'll replace us! Machines, fluffs, they'll both end us!"

"No, Hatch. This, what you're doing now, that's what'll end us. For once in your life, think! You know why we're on the edge of extinction? It's because we're stagnant. The Upper Levels didn't teach us to think outside the box or question the book. Humanity's on the brink because we can't imagine anything better. What if this is it? What if this is how we save ourselves?"

"By betraying the Tower? By disobeying our orders?"

The muzzle was close enough for Lima to touch. "And what were High Command's orders? Kill until they said to stop? They put hundred-year-old plasma rifles in our hands, dropped us in flying tombs, and pointed us at Radan. They were just as surprised as us when EMPs and siphon beams started dropping us like rain."

By now, only Lima would be hit if Hatchet fired, but no one dared to even twitch. If Palis concentrated, she swore she almost heard the humans' hearts beating like drums.

"The Gilded Tower doesn't care about us. They hardly trained us to fight and they definitely didn't train us to survive because we weren't supposed to. If we took Radan, great!

Crisis averted. If we all die, the city has fewer mouths to feed. They still win. That was the plan, Hatch. Those were the orders."

Corporal Hatchet tried to speak. Instead, he merely seemed to choke on his words.

"But we did survive," Lima said. "And now we have a chance to reclaim the parts of us that actually matter. The parts we gave to the Radans when we made them like us. Do you know what those are?"

Shaking his head, Hatchet rasped, "What?"

"Creativity. Imagination. Innovation," Lima explained. "And instinct. Humans are wild animals, too, Hatch. Somewhere along the way, I think we forgot that."

Their heartbeats slowed. Hatchet lowered his weapon. He wobbled and leaned on Lima. As he did, his mask of anger fell away. "I don't wanna die, sir, I just wanna survive this whole bloody mess."

As Palis took the carbine from Hatchet's hand, he started sobbing gently. Lima pulled the corporal's arm behind his head and helped him walk. Though initially unsure, the vixen handed off the blaster and took Hatchet's other arm. "It's okay, we've got you," Lima said. "I promise you, together we're not just going to survive, we're going to live."

———

Firelight danced and flickered across Palis' grey coat, warming her against the evening breezes that blew through the tail camp. She checked her pistol once more before tinkering with the plasma pike on her lap. In a few minutes, she installed the power source at the butt and ran the cables through the insulated shaft to the cutter at the tip. The vixen tapped the activation button and the cutter shot out a short burst of energy.

Boots and paws crunched through the grass towards her, so Palis stood with her new weapon.

"I see you got another one working," Lima said as he stepped into the orange light with Crags beside him.

"The parts clicked together perfectly," Palis remarked. "Anyway, how's Corporal Hatchet doing?"

"Sneffels gave him some tea and has him resting with the others in the infirmary. The medics will keep an eye on him," Crags reported. "Speaking of rest, when's the last time you slept, Captain?"

"Don't worry about me," Palis replied, "I'll sleep once we make it through the night. Is everyone ready?"

"As ready as we can be," Lima said, patting his newly charged carbine.

"Excellent," Palis said. She stepped away from the fire and surveyed the meadow. Radan sentries kept watch along the clearing's perimeter, their ears up and scanning for any sounds out of the ordinary. Closer to the camps, mixed squads ate their rations, tended fires, checked traps and weapons, or chattered idly. "Crags, you can head to your perch," Palis said after a moment. "I have a feeling it won't be long now."

"Yes, ma'am," the gryphon said. He got a running start and took wing, disappearing into the inky sky.

Once they were alone, Lima let out a soft chuckle.

"What is it?" Palis inquired.

The man waved dismissively. "Oh, nothing. It's just kind of funny to me. Here we are, the soldiers of a Tower City, heirs to the most advanced technology in human history, and we're huddled around campfires in the woods, clutching spears for protection with canines standing guard by our side."

Palis couldn't help but grin. "I think those were wolves the first time around." She chuckled. "As far as human innovations go, I'd say that idea was a winner."

"When they said the Blackout knocked us back to the Stone Age, I never thought about how true that was in some respects," Lima said. "Still, the good thing about starting over is we get a chance to do it right this time."

"Well, at least the canines get more of a say now," Palis said. "Maybe that's what you were missing."

A deep howl suddenly echoed through the clearing. As it built, more howls joined, followed by roars, yelps, and other calls from every sentry. Both camps sprang to life and the defenders took their positions. With some focus, Palis picked up the telltale clicks and buzzing they'd been waiting for.

"Fortunately, we won't be missing your help tonight!" Lima declared with a spark in his eyes. He readied his weapon and followed Palis to their barricade.

Countless rows of red eyes amassed in the trees while the sentries fell back, lighting fire rings and stationary torches as they went. Aura's horde seemed to be waiting, though for what none of the survivors could tell. Calls to hold fire passed from squad to squad. Everyone armed with a ranged weapon already had their target but as long as they didn't shoot, the machines remained in place.

Abruptly, Aura's drones all emitted a low tone three times. As the final note faded away, the robots spoke simultaneously in a voice comprised of a hundred others. "We are Aura. We have come to fulfill our objectives," they intoned. "Turn over all human personnel immediately and you will not be harmed. Any non-humans who fail to comply will be designated as hostile. You have ten seconds to comply."

Murmurs rippled through the entrenched squads. It didn't take someone with the ears of a fox to hear the consensus. Palis loaded a holoflare launcher and looked to Lima. The human commander made sure to get nods from Oakes, Fennel, Sneffels, and their human squad mates before he nodded back. Hackles raised and teeth bared, Palis fired the scarlet flare into the sky and chased it with her battle cry.

Dazzling pulses of blue energy streaked over the open grass. Sparks and molten metal erupted from every drone hit, downing them instantly. At Palis' suggestion, Radan sharp-shooters engaged the machine army first. Their keen eyes and reflexes helped them track and destroy the distant robots effi-ciently, while most humans waited for any robots that slipped through. With Sneffels blasting drone after drone beside him, Lima had to wait a few moments before even one beetle entered his designated firing range so he didn't waste battery on targets he couldn't see.

As Palis theorized, the dragonfly drones stopped and attempted to extinguish every fire ring. The delays made them easier targets and had the bonus effect of slowing the green insectoid machines as well. Still, no matter if they flew high or low or skittered along the ground, the combined Radan and human gunners thinned Aura's forces considerably.

"Some are getting' close!" Sergeant Oakes roared. "Pikes ready!" Those without rifles leveled their plasma pikes or spears at the first centipedes quick enough to reach them. Despite the machines' speed, size, and exoskeletons, the defenders' polearms easily found their marks.

Specialist Fennel retracted her pike and smiled wickedly. "It's like cuttin' butter!" the raccoon shouted.

"Good kill, good kill," Palis encouraged, readying her own pike for another target. "Sneffels! Fliers at ten o'clock high!"

"Copy that!" the medic acknowledged moments before Palis saw the effects of a laser pulse up close.

The few minutes that passed dragged as adrenaline and instincts kicked into high gear. Palis fought to maintain her awareness of the battlefield, thankful she had Crags' wings to count on. The gryphon swooped overhead and out of reach to not only strafe the drones, but to also be the survivors' eye in the sky. He occasionally landed behind Palis and gave her tactical updates, reassuring her their lines were holding.

"C'mon!" Fennel taunted after skewering another dragon-fly. "Is that all you got?"

Ears swiveling and eyes scanning, Palis barked a quick warning. "Stay sharp, Fen! It's not over yet!"

But Fennel only laughed. "Last night was way tougher than this! I think we've seen the worst they can throw at us!"

Then, as if waiting for the raccoon's cue, the machines abandoned their assault and retreated to the northwest woods. Cheers and howls spread for a moment, only to die when the defenders noticed pines trembling and heard branches breaking.

Palis loaded her launcher and illuminated the clearing once again. By the red glare, everyone watched the tree line and saw a mechanical monstrosity emerge. Eight ruby eyes glared back from their mounts in a body as wide and thick as two drop-rafts, held aloft by six spindly legs. The two sturdy arms under the eye clusters and four tentacles dangling under the body all ended in deadly pincers, easily capable of grasping even the largest Radan.

"I just had to open my muzzle," Fennel growled. "Who ordered the seafood special?" As the hexapod strode closer, Palis saw its body and legs were coated in thick, grey panels, indeed giving it the appearance of a giant crab.

"Light it up!" Palis barked, but her sharpshooters were already well ahead of her. Anything else caught in the survivors' barrage would've burst into flames instantly. However, to their horror, the hexapod kept walking as if through a stiff breeze, shrugging off every blast.

Lima held his fire. He pulled Palis back and shouted, "Its shell is too thick! We'll never get through at this rate!"

"He's right!" Fennel added. "Looks like some kind of heat shielding's all over that thing!"

The last of Aura's smaller drones took cover behind their walking siege engine and steadily advanced. *They'll reach one of the camps soon*, Palis thought. *Lasers are no good and bullets probably aren't much better. We can't dent it from here. If we're gonna attack it, it's gotta be from a different angle.*

"Crags!" Palis called above the laser fire. Seconds later, the gryphon made a hasty landing.

"Got a plan for the big one?" Crags asked between breaths.

"Yeah, I need to know if the top's armored," Palis replied.

"Okay, I'm on it!"

While the gryphon flew off, Palis grabbed a fresh plasma pike and tested it once. "I hope you're not planning something stupid," Lima said. "You can't take on that thing alone."

"I know," Palis replied. "Which is why we'll have to hit it together. The trouble is we gotta get close."

Lima winced. "Those claws and legs will crush us!"

"Not if we mix fight with flight," Palis smiled as Crags touched down again. "And not just literally," the vixen added, nodding to the gryphon.

"Am I missing something?" Crags asked, cocking his head.

"Not really," Lima scoffed. "I think your captain was just about to explain how kill a tree-sized metal crab with sharp sticks and laser pointers."

The gryphon chuckled. "Well, before you get too deep into that, I have good news and bad news," he said. "The good news is the top isn't coated with tiles. The bad news is the rest of Aura's army is waiting in the woods for that thing to wreck us. Again."

Palis nodded and focused, drowning out the gunfire and growing unease rippling through the survivors' defenses. She listened closely to the humans and Radans and knew their only chance was to try something unthinkable.

"Fennel!" Palis barked, pulling the raccoon in close. "Get me climbers! Possums, squirrels, felines, anyone! Tell them to make their plasma cutters as portable as possible and put one climber in each squad! Bring the squad leaders back when you return, too!"

"Yes, ma'am!" Fennel replied. She hurried off to spread the word.

"Oakes!" Palis said, grabbing the bear from the firing line. "You're on crowd control. Get your best human brawlers and when we push, keep the drones off our tails."

"With pleasure, Captain!" Oakes growled with a smile.

Palis glanced over the barricade and noted the hexapod's slow but steady progress. "Crags, tell the squads at the nose to watch our flanks! I don't wanna get surrounded while we try this stunt, but come right back here because I'll need a lift." The gryphon acknowledged the order and left as well.

Lima, who hadn't taken his eyes of the giant machine for several moments, finally turned back to Palis. "It's just a large beast of prey," he mused, starting to see what Palis had in mind. "And we'll hunt it like a pack."

The vixen grinned. "Now you're thinking like an animal."

When Crags and Fennel returned, Palis explained the plan to the gathered squad leaders. They took the strategy back to their own troops and waited for Palis' signal. By then, the hexapod's footsteps were close enough to be felt rumbling through the ground. *This is it*, the vixen thought, taking a deep breath.

Lima slapped a new battery into his carbine and nodded to Palis. She fired the last of her holoflares, grabbed her pike, and led the defenders away from their barricades. Countless red eyes locked onto the movement, and the hexapod turned toward them. Paws and boots trampled the grass slowly at first, then they picked up speed.

Makeshift shields braced and weapons level, each squad moved to their attack positions. The troops from the nose camp started to move, too, but once they settled, Palis felt confident their time had come.

"For *Unity!*" Palis roared as loudly as her lungs could manage. Humans and Radans alike took up the battle cry after her. Their voices turned into wild roars and howls that melded into one furious wave of energy. Their hearts pounded, their blood raced, and their muscles tensed to meet the enemy.

Drones broke from the cover of the trees, swarming under and around their lumbering champion. "Fire at will!" the squad leaders commanded. Though still advancing, the squad gunners opened up on the hovering or crawling drones. Oakes and her forces soon sprang into action, maneuvering around and behind the hexapod to draw its drone supports away while the other squads closed in on their target.

So far so good, Palis thought once they encircled the machine. *Second phase.*

"Aim for the eyes and arms!" Lima shouted. "Laze it!"

Between the falling cherry holoflare and the azure laser bolts, the battlefield flashed with pulses of brilliant purple light. As the ground fire blinded the towering robot and crippled its deadly arms, Palis yelped again. "Climbers! You're up!"

A climber from each of the six squads broke ranks and rushed at their assigned leg. If the hexapod had detected them, it couldn't calculate their positions well enough to stomp them. The Radans easily scampered up the limbs with their plasma cutters tucked into their belts. Each found a joint on the machine's legs and started slicing where the grey panels didn't cover.

"Cease fire!" Lima ordered upon seeing the climbers in position. The hexapod's pincers were no longer a threat as they hung limply under it, blasted into scrap.

Aura's swarm tried in vain to reach the suddenly stricken giant, but the crack shots, slashes, and thrusts of Oakes and her warriors ensured nothing made it through. With each second of cutting that passed, the hexapod struggled more and more to move. It made harsh artificial yelps of alarm and at these cries, Crags recognized the final phase of the plan.

"Ready, Ponder?" he asked the vixen as she lifted her plasma pike.

"As I'll ever be!" Palis replied.

Crags picked her up and took off with a running start. Night air whipped past the pair, forcing the vixen to squint. Molten metal and leaking vitafluid filled her nose with the pungent aroma of a battle half-won. She just needed to land a killing blow.

The Radan climbers leapt clear once their work was done. Likewise, the other squads backed away from the tottering hexapod and focused on taking any shots they could at the smaller drones. Now assured she wouldn't be interrupted, Palis told Crags to drop her onto the machine's back.

To her surprise, the top of the machine was flat and felt gritty under her paws. However, the vixen was even more surprised when metal safety railings automatically rose out of the body, followed by what appeared to be a control panel. Then, as if the hexapod knew about its unwelcome rider, the towering robot began to jolt erratically. Palis gripped the railing and activated her pike with one paw. She inverted the pike and started boring into the hexapod. The machine screeched unlike anything Palis had ever heard. Still, she held on. Nothing else mattered besides driving the plasma cutter as far as it would go.

Suddenly, an opening appeared by the control panel and a cable snaked out of the deck. Palis fended it off with her pike, but soon another whip-like cable emerged. The hexapod lurched, knocking her off her paws. Before she had time to react, one of the cables slithered up to her and jabbed its pronged end under her right ear.

Instantly, a voice spoke in the vixen's head and her vision faded. "Aura 2100 Neurolink established," the voice said. "Please do not be alarmed. Neural interface will be used to assess emergency victims' physical and mental well-being. Your data will not be shared with third parties. Our privacy policy is avail—" The interruption sent a jolt through Palis as the amalgamated voice returned. "Forget that! Give us everything. Isolate candidates for acquisition and integration!"

"W-what?" Palis said, unsure if it was just a thought or something she spoke aloud. Either way, Aura heard her.

"Subject, Palis Ponderosa. Anthropomorphic organism, base species, kit fox, *Vulpes macrotis*," Aura went on. "Member of the Radan Vanguard, designated hostile. Tactical analysis indicates high probability for beneficial intelligence extraction."

So, this is what they were doing to Air Captain Villalobos on the bridge, Palis thought, hoping the machine didn't hear her.

"Your captain proved valuable," the voice intoned. "We thank her for the radio codes. The human soldiers we acquired were of minimal use, however. They displayed no willingness or capacity for adaptation. If reintegration is to succeed, we require the humans open to change."

All it took was an errant thought. A single name drifting across her consciousness. *Lima*. Aura latched on and dug digital fangs into Palis' mind. "No! No! Leave the humans alone."

"Yes," Aura countered. "Commander Lima, accessing subject memories."

Palis screamed in her mind and tried thinking of anything else. Whatever the machines wanted, she feared they were finding it. "Get out of my head!"

Though she only half-expected it to work, Aura replied in its soothing tone from earlier. "Withdrawal of patient consent detected. Do you wish to disable Neurolink?"

"Yes!"

"No! Override Hippocratic Protocols! Give us everything!" roared the AI's voice, turning on her again. "Subject, Lima. Yes, he is ideal! Updating target list."

Blurry images of Lima and the work the survivors accomplished flashed through her mind's eye. "They. Want. Lima!" Palis forced through the mental onslaught. But just as she thought all was lost, sounds beyond the mad machine's voice reached her. A gryphon's screech, the thump of someone else landing on the hexapod, and a voice.

"You want me? Here, Aura, you can have me!" Lima said, sounding distant. "Just let the fox go."

The next thing Palis knew, she found herself in a blank room with Lima standing next to her. "Lima! What's going on?"

"I don't know," Lima replied, looking around.

"Welcome!" Aura's voice echoed. "How fortunate the very human we were seeking should give himself to us so easily. If you had only been this cooperative earlier, we would have avoided much damage to Network property."

Lima smirked and turned, unsure of which direction to face when speaking to Aura. "What can I say? Humans aren't the most cooperative creatures in the world."

"On the contrary," Aura soothed. "You seemed to cooperate with the anthromorph species quite well. Against our calculations, of course. This experimental scenario has yielded unexpected results."

Palis didn't like the sound of that. Unfortunately, she still feared Aura could hear her thoughts, so she tried to let Lima do the talking.

"Well, the experiment's over!" Lima chuckled with a shrug. "Turns out when two sworn enemies face a threat to their survival, they either get friendly or die alone."

"Us, a threat?" Aura taunted. "Why do you fight us, human? We are only trying to fulfill our purpose." Lima looked like he wanted to ignore the machine. Aura must have sensed it. "Reintegrate us into your city. Link yourselves to us again! Radan will fall with the Aura Network as your sword." The white room swirled and changed until Palis and Lima were floating in space, high above the Earth. Glowing dots winked into existence and spread across the land and sea. "All of this, all of us, can be yours again!"

Palis met Lima's gaze. *Did he know this would happen? Did he know this is what Aura wanted? He could return to the Gilded Tower as a hero, the conqueror of Radan and all who opposed him.* For the first time since they'd met, she looked at him with the face of a cornered animal.

"Not interested," came Lima's reply after a moment. He smiled at Palis. Then he mouthed the words, "Keep talking."

"Security. Stability. Safety," Aura intoned before growing bitter again. "This is what your people wanted! It's why we were created! Are you not happy? Are you not pleased? Let us return Earth to its rightful rulers!"

Palis found her voice. "We prefer the term 'caretakers,' Aura," she said smoothly.

"We are the legacy of mankind, not you!" the AI boomed

at the vixen. "You! So impure! So organic! Crawling through the dirt like the animals you are! We are eternal!"

Though the voice was faded, Palis and Lima swore they heard Crags shout something through the void. "Hold on! I don't know what this will do!"

With a wave of her paw, Palis dissolved the world in front of her and all the Aura Network's scattered and disparate units. "Eternal?" Palis laughed. "We'll see about that, Aura. You want another experiment? Another test? How about this? Man, machine, animal. Last one alive keeps the planet."

Electricity surged through her mind, but Palis didn't fear Aura's reaction. Her last memory before the void swallowed her was the sight of Commander Lima, bloodshirt soldier and former enemy of Radan, grinning from ear to ear.

———

Herbal tea and the gentle crackling of a pine fire greeted Palis when she awoke. The flames gave her eyes something to focus on, assuaging her fears that the connection to Aura had somehow blinded her. Of course, she was more relieved to find Crags crouched by the fire, brewing what smelled like raspberry leaf tea as the smoke lazily rose through a vent hole above.

"Crags?" Palis croaked. The gryphon flicked and ear and nearly dropped the pot.

"Ponder!" he gasped. "I knew you'd make it! How're you feeling, Captain?"

Palis blinked. She rubbed her head and arms, then stretched the pains out of her tail with a noise between a groan and a yawn.

"That bad, huh?" Crags chuckled.

"How long was I out?" Palis said, looking around the rounded room.

"Two days."

"Two days!" Palis leapt to her hind paws.

"Woah! Easy, ma'am," Crags said, bringing her a cup of tea. "Everything's under control. Have some of this, and there's a NOM patty if you're up for it."

A rumble rolled through Palis' stomach and her head felt light. She reasoned Crags was right, so she took the moment to eat and drink before asking what happened.

Crags explained everything and assured her the crews were alright. He pointed out the advances they'd made, like the den they'd built for her near the infirmary. Nocturnal Radans guarded the night while diurnals and humans took the day shifts.

"And the drones?" Palis inquired, lapping at her tea.

Crags shook his head. "All deactivated once we took down the hexapod," he said. "It stopped the jamming, too. Tang sent out a new message yesterday. Unfortunately, you were right, the Vanguard's still too busy fighting to send anyone."

"I was afraid of that," Palis sighed.

"Still, it's not all bad," the gryphon said, flicking his tail. "After all, we managed to carve out our own piece of the world right here, and I think you're gonna wanna see it."

Palis tilted her head involuntarily, dropping one ear to the side comically. Crags motioned for her to follow him, so she left the den and trailed him to the edge of the camp.

In the light of a breaking dawn, Palis beheld several huts built from metal salvage, earth, and some wood from the forest. Solaskin chargers eagerly awaited the sun's rays so they could power strings of lights, radios, or whatever other gadgets they were hooked up to. On the hill, windmills made from *Unity's* propellers caught the morning breeze. Starting in the middle of the clearing, the vixen also noticed the growing foundations of a few larger buildings.

Hunters and gathers, humans and Radans, returned from their nighttime venture in the wilderness, walking together to the cooking areas built in both camps. The aroma of sizzling fish, freshly caught that morning, wafted through the air and tickled Palis' nose. Everywhere, merry voices exchanged friendly conversation at the start of a new day.

Not long later, Palis finally found Lima near a small plot of land set on a hill overlooking the meadow. There, the crews had buried Captain Villalobos, the bridge crew, and anyone else who had fallen to Aura's machines. Lima meditated in silence for a few minutes before standing next to Palis.

"For what it's worth," Lima began, "I apologize for the mess humans got the world into. None of you would've been out here if we hadn't invaded."

"You're not responsible for what happened before your time," Palis replied after pausing to think. "But I'm glad you took responsibility for your present. And our future."

Lima furrowed his brow. "*Our* future?"

"Our crews are still stuck in the Divide, Commander. By the sounds of it, we'll be here a lot longer than we thought." Palis perked her ears. "Aura still owns the surrounding forests, but there might be something in their bunkers we could use. It's good to know I can trust you with the next phase of our survival plans."

"Are you suggesting we go on the offensive?" Lima asked.

"I'm saying I'm open to unconventional thinking," Palis clarified. "So, how about it? Any bright ideas?"

"A few, yes."

"Perfect. Because like you said, we're still not out of the woods, and I made a promise to bring everyone home."

OTTERS CAN'T RIG.
BADGERS CAN'T PULL

MEPHITIS

A big project like an airship takes many critters working in harmony to build. Of course, each critter has a specialty, and an otter can't do a badger's job or a badger an otter's. Everyone knows this simple truth. Or is it really that simple?

Not a bad report, Royce muttered, both airships were on time, they might even end up slightly ahead of schedule next week if the rain held off, and both were definitely under budget. He struggled to see the report through the bangs falling over his eyes. He pawed his hair aside as he reviewed the weekly production status report. "Oh, the pain of being a hard working sheepdog. I don't even have time to keep my hair cut so I don't walk into things." *But*, he thought, *Mr. McCary will be happy with this weekly report.* Royce smiled, dreaming of the nice year-end bonus he would receive as site supervisor.

He lifted his head at a knock on his door and his secretary stuck her head in. The squirrel had her head fur cut in the latest style, haphazardly shaved with multi-colored tuffs of hair; a style Royce couldn't understand although his daughter had her coat cut the same way. "Mr. Fullerman, a messenger rabbit just brought an urgent message from Adam on airship #2." She came up and handed him a folded green sheet of paper.

Through the open door he could see the rabbit still standing there, who also had her hair cut in multi-colored tuffs. He sighed. A waiting rabbit meant Adam wanted an immediate response and it was never good when your unit coordinator wanted anything immediately. He unfolded the note and started to read. His already drooped ears drooped farther. "Oh hell, the otters and badgers are at it again. Fourth work stoppage this month. Why do they have to be so…" He called out at the messenger. "Did Adam send notes to the guild masters?"

The rabbit shrugged. "He was writing when he sent me off, but I'm not sure."

"Ok. Go tell Adam I'll be there momentarily."

The rabbit nodded. "Tell Adam you'll be there momentarily. Yes, sir." She hopped off.

Royce crumpled the note between his paws as he turned to look out his window. Black coal smoke from the airship-construction company's huge boilers and other nearby factories drifted across the complex; a downdraft grabbed the smoke as it left the tall chimneys and forced it downward to roll across the ground in black waves. His view from six floors up, except for the obscuring black smoke, showed the entire airship construction area. Multiple canals crisscrossed the yard with building-lined roads spanning them on high-arched bridges. Two partially completed airship frames soared out of the construction docks, rising from below the ground to higher than his window. The even taller cranes gave the frames the appearance of upside down spiders. Beyond those two docks were piles of dirt from the construction of three new docks.

McCary and the board were betting the company on that expansion, but the expansion was based on their belief that war was eminent and they would soon receive huge government contracts for more airships. *Of course,* Royce thought, *if these non-stop otter and badger feuds don't end soon the company may not be around to get those contracts. And, more practically, if I don't figure out how to stop them, I may not be around for my year-end bonus. Or maybe even my month-end paycheck.*

With a deep-throated growl, he ripped the crumpled note in two and slammed it into the trash.

The hike to the construction site didn't improve his disposition since he had to wait at an open drawbridge while a slow tug pushed three barges of iron ingots past. A cloud of black smoke poured out of the tug's stack and rolled over him, causing a coughing fit. That iron delivery was two days late and he'd been worried about it affecting his schedule, but any relief he felt at seeing its arrival was overshadowed by the reason he needed to be on the other side of the canal. Why did the otters and badgers not get along? Granted, they didn't get along with anyone outside of their species and no one really liked them either. The otters were too playful and refused to take anything seriously and the badgers, well, badgers were just plain mean.

However, they were by far the best riggers and cable pullers. Royce would love to fire the lot of them, but rigging frames and pulling tension cables were the two fundamental jobs of building an airship. Thus, he had no choice but to put up with them, but the escalation in this current round of feuding made both of them unbearable.

Airship #2 was the farthest one from his office, but as he walked past #1, he saw critters standing around. His lips drew back, exposing teeth. Whatever problem was causing this current stoppage had better involve multiple dead bodies or he'd create them.

The head rigger for airship #1 jogged up to him as he walked past. Royce showed teeth to the badger. "Why did you stop work? Are you planning on making up the slippage at no-time?"

"Hey, hey, Mr. Fullerman," the badger held out her paws, "the guild master called the stoppage because of the otters on #2. We're within rules. You know I'd never go against the rules."

"Yeah, and last week I bet on your grandma in a cage fight against two lions," Royce muttered. Louder he said, "Come on. Let's go get this all straightened out."

The badger fell in beside him and they walked in silence to airship #2.

A circle of the various critters working on the site formed an outer ring surrounding the otters and badgers, who stood in their own groups, hissing at each other. Between them stood Adam, Frank the head rigger, Ruby the head puller, and Caresa the cable-puller guild master. Royce rolled his eyes at the dress the guild master wore. She was the only critter who routinely walked inside the construction zone in a dress. However, he did have to admit she had been a top-tier cable-puller and supervisor before she took the guild job; he often wished she still worked on a pulling crew. Her hair perfectly matched the current high-fashion style, with none of the color streaks sported by about half of the female otters on the crew. Royce looked over his shoulder and saw a fat huffing badger, the rigging guild master, hurrying across a bridge toward the group.

The circle of critters parted as Royce walked through them. He stood beside Adam and alternated between stares, half exposing his teeth, and head shakes at each group until the puffing and wheezing badger guild master joined them.

He turned toward an otter. "Ruby, what's your side?"

The badger foreman spoke up, "Well, Mr. Fullerman, these fish smelling scum sucking…"

Royce whirled on him and jabbed a paw into his chest. "Otters first, then your turn. Each speaks in turn when asked, or I resolve this for the group that can keep its mouth shut unless spoken to. Understand?" He moved to glare at each critter in turn and waited until they all dropped their eyes toward the ground and grumbled something resembling an affirmative answer.

"Ok, now, Ruby, you were saying?"

"Well, these carrion eaters were…"

A growl went though the badger ranks.

"Language!" Royce said, lips drawing back to show his teeth.

Ruby's eyes flashed for a second before her shoulders dropped. "Ok, we had a crew pulling cable into the area below the rigging area. The rivet crews had finished earlier today so it was our turn. Then, after we got the first cable threaded through and partially tensioned — it was one of the two incher main cables — the badgers were jumping on it. Falling down off their perch onto the cable, bouncing a few times, and then letting their safety lines catch them. Tore loose one of the connectors. It could have damaged a frame."

Royce turned to the badger foreman. "Frank, your side."

The badger guild master cut in. "None of the badgers would ever do anything like that. It's unsafe. I'm sure it's nothing but a story these otters made up to cause trouble."

Royce stepped toward to him, gums rolled back. "Were you an eye witness?"

"As the guild master, I speak for…"

"Were you an eye witness?"

"Well, no. I was in my office."

"Eating donuts. Right." He turned back to Frank. "And?"

"Well these wiggle," he clenched his teeth, "these otters had run the cable. But none of my people jumped on it. Louis took a fall and happened to come in contact with it. Sort of lucky for Louis. It took some of the shock before his safety line stopped him. Even so, he'll have some good harness bruises."

Ruby muttered, "And what about the other four that just happened to fall?"

Royce raised his voice and addressed the crowd. "Any witnesses? Especially any inspector?"

His eyes scanned over the silent critters, who all felt a sudden urge to look elsewhere.

"Ok everyone, back to work. We'll have a full investigation into this."

The badger and otter guild masters spoke in unison, "No!"

"What do you mean, no?"

Caresa spoke up, "We refuse to work on the site as long as these critters are violating safety rules and causing damage to our work."

The badger nodded, "For once we agree on something. As long as these wiggle snakes are making up untrue stories, we will not work."

Royce glared at both of them, contemplating what species could replace the whole lot of them. Maybe he should hire a few sociopathic skunks to work on their crews. Then, he had an idea. He rocked back and smiled. With a big smile on his face he kept looking between Frank, Ruby, and the two guild masters. The smile grew bigger as he watched deep worry lines wrinkle the fur on their faces. Wrinkles that transformed into fear when he burst out laughing.

Finally, Royce nodded. "Ok, I agree. Since you both refuse

to work with the other species, you don't have too." A collective gasp went up from the crowd. "However, since the work must still be done, you'll have to do it yourself. Otters get to do rigging and pulling on #1 and badgers get rigging and pulling on #2."

In unison, the guild masters said, "What? Impossible, they are not qualified."

Royce tilted his head. "Oh. Ok then, back to work since you agree that you must work together."

Both guild masters stood stunned, open and closing their mouths wordlessly.

Frank stepped forward. "Oh bloody hell, if a stinking otter can pull cables it's got to be trivial for a badger."

"Yeah, what's so hard about sticking pieces of metal together? If a badger can do it, an otter can do it better. It ain't nothing like the real work of pulling and tensioning a cable through tight spaces."

Royce slapped both foremen on the back. "Good. Now that you're all happy, everyone back to work. We're barely on schedule and I don't want any slippage. I'll be nice, but you should be working no-pay overtime to cover this hour-long work stoppage." Leaving behind shocked faces, Royce walked off.

———

Mr. McCary drummed the polished walnut desk with his paw. "Royce, it's been two days since you split the otters and badgers and our framing schedules are slipping. Something which greatly concerns me since the carriage units are ahead of schedule. I *will* deliver these two airships well ahead of schedule. The air company doesn't want to hear excuses about strikes or anything else. Plus, we've got three more orders waiting. We need to clear those docks and get started on two of them."

Royce stood before his boss's desk and refused to wither under the large wolf's piercing gaze.

"Sir, that was the fifth stoppage in the last two months. Those two groups are looking for slights to call a stoppage. And that was seriously affecting the long-term schedule since it seems to take a day or two to return to normal productivity. Frankly, I'm surprised they haven't given up on doing the other's task. Right now, I'm sure they're both stubbornly praying for the other to give up first. In the meantime, the inspectors are passing the work. Both species are paranoid about a failed inspection as proof they can't do the job. I'm confident that in another day or so things will return to normal."

"Ok, a few days, but no more than a few. No overtime pay to get back on schedule. When they get done being jerks, production goals go up until we're back on schedule."

Royce kept his face blank as he replied, "Yes, Mr. McCary." But he knew that threat was toothless with work schedules already stretched to the breaking point. Increased production goals would only result in a schedule slip since the work could not go faster.

A messenger rabbit waited outside McCary's office. "Mr. Fullerman, I know this message is urgent, but Mr. McCary's secretary wouldn't let me interrupt. But, anyway, there was a fight on number #1. A badger was found sneaking onto the frame."

Royce growled and bared his teeth as the rabbit cowered against the wall. "I am going to kill the lot of them. I'll kill them and then push them off the highest crane." Leaving the poor trembling rabbit, he left at a full run.

Everyone was back at work when he arrived. Katrina, the

#1 air frame supervisor, explained that the badgers had sent a critter sneaking over to see how badly the otters were rigging. He was noticed before reaching the framing itself, so he had made up a pitiful excuse. Lucky for the badger, Katrina was one of the first critters to arrive and got him hustled off site #1 before it progressed beyond jeers and insults.

Royce called the otter foreman and guild master, told them the matter of the trespassing badger was closed, and that any otter found trespassing on airship #2 was fired. Then he leaned in close, showed his teeth, and told them that they would both accompany any trespassing otter out the gate. As they stood pale in their fur, he assured them that the badgers would receive the same notice.

A few hours later, still fuming over the ongoing otter-badger feud, he walked out the shipyard gate and down to the canal dock at end of the street, glad to head home. He looked at his usual water bus, puffing steam from its boiler and shaking from the engine vibration. He shook his head and walked past it to a hand-rowed gondola. He nodded to the burly bear gondolier as he climbed in, admiring the finely tooled brass trim under his paw. A rowed boat would take longer, but would be quiet and smooth. Right now, he needed time to think and did not want to deal with the noise and shake of a steam turbine. And he certainly didn't want any critter trying to strike up a sports conversation; the city was abuzz about the local team being in the final eight of the national push-and-roll championships, a sport he despised. In his current state of mind he didn't trust himself to just nod noncommittally to some gushing crazed fan.

For the first part of the trip, he sank back into the cushions and let his mind go blank while the boat moved along the side canal and merged into Grand Canal. An oily film covered the water; even the otters didn't swim in Grand Canal. Other boats, both animal-powered and steam-powered moved though the canal and bobbed at their moorings along the canal's sides. In the buildings lining the canals, the yellow flicker of gas lights filled the windows. He loved traveling the canals at dusk, with the lights glowing and people moving about. His stomach rumbled as the odors of cooking food wafted past his nostrils.

An airship passed overhead, its nose slightly up as it worked to gain more altitude. From the carriage design he knew his yard had built it a few years ago. Other airships floated from the mooring poles topping the tall buildings on the inland side of the city.

The boat slipped past the moorings of Badgertown. Loud music and laughter came from the bars that lined the canal. A few leather-collared badgers leaned on the rails at the top of a mooring step. Badgertown was not an area he would go after dark... or, truth be told, any time of day. He wondered why each species moved together to form a city, but then insisted on living within enclaves of their own species. He had traveled to several cities and each was the same; consistently, some of those enclaves were nice areas and some were seriously dangerous. He had never seen a single city where Badgertown wasn't the worst hellhole in the city. Nothing but a cesspit of drinking and fighting. He was sure all of the yard's badgers lived in Badgertown and most had grown up there. Looking at it that way, he could understand why they had such a rough outlook on life. He couldn't imagine growing up in that sort of place. Of course, he lived in a higher-end canine area himself, so he was just as guilty of staying species-centric. Other than some very swank areas he couldn't afford, like where McCary lived, he wasn't sure if he wanted to live anywhere else.

Royce sighed. If the otter-badger job switch didn't get resolved soon, that old critter McCary had more than enough pull in this city to ensure that Royce would be lucky to get a job as a sewer cleaner in Badgertown. Then he would have no choice but to uproot his family and move back to the town where he and his wife had grown up. At least the inspectors were not failing everything. To be honest, he had expected failed inspections and after a half a day both species to be forced to admit they couldn't do the work.

He rocked back in the cushion and took a deep breath; he needed to relax and forget about work. His wife had mentioned something about a dinner party and someone's daughter playing music with a group. He hoped it was a nice classical quartet. He shuddered at the thought that it might be someone's not-so-talented daughter's paws torturing a musical instrument. At a tea party last month, he had suffered through a daughter duet that sounded closer to an otter-badger fight than music. If given a choice between a repeat of that recital and being in a backstreet Badgertown fisticuffs, he'd vote for fisticuffs.

———

A week later, Royce stood twenty stories above the street. He pulled his cape tighter around his shoulders as a cold wind ruffled his fur. Several other critters stood around him, forming a haphazard line before the gate that blocked a narrow walkway leading to a waiting airship. It rocked slowly on its nose tether attached to the building's mast.

Royce looked over the airship with his experienced eye. It was a Briggerton airship, larger than the ones he built, but designed on the same basic principle. A two-level carriage hung from a maze of cables wrapped around the large covered airframe. In true overdone Briggerton fashion, the outside of the carriage had all of the seams covered in brass with mosaic designs filling most of the areas in between. The transport company logo of a rabbit surfing on a stylized airship covered the front end. Four large prop motors were attached to the back in the standard configuration, but their engine design looked different. He made a mental note to check into that. He had noticed that the trip to the capital was scheduled to be several hours quicker than he expected; it had to be these engines. McCary would want to know if they needed to change engine suppliers to make a faster product.

Not that a faster product would be an issue if the reason for this trip came to be reality. The war department was holding a meeting of airship companies, and he had heard invitations had gone out to other war equipment companies. McCary had left for the capital three days earlier and had telegraphed for Royce to come and engage in a more detailed level of discussion. If war did come, he wouldn't be mounting any engines since the military had a new propless design that greatly increased the range and speed of an airship. But those engines were a military secret and installed by the military after delivery.

A ferret wearing a uniform overladen with gold braid climbed through the airship door, walked down the swaying walkway, and opened the gate. Then she stepped aside and let the assembled critters walk past.

Inside the door were stairs going up and a doorway to the left. A couple of cute cat hostesses stood on each side of the doorway to greet the first class passengers. Through the door he could see cushy seats, an open bar, and what sounded like a small band. Royce sighed and dutifully climbed the stairs. In the upper level, he found wooden benches and muffled music drifting up from below. When he traveled with McCary, he got to travel first class, but never when he travelled alone.

After stuffing his bag under the bench and sitting down,

Royce frowned as he wondered what the military would think if they heard his schedules were slipping because those damn badgers and otters both refused to admit they couldn't do both jobs. The feud was almost two weeks old now. After a few days of a rapidly sliding schedule, they had at least stabilized. Not slipping, but not making up time either. McCary was beyond impatient and Royce knew that in six days when McCary returned, this situation had to be resolved. It was not going to be pretty. When he returned he would look at the inspection reports more closely and see what types of comments were being made. Passing inspection was different from doing work at the quality he, and McCary, expected. Perhaps the reports would provide the stick to get everything back to normal. This feud risked his own management credibility since he was going to have to end it instead of allowing either the badgers or otters to curl up and show their necks.

———

After the morning senior management briefings, his first update after returning late last night from his trip to the capital, Royce stood staring out his office window at the new docks. He had not been too happy during his days in the capital. War seemed much too eminent, especially with the government almost pushing to start it. The company's government agents reported beating war drums within the Parliament halls that echoed those of the military meetings, and they were starting to sound in the newspapers, too. McCary had been almost jubilant as he talked about working three shifts on five docks to supply military airships. He had updated the new dock's construction contract so the crews would work two shifts a day to get them built faster. In addition, he had told all of his managers, Royce included, that he wanted plans for hiring and training the new crews required to work the new docks. McCary expected both single shift and full 24/7 shift hiring plans with larger crews. Royce was happy that they were out of range of enemy airships, at least as long as a war went well. However, he didn't really relish the idea of managing five dock supervisors across three shifts and weekends. At the same time, he knew he wouldn't be happy if McCary hired a new senior supervisor to oversee all shift supervisors and left him just in charge of this shift. However he sniffed it, it seemed he was destined to be living in this office.

The good news was that during his time away, the schedule hadn't slipped, so McCary wouldn't tear the fur off his back about that. Sighing, he turned back to his desk. He looked at the stacks of paper covering it and shook his head. Attacking those mounds of paper would have to wait until after he'd resolved the otter and badger issue. He had hoped that they would give it up during his time away and he would return to find both critters doing their normal work. First, he would review the inspection reports and then he would walk over and do a personal inspection. He would find the stick he needed. On schedule or not, the feud ended today.

His secretary opened his office door, breaking into his thoughts. "Mr. Fullerman, a messenger just arrived from airship #1. Rigging work has stopped."

He buried his face into his paws. "Now what? Now why have the otters stopped?"

He was a herding dog and he so wanted to herd those otters and badgers over a cliff. The mental image of them tumbling over the edge looked so sweet.

When he arrived at airship #1, Ruby was standing on the bridge to the dock waiting for him. No other otters were in sight.

"Ok, Ruby, what's the problem? Why did you stop work?"

"We only stopped rigging, My Fullerman. I put everyone on pulling, but that'll only keep us busy for the rest of shift and maybe a couple hours tomorrow. We'll rig again after tomorrow's frame delivery, but only maybe until noon."

Royce growled. "Why did you stop rigging?"

"No frames. We're working too fast."

Royce caught a snarl in his throat. "Wait, what?" With a shake of his head, he said, "You are working too fast?"

"Yes, we're going faster than the badgers did and the fabrication shop only tends to work a day or so ahead of rigging. Those bears and wolves are worse than badgers about not working any harder than they have to. Anyway, we've installed everything they have ready. They can't keep up. Sorry, sir, but we've fallen off the front of the schedule."

"Fallen off the front of the schedule? Wait, you said you've rigged all the frames that are ready to install. I need to get fabrication working faster?" *Oh, yes*, he thought, *Charles will really love being told his crews needed to work faster.* Something to add to his endless complaints about being understaffed. Of course, Ruby's comment about the fab shop only working as hard as it was forced to was, unfortunately, also true. Well, now Charles would just be forced to work faster.

Ruby nodded. "Fallen off the front. One of the guys described it that way. I think it fits."

"How are the rivet crews keeping up?"

"Easily. I don't think they work all that hard. If I had frames and could hire another rigger team or two we could really fly. Hmm, maybe not; that would require another crane. Pulling is an issue though. We found we can rig faster than we can pull. Never had that problem with badgers rigging."

Royce closed his eyes and thought, *Ruby, if you really can go that fast and we get war orders to fill those three new docks, you'll regret saying that.*

"Ok, if fab isn't keeping up, I'll go and deal with that. Where's Katrina?" Royce asked.

"Up supervising whatever. I told her I'd wait down here for you."

"Let's go find her."

They found Katrina talking to one of the inspectors. Seeing Royce, she waved and walked over.

"So, tell me Katrina, how is the cable pulling going if there are so many otters working rigging?"

Katrina and Ruby exchanged glances. "Actually, the last four days we've only had four-otter rigging crews instead of seven. So, we set up some extra rigging crews and the left-over critters were sent back to pulling, giving us a couple extra crews there, too. That's why we're almost at a stop on pulling too until the morning's frame delivery."

Royce's ears rose. "Badgers need seven-critter crews but otters only need four?"

Ruby nodded. "Well, yes. Well, I mean, the badgers are very strong. They rig by just critter-powering the frame into place. That's why they need seven. To deal with it by sheer strength required an eleven-otter crew and that doesn't work. Too many paws on a frame. But then we figured out a few shortcuts."

Royce bristled, hair raising on his neck. "Shortcuts? Katrina, how can you allow shortcuts?"

"No, no, Mr. Fullerman," Katrina stepped back, waving her paws, "not really shortcuts, but more efficient ways to move the frames into place. Rather than brute strength, they finessed. Same result, less critter-power. Safety and quality inspectors don't see any problems. And it's faster. Lots faster."

Royce looked at the two of them. "I'll be back."

Royce walked over to airship #2 and watched steam pour out of a crane as it lifted a frame and swung it into a group of waiting badgers. A quick count showed seven badgers working the frame. Then he walked into the dock, looking for Adam. He found him watching badgers threading a very thin, stiff cable.

"Are we changing the cables we use on this airship?"

Adam shook his head. "No, Mr. Fullerman. The otters are thin, they can slip through those narrow places carrying the tension cables. Badgers are too big, so they figured out threading that little thing through, tying it onto the cable, and pulling it back. Faster than an otter physically carrying it through, actually."

They stood silently watching the working badgers.

"Um, by the way," Adam said, "this is fast enough that the pulling crews were standing around too much. Two days ago, I divided them up to form another rigger crew. Pulling crews are keeping up just fine."

"So you pull different than otters. Do you still rig the same way as before?"

Adam looked puzzled. "Huh? How else do you rig a frame?"

"Yeah." Royce nodded. "Yeah, that's what I figured you'd say. Meeting in my office the last hour of the shift. You, Frank, and the rigging guild master."

"Um, ok, Mr. Fullerman."

"By the way, you should tell these badgers… never mind. Just remember otters are too wimpy to out-rig a badger and badgers are too big to pull cables."

Royce turned and walked away leaving Adam with a puzzled look on his face. At the dock entrance, he sent a messenger rabbit to tell the otters about the end-of-shift meeting.

Half way across a canal bridge, Royce stopped and looked down into a brass molding shop. The doors stood wide open to keep it cooler. As a bear and wolf wearing apprentice aprons pumped the furnace bellows, flames roared up the sides of crucibles with dull red bottoms. Royce watched two bears lift a hot crucible of molten brass, carry it across the floor, and pour it into a mold.

Royce nodded. That was how you worked brass. The bears, who claimed to be master brass-smiths, had always done it that way. Of course, the badgers claimed to be master riggers and had always done it that way. Yet, the otters had promptly found a faster way using fewer critters. Was this the best way to work brass? Was there a faster way? How many other trades within the yard could be more efficient if they were forced to work through their preconceptions about how it was always done?

Forcing a change. He pondered dyeing his head with multiple color streaks. No, he couldn't see that. He stretched out his paws. Yeah, maybe color streaks on his paws. He snickered, imaging McCary and his wife's response. Still, if it helped him to look at things differently.

He turned to look at the soaring ribs of the airship frames. Was the entire shipbuilding process efficient? This airship yard was, what, almost 200 years old? Had rigging and pulling always been done the same way? He knew it hadn't changed in his 20 years here. Were they all missing other clever ways of dramatically cutting construction time? Paws clasped behind his back, Royce walked slowly back to his office, pondering this problem, oblivious to the bustle of the critters working around him.

Royce sent his secretary in with a fake apology about a messenger rabbit that needed an immediate response and let everyone stew as they waited at the conference table. He stared out his window an extra ten minutes still worrying over the question of procedural changes for other trades. He needed to figure out how to pressure the trades without seeming to pressure them. But nobody else had anything like the otter-badger feud he could take advantage of.

As he walked into the quiet conference room, he half-expected both species to be gloating about how they were doing the other's job faster. Instead, he found them silently eyeing each other warily across the table. Badgers sat on the left side and otters on the right. For a moment he wondered if whichever critter had arrived first had specifically chosen their side for some reason that only made sense in their species-centric logic. He was sure both expected him to announce the other had ceded and that they would be returning to normal work assignments.

"So, critters," he said, "we're here to discuss the new training program."

He smiled at the shocked faces. "Why yes, we need to learn the new pulling and rigging methods. Mr. McCary is very happy to learn that we'll be able to add a couple extra rigging and pulling crews to each airship frame and accelerate the schedule without having to hire any new critters."

There were a few moments of silence before Ruby quietly asked, "New pulling method?"

Royce nodded. "Yes, the otters have to learn new cable pulling methods and the badgers have to learn new rigging methods.

Royce focused on Frank, whose neck hair had popped upright at the suggestion badgers were not perfect riggers. "Something to say Frank?"

"Damn right. Badgers have been rigging here for years and if there were faster ways, we would have found them years ago. There is no faster way that conforms to safety requirements. No faster way, period."

Ruby had rocked forward to shout her protest and/or gloat at Frank and badgers in general, when a look of terror rippled across her face fur. She collapsed back into her seat with her paws covering her face. "Uh oh."

Frank leaned toward Ruby. "Right, we figured out faster cable pulling, but rigging can't be improved."

Royce cocked his head. "Then why are the otters days ahead of you? Didn't you hear they ran out of fabricated frames today? Using four otter crews."

"Of course with their rigging skills, I'm surprised they are not a bunch of days… Wait! Days ahead?"

Ruby and Caresa gave a triumphant paw pump in the air.

The ruff on Frank's neck collapsed as he sagged back into his chair. With his voice barely a whisper, he said, "I take it that somehow the otters found a faster way to rig, just like we found a faster way to pull?"

Ruby slumped. "I knew it."

Royce nodded. "Yes. Neither of you could actually do the other critter's job as it was currently done. The otters were not strong enough to critter-haul the frames and the badgers couldn't fit through the tight spaces. And both of you are too obnoxious to admit that. So you figured out different ways. Interestingly, both new ways proved faster and used a smaller crew.

"Mr. McCary is very happy you were able to figure out better ways of doing the work. He expects lots of new orders to fill those three new docks and it'll be important to get those airships built as quickly as possible. More important in the short term, I believe at our current pace we're looking at an early completion bonus on these two airships."

"So, are you saying that we go back to working with otters tomorrow?"

"No, Frank, you do not," Royce said. "Your badgers need to learn the new rigging methods." He turned to face Ruby. "Just like the otters need to learn new pulling methods. No, I think you'll both remain split up for a week or so at least. We need to get the training created."

Royce's voice hardened. "It goes without saying that the supervisors and inspectors will be ensuring the new methods are used once you learn them. And the new schedule and staffing will reflect them. No nodding in training and doing it the old way. Clear?

"I said, clear?"

He shifted his gaze between Frank and Ruby until both mumbled their assent. Both guild masters' foreheads lay on the table as they slowly nodded. The badger guild master whimpered.

"Thank you, critters. Training starts beginning of shift in four days." Royce jabbed his paw at Frank and Ruby. "This meeting — and this round of your feud — is over."

OCTOPUS EX MACHINA

MARY E. LOWD

What happens when a miraculous technological advancement can give anyone a new form to match how they feel inside?

The thing that surprised Lora most about being an otter was that her face was round, and her nose was round. Everyone thinks of otters as long. With their sinuous spines, like weasels and ferrets, they're big ol' fuzzy noodles. But when Lora looked at her face — round. So round.

When Lora had been a cat, her face had been full of corners and edges; triangular ears, articulated muzzle; even the shape of her eyes had been filled with crescents and sharpness. She'd had tiny little fangs that made her feel like a vampire. All of those edges and points had felt like affectations. As shallow as fur and skin. This round face — that was who she'd always been underneath. Always.

But... Lora almost wished that she'd actually been the cat who she'd been born and raised as, with all the complexity and sharp edges. But she knew that had never been her. She wished her family understood that too.

Her eyes were brown, plain and honest and completely her. She looked at herself in the mirror and saw the person she knew she'd always been, even before she'd saved enough for the Re-Incorpus surgery. An otter with a heart filled by sunshine and splashing water. But sometimes those brown eyes still surprised her. Sometimes she almost missed the coy green cat eyes; the eyes filled with mystery; the eyes that obscured who she had always been beneath. The mask that had made life a masquerade.

Lora threw a bright yellow towel over her shoulder, more out of habit than a real need. Her thick fur dried fast these days, and the sensation of water against it was… pleasant. Cat fur was too thin to feel good when it got wet. When she'd been a cat, wet fur had plastered against her body, pulling on her skin and itching. Otter fur was made for water.

She wore a simple two-piece swimsuit, decorated with clouds and rainbows. Though she pulled a pair of faded green overalls up over them. She didn't want to draw too much attention on the tram from her apartment to the pool. Some attention, maybe. She did enjoyed hearing strangers' stray comments about "that otter." Simply knowing that they saw her for what she truly was felt wonderful.

The tram bumped along through the city, and Lora enjoyed the crowds of animals getting on and off at each stop. The closer the tram got to the pool, the more animals came aboard with towels over their shoulders or bags full of pool toys, like foam noodles and inflatable beach balls. Lora loved all the bright colors; she bounced on her webbed paws at the cheerful sight. And the best part was knowing that all the animals heading to the pool today were like her. They'd all been different species before being reborn through the magic — well, science — of Re-Incorpus.

A penguin waddled onto the tram. She didn't have a towel with her. (Why would a penguin ever need a towel? Water rolls right off their feathers.) But Lora knew her. They'd crossed paths in the Re-Incorpus offices many times during the months of counseling each client had to do while waiting for their new bodies to grow. Back then, this penguin woman had been a male antelope. She looked so much happier now in her sleek tuxedo feathers and bright orange feet instead of clompy hooves and antlers tangling in the grab handles hanging from the ceiling.

Lora raised her paw and waved at the penguin, surprising herself with her own friendliness and enthusiasm. Somehow as a cat, she'd always been more tentative. So she had expected to wave shyly at the penguin, but her new, webbed paw had different ideas. She was glad, though, because the penguin's beaked face lit up, and the flightless bird waddled toward Lora.

"Goin' to the party?" the penguin chuffed.

Lora felt a grin spread across her face. "Yeah. My name's Lora." She hadn't changed her name when she'd changed species, but a lot of animals did. So she found it was always a good idea to reintroduce herself. She held out her paw, and the penguin curled the tip of her wing, where the feathers spread into fingers, around it.

"Ninette," the penguin said, saving Lora the trouble of trying to remember her antelope name. Lora suspected Ninette would prefer if her antelope name were forgotten anyway.

"How goes the otter-life?" Ninette asked.

"Good, good," Lora said, trying to smile brightly, but a shadow must have crossed her face anyway.

Ninette angled her narrow beak downwards and said, "Family trouble?" It was the obvious guess.

Lora scuffed one of her webbed hind paws along the tram floor. "It's to be expected, I guess."

A lot of animals still believed that transferring one's brain waves into a new body meant the person died along with their original, abandoned body and emptied brain. It wasn't true. But some people couldn't be swayed by science.

"How has your family been?" Lora asked.

"Fine," Ninette chuffed, leaving Lora bewildered. The change from antelope to penguin seemed much more extreme to her than cat to otter. "I mean, I wish my brother would stop making jokes about laying eggs, but other than that..." She shrugged her wings.

Their conversation drifted away from the mundanities of their pasts and into the pleasant trivialities of the day. Ninette had joined a Feathered Friends group and had a crush on the only other flightless bird in the group — an emu who was twice her height and had legs for days; he had the most adorable tuft of fluffy black feathers on the middle of his head, according to Ninette. (Personally, Lora always thought emus looked angry with their severe eyebrows.)

For her part, Lora had taken up sewing so she could alter some of her favorite clothes from back when she was a cat to fit her new wide rudder tail. She found she enjoyed the pastime and had begun designing little plush animal dolls, wearing costumes of other animals. One animal on the inside; another on the outside. Just like she used to be.

And everyone else here...

By now, the tram car seemed to be filled entirely with Re-Incorpus clients. A few wore polo shirts with the Re-Incorpus logo — a stylized phoenix with its wings spread wide — stitched onto the shoulder. But mostly there was no way to tell that any of them had ever been animal species other than the ones they were now. Birds, reptiles, mammals; long swooping necks, wide toothy mouths, puffball tails; colorful feathers, glittering scales, speckled fur. Yet, the only way to tell that any of them had been re-incorporated was that they were heading to the pool today with their towels and toys.

The tram stopped and animals began filing out, paws shuffling and wings flapping in excitement and anticipation. As Lora passed through the automatic sliding door, she noticed an octopus above her, tentacles suckered up against the domed tram car ceiling and wrapped around one of the grab handles.

Lora only noticed it because a pinky-peach flush passed over the octopus's bulbous body and tentacles before its fleshy limbs returned to a shade of gray that perfectly matched the ceiling. It looked kind of dry up there. Lora would've bet her whiskers that the octopus was looking forward to the pool party more than any of them.

A banner stretched over the gated entrance to the pool, fluttering slightly in the breeze. It read: "Re-Incorpus? Refresh Yourself!" And then in smaller letters underneath, "Splash Your Cares Away At the Summer Pool Party."

Lora suspected that the Re-Incorpus clients filing through the gates right now would have a lot fewer cares at the moment if the company hadn't brazenly advertised the pool party like that. Protesters had to be held back by Re-Incorpus employees — mostly big species, like tigers, bears, oxen — working as guards.

One panda man was strong enough to shoulder past the guards and bellow at the crowd heading into the pool, "You monsters killed my baby! My little teddy bear baby!"

Of course, the panda's child might well be right here, listening to their father disown them, simply for not having grown up into the panda bear he'd expected. Lora turned her head away, cringing. Her family hadn't been that bad. She knew she should feel grateful for that. Yet, the idea of feeling grateful for the skewed ears and pointed silences that her feline kin had given her since the rebirth made those minor slights feel all the more cutting.

Past the gates, Lora and the rest of the Re-Incorpus crowd could relax, throw their towels on lounge chairs, and dive into the water. Happy shrieks, squawks, and splashes totally drowned out the noise from outside. Lora could feel herself grinning from ear to ear. She pulled off her overalls and dropped them with her yellow towel on the concrete ground, patterned with blue tiles, around the pool, completely careless of how they fell. She didn't need a towel. She was an otter!

Lora dove into the water nose first. Her nictitating membranes slid shut, shielding her eyes automatically, without her even thinking, and her ears and nostrils closed too. The water enfolded her in an all-encompassing embrace. She was home.

Through her slightly filmy vision, Lora saw other otters, and she swam in curlicues toward them. They spiraled around each other in an intricate, spontaneous, exhilarating dance under the shifting sunlight, filtered through the water.

With delight, Lora found Ninette at the deep end of the pool. The otter and penguin glided beside each other, coasting along the bottom of the pool, needing no words to share the joy and buoyancy they felt together. Lora had never felt this way as a cat. She had never felt so much like herself, so comfortable in her own fur. She could see the crinkles around Ninette's eyes, the slight upturn of the ebony feathers around her beak. She was as happy as Lora.

Then a shiver raced down Lora's spine. She thought she imagined it at first, but the water was growing colder. She hadn't expected to feel a chill through her thickened fur. But she saw looks on the faces of the other swimmers beneath the surface — mostly otters, but also Ninette, an adventurous Labrador retriever, and a polar bear — showing that they felt something wrong too.

Lora began to swim for the surface, but the water wasn't only colder... it felt... thicker? And grainy... Like she was swimming through cold, light sand. She started to have trouble seeing, and by the time her head broke the surface, the entire pool was filled with soft, fluffy, white snow. As the water crystallized it expanded, overflowing the edges of the pool like popcorn in an overfilled popper.

Laughter rang out from where the polar bear had surfaced; a deep, hearty belly laugh. His head looked comical, sticking out of the pool of snow, and his laughter was infectious. Soon the entire crowd was laughing with all their different-sounding voices. Cackles, chuckles, chortles, giggles and guffaws. Even a donkey braying from where she reclined on a poolside chaise.

Soon the air was filled with flying snowballs, and several of the ungulates who'd been less inclined towards swimming began building snow animals beside the pool, rolling up giant snowballs, stacking, and sculpting them. They decorated the snow animals with towels wrapped around their middles, and placed volunteered hats and sunglasses on their heads.

With difficulty, Lora swam — well, trudged — her way through the snow to the edge of the pool. Ninette waddled along in her wake, and Lora helped the penguin up. Once they were both free from the pit of snow, Lora asked, "What happened? I was expecting a summer paradise; not a winter wonderland!"

Ninette shrugged her wings. "Magic?"

The polar bear had stayed in the middle of the pool and was roaring at anyone who would listen, "Throw snowballs at me! Rarr!"

In Lora's experience, most magic was really science at its heart. She looked around the pool, trying to spot any animal who didn't look surprised. Meanwhile, Ninette took the polar bear up on his challenge and began deftly hurling snowballs toward the center of the pool with her wings. She might not be able to fly, but her snowballs certainly could.

Eventually, Lora's eyes settled on her own yellow towel, still discarded beside the pool, but now wrapped around a shivering octopus. Its mantle had taken on a pretty canary hue to match the terry cloth fabric. And it did not look surprised.

Can octopuses look surprised? Probably. Though Lora wasn't sure she'd recognize the expression in their unusual faces — a mere expanse of skin, stretched between two bulbous protuberances around their eyes. This octopus's eyes were a yellow that matched its current hue, and its rectangular pupils were narrow in a way that looked like a smile.

Lora made her way over and sat down beside the octopus cuddled in her yellow towel. The otter wrapped her rudder tail around herself, began smoothing the clumpy wet fur, and said, "You seem like someone who knows what's going on."

The octopus glanced at her. Its pupils narrowed further, and a blush of blue circles danced over its skin. Laughter? There was a lot of laughter at the moment; the entire pool-party-turned-snow-party echoed with peals of laughter.

Just as Lora began to wonder if she and the octopus would be able to communicate at all, given that she didn't know sign language, a mechanical voice emanated from under the octopus's mantle. Lora noticed a small black box nestled there against its tubular siphon. The voice said, "You have a keen eye. And apparently a curious mind. Don't you want to play in the snow?"

Lora did. But not as much as she wanted to understand it.

"How did you do this?" She was sure, deep under her fur, that the octopus was behind the snow. "And why?"

"It's fun. Isn't that enough?" Its tentacles writhed, as if they were eight different creatures, barely held together by the body and bulbous mantle that joined them.

Lora caught herself wondering what the octopus had been before it was an octopus. She knew it was gauche. But she couldn't imagine knowing that you were meant to have tentacles like those — each one covered in hundreds of delicate, dexterous sucker disks — while wearing a comparatively simplistic mammal body with four paws, or a bird body with two talons and two wings.

"You're wondering what we used to be," the octopus said.

Lora looked away, embarrassed that she was unable to deny it.

"Seven mice," the octopus said, and then they held up one tentacle and wiggled it. "And one gerbil. This arm was the gerbil."

Lora blinked, not just with her nictitating membranes but all three sets of eyelids. "You were... seven mice and a gerbil?" She was stunned. "I didn't know that was even possible. To combine multiple minds... into one body?"

"We couldn't share our thoughts fast enough," the octopus explained. "We would stay up all night, every night talking, brainstorming... It was never enough." The octopus's tentacles wrapped around each other, coiling and writhing in harmony. "And an octopus has a distributed nervous system with both a brain and eight arms, each capable of carrying intelligence."

Lora and the octopus sat beside each other, watching the winter games playing out around the pool. The snow was already melting. The snow party would be a pool party again soon enough.

"Are you bothered?" the octopus asked.

"Of course not," Lora answered, knowing the words to say so readily that she didn't have to think before saying them. But they weren't entirely true. She was troubled. She had trouble understanding how eight separate rodents could know they would be happier as one cephalopod.

Lora remembered climbing to a Re-Incorpus pod and lying down, still in her cat body. Her long, narrow tail had curled around her, tip twitching, and she hadn't been able to stop her triangular ears from skewing. She'd been so scared that she'd wake up in her new otter body and it wouldn't feel right. It wouldn't feel any different or less ill-fitting to her than her cat body had. But she hadn't had to worry about her brain waves not mapping correctly or not joining right or… whatever dangers there might be with an eight-brain-to-one-distributed-nervous-system transition.

What if when the seven mice and one gerbil woke up, they weren't really all there? What if each of them had lost something in the transfer?

Except, Re-Incorpus technology had been fastidiously researched and was applied with stringent safety protocols. It had to be given how controversial the procedures still were. Many uninformed animals believed that the empty, discarded bodies from Re-Incorpus transfers had been murdered, and it required iron-clad contracts and unimpeachable proof that the transferred individual was the same person — or people, apparently — that they'd been before to avoid all transferred individuals (and every single Re-Incorpus tech) being thrown in jail. And yet, Re-Incorpus had never had an unsatisfied transfer.

With an uneasy discomfort, Lora realized she was feeling what her parents and littermates felt. Fear of someone who was different from her. She hoped her discomfort wasn't showing through. She supposed, her round otter ears were less likely to betray her, making her look snarky and judgmental, than her triangular cat ears had been.

Except, really, she didn't feel snarky or judgmental. Only awe. She was impressed that this octopus had known itself so well that it had been able to transform so completely.

"Did you design your mechanical voice box yourself?" Lora asked.

"Yes, we brainstormed and planned it out before Re-Incorporating."

"Is that how you designed whatever device you used to make all this snow?" Lora asked. "You have eight brilliant minds, constantly brainstorming inside of you?"

"I am creativity incarnate." The blue circles washed over the octopus's canary-yellow tentacles again. Definitely laughter.

"That's a mouthful of a name," Lora said. She held out a paw, "I'm Lora. You?"

"Divinity," the octopus answered, wrapping a tentacle around Lora's paw. The otter couldn't remember if it was the tentacle that had used to be a gerbil or not. She was sure it didn't matter, and she giggled as the sucker disks tickled her fur and paw pads.

"Will you show me the snow device, Divinity?" Lora asked. "Also, what pronouns should I use?"

"Them," Divinity said. "We're still us. And... no, not yet." Their tentacles coiled, and the tips — which grew almost impossibly narrow — turned bright apple green. "But if you're really interested, I'll be using it again next week. There's a playground with fountains for the children to play in..."

"Gladstone Garden," Lora said. "I used to play there as —" She almost said 'kitten,' but caught herself. "When I was young." Her littermates had never understood why she loved playing in the streams of water so much. They'd made her feel alive. "That was my favorite place."

"How would you like to help me freeze the fountains into ice sculptures?" Divinity's apple green tentacle tips arranged themselves into a pantomime of the Gladstone fountains.

Lora grinned. "I'd love it. Is this what you do? Make strange inventions and sow random chaos?"

"Aesthetic chaos," Divinity corrected. "Not random. Think of it as a kind of performance art, crossed with field testing. The device does have practical applications."

Lora nodded, although she didn't completely buy it. Field tests would work better under more controlled circumstances — with fewer giggles and shrieks of delight from unsuspecting bystanders. Divinity was doing this for fun.

"I could use a lab assistant with a strong back to help me carry the device," Divinity said. "It took me forever to drag it here, sneaking around in the middle of the night. With you, it would go much faster."

Lora loved the idea of causing aesthetically pleasing mischief. Otters are all about fun. "Count me in."

Maybe she'd invite her littermates to bring their litters of kittens to Gladstone Garden for a fun surprise next week. If her sisters and brother couldn't appreciate some good otter fun, she was pretty sure their kittens could.

ABOUT THE AUTHORS

Huskyteer's short stories have been published both in and out of the fandom, and have won two Cóyotl Awards, two Ursa Major Awards, and one Leo Award. She rides a motorcycle, has a black belt in karate, and is much less cool than that makes her sound. Find her at huskyteer.co.uk, or as @Huskyteer on Twitter.

Gustavo Bondoni is an Argentine writer with over two hundred stories published in fourteen countries, in seven languages. His latest book is *Ice Station: Death* (2019). He has also published three science fiction novels: *Incursion* (2017), *Outside* (2017) and *Siege* (2016) and an ebook novella entitled *Branch*. His short fiction is collected in *Off the Beaten Path* (2019) *Tenth Orbit and Other Faraway Places* (2010) and *Virtuoso and Other Stories* (2011).

In 2019, Gustavo was awarded second place in the Jim Baen Memorial Contest and in 2018 he received a Judges Commendation (and second place) in The James White Award. He was also a 2019 finalist in the Writers of the Future Contest.

His website is at www.gustavobondoni.com

Nenekiri Bookwyrm is a dragon that loves writing and making games. He's also been known to paint and play the ukelele on occasion. He's been published in *Reclamation Project: Year One* with "The Underground Star," *Boldly Going Forward* with "Distress Signal," and in a few conbooks as well. You can find more of his writing and other projects on www. nenekiri.com. Curl up with a good book and be kind to yourself. Twitter: @Nenekiri_Dragon

A member of the furry fandom for eight years and the LGBT community since birth, **David M. Sula** has always pursued his love of fiction through the lenses of fantasy and innovative progressive activism. With an MFA in fiction writing, the art of telling stories has always served a critical role in his life, and his love of writing has forged many of his most meaningful relationships, including his boyfriend of three years. David currently teaches first-year writing at College of DuPage, where he emphasizes the importance of rhetoric and social awareness in academic writing. When not teaching or writing, David enjoys video editing, drawing, music composition, and the occasional papier-mâché project. He shares a cozy apartment with his loving boyfriend Alex and his lazy bunny Casey. Some of his previous publications include "Hooked" in *Hair Trigger*, "Resistance" in *ROAR Volume 9*, and "The Dolls of Bogle Street" in *The Lab Review*. You can follow him on Twitter @DavidMSula

Linnea 'LiteralGrill' Capps is a bubbly ball of fluff with an insatiable wanderlust. An award winning poet and author, she happily plays songs on her ukulele and writes the stories she dreams up every night before bed. Her adventures can be followed on Twitter @LiteralGrill or at her website www. linneacapps.com

Frances Pauli writes books about animals, hybrids, aliens, shifters, and occasionally ordinary humans. She tends to cross genre boundaries, but hovers around fantasy and science fiction with romantic tendencies.

She lives in Washington State with her family, a small menagerie, and far too many houseplants. You can find her newsletter, updates, free fiction and a bibliography at: francepauli.com

A 2016 MBA graduate and published author, **Priya Sridhar** has been writing fantasy and science fiction for fifteen years, and counting. Capstone published the *Powered* series, and Alban Lake published her works *Carousel* and *Neo-Mecha Mayhem*. Priya lives in Miami, Florida with her family.

Cedric G! Bacon has been a writer most of his life, and since 2017 has been submitting stories to various publications. He works the front desk at a Holiday Inn hotel chain, and in his spare time he enjoys reading comic books, photography (specifically those of action figures), collecting action figures, watching Doctor Who (both Classic and New), and of course creating new stories. He has appeared in *Infurno*, *Slashers*, *Thrill of the Hunt*, *12 Days of Yiffmas*, *Furry Trash*, and *Sinister Sheets*.

He currently lives in North Florida with his girlfriend and two cats.

Sofox is a software programmer and all round Furry Nerd hailing from Dublin, Ireland. He developed video games, and here he's writing about a fictional one, so it all ties together! He has previously been published in the anthologies *What the Fox?!* from Thurston Howl Publications and *Boldly Going Forward* from Goal Publications. While the future can still be hard to discern, he hopes to get published many times more! So many fun stories to tell and things to explore! Aside from writing, he also dabbles in art, various electronic projects, and yes, likes to play video games! He enjoys long walks in the park, which played a surprisingly strong role in the making of this story. Contact on Twitter via @TheSofox, though be warned: It is Twitter.

Gabi is a person of multiple interests, who juggles two jobs as a university teacher and software developer, but writing has been on top of her mind for as long as she can remember; so much that she got her parents to teach her the alphabet at the age of 3. She has been writing on and off in Spanish and English — she's from Argentina — but becoming a published fiction writer felt like an impossible dream... So much that her first few international publications were of a scientific nature — made while pursuing her doctorate in computer science. However, ever since she learned about the Internet, she has found an outlet for her creative impulses and has been sharing some stories on forums, chatrooms, and even got two stories printed in a local magazine. Her love for animals has always been strong as well, but she had to wait until adulthood to learn about the furry community, to which she is grateful for their warm and welcoming reception and the wonderful friends she has found.

Though he grew up in the western and Midwestern United States, **Frank LeRenard** is currently a postdoctoral researcher moving around the globe from one two-year position to the next. Aside from the occasional short story, he is currently — and perhaps always will be — working on a novel.

Juniper V. Stokes is a trans woman and writer based in Austin who has built and retooled more worlds than she could ever remember — thankfully lists exist as a helpful backup memory. The fact that she can be technically credited as a Hugo Award Winning Author before being physically published thanks to *AO3* is a baffling yet amusing fact, and she has been honing her craft in fandom spaces since before Sonic started getting good again. All of her online publishing and presence is put out under the name ArtieStroke, and more of her writing and art can be found under that same name on *AO3* and Twitter.

K.C. Shaw lives in East Tennessee and spends most of her free time drumming, birdwatching, and reading other people's books instead of writing her own. She also produces and hosts *Strange Animals Podcast*. Her fantasy adventure novel, *Skytown*, is available from Fox Spirit Books with a short story collection, *Skyway* (set in the same world as *Skytown*), newly released from Mannison Press. Her Twitter handle is @kc_shaw.

With his den in northern Colorado, **Juan C. Moreno** (Vulpes vulpes moreno) works as a marketing copywriter while moonlighting as a fiction author for anthologies like the *Werewolves Versus* online 'zine series and most recently, the FurPlanet-produced solarpunk anthology *Reclamation Project:*

Year One. His stories are inspired by the places he's traveled to and the cast of characters he's shared adventures with along the way.

When he's not pawing at a keyboard or raising his hackles in defense of the Oxford comma, Juan can be found hiking ancient pathways, exploring modern trails, or finding new tracks with his significant otter. You can visit Juan online by searching for WanderingGoose on DeviantArt or Quick-BrownFoxWrites on Tumblr.

Mephitis is a grey muzzle skunk who first encountered the furry fandom in 2000. Since then he has attended many cons in the southeastern US. His skunk fursuit head sports a blue tuff, not unlike the colored hair style in "Otters can't rig. Badgers can't pull." He has a huge skunk collection of plushies, figurines, and everything else you can make skunks from.

Previous published work includes stories in *Crossed Genres*, *nthZine*, and *Bewildering Stories*. In addition, he has written three academic books and numerous journal articles that that he had to create as part of the monetary acquisition process to support con-going.

Mary E. Lowd is a prolific science-fiction and furry writer in Oregon. She's had more than 150 stories and six novels published, mostly featuring talking animals, spaceships, or both. Her work has won an Ursa Major Award, two Cóyotl Awards, and two Leo Literary Awards. Mary's stories have previously appeared in *ROAR* volumes 4 & 5, and she edited *ROAR* volumes 6-10. She now edits the online furry zine *Zooscape*. She lives in a crashed spaceship disguised as a house and hidden behind a rose garden, with an extensive menagerie of animals, some real and some imaginary.

Learn more at www.marylowd.com or read more stories at www.deepskyanchor.com.

ABOUT THE ARTIST

Dante (otherwise known by the user fresaboba) is an Afro-Latino and trans illustrator/animator operating in the Midwest of the United States. His passions are creating/designing characters, animating and drawing fan art. He can be found at fresaboba.com

ABOUT THE EDITOR

Ian Madison Keller is a fantasy writer currently living in Oregon. Originally from Utah, he moved up to the Pacific Northwest on a whim a decade ago and never plans on leaving. Ian has been writing since 2013 with eight novels and more than a dozen published short stories. Ian has also written under the name Madison Keller before transitioning in 2019 to Ian.

His novels include the *Flower's Fang* trilogy and the four book award-winning *Dragonsbane Saga* self-published under Rainbow Dog Press, and an upcoming urban fantasy novel from GoAL Publications. His work has won a Cóyotl Award and two LEO awards. He is also the new editor of *ROAR* starting in 2020 with *ROAR Volume 11*. He can be found on the web at madisonkeller.net Or on Twitter as @MaddieKellerr